DEATH *on a* PALE HORSE

ALSO BY DONALD THOMAS

POETRY
Points of Contact
Welcome to the Grand Hotel

FICTION
Prince Charlie's Bluff
The Flight of the Eagle
The Raising of Lizzie Meek
The Blindfold Game
Belladonna: A Lewis Carroll Nightmare
The Ripper's Apprentice
Jekyll, Alias Hyde
The Arrest of Scotland Yard
The Day the Sun Rose Twice
Dancing in the Dark
Red Flowers for Lady Blue
The Secret Cases of Sherlock Holmes
Sherlock Holmes and the Running Noose
The Execution of Sherlock Holmes
Sherlock Holmes and the King's Evil
Sherlock Holmes and the Ghosts of Bly

BIOGRAPHY
Cardigan of Balaclava
Cochrane: Britannia's Sea-Wolf
Swinburne: The Poet in his World
Robert Browning: A Life Within Life
Henry Fielding: A Life
The Marquis de Sade
Lewis Carroll: A Portrait with Background

CRIME AND DOCUMENTARY
A Long Time Burning: The History of Literary Censorship in England
Freedom's Frontier: Censorship in Modern Britain
Dead Giveaway: Murder Avenged from the Grave
The Victorian Underworld
An Underworld at War: Spies, Deserters, Racketeers and Civilians in the Second World War
Villains' Paradise: Britain's Post-War Underworld
State Trials: 1. Treason and Libel; 2. The Public Conscience

DEATH on a PALE HORSE

SHERLOCK HOLMES ON
HER MAJESTY'S SECRET SERVICE

DONALD THOMAS

PEGASUS CRIME

NEW YORK LONDON

For Tony Horner

—◦—

DEATH ON A PALE HORSE

Pegasus Books LLC
80 Broad Street, 5th Floor
New York, NY 10004

First Pegasus Books paperback edition December 2014
First Pegasus Books hardcover edition March 2013

Interior design by Maria Fernandez

Library of Congress Cataloging-in-Publication Data is available.

ISBN: 978-1-60598-621-0

10 9 8 7 6 5 4 3 2 1

Printed in the United States of America
Distributed by W. W. Norton & Company

CONTENTS

HISTORICAL NOTE

22 January 1879: Annihilation of British Armoured and Infantry Column by Zulu Tribesmen, Isandhlwana, South-East Africa.

1 June 1879: Assassination of Louis Napoleon, Prince Imperial and claimant to the French throne, at the Blood River, Natal, South Africa.

12 June 1879: Captain Jahleel Brenton Carey, commander of the Prince Imperial's bodyguard, tried and convicted by General Court-Martial at Blood River Camp, for "Misbehaviour in the face of the enemy."

16 August 1879: Court-martial verdict quashed.

28 January 1881: Transvaal Boers first defeat of the British Army in South Africa.

27 February 1881: Decisive victory of Boers at Majuba Hill.

5 April 1881: Great Britain concedes independence to the Transvaal.

22 February 1883: Death of Captain Jahleel Brenton Carey in India "under mysterious circumstances."

31 December 1887: *Reichsanzeiger* revelations of criminal attempts to provoke a European war, Germany and Austria against Russia and France. Despatches forged in the names of Count Bismarck, Prince Reuss (German ambassador in Vienna), Prince Ferdinand of Bulgaria, and his sister the Comtesse de Flandre, also sister-in-law to Leopold II of Belgium.

29 March 1889: Floating wreck of the paddle-steamer *Comtesse de Flandre* sinks in deep water off Ostend.

PART I

The Documents in the Case

MEMORANDUM

From: Permanent Secretary for Cabinet Affairs
To: Provost Marshal General
Date and Source: Cabinet Office, 20 August 1894

Subject: *The Narrative of Colonel Rawdon Moran,* a paper dated February 1879

My Lord,
By dispensation of Her Majesty's Privy Council, I enclose for your confidential information a copy of a report compiled for his criminal paymasters by Colonel Rawdon Moran.

Your records will confirm that this officer was never brought before any recognised civilian or military court. Yet he remains the one agent identified in a criminal conspiracy which to this day endeavours to undermine the British position in Southern Africa. The wealth of newly discovered gold fields and diamond mines in the Transvaal was to be his particular prize.

An illegal arms traffic via the Congo Free State was to be the means to that end.

In his departure from the British Army, Colonel Moran had suffered a terrible injury at the hands of fellow officers. Who shall say that it was not deserved? He swore at the time that he would be revenged upon them and their comrades many times over. And who shall say that he was not?

The attached manuscript describes certain remarkable events in Zululand, South-East Africa, on 22 January 1879. It is a curious document, for he adopts a literary style. As a young man, Moran was a hunter of big game whose bag of Bengal tigers has never been exceeded. He was the author of his own tales of adventure. Such titles as *Heavy Game of the Western Himalayas* enjoyed a steady sale on his return to London. Yet he must have feared the consequences, if this account of treachery at Isandhlwana ever fell into the wrong hands. Therefore he writes his account as a detached observer or story-teller, rather than as one who was present and participating at the scene. In truth, Colonel Moran alone was the Hunter, the observer and the mysterious horseman of his own narration.

This report, made to his criminal associates, was found among the effects of one of them. Professor James Moriarty, a mathematical scholar and a suspect in several crimes, died in an unusual accident at the Reichenbach Falls some months ago. But for that accident, Moran's account would be known only to those who presumably employed his services.

My disclosure of this document to yourself was sanctioned yesterday at a meeting of the Privy Council. As I am sure your lordship will be aware, only the Sovereign and one other member need be present for a meeting of the Council and for its decisions to be valid under the constitution. Her Majesty is insistent that the fewer people who know of this matter at present, the better.

Accordingly, Lord Rosebery, as Prime Minister, and I waited upon the Queen at Osborne House, Isle of Wight, yesterday evening.

Colonel Moran's case may now be regarded as closed. However, in the interest of military intelligence, Council deemed it advisable that you should have sight of this narrative before it is filed for indefinite retention among the confidential State Papers. I hardly need add that you have not been authorised to communicate the contents of this document to any other person.

My courier, Sergeant Albert Gibbons of the Royal Marines Despatch Corps, will attend you while you read it, and will convey the paper to me again when you have done so.

I have the honour to remain, sir, your obedient servant,

William Mycroft Holmes, PC, KBE

STATE PAPERS

CRIMINAL RECORDS Moran 1879/3
DOCUMENT NOT TO BE REMOVED FROM THE FILE
The Narrative of Colonel Rawdon Moran
February 1879

A brown minullus hawk rode high and alone above the silence of the arid plain. Its wings drooped in an easy curve against a green flush of African dawn. Below it, the broad lowland marked by a dry river donga lay in shadow, while the early sky gathered reflected light. In the growing day, not a breath of dust stirred the wild grass and mimosa thorn. The bird shifted a little, an alignment of patient grace, as the dismounted horseman watched and listened.

The scene was everything that this hunter had expected. That morning, for the first time, a distant accompaniment to the wakening day rose from a ravine of the eastern hills. The sound drifted across the tall parched grass where the rider lay concealed. Its continuous humming was subdued but undulating, like a swarm of countless bees. Carried higher in the warmer air, it began to take on a human resonance, the prayer of warriors intoned before battle.

At that moment a yellow disc of sun began to break on the high ridges of the eastern plateau and the Malagata range. Seeking warmth, the brown hawk broke away and soared into the clearing sky. It had seen what the hunter in the grass could not. He lay and watched a little longer while new light from the eastern ridge splintered the shadows across a massive rock-face in the west, working down the slope.

The few European travellers who had seen the summit of this pale rock, rearing like a carved head from the neck of its col, had compared it to a silhouette of the Sphinx. But the warriors of Cetewayo knew nothing of sphinxes. It had been named for them by men whose trade was the slaughter of herds. Cow-Belly. Isandhlwana.

The sun had now risen clear of the eastern hills. Its cool light travelled quickly down the western slope of the col until the wide plain came into full view. At the foot of Isandhlwana, protected at the rear by the great rock itself, stretched the silent camp of an invading army. Lines of neat white bell-tents ran as trimly as the streets of a new-built town. Behind them, where the rocky ground sloped up to the col, row upon row of ox-drawn supply-wagons held food and drink for two thousand men. They also carried enough ammunition to kill every man and woman between the Buffalo River and the Cape.

To the left of this camp, four Royal Artillery bombardiers in dark tunics and caps kept watch over a battery of seven-pounder field-guns. Half a mile before them, in the open terrain of grass and thorn, the approach from the northern plateau was guarded by mounted vedettes of the Natal Volunteers in their black tunics, and by red-coated pickets of Her Majesty's 24th Regiment of Foot, from the valleys of Wales.

The camp began to stir as the first white smoke rose from its field kitchens. Through his lenses, the hunter in the grass watched the first bearded infantrymen of the Volunteers forming a queue with their mess-tins for pressed beef, hardtack, and tea. As the sun's warmth began to penetrate the cold air of the plain, a long mounted column was forming up by the main body of the tents. Sound carries far at such an hour and in such stillness. The shifting and snorting of horses, the clink of bridles, drifted through the clear air towards the eastern slopes.

"Walk march!"

The call rang out, repeated down the length of the column. In perfect order, this mounted patrol moved out across the brown pasture, withered by sun and wind, towards the Malagata foothills.

At the scarlet column's head rode several men whose white helmets bore the gilt insignia of the British General Staff. The dismounted horseman in the grass recognised them all. Foremost was Lieutenant-General Lord Chelmsford of the Grenadier Guards, Commander-in-Chief of the British Army at the Cape. He sat tall and slim in the saddle, with the high-bridged nose of a born aristocrat. Chelmsford had led his troops in the Queen's wars from the Crimea and Abyssinia to Bengal and the Punjab. Leaving the rest of his regiments in the safety of the camp, he now rode out at the head of his patrol to scout for an elusive enemy.

Among his subalterns and aides-de-camp, he was immediately followed by a tall languid dandy with a sneering drawl. The patient hunter also recognised this creature. He was one who spent his London furloughs as a gambler in Chelsea's Cremorne pleasure gardens and as whoremaster in the Regent Street night-houses. His features profiled the spoilt beauty of a bankrupt Apollo.

In the small hours of darkness, the hunter had come and gone from his enemy's camp, passing the sentries as easily as a shadow crossing the moon. Now lying hidden from their view at sunrise, he lacked the means to check his own appearance. He imagined it would suggest his last hours in the dying-room of a fever hospital. Despite the new warmth of morning, the sharp rat-like bite of the cold night had gnawed his bones. Sometimes he shivered until his teeth rattled like a zany's. There were spasms in which the hands that held the field-glasses shook too hard to hold them steady and his eyes watered with the chill. In the last hour before dawn, it had seemed that day would never come.

Chelmsford's reconnaissance raised a slow wake of dust in its progress to the farther hills. The camp had now lost its commander and most of its mounted troops for the rest of the day. Its position would be held until dusk by the general's subordinate, Colonel Henry Pulleine, and his 24th Regiment of Foot.

The climbing sun burnt off the remaining drifts of morning mist. From its eastern ravine, the hunter heard that strange bee-like humming ebb and die, as if at the approach of the cavalry patrol.

With talons folded in its warm plumage, the observer's quiet companion swooped and soared again. It hovered low above an isolated hill that stood in the centre of the plain between the eastern ridge and the camp at the foot of Isandhlwana. This splendid bird showed no fear of the man. A body lying prone in the tall grass of the slope could do it no harm.

Avoiding the sun's reflection on the lenses of his field-glasses, the observer raised himself to inspect more fully the camp across the plain. He felt the dry flesh shrink on his face and the skin burn red on the points of his cheek-bones, under a ragged beard. The water-bottle beside him had been dry since the previous dusk, but he opened it from time to time and sucked at the cooler air of its interior, a substitute for water itself.

Then, stiff and ungainly, he stood up. It mattered nothing if they saw him now. With dawn and daylight, the time for suspicion was past. Twenty yards away, the dappled mare arched her neck and got slowly to her feet from the flattened grass. Everything was in place for the event that must follow, though the drama was not yet of his making. The period of his allotted patrol as a Natal Volunteer was not quite over, but he could move freely until the time came for his withdrawal through the camp itself. He had an hour in hand as he led the mare in an eastern semi-circle to the near side of the ravine. There was silence now on all sides. By night, the perimeter guards were alert for a footfall or the brushing of grass. In the safety of daylight, no one below would pay him the least attention.

He worked his way carefully along the plateau until he could see the approach to the isolated Conical Kopje from east as well as west. Then, as he drew closer to the ravine, he heard again that strange, unaccountable buzzing. The mobilisation of a nation of bees. But still there was no movement to be seen on the plain below, nor on the ridges about him.

As he ambled to the east along the plateau, with the lazy progress of a Volunteer, his stony path ended presently at the sharp edge of the ravine, dropping five hundred feet to the level of the foothills. He walked the horse to the lip of this chasm. The sound of the hive grew louder until he stood behind chest-high scrub, where the ground sloped rapidly down. He looked through a gap in the branches into this narrow gorge and saw what he had known he was going to see.

A less-experienced observer might have thought that the sun and shade had played a trick upon his eyes. Where stretches of withered grass should have clothed the limestone slopes on either side of this declivity, the entire face of the ravine for a mile or more was dark and smooth, hung here and there with oval shields of animal hide. At several points, the sun caught polished metal. The humming that had echoed in the warmer air grew louder and more insistent. It was the warning of an army disturbed, of its warriors waking to the dawn of battle.

A stranger might have stood in admiration, for the carpet that covered the sides of the ravine was living and human. The massed battalions of a great Zulu battle force, perhaps ten thousand strong, lay or crouched in the concealment of this rift in the hills. Such was the flower of Cetewayo's tribes, young men who had yet to earn the prize of a woman by dipping their spears in the blood of an enemy.

He stepped back cautiously for better concealment. Here and there the first ranks were rising slowly, stiff from rest but impatient for combat. Isandhlwana was to be the arena of the young men's initiation. The washing of the spears. All their lives had been lived for this day.

Despite his own preparations and the care of his planning, a sudden fear at the sight of such numbers stung him like the shock of an icy plunge. But the lore of nature had taught him that there is no enduring courage without fear and its conquest. As he mounted the dappled horse, a last low-pitched humming was lost in the rustling of grass. The mighty army crouched together and quietly murmured its battle-cry.

"u-Suthu! u-Suthu!"

Putting spurs to the grey mare, its rider came jauntily down the slope like a returning scout, recrossed the plain, and passed through the outer picket-line into the 24th Foot's quiet camp. No one barred his way. It was enough that he wore the dark serge patrol-jacket and cord breeches of the Volunteers, a wide-awake hat, broad-brimmed with a silk band. No Volunteer would choose to ride the veldt by darkness. Where else could a man in such clothes come from but a night patrol? The picket captain had checked the horsemen of a patrol out from the camp before dusk. Many a rider now passed through the forward line of the 24th Regiment of Foot with less notice taken of him than if he had been a stray dog from a deserted kraal.

For a moment more, the plain was silent. The first chant from the tribes had been too deep in the ravine to carry this far. The returning horseman dismounted, walked his horse past the headquarters tents, and tethered the mare to its rail. So far as the smartly uniformed imperial riflemen were concerned, he might not exist. Yet the plan he had proposed to his confederates was now unfolding as effortlessly as a flag in the wind.

He let his loitering footsteps carry him past the tent of Colonel Henry Pulleine of the 24th Foot. Pulleine was the only man with the rank to be camp-commander in Lord Chelmsford's absence. His Natal Volunteers supplementing the regular infantry consisted of mercenaries, freebooters, and bounty-hunters. They were apt to be known for indiscipline and brutality. Their commanders despised a gentleman like Pulleine as instinctively as he deplored them. With a facetious irony, they called themselves "Pulleine's Lambs."

The flap of the colonel's tent was open by this hour of the morning, revealing his stocky, moustached figure as he turned from a long mirror. He had been standing before it while his batman adjusted the scarlet tunic with its gold-fringed epaulettes. The servant executed a running backward bow and retrieved Henry Pulleine's white pith helmet from its place on a chest of drawers. A sword hilt glittered like new silver as the colonel buckled on his white belt. Equipped for duty, he turned to the opening of the canvas.

Before walking forward, he had picked up several company reports laid on a trestle table by his adjutant. Now he put them down again. A blond giant in the regular scarlet and blue of the 24th Foot, his peaked cap clasped under his arm, had pushed before him.

"Sar' Major Tindal, sir. Permission to report loss of mess equipment, sir!"

"Loss?" Pulleine glanced at him, not understanding. He turned back and looked down at the company commanders' reports on his desk again but appeared to find no explanation there.

The anonymous horseman kept his inconspicuous distance from the conversation. He made a convincing play of piercing a further hole in his belt with an awl from his knapsack, maintaining a frown of concentration. It surprised him that they had noticed their loss already. Not a syllable of the words between the two men escaped him. Pulleine shook his head.

"Very well, sergeant-major. Loss of what?"

Tindal was quiet and confidential. Like many of his regiment, his voice retained the low lilt of his Welsh valley.

"Owain Glyndwr, sir. Missing from the mess-tent, sir."

"Nonsense. What the devil would anyone want with him?"

As even the Natal Volunteers knew by now, Owain Glyndwr was a piece of regimental mythology, the mummified head of an Abyssinian sharpshooter, brought back as a trophy after the storming of Magdala in 1867. Pickled by the surgeon-major, it had become an object of veneration to younger officers in the boisterous aftermath of regimental guest-nights.

"Not nonsense, sir," said Tindal quickly. "He's gone. And Dai Morgan do say someone was creeping about last night when Mr. Pope's dogs did bark. Perhaps a native spy was out in the hills, sir."

Pulleine looked up and scrutinised the sergeant-major a moment longer before replying.

"Sar' Major! Inform Private Morgan and anyone else to whom it may apply that the purpose of this expedition is to repulse a Zulu invasion of the province of Natal. I will not have any officer or batman playing the fool at a time like this. If I hear more of this matter, or if I find that Private Morgan has laid his hands on an unauthorised rum-ration again, he and you will be visited as if by the Wrath of God. Is that plain?"

"Sir," said Tindal smartly.

"Very well, sar' major. Dismiss!"

Pulleine was still standing in the opening of the tent as the bugles blew "Column Call" and the regimental NCOs prepared to call the names of the men who had fallen in by companies. The colonel shouted across to one of his subalterns.

"Mr. Spencer!"

As he watched them casually, the hunter identified Spencer as the fair-skinned young captain who went everywhere with a pet terrier running at his heels. Spencer now crossed to the colonel's tent and saluted self-consciously, the fair skin colouring a little under the trim line of his ginger moustaches.

"Mr. Spencer, as orderly officer last night, please explain to me this report of the removal of Owain Glyndwr from the guard-tent!"

"Sar' Major Tindal is investigating it, sir. Someone seems to have taken the head from the mess trophy-case in the small hours of this morning."

"I am aware of that, Mr. Spencer." Pulleine rested his hand on his sword-hilt in the brightness of the African sun. "Be so good as to find the culprit, put him in close arrest, and bring him to me at defaulters' parade tomorrow morning. Understood?"

Spencer hesitated. Unlike his brother captains, he seemed a diffident young man who took awkwardly to the self-assurance of professional soldiering.

"With respect, sir."

"Well?" Pulleine released the hilt and adjusted the angle of the scabbard again.

"The men suspect an intruder in the camp last night, near 'B' Company lines."

"The devil they do, Mr. Spencer! Then why, in God's name, was something not done at the time?"

"Morgan reported a wide-brimmed hat. Whoever he was, he was close to the wagons and the guard-tents."

"Mr. Spencer," said Pulleine softly, "almost every Natal Volunteer wears a patrol-jacket and a wide-awake hat. How could one of them—or more—fail to be in the area? You must do better than that, sir."

Spencer was not so easily defeated.

"Mr. Pope's men saw something as well."

"Mr. Pope is now out on picket-guard. You may speak to him when he's relieved. Meantime, let me have no more cock-and-bull stories. This is regimental mischief, you may be sure of that. Find the culprit and put him in detention. I have no doubt that he can be named easily enough."

Spencer saluted, called his terrier to heel, and marched back to the waiting lines of the parade square.

The hunter's curiosity was satisfied. He promised the world that it had not seen the last of "Owain Glyndwr." Across the camp ground, bugles finished blowing and the NCOs began to call the names of the men who had fallen in by companies. The sun rose higher in the burning-mirror of the sky, its heat shimmering distantly from the stone ridges that overlooked the plain on all sides.

Presently, a trail of dust drifted from the west, where the Buffalo River marked the frontier dividing Natal from Cetewayo's Zulu Kingdom. Across this rough terrain moved a column of mounted detachments, a further company of infantry, and a rocket-battery with its strange launching-troughs drawn on limber wheels. The scarlet tunic'd foot-soldiers and the monocled cavalry officers in dark blue were preceded by a regimental band playing *Men of Harlech* in march time. The sun fired the silver instruments of the bandsmen, giving this support column of Durnford, the junior colonel, the air of a bank holiday carnival.

Among the horsemen, Durnford was easily picked out by the sleeve of his withered left arm pinned to his tunic. Presently he dismounted on the garrison ground at the centre of the camp and strode across to report his arrival to Pulleine. The patient onlooker waited until he saw Durnford leave Pulleine's tent twenty minutes later, after a delayed breakfast of beef and porter. The horsemen of the column were formed up again for a sweep across the plain from west to east, to root out any forward positions of the tribes in the foothills.

Pulleine had every reason to feel confident. The battalions of the tribes carried no arms beyond their shields of animal skin stretched over light wooden frames and their metal-tipped spears or assegais. Looking about him, the colonel saw a park of British wagons holding half a million rounds of ammunition and enough of the latest quick-firing Martini-Henry rifles to equip two thousand infantry. There was a rocket-battery, and a Royal Artillery battery of seven-pounder guns, as well as the new continuous-firing Gatling guns mounted on limber wheels.

It was the rifles that would stop an attacking formation by a wall of timed-volleys. Even at five or six hundred yards, the aimed and coordinated fire of trained infantry using the Martini-Henry would be lethal to any assault.

Durnford's horsemen were moving leisurely towards the eastern foothills. Now it was the senior man of the Natal Volunteers, Boss Strickland, who grinned and elbowed his way through a cheering mob of his men about the guard-tents. Their clothes were shabby by contrast with the spotless white-and-scarlet of the British regiments, but their self-confidence was at a peak.

The hunter moved aside and remained in earshot by unobtrusive attendance to his tethered mount. He could hear easily enough the loud argument that developed as Strickland entered the colonel's tent. Pulleine had come to defend Natal, but Strickland and his friends had followed him for booty. These mercenaries were anxious to be off the leash and into the villages. Strickland's tone was half a drawl and half a sneer. Pulleine's reply was breathless with exasperation.

"Once and for all, Mr. Strickland! This camp is to be held securely until Lord Chelmsford returns. Then you may seek his leave to do as you please. Those are my orders—and your orders."

"Supposing his lordship ain't back this side of dark?"

"He will be."

"Supposin' he ain't?"

Pulleine made no reply.

"All right." Strickland had moved so that he was now almost blocking the tent-opening with his bulk. "Then supposing I was just to ride my men out. Shoot us in the back, would you?"

Pulleine swung round.

"I'll do better than that, Mr. Strickland. I'll court-martial you!"

Strickland laughed as if it was the best thing he had heard in months.

"No, you won't, Pulleine. Not me. I ain't one of your regimental flunkeys. Court-martial me? If you was to do that, my friend, you wouldn't get back over the Buffalo River alive. There's fifty men 'd see to that."

Strickland showed the manner which had served him so well in the Durban markets and the diamond mining settlements of the Transvaal.

"I'll tell you what though, Colonel. I'll go half way with you. We'll take a patrol along the north plateau presently. No further. From there, we can survey the front of the Conical Kopje and see the back of it. We'll sit quietly there until Lord Chelmsford comes back safe. After that, we'll press on. Not before."

Pulleine hesitated, but Strickland gave him no respite.

"Give our fellows a square deal, Pulleine, or I shan't be answerable for 'em. I daresay this stolen regimental mascot nonsense is up to one of them. I'll give you that. But let them alone and there's enough in a quick swoop to keep them happy for a month or two."

Pulleine hesitated. Long years of military command had accustomed him to deference and dignity. Men of Strickland's cut were beyond him. How far did his authority extend over this civilian riff-raff?

"Very well, Mr. Strickland. The northern plateau and no further. You will take the heliograph. You will respond to all signals flashed from this camp. In the event of a recall being sounded, you will return at once."

Strickland pushed aside the tent flap, still grinning. Presently the bearded mercenaries of Pulleine's Lambs rode two by two towards the north plateau, escorted by Captain Shepstone of Durnford's mounted detail. They passed the forward line and a red-coated picket of the 24th Foot, commanded by Lieutenant Pope. Presently they caught up with a mounted vedette of the Natal Cavalry on the eastern slope.

Heat had stunned the plain into silence and stillness. At the western end of the camp, under the great rock itself, the lines between the tents were now almost deserted. Far out across the plain, the pickets and vedettes of the forward posts wilted in the glare. The rocket-battery with its trough-like launchers was almost level with the Conical Kopje as it approached the camp. On the eastern hills and the Malagata range to the south, there was still no sign of Lord Chelmsford's column.

The mercenary riders of the Natal Volunteers had begun to pick their way leisurely through the fierce light that shone back from pale stone ridges. They were across the dry and broken course of the river donga, its boulders scattered along the plain from north to south.

Presently they were far enough forward to look down on the approaches to the Kopje. As they dismounted to wait for Chelmsford's return, it was possible to see through field-glasses from the camp that Strickland, distinguished by the white band round his wide-awake hat, remained on his horse. Perhaps in the stillness he was puzzled by that strange, unaccountable buzzing of a vast army of bees.

Presently he could be seen dismounting cautiously and guiding his horse to the sharp edge of the ravine, where it dropped to the level of the lower hills. He walked alone to the lip of the rift, stood on the edge where the ground sloped away, and looked into the narrow gorge.

A moment later, he was seen with his foot in the stirrup, turning his horse about. He flung himself astride and spurred at full pelt upon the astonished patrol of Pulleine's Lambs, stretched in the grass, talking and laughing.

The message, though out of earshot from the camp, was never in doubt.

"Ride for your lives! The tribes are in the ravine! Thousand on thousand of them! Ride for the camp or we shall all be lost!"

The puzzled vedettes on the camp perimeter saw through their glasses the Volunteers snatch at their bridles, jump for their stirrups, and gallop in wild retreat down the slope of the plateau. Still Cetewayo's warriors lay low with perfect discipline while the British camp was quiet and unprepared for an assault. Something like a battle-cry now sounded thinly at this distance. Then the first ranks of the tribesmen rose silently into view along the ridge with their oval shields and assegais. At the two ends of their great line, the horns of the formation forming the Zulu impi were coming down towards either side of Pulleine's men while the centre pinned the defenders down. Worse still for Pulleine, he was to be trapped with his back to the mountain.

Watching this across the quiet veldt, the horseman stood by his dappled mare and heard a sharp but distant crackling of rifles, like dry twigs in a fire. It seemed the best thing to be up and gone. As he mounted, Pulleine was in the opening of the tent again, tunic unbuttoned and a towel in his hands.

"Sar' Major Tindal!"

"Firing on the north plateau, sir. Mr. Strickland and the mounted detail riding back!"

"Mr. Spencer!" Pulleine roared at his junior captain. "Sound the Alarm and the Fall-In. Keep your glasses on the north plateau and report!"

The colonel turned back into his tent, buckling his belt on, testing the angle of his scabbard and revolver holster. The onlooker knew what must happen next, as surely as if he had rehearsed it all himself. In a final glance, he saw that Pulleine's eyes appeared set with anger, as surely as they would soon be stilled in death. The colonel was no doubt composing the phrases he would use when Strickland reappeared. Despite the injury that still seemed secretly to burn his flesh, the watching hunter felt no hatred, rather a cold satisfaction at what must happen. The dice had rolled. The outcome was no more to him now than the stars in their courses, the shining masters riveted in the sky. He untethered the dappled mare from the fence and led her away, glancing back from time to time.

Somewhere among the tents, a boy bugler of the regimental band sounded the Alarm and, after a moment's pause, the Fall-In. The heat of noon rang with the shouts of NCOs, of troopers cursing as they buckled on their webbing while they ran. In a moment more, the air sounded to cries of "Company, A-ttention! Right dress!"

"Sir!" Spencer's words carried as he ran towards the colonel's tent, his voice steady but its pitch high, "enemy now in force on the north plateau! The ridge is thick with them!"

"Very well, Mr. Spencer. Companies to their positions on the perimeter. Where are Colonel Durnford and his troopers?"

"No sign, sir."

"He may find himself cut off. He and Lord Chelmsford." Pulleine's face was still tense with anger. "I'll be damned if I don't have that fool Strickland court-martialled!"

But his tone of voice and the unease in his eyes suggested that he now thought himself the greater fool of the two. He took his field-glasses from their case again, glancing across to see that the companies of the 24th Foot were doubling forward to their positions. Then he strode off to survey the perimeter defences. Lieutenant Coghill, acting adjutant in the absence of Chelmsford's party, caught him up.

Watching from the saddle, the hunter knew that the field-glasses would prove that Spencer had been right. For almost a mile along the edge of the northern plateau, the horizon-line had become a dark undulating mass of humanity. They had come from nowhere, as it seemed, for the night patrol had reported nothing. Metal tips of their razor-sharp assegais glittered in strong light, and at this distance the tawny-coloured animal skins covering their shields seemed to float on their bodies like debris on a tide.

At the nearer end of the plateau, Strickland's men were still careering in panic towards the camp in a motley stampede, a retreat as undisciplined as a donkey-race. The rocket-battery would never limber up in time to withdraw. Though well-armed, it was about to be marooned in the centre of the plain. But Durnford's mounted column was now riding back in good order from the eastern foothills. Its men began to dismount and take up a defensive line just forward of the main camp, where the boulders of the dry river donga offered good cover for the riflemen.

Pulleine's voice still carried across the lines.

"I want Mr. Pope and his platoon brought in now! If the tribes attack down the slope, they'll be on top of the pickets before we know where we are."

Coghill saluted and rode away.

Strickland and his Volunteers were at last cantering across a flat stretch of plain towards the camp. Durnford's riflemen were in place, making their forward line of defence among the rocks of the donga. The companies of the 24th and the other regiments still under Pulleine's command formed a formidable double rampart across the approach to the camp perimeter. With its Martini-Henry breech-loaders, this red-coated infantry presented a constant wall of fire. The kneeling sections fired first and those standing behind fired over the first rank's heads while those kneeling reloaded. The aim was sure, disciplined, and regular. Even at quarter of a mile, the effect of such volleys would make a shambles of the close-ranked battalions of the tribes.

By now, the rocket-battery was isolated. Its launching-troughs on their limber-wheels stood well ahead of the main defensive line. But the camp was secure beyond question. Indeed, at the sight of the double line of infantry, the tribal army at the plateau's foot appeared to hesitate. The massed bodies swayed a little, side to side, while a hymn-like chant rose slow and mournful to the white heat of the sky.

"u-Suthu! u-Suthu!"

Sometimes the warriors would make a brief demonstration with shields and spears, beating the rhythm of a tattoo, only to

withdraw. Whatever their chiefs promised, even this phalanx—
a mile long and eight or ten men deep—faced slaughter at the
hands of mechanised weaponry. The artillery battery was now
trained on their approach.

Pulleine lowered his field-glasses as Coghill returned. The
hunter glanced again as his mount rambled on inconspicu-
ously. Chelmsford would be five miles to the south-east by now,
following the Malagata range. Coghill had his despatch-book
and pencil out. There was only one message to send, and the
mounted hunter could echo every word.

"Return at once with all your force. Zulus advancing in force
from the left front of the camp."

The hunter had seen and guessed enough. With Strickland's
return, there were scores of men in uniforms identical to his, Natal
Volunteers scattered throughout the camp. Once again, no one
would pay him the least attention. It was all just as he had calculated. He saw that a mounted messenger and three escorts, one of
them a black-coated guide, were making their way to the western
perimeter by the foot of the col. He had only to follow at a distance,
apparently bringing up the rear as one of the despatch riders. Best
of all, Her Majesty's infantry had been taught that he would not be
worth challenging as though he were a British "regular." The ruffians
of the Volunteers did not count as true soldiers.

Behind him, he heard a single battle-cry of the human tide
as it burst from its line on the plateau and surged in mass formation down the slope to the plain. Then it came on silently
and in perfect order, the war-chant stilled. Glancing back, he
saw that the individual warriors were almost distinguishable.
Their advance spread and formed a human phalanx across the
scorching grassland. Then Cetewayo's young men broke into a
slow rhythmic run, with all the professional precision of British
regiments moving in double-time.

Despite the apparent security of Pulleine's main position,
the rocket-battery had delayed too long. Major Russell, his

bombardier, and the eight troopers had chosen to make a fight of it. Among the pack mules which carried their equipment, two launching-troughs on limber wheels were now aimed directly at the advancing tribes. Two steel-cased rockets had been laid in place and two troopers were lighting the fuses by hand. The stillness of the plain was rent by a demonic shriek as the first of the projectiles shot from its launcher, trailing plumes of white smoke and sparks. High above the oncoming force, it went into an erratic spin, plunging harmlessly into the hillside beyond with a dull thump of explosive power and a slow drift of blackened smoke.

But the second shell flew low and straight, detonating in the mass of the tribes with terrible effect. A cheer went up from the rocket battery as the launchers were reloaded. The ranks of oncoming attackers hid the scene for a moment. But something had gone amiss. It seemed that the next missiles failed to ignite. Two rocketeers tried vainly to light the fuses, the rest turning to hold off the attack with rifles and service revolvers.

Almost before the danger was evident, the major and his bombardier and troopers vanished under a wave of bodies and spears. Several times the sun caught the tips of assegais held aloft in a powerful fist. There was a shout of victory from the pressing tribes, drawing back after conquest, a severed head dancing high on the shaft of a spear. Round the overturned limbers, the bodies of the nine soldiers lay torn and dishevelled.

With such a sight before them, not a single face from the camp was turned towards the fugitive as he swung away from the despatch party. Abruptly, he spurred forward to put the shelter of the col between him and the fighting. From the concealment that the tall grass offered, he now saw the dark wall of the impi turn towards the main defensive line of Pulleine's men. At the isolated donga, where his riflemen lay behind whitened boulders, Durnford alone stood upright, his left sleeve pinned to his tunic, his right arm brandishing his sword as he shouted encouragement to his men.

At about two hundred yards, Durnford's rifles opened fire, volleys aimed with a force and precision that might have equalled an artillery salvo. Twenty or thirty of the tribesmen went down, swarmed over by the mass which pressed on from behind them. At the foot of the plateau, the Royal Artillery battery loaded its guns again with case shot, lethal slugs of metal capable of bringing down attackers by the dozen.

Durnford's forward line began a careful withdrawal to the main perimeter, in order to secure their flank. The riflemen of the 24th Foot covered their retreat with the same precise ear-stunning volleys, each of which caused the oncoming wave of the attack to halt and recoil a little, leaving a line of fallen warriors at its feet.

To those who had faced the ordeal of the Russian guns at the Alma or the bloody hand-to-hand carnage in the mist and mud of Inkerman, this skirmish at Isandhlwana had no more promised a proper battle than a rabbit-shoot or a battue of pheasants. The double-ranked companies of the 24th were so little concerned that men were chattering and laughing as they fired, pausing to reload from white blanco'd cartridge-pouches. Several officers walked up and down the line encouraging their men, voices carrying through the heat in the intervals of the crashing volleys. "Well done, Captain Pope's company! . . . Good shooting, the 24th!"

The hunter dismounted behind the rocks on the lower slope of the col. He saw that the first ranks of the attacking tribesmen were closer to the camp perimeter now, though at a range of well over two hundred yards. A few of the veteran warriors set an example to the youths by dashing forward and launching their six-foot assegais, light spears that flew with a faint *whoop!* through the air. The steel points bedded deep in the earth, but no more than half the distance from the British perimeter.

Presently, the attacking line surged forward again with a rising murmur of voices, lapping the entire length of the defence. Again it drew back before the volley-fire of the imperial regiments, the battle hymn falling to a low howl. To the north, however, one horn of the impi was trying to encircle the flank of the 24th Foot, while case-shot from the seven-pounder guns of the Royal Artillery defending that sector filled the air with a hail of metal.

In the wagon-park, to the rear of Pulleine's position, the cooks and quartermasters had come out, as if to watch a football game. The regimental band was formed up in the safety of this garrison ground. In battle, these musicians would serve as ammunition-bearers. The observer on the col turned his glasses upon this enclosure. That was where the engagement would be lost or won, but not yet.

Strickland and his Volunteers had fallen back to hold a line on the left. These were the sharp-shooters and harriers of the veldt. Recovered from their fright on the plateau, their steady carefully aimed fire brought down rank after rank of attackers. The great tribal phalanx wavered and, for a moment, the advance seemed to fall away again. But the experienced warriors had taught the new recruits well. The survivors of the Uve and Uncijo battalions had learnt to drop to their knees as the volleys were fired, but then rose again to launch their spears.

Even so, the Uvi battalion came to a halt, kept down by shots that sang and whipped overhead. Promised that the enemy's bullets would slide off their skins without harming them, the young warriors were losing heart. Tales of white birds that flew above and dropped fire from the sky were proving true. Soon there might follow attacks by dogs and apes, clothed and carrying firearms on their shoulders, of which their elders spoke.

Then, as quickly as it had begun, the lull ended and the attack was resumed. Stung by its losses, the Uvi rose from the grass and flung its ranks upon the riflemen. The most powerful warriors were now in range with their assegais. Like a shaft from the sun, a six-foot spear flew with the speed of a hawk and sank into Strickland's back as he turned to reload his rifle. His men would hear a sharp crack as the tip fractured his rib-cage. Pinned through the body, his face pressed to the earth, the gang-master of the markets and the mines was dead at once.

Here and there, the disciplined fire of Pulleine's Lambs faltered as the spears flew among them. Two mercenaries were carrying Strickland's body back to the regimental lines. The patient observer on the col heard the rifle fire on the northern perimeter die away. From time to time, red-coated infantry had grounded their weapons and were glancing round behind them. Presently the crackle of shots broke out again but now it was uneven and the delay had been costly. In the scrimmage, the attacking force had become so dense that it sometimes eclipsed the view of the action. To the south of the line, the tribesmen were still running forward at a steady trot, only to fall under the swarm of bullets. But to the north, more of them were pressing against the front line of the regiments.

Pulleine had been given his command of the 24th Foot because he was one of few experienced in such warfare. Had the hunter been in his position, he too would believe that he need only hold firm for a little longer before the warriors must have thrown the last of their weapons. Each man carried five or six. Then the Zulu line must fall back—or die.

From the col, the precision glasses easily covered the wagon-park and the ammunition carriers, immediately below and on the nearer edge of the camp. In this tented space, the wagons were now surrounded by a jostling swarm of bandsmen with their blue caps held out, drummer boys and buglers who acted as runners to re-supply the infantry during the action. Anyone but the observer on the col might have wondered why they were not already running to and fro to feed the cartridge pouches of the regimental lines.

At the centre of the impatient musicians stood a score of oblong roughly made wooden crates that might need two men to lift them by their rope handles. Each was stamped in black with the crow's-foot insignia and initials of the War Department. They were of a conventional cargo pattern, crude but strong, with tight copper bands holding the lids down. Steel screws, rusted into place, had been sunk through each band. Inside the crates, there was a weatherproof lining of silver foil to protect the rows of waxed-paper cartridge packets, keeping out damp and preventing an accidental spark from the friction of metal against metal. Each packet, when torn open, would yield a cache of calibre .450 cartridges for the breech-loading Martini-Henry rifles.

Scanning the line through his field-glasses, the hunter made out that something had gone badly wrong with the Royal Artillery battery, forward of the perimeter on the northern flank. He was not surprised at this, though it was something of a bonus, a tribute to the incompetence of whoever had left the gunners there. Perhaps it was simply that Cetewayo's inexperienced young warriors had learnt the lesson of the battle more quickly then anyone had expected. By their movements, it was plain that they knew that lesson now.

After a shell had been fired, the iron monster that belched fire and smoke was powerless against them for almost a minute while it was loaded again. At the moment of its discharge, they had only to drop flat on the earth in the long dry grass until the flight of the thunderbolt passed over them. The weapon that fired it was then at their mercy, as they rose to their knees, to their feet, and surged forward again with spears poised to take their revenge.

Each time the artillery gunners reloaded, the officers of the beleaguered battery were striving to keep the tribes at bay with revolvers and swords. But during these pauses, the weight of numbers had begun to tell. In this reversal of fortune, the artillerymen were also in danger of being overwhelmed, cut off in the path of a continuing advance.

The only recourse was to save the guns, and the order was given. In a rapid manoeuvre, the teams struggled to get their field pieces to their horse-drawn limbers and then back within the camp perimeter. The dark-uniformed crews at each of the seven-pounders began hauling them away. Training and discipline accomplished this in less than half a minute. On the right, the 1st Battalion of the 24th Foot, on Pulleine's order, opened a covering rifle fire on the tribesmen as they swarmed round the retreating gunners. Drivers whipped up the horses while gun-crews jumped for a seat on the limbers. A spear, launched at short range, pierced an artilleryman's back even as he snatched for a hand-hold. At a distance, his cry was audible but brief.

The limber wheels lurched and jolted forward over uneven ground, their crews and passengers hacking at the heads and hands of the tribesmen following them. Elsewhere, the last of the gunners ran alongside the vehicles, the warriors close behind them.

A retreat by British artillery in the face of the tribes was a reverse, but it was not yet the rout that the hunter had envisaged. His glasses showed him Colonel Pulleine striding back to his tent, then pausing. He was looking up at the skyline, the hills above the plain. What could he hope to see there, in the white glare of noon? Perhaps Lord Chelmsford's column returning. But as he looked to left and right, he would sense a growing stillness across the field of battle. And in that stillness the colonel would know, as the quiet observer had known for many hours, that he and his entire force were doomed to die.

To the south, on the right of the position, the red lines of the infantry were still holding firm, for the attack had been lighter. On the left, where the artillerymen had found refuge, the crackling volleys of the rifles sputtered and died. The forward ranks were almost face to face with the enemy. A metallic rattle and scraping followed the chilling command that echoed down the lines of white helmets and scarlet tunics from officers and NCOs:

"Company—Fix bayonets!"

Pulleine must have wondered how it could have come to this. Perhaps he might guess. More likely, he would die and never know the reason. With the precision of a guards regiment on a drill square, the endangered platoons and companies had drawn bayonets in unison, counting three as the steel flickered bright in the sun, then clipping them in a single movement to the hot barrels of the rifles.

With a howl of expectant triumph, Cetewayo's warriors flung down their shields, raised their fine-honed assegais in powerful fists, and rushed upon the redcoat line. The bayonets of the 24th held them for an instant. But as each rifleman sank his blade under the breastbone of an assailant, a new wave of the warriors broke over his position. Before the bayonets could be withdrawn, the first riflemen were cut down by the Uvi and Umcijo.

The 24th infantry pulled back, leaving dead and wounded on the rough grass over which the line of the advance swept forward. The Natal Cavalry, fighting on foot, though entirely unprepared for hand-to-hand combat, was the next in danger of being cut off as the 24th fell back. But many of these dismounted riders turned, found their horses, and galloped for safety in the hills. Another gap in the northern flank was now undefended. The remaining artillery pieces stood forlorn and isolated in the wake of the advance.

The watching horseman again turned his field-glasses to the wagon-park below him. The orderly queue of blue-uniformed bandsmen had become a rabble of musicians, cooks, batmen, grooms, and orderlies. The tailboard of every ammunition wagon was down and a dozen of the heavy wooden boxes with their rope handles stood in two lines. Quartermaster Bloomfield was struggling with a powerful turn-screw to twist the thread of one of the steel bolts, sunken and rusted into the oblong boxes, holding the copper bands and heavy lids in place. There was a shout across the yard.

"The turn-screw drivers are too narrow! They're not Boxer calibre!"

"They surely must be! They were checked!"

"God help us, we have been given the wrong calibre for .450 ammunition crates!"

Another shout rang back.

"Then the boxes must be broken open, Mr. Bloomfield! A mallet or rifle butt! Nothing metal. There must not be a spark! Make a start! Some of these packets are to be carried half a mile to forward companies."

This reply had come from a supply officer, whom the onlooker identified as Lieutenant Smith-Dorrien. His disorganised queues of bandsmen and supernumeraries now scattered and began to attack the abandoned boxes. At the far end of the transport-park, there was a sound of hooves. Captain Bonham and two corporals of the Newcastle Mounted Infantry appeared at a gallop. Bonham swung round to face the supply officer, his voice carrying through the warm air.

"Mr. Smith-Dorrien! Captain Wardell's compliments. H Company's ammunition is exhausted. The 24th must abandon their present position and fall back almost to this point unless you can give our runners cartridges to carry back this minute. If you cannot do it, let us have the boxes and we will break them open!"

Smith-Dorrien straightened up.

"No, Captain Bonham! There must be order. There cannot be order if the boxes are taken away! Some companies will have too many cartridges and others too few."

"H Company has none at all, sir! If we fall back, the northern flank cannot hold out! The artillery has been routed. My message is a command from Colonel Pulleine, sir. It is not a request!"

"Then open them here! Your mounted men may ride back with enough packages in your saddle-bags to carry on. It will be quicker than carrying heavy boxes such a distance!"

This concession was a signal for general disorder. The supernumeraries and infantry runners pushed forward in a scrum to drag the remaining boxes over the tailboards of the wagons. The scene was one of looting. Despite Smith-Dorrien's warning of metal striking a spark on metal, a bayonet flashed as it stabbed down to prise a thick wooden lid from the carcase of a heavy box. Elsewhere, iron hammers were being used to smash in the lids and sides.

There was a cry of relief as several lids sprang loose under the pressure of bayonets. A crowd surged round the quartermaster in possession of a broken box. The metal foil was ripped back. Caps or helmets were held out as wax-paper was torn and the brass cartridges tipped out in a stream. From the col, the view stretched far beyond the enclosure of the wagon-park. It needed no field-glasses to show that the amounts of ammunition would be too little and too late. Captain Bonham and his corporals raised dust as they turned and galloped off with the first consignments.

The warriors had broken the line to the south, where Durnford's surrounded position had now been overwhelmed. The tribesmen were in among the first tents. A well-aimed spear brought Bonham from the saddle. As the captain fell into the path of the next rider, his corporal's horse reared and threw him at the feet of his killers. Only the second corporal charged his way through. The bandsmen carrying the first heavy box got no further. From the hill, it was plain that the horns of the Zulu impi had almost closed round the rear of the British position. If Pulleine was still alive, he surely knew the end had come.

Unaware of the extent of the disaster, two men in the dark tunics of quartermasters were shouting at each other. Officers joined in. Smith-Dorrien had broken open a new box. He was tipping cartridges into twenty or thirty helmets and haversacks held out for him. Bloomfield shouted from a nearby wagon, "For heaven's sake, don't take those, man! They belong to our battalion. It's all we have left!"

"Hang it all!" the young subaltern called back. "You don't want a requisition order at a time like this, do you?"

With the first breach, the line which had held against the impi's weight began to fragment. Its men now found the attackers at their backs and feared they would be cut off. The 24th Foot, with Pulleine still alive and assuming direct command, drew back in a semblance of orderly retreat. The men at either end of the line fell away first and fought to the end among the tents of the company lines. Pulleine tried to keep the main body intact, ordering them back to the lower slope of Isandhlwana. Beyond the wagons, the boulders and low ridges might afford a defensive line.

As they withdrew, the men snatched ammunition pouches from the bodies of the fallen. Ironically, now that the camp was being overrun, the survivors found cartridges enough to supply themselves. Their tactic must surely be to defend a position among the rocks of the lower slope, saving ammunition, holding this makeshift redoubt until Lord Chelmsford's return with the mounted column. Yet even that defensive line was soon being infiltrated by the warriors of the tribes.

The last stage of the battle was one of universal confusion. Infantrymen were fighting in isolated groups. Back to back, in shrinking squares, the riflemen fought on with bullets and then with rifle-butts and bayonets, falling one by one. Among the tents and wagons, the British and the Zulu warriors carried on a random struggle of individual encounters. The watching horseman saw a sailor of the Naval Brigade, wounded in the leg, fighting madly with his cutlass against the encroaching warriors, his back to a wagon-wheel. One dead tribesman lay across his feet, another at his side. A moment later, a third who had crawled under the wagon pierced him through the body from behind.

There was a glimpse of Pulleine in the chaos, looking about him for his company commanders. Captain Pope and a dozen men still contested the thrust of the advance. His men fought with fixed bayonets, clubbing with rifle-butts until an assegai stabbed Pope through the breast. Still on his feet, he tried vainly to pull the shaft from his body while the powerful arms of the advancing tribes bore him down.

On the far side of the wagon-park, Captain Younghusband and the remnants of C Company had turned one of the wagons over in preparation for a last stand behind its shelter. Younghusband was passing down the line of survivors, shaking hands with each in a solemn farewell. A moment later, the warriors had swarmed over the shattered wagon, bringing down the captain and the last of his platoons.

The time had come for the horseman to draw a little further up the col, beyond the point that any reconnaissance by the tribes might reach in the wake of their victory. He had scouted the ground two nights before and knew the path that would take him higher while keeping out of immediate view. Not that those engaged in the dreadful hand-to-hand combat below would have much time to survey the hills above them. He led the dappled mare quietly, glancing down from time to time as opportunity gave him an aerial view of what was taking place.

Durnford and a dozen or so of his troopers held out briefly at the foot of the col. Their ammunition spent, they thrust and repelled the black battalions for a while with their bayonets. Then the leaders of the Uvi and Umcijo, splendid in their head-feathers and leopard pelts, seized the bodies of their own dead and bore them like a battle-ram onto the bayonet blades. Before they could free their weapons, Durnford and his men were overwhelmed.

Pulleine again trained his field-glasses on the ridges, no doubt in a dwindling hope of seeing Chelmsford's column riding hard to the rescue. He saw nothing but a deserted horizon of rock against the blanched heat of the sky. Had the colonel known where to look, he might have glimpsed a messenger of fate standing by a dappled mare.

Pulleine was not that witness's personal enemy. Had there been means of paying tribute to a fallen foe, the hunter might have availed himself of it. As it was, the scene below confirmed that the commander of the camp knew hope was gone and that he must nerve himself for what remained. Pulleine could not see, as the watcher on the col could see, that even in the wagon-park Quartermaster Sergeant Bloomfield was dead, sprawling on the tail-board of an ammunition wagon. A drummer-boy of the 24th had been slaughtered and left dangling by his heels from a wagon shaft.

Alone among the doomed survivors, Colonel Pulleine had a purpose to fulfil. In a few hours, Chelmsford's column would return and the debris of defeat must be sifted. The past half hour had seen a disaster without equal in British imperial rule. Two thousand men, armed with the latest rifles, field-guns, a rocket battery, and Gatling guns had been wiped out by barefoot tribes with spears and shields. Pulleine must surely have sworn to himself that the world should know the reason.

As the hunter watched from his refuge, Pulleine, bareheaded and with his tunic open at the top, drew his revolver and moved cautiously towards the guard-tent. Even among death and tumult, parts of the camp were still untouched by battle as the tribes swept through. The guard-tent was one of them. The last of the subalterns, Lieutenant Teignmouth Melvill, was standing by it, distributing the final packets of cartridges to half a dozen riflemen prepared to make a dash for the river.

Pulleine would not join them, having a more important duty to perform. But first, as though Chelmsford might still appear on the ridge, the colonel used the grace allowed him to look slowly for a last time along the skyline. At some distance, the hunter now revealed himself. He mounted, edged the mare forward into full view and came to the salute. Pulleine stopped and, whatever he may have seen in his last bewildered moments, the two men looked directly at each other. The colonel handed his field glasses to the young officer beside him and gestured at the hillside.

When they had inflicted their injury upon him, it was the mark of hellfire. Now he gave them back text for text, speaking as Pulleine's field-glasses swept across the rocky slope once more. The grey mare pricked her ears up at her rider's voice.

"And I looked, and behold a pale horse, and his name that sat on him was Death. And Hell followed with him!"

In his mind, Pulleine echoed him as his adjutant handed back the glasses.

"What do you see, Mr. Melvill? What do you see, sir? Do you not see death, Mr. Melvill? Death on a pale horse!"

A moment later, he knew that Pulleine was giving the last order of a British commander defeated in battle, when hope was gone and his men lay dead about him. The regimental colours of the 24th Foot were safe at Helpmakaar, but the flag bearing the Queen's Colour and the regiment's insignia, embossed in gold on the Union Jack, was now brought from the guard-tent, still rolled and cased in its cylindrical sheath. It was the symbol of the regiment's battle honours at Talavera and in the Peninsula, Cape Town, and Chillianwallah, Wellington's wars and the Queen's imperial conquests.

Pulleine was handing the cased flag to the pale lieutenant. The watching horseman echoed in his mind the words he would have used in the colonel's place.

"Take my horse from the lines, Mr. Melvill. Save the colours, if you can. Ride out across the saddle of Isandhlwana. Make for the Buffalo River and a crossing to the camp at Rorke's Drift. God speed!"

Whatever the exchange, the two men shook hands. Melvill saluted and doubled away to untie the colonel's horse. Through the stench of death and cordite in his throat, Pulleine came unharmed to his own tent and disappeared from view. Even if he heard the feet of his pursuers, the thought of what he must do might still hold his fear in check.

When the victors had withdrawn from the camp with their booty, the horseman on the col would ride down to see for himself what had happened in that tent. In the meantime, he had only to wait. He watched from above as several of the tribesmen approached the regimental lines. Whatever Pulleine had to do would be done by now. Before his enemies could enter, he appeared briefly in the opening of the canvas flap, his revolver in his hand. The warriors hesitated at the sight of the gun. Pulleine fired and the first man sank to his knees. The others drew back behind a further tent, trusting to its shelter. But there were no more shots. Pulleine's revolver was no doubt empty and only his sword remained. The tribesmen rose and moved forward.

It was several hours before the battalions of Cetewayo withdrew.

From above and at a distance, the looted camp presented a curious sight. Here and there a red-coated figure moved about the wagon-park or in the company lines. Over the tented army the British flag on its staff stirred perceptibly in the slight breeze of the coming dusk. Everything appeared to be in good order, as if the lines were quiet but a few of the men were moving about. If Chelmsford's column had been anxious at the despatches from Pulleine or had heard the sound of cannon fire from Isandhl-wana, seven or eight miles off, they would be reassured by their first distant sight. If it was Chelmsford's decision to extend his reconnaissance until twilight, he might feel vindicated.

So far as his riders could see at a distance, there would not be a Zulu anywhere near the camp. The first suggestion of disorder would probably be the sight of figures in red tunics, apparently from the native regiments, running from the tents of the officers' compound with bottles, dressing-mirrors, and ceremonial swords. There might even be an exchange of shots before the looters and their trophies disappeared into the dusk. Only when the column reached the perimeter would they have a full sight of the bodies from two armies, concealed at a distance by tall grass.

Unbelieving at first, they would see men whom they had taken leave of that morning now lying open-eyed in death. For all of them, it would be their first experience of a British defeat. What they saw around them would seem like the end of a world. On the garrison ground at the centre of the camp, a reconnaissance would reveal the heads of a dozen of Pulleine's officers set on the ground in a ritual circle, staring blindly outwards across the darkening veldt.

During his own reconnaissance, the hunter had found boxes and sacks of stores broken in the grass. Flour and biscuits, tea and sugar, oats and mealies had been scattered on the earth. The wagon-park was a tableau of confusion. Some of the vehicles had been over-turned, others thrown out in all directions. Some of the horses had been killed and some of the oxen lay dead beside the carts. A few were still alive, standing upright in the yoke as if yet awaiting the commands of their drovers. The horseman who had watched the drama had no quarrel with these beasts. He unharnessed them and set them loose to take their chance.

It would be beyond the capacity of Lord Chelmsford's patrol to bury so many dead. Stone cairns must be erected over the worst horrors for decency's sake, but no more. To make even a tempo-rary camp here would be unthinkable. Therefore, as Chelmsford knew, he could only gather as much evidence of the disaster as quickly as possible and then retire to Rorke's Drift. To search the tents of the officers' compound for papers and messages would be a priority. There might be some last signal to explain what had happened at Isandhlwana in those dreadful hours.

The hunter's reconnaissance centred on the wagon-park and the guard tent of Colonel Pulleine. Only a far greater prize would compel a man to explore the rest of the charnel-house the camp had become. In the wagon-park it was not necessary to replace every one of the useless ammunition turn-screws with the originals which he had removed during the previous night. Just enough of those originals must be found there to obscure the criminal cause of the catastrophe for the time being.

Pulleine's tent was the final scene of the hunter's revenge. A scattering of glass fragments on the carpet; a smell of gin.

The colonel had fallen after a struggle in his outer tent or day-quarters, where his body lay. Having fired the last chambers of his revolver, he must have fought with his sword until he was impaled twice in the back—through the tent wall. The blows had thrown him forward across the rosewood desk.

In this case, the looters had been too preoccupied at first to attack the body. The drawers of the desk had been wrenched out and smashed. A silver locket lying on the carpet had been overlooked by the victors. It held a woman's picture, probably a woman who had been young ten years before, with a background of summer trees.

No doubt the colonel had spent his final moments at the desk, writing a last testament as his killers closed in—giving as many details of the disaster as possible for the benefit of Lord Chelmsford. Such pages lay under the desk-blotter in an envelope addressed to the Commander-in-Chief at the Cape. The looters had paid no attention to it, and the hunter found the pages intact.

It would have been imprudent to preserve such a testament in any form. At the same time, the least sign of smoke or flame might attract attention. It was enough for the hunter to tear the pages into irregular fragments, crumpling each in his hands as he rode away and, at a distance, scattering the pieces to the breeze of a warm African dusk.

At the ruins of the guard tent, he had also allowed one concession to vanity. Before mounting his horse, he drew a plain card from his pocket. He wrote five words upon it, as though it had been a *carte de visite*, and tossed it into the ruined canvas structure. It did not even matter if the words were never found, so long as they had been uttered. The author had set a title to his masterpiece of devastation. *Death on a Pale Horse*. Let the gods of battle decide whether it should ever be read—and what the world would make of it.

Riding towards the eastern ridge, he dismounted on the slope where the tall grass had been flattened by his grey horse that morning. At the foot of a thorn-bush, the pale earth was scraped into a mound that might have been a substantial ant-hill. Scattering the crumbs of soil, he uncovered an object wrapped in sacking, something the size of a football or a child's tin drum. He had been well paid and he had kept his bargain. Those who doubted him should face the dead stare of Owain Glyndwr's one remaining eye.

He looked around him once more. There was no sign of scavengers in the camp nor of Lord Chelmsford's column as the sky began to cloud over. To the superstitious, it might seem curious that a night wind had begun to moan by daylight in the singing-thorn, like an anthem for the fallen warriors of two armies who lay in such numbers on every side. Yet between its gusts, the silence of the darkening veldt was so profound that it was possible to hear a single tribesman singing somewhere on the kopje, drunk on the liquor of the defeated.

WAR DEPARTMENT RECORDS

[PROVOST PAPERS WO/ 79/4281]

Provost Marshal Cape Colony

> To: Major The Hon. Lord Worsley
> Adjutant to Commander-in-Chief,
> His Royal Highness the Duke of Cambridge,
> Horse Guards,
> Whitehall
> London SW

Sir,

I have the honour to forward for your attention the enclosed despatch form. It was found wedged and concealed within the black leather rim of the right boot, when the body of Colonel Henry Pulleine was recovered by the Provost patrol and burial party at Isandhlwana on 20 May last. The form had evidently not been discovered by the colonel's assailants after his death.

Colonel Pulleine was well acquainted with Zulu customs. Contrary to popular belief, the tribes are usually averse to slaughter. After the ritual of the Washing of the Spears, they believe that any further act of killing a foe in battle contaminates the spirit of a man. They are therefore required by their belief to take an item of a dead enemy's clothes and wear this until a rite of purification has followed battle. Colonel Pulleine also knew from experience that tunics or uniforms are often taken from the dead but boots never, for the tribes go barefoot. His chosen place of concealment for this slip of paper is significant of that.

By the time the colonel wrote his message, he must have known what his fate would be. He also knew what might happen to his body after death. Regarding the enclosed message as of the greatest importance, and being a man of supreme valour, he did all in his power to convey its contents safely. You may deduce from the appearance of the paper and from the evident haste of the writing that he had only a matter of seconds to complete and conceal it.

In remaining your lordship's obedient servant, I have the honour to request that His Grace will give the message from this brave gentleman the immediate consideration it deserves.

/s/

[Enclosure] *CAMP ISANDHLWANA, 22 JANUARY 1879, 1.35pm*

WE ARE BETRAYED . . . FOR GOD'S SAKE LOOK AFTER OUR PEOPLE . . . GOD SAVE THE QUEEN . . .
    —Lt. Col. Henry Burmester Pulleine, Officer Commanding
    Her Majesty's 24th Regiment of Foot

METROPOLITAN POLICE FILE—
MEPO 3

ACC/ Personal File/Sir Melville Macnaghten

221b Baker Street
London W

Sir Melville Macnaghten
Assistant Chief Constable,
New Scotland Yard
London SW

30 August 1894

My dear Sir Melville,
It comes a little late for me to forward to you the following details of Colonel Rawdon Moran, *alias* "Hunter" Moran, formerly of Her Majesty's Indian Army. However, you may care to include the following information in your files. I suggest that it is pertinent

to the dossier of his younger brother, Colonel Sebastian Moran. He it was who died this morning on the gallows at Newgate Gaol for the "Park Lane Murder" of the Honourable Ronald Adair. I myself played some small part in the resolution of this mystery.

Unlike his younger brother, Rawdon Moran never incurred a criminal conviction for his many crimes. He was born in 1840, elder son of Sir Augustus Moran, who had undertaken several diplomatic missions to the court of Persia and the Sublime Porte on behalf of Lord Melbourne's administration.

I know something of Sir Augustus Moran. He and my father, Siger Holmes, were on opposite sides of the business when Edward Oxford made his attempt against the life of the young Queen. The shots were fired on Constitution Hill in the third year of her reign. My own narrative of this affair, taken down from my father's own words, must lie where it is a little longer.

Sir Augustus Moran was obliged to withdraw to exile in Hanover after the attempted assassination. His elder son Rawdon remained in England. Indeed, he attended both Eton and Oxford. As a young man, he left Magdalen College before his time, following a pistol duel with another undergraduate. He subsequently acquired a noxious reputation in London's sporting life.

After the father's disgrace, it was impossible the elder son should find a place in a fashionable regiment. I believe in 1863 he was refused when he tried to buy a captaincy under the Earl of Cardigan in the 11th (Prince Albert's Own) Hussars. His father had served in that corps as a young man. Making his way to India, where his ancestry was of less interest, Rawdon Moran first served as commander of an Indian bodyguard to the Rajah of Kalore with the local rajpoot rank of "colonel." Long after his dismissal by the Rajah, Moran habitually made civilian use of the title this rank had given him.

He subsequently returned to direct allegiance to the British Crown and bought a place in the unfashionable corps of the 1st Bangalore Pioneers. He distinguished himself on active service in the Jowaki campaigns and was mentioned in despatches after the battle of Charasiab. Whatever his regrettable moral reputation, his personal bravery under fire cannot be questioned. When the ammunition was exhausted and the position appeared hopeless, he and his company of mercenaries defended the wounded in the field hospital by beating off the attackers with trenching tools and killing a dozen of them. In the aftermath of his recognition, he transferred to the regular Army in the 109th Regiment of Foot, subsequently known as the Albion Fusiliers.

Rawdon Moran was reputed to have a nerve of iron. The tale of how he and his younger brother, Sebastian, crawled down a culvert after a wounded man-eating tiger became a legend in the brotherhood of big-game hunters. Its truth is vouched for by five independent witnesses.

Certain other of his attainments are beyond doubt. This *soi-disant* colonel, for he still used that title as though he owed it to Her Majesty rather than to a local nabob, was the best heavy-game shot that our Eastern Empire has ever produced.

So much may stand to his credit. He was also endowed with a perverted ingenuity and a warped moral instinct. Like his father, he was an aberrant growth from an honourable ancestral tree. Discreditable stories were told in Bengal. They asserted that

Rawdon Moran was a cheat at the gaming-table and an evil demon in the lives of several women. I believe, from the facts before me, that the unexplained self-destruction of Mrs. Stewart of Lauder after a matrimonial scandal fifteen years ago also stands to his account.

Though a cheat at cards and in financial matters generally, he was fierce and indomitable. To challenge him to a duel with pistols would have been madness. He had proved his skill on regimental mess nights by putting five successive pistol shots through the centre of an ace of spades at a range of thirty-seven paces. These bullets, from a .22 target pistol, were so closely placed that they entered one on top of the other, leaving a single hole. A man would therefore accept his losses rather than confront such an antagonist on a charge of dishonesty.

It was his conduct with women that ended his Indian career. You will no doubt recall the tragic case of the young military wife, Mrs. Emmeline Putney-Wilson. She it was who attempted to poison her infants and then hanged herself after the scorn and humiliation to which he exposed her. A clandestine "subalterns' court-martial" of the 109th Foot convicted him of conduct unbecoming an officer and a gentleman. A permanent injury was inflicted upon him by the officers of this "court," rather worse than being drummed out of the regiment to the accompaniment of the "Rogues' March." His departure in this manner made India too hot to hold him.

Returning to England, via the Zulu and South African Wars, he nursed a passion for revenge against the world and those to whom he owed his injury. London did not yet know the worst of him. He posed there as the gallant Indian officer he had once been. Indeed, he boosted his reputation by two books of reminiscences written by a journalist on behalf of himself and his brother. *Heavy Game of the Western Himalayas* appeared in 1881 and *Three Months in the Jungle* a few years later. He lived in the West End, with some extravagance, just off Bond Street. The clubs knew no positive ill of him. Until his death he remained a member of the Anglo-Indian, the Tankerville, and the Bagatelle Card-Club.

About the year 1884 he was sought out by the late Professor James Moriarty. Two or three years earlier, this luminary of crime had been dismissed with ignominy from his post in mathematics at one of our ancient universities. His offences were such as the college authorities could not get themselves to describe. The Professor got wind of the Indian scandals but also read of Colonel Moran's courage and enterprise.

These two scoundrels struck inspiration from one another. Professor Moriarty seldom exposed himself to danger but used Rawdon Moran as his brilliant aide-de-camp. Their network of infamy embraced the Transvaal diamond swindles of the 1880s and the so-called Pall Mall "white slave" conspiracies of 1885-6. In the course of his South African activities in the sphere of Illicit Diamond Buying, Moran left a foolish but innocent young woman to face the gallows on his behalf for the death of her master, Andreis Reuter. At my prompting, my brother Sir William Mycroft Holmes, Permanent Secretary for Cabinet Office Affairs, intervened successfully with the Transvaal government to save her life.

Your predecessors have been sceptical of my belief in a criminal brotherhood organised for war against society. I remain convinced of its existence, upon positive evidence, and could name most of its leaders.

Some of those names belong to men high in society and public life. The great prosper. As in the world of angling, it is the smaller fry who are generally caught.

Long before my own encounter with the Professor at the Falls of Reichenbach, I knew that James Moriarty could not be working alone. In the 1880s, I had also encountered Rawdon Moran. For my own safety, it became necessary that I should either leave England or that I should draw this most intrepid and resourceful of hunters into a trap of his own devising.

It was never easy to lay a snare for him. Despite his vicious conduct and repellent views, Rawdon Moran had shown himself a man of few weaknesses. He was, however, an habitual gambler at cards, notably at the Bagatelle Club. It was in his nature to cheat. He accomplished this less by sleight of hand than by judging the characters of those with whom he played.

It was characteristic of Moran that, when he had no need of money, it was his instinct to play false for the love and excitement of the thing. In cheating at baccarat, as in staking his life in a big-game hunt or a criminal venture, the thrill of the risk was more than half the reward.

The details of his career and "disappearance" have never been made public. You may now gather the story of this from Dr. John Watson's narrative. Its first chapter leads back to a time shortly before Dr. Watson and I were first acquainted. Even before that acquaintanceship, a common link was provided by the criminal activities of our adversary. These at least have been put an end to. You may rest assured, however, that, as nature abhors a vacuum, Rawdon Moran will have been replaced by now.

Should there be any further point upon which I may assist you, my talents such as they are remain at your disposal.

> I have the honour to be, sir,
> Your humble servant,
> William Sherlock Scott Holmes.

PART II

The Narrative of John H. Watson, M. D.

1

*M*y reader will readily understand that the foregoing documents have never previously been published for the world to read. The account of Isandhlwana remained classified in the criminal records of the State Papers under the name of Rawdon Moran. Other papers lie in a confidential War Office series detailing the activities of the Provost Marshal's corps, as our military police are known. Strict procedure under the Official Secrets Act of 1889 allows every Home Secretary to judge whether such papers shall be closed to the public for fifty years, or a hundred years—or for ever.

I am grateful to our late Prime Minister, Mr. David Lloyd George, who decided that after forty years had passed, the disclosure of reports from the field of Isandhlwana would no longer constitute a threat to national security nor embarrass the government of the day.

Sherlock Holmes had of course shown me his letter to Sir Melville Macnaghten at the time that he wrote it. However, I did not actually meet Holmes for almost two years after the catastrophe at Isandhlwana and my own arrival in India. I had qualified as a medical man at St. Bartholomew's Hospital in June 1878. Next month, I joined the Army Medical Department and undertook the customary short course in military training for medical officers, at Netley, near the Aldershot Garrison. I trusted that this additional qualification might one day transform me into a full regimental surgeon-major.

At the end of that year I was still a humble assistant with orders to join the 5th Northumberland Fusiliers, then stationed in India. All eyes were on India just then, for she was regarded as the jewel in our imperial crown. The voyage to the East had been shortened by the opening of the Suez Canal. Southern Africa remained important principally for the newly discovered riches of gold and diamonds, rather than as the principal route to Bombay.

If India was vital to our interests, Afghanistan was scarcely less so, at the time I left Netley for my military service. Under the leadership of Lord Beaconsfield, our rulers were convinced that Afghanistan was once again in peril from its Russian neighbour to the north. A British embassy had been refused entry to Kabul. However, a Russian mission was soon after received with honour. The Viceroy of India, Lord Lytton, warned the government at home that he would take independent military action if necessary, as the constitution entitled him to do. If he did not, we should wake up to find the Russian Bear on the North-West Frontier of India.

Before the year's end, I was among five hundred reinforcements of all ranks, marching through the streets of Portsmouth from the railway station to the docks. How popular we were! A regimental band was playing *The British Grenadiers* and *The Girl I Left Behind Me*. Crowds at either side were so dense that you might almost have walked over the heads of the people. As for patriotic shouts, it was all "Remember Old England depends on you! . . . Give them plenty of cold steel! . . . Keep your pecker up, old boy, and never say die! . . . We'll not forget you!"

As yet, there had been no fighting. What they thought we were going out there for, I do not know. We marched into the dockyard and, as the gates closed behind us, a thousand voices shouted "Farewell! God bless you!"

There was no speedy passage for us through the Suez Canal. We carried an infantry regiment to reinforce Lord Chelmsford at the Cape. The troopship *Clyde*, a decommissioned P & O liner which had seen better days, was our transport as far as Cape Town. Belowdecks, men slept in hammocks slung from the beams. Some preferred to huddle in blankets on the deck. Everywhere we breathed coal dust and hot oil, while the paddles beat their rhythm alongside the hull. The heart of the ship was the deep well of the engine-room. There was little to do but stare mesmerised at the massive and polished hammer-heads of three pistons driving forward and back, mile after mile, day after day, night after night.

We spent Christmas Day near the equator. Early in January we dropped anchor with white buildings and the mountain behind Cape Town on our port beam. There was not much talk ashore of Afghanistan, which was still an ocean away from us. A number of regiments, including my own Northumberland Fusiliers, were rumoured to have advanced from India through the mountain passes into Afghan territory—but whether that was true, who could say? At the Cape, all the talk was of an invasion of Natal by the Zulu tribes to the north of us, under their King Cetewayo.

The drums were beating for war on both sides in Natal, and the newspapers were full of it. Cetewayo had told Sir Henry Bowler, "While wishing to be friends with the English, I do not agree to have my people governed by their laws." It was a delicate balance. If there was war with the Zulus, what would prevent the Dutch settlers of the prosperous Transvaal stabbing us in the back by declaring independence from British rule? With one war on our hands, our resources would not permit us to fight on a second front.

My greatest fear was that I might get conscripted for this war in southern Africa and never see the wonders of India or the regiment I had been assigned to. It was not the life I had joined the Army for.

Under this gathering cloud, I met a young Army captain whose acquaintance I had made on board ship. He was now attached to Lord Chelmsford's infantry column of some four thousand men which was about to confront Cetewayo.

"Hello, doc!" this young spark greeted me cheerily. "You coming to the picnic in Zululand with us?"

"Not if I know it!"

How fortunate I was. A few weeks later the bones of this poor young fellow and more than a thousand others were picked clean by vultures from the skies above Natal. I should almost certainly have been cut to pieces with Colonel Pulleine and the 24th Foot. As it was, I boarded the trooper *Londonderry* and reached Bombay before I heard of Isandhlwana.

On a hot and dusty morning, I reported to brigade headquarters in Bombay. There was utter confusion in the Movements Office as to what was going on in Afghanistan. I asked a transport officer how I might best catch up with the 5th Northumberland Fusiliers. I understood that they might already be garrisoned in Kandahar, on the far side of the Khyber Pass. This chair-bound Irish major looked at me irritably. He spoke as though the pandemonium in his office was all my fault.

"Has no one told you, mister? Your travel order should make it clear. The Northumberlands no longer require an assistant surgeon. It is the Berkshires who are in need. Assistant Surgeon Mackintosh has been invalided back to the depot at Peshawar with dysentery. You will exchange into the Berkshires at your earliest convenience. Draw travel warrants and your pay draft here. The railway does not run as far as Peshawar. Requisition a seat as far as Lahore on tomorrow's Delhi train. Make arrangements when you get there. Now, who's the next man?"

Such was my welcome to active service. I set out the following morning on the first stage of my journey in a saloon coach of the Bombay, Baroda and Central India Railway. This was one of several coaches reserved for British officers. With wide windows, easy chairs, and clubroom tables, it was the type of train which, in England, carries young swells with their picnic hampers and servants to a fashionable race meeting.

From the pages of the newspaper behind which I retired, I gathered that the situation in Afghanistan had deteriorated since the last news reached England. The rebel leader Ayub Khan had gained the upper hand, and our expeditionary force had been obliged to move forward with speed. A good many officers from all over India now filled the carriages of every train destined for the nearest junctions to the North-West Frontier. In those days, the line stopped short of the Khyber Pass. I should have to join a mounted column for the journey beyond Lahore. My imagination was full of the high snow-covered peaks of the pass and the white-walled city of my destination. Not so long ago, Kandahar had been the capital of Afghanistan.

As we travelled north, there was a curious interlude. I could not see that it concerned me at the time—so much the worse for me. At every stage of this northward journey, I was increasingly preoccupied by the petty discomforts which anyone who has travelled by military train in India will recognise. Black horsehair is used as upholstery in these saloon carriages because it is easily cleaned and hygienic. Unfortunately, in that heat, it becomes a refined torture after a very little while. The firm stuffing gradually feels more like compressed bramble thorns, and its effects upon the body grow more acute with every passing mile.

I was not alone in my restless discomfort. The train to Lahore was far too crowded with our troops for anyone to have a carriage to himself. I found myself sharing with a captain and two lieutenants from a regiment I shall not for the moment name. The lieutenants answered to the names of "Jock" and "Frank." Both had come aboard in mufti. Their regimental blazers and white flannels equipped them better for a picnic on the banks of the Thames than an encounter with Ayub Khan's murderous Jezails. I should guess that they were no more than twenty-one years old: they could not have more than a couple of years service between them.

After my seven years spent walking the wards of St Bartholomew's Hospital, the gap in our age and experience made them seem frivolous and vexatious. They were like excited schoolboys on a holiday. The uniformed captain, whom they called by his surname, Sellon, was a little older and far more sober. He glanced at me from time to time, as though suspicious of who I might be and what I had come for.

Sleep helps to pass the time but I was soon glad of conversation to take my mind off the horsehair padding. The lieutenants and I exchanged small talk. From the first, it was evident that I was not their type but they regarded me with friendly curiosity. They were going no further than Peshawar but knew a good deal about the regiments there. When they asked me the name of my unit, I said that I thought it would be the Berkshires.

"Jock" and "Frank" made grimaces and sounds of approval. Jock went so far as to shake me by the hand. The Berkshires, he assured me, were as fine bunch of fellows as ever lived. It would be "rather a lark" fighting alongside them.

"I came out here straight from Cambridge," Jock added with an ingratiating grin. "I was only up for a year. I can't say I did much work there and it seemed rather a waste of time. My father thought so as well—after all, the bills come pretty steep at Kings and he was footing them, poor old fellow. So here I am, as the poet says."

Captain Sellon stared at these two without comment. They looked the sort of expensively educated young mutts whom Holmes once said could talk and could think but unfortunately could not do both at the same time. I thought it would do no harm to toss them a scrap of biography.

"I was posted out to the 109th Albion Fusiliers originally, then the Northumberlands, but it seems both are already suited."

There was an exchange of looks between them, just as if I had made a bad joke. What on earth had I said? I waited for them to tell me. Jock and Sellon merely stared at me; but Frank, a rather slight youth with dark curly hair, smiled.

"Then I daresay you won't mind a change to the Berkshires. What? I should think anybody would. Eh?"

They spoke as if we were all sharing a secret. I had better know the truth of it.

"I'm sure the Berkshires will prove a fine regiment."

"Rather," said fair-haired Jock. Captain Sellon now turned and stared out through the window as if to avoid discussing the matter. But his two lieutenants had not an ounce of discretion between them. They were plainly itching to impart some scandal to see how I would take it.

"Whereas the 109th . . ." I began.

Sellon turned from the window.

"What do you know about the 109th? The Albion Fusiliers?"

"Nothing, in so many words."

Frank and Jock began to laugh, whether at my curiosity or stupidity I cannot say.

"If you have not heard," said Sellon, without a trace of a smile, "you must be the only man from Mitchni to Mooltan who has not. Perhaps that is for the best."

"Heard what?"

Jock could not quite resist the chance. He gave a chuckle.

"The subalterns' court-martial in the 109th. That was a ripe one!"

For whatever reason, Captain Sellon favoured him with a full-faced glare. Jock was grinning too hard to notice.

"I have just come from regimental surgeon's training at Aldershot," I said firmly. "All this is new to me. What on earth is a subalterns' court-martial?"

The two lieutenants jostled each other a little and smiled politely. Captain Sellon intervened accusingly, as if I should have known better.

"A wholesome way of teaching a fellow manners, sir. I cannot condone it, but it may sometimes be the only way to avoid a regimental scandal. It is a court made up of junior officers to try a defendant privately. Let us leave it there."

I found it odd that Sellon should be so touchy while Jock and Frank could hardly contain themselves. They had no wish to leave it there!

"Privately?" I asked.

"Mess jackets and medals at midnight," said Frank with a helpful grin.

Sellon waved him aside. He proved to be the authority, but I noticed that he blushed a little as he spoke.

"Several years ago, doctor, there was a new young fellow in my brigade who thought himself a bit above the other lieutenants. He liked to swank and insisted on wearing a medal ribbon given for native Indian service. Not a British decoration. One does not wear such a trinket at a formal mess dinner. You understand that, no doubt. They warned him twice, to no avail. The third time, his junior comrades constituted themselves a court-martial and tried him in the mess at three o'clock in the morning. They sentenced him to have the letter 'S' for 'swank' shaved on the top of his head. It was done then and there. Two or three of them sat on him and another did the shaving. The hair grew back in a few weeks and no harm done. But they took the bounce out of him and he turned into a decent enough fellow. I promise you, he learnt his lesson."

Jock leant forward.

"Before we came out from England, I heard of a man in the Brigade of Guards, no less. He was seen walking down the Strand in a boater that a fishmonger might wear, rather than a proper top hat. They tried him in the mess. Then they stripped him and made him run a circuit of the dinner room under the gauntlet of their belts. There were two other new officers, sprogs they call them in the guards. They refused to enter for the regimental sports. The same thing happened to them."

Perhaps it was no more than I expected, but there was more to come from Captain Sellon, though he sounded impatient to have the thing over with.

"These things exist because of defects in the legal system. You know, I presume, that an ordinary regimental court-martial is only empowered to try non-commissioned officers and other ranks. Its officers have to be dealt with in public at a general headquarters court. A trial like that makes a lot of noise and does no good to morale. Have you not been taught that—doctor?"

"I can't say I have been. Justice ought surely to be dispensed in open court."

He gave a short exasperated sigh.

"To be sure. As it is in England. Out here, any public trial may smear the regiment in the eyes of our own people and the Indians as well. Let me show you. A crime need not be great in order to bring disgrace. Sometimes it is only military incompetence or perhaps insubordination. Of course it may be something more serious. A young officer as mess treasurer may embezzle part of the funds. Even worse, it might be some kind of offence against a woman. Imagine what the story would do to that woman if it were spread all over the native newspapers! Oh yes, doctor—there is a press for the Pandies out here as well as our own. The trouble-makers know how to use it. Well, then, say a young man has gone wrong but simply needs a sharp lesson. A subalterns' court-martial, junior officers who are his equals, administers that lesson to him in private. It is irregular, but it is found to be useful."

"I have never heard of such a thing before," I said. I did not add that the more I heard of it, the less I liked it.

"Did they teach you so little of Army life at Aldershot?" Sellon inquired.

He was quite right. No one at Netley Hospital had thought it necessary to inform me of these military curiosities during my medical training. He still looked at me for all the world as though I might have been an impostor in uniform. Who was he? He seemed remarkably well informed about military law.

"How long have you been in the Army, sir—or in India at least?" he inquired laconically. "Not very long, I think!"

I protested at this.

"A trial of whatever kind must be a matter for judicial authority. There must be proper rules, a report, and an appeal procedure."

Sellon continued more slowly, as if determined that I should understand every word.

"These trials are not reported. They are not officially spoken of. Any commanding officer will know when one is taking place. The rumour mill sees to that. Sometimes he may even be called to give evidence. But he has no official knowledge of its proceedings, its verdict, or its sentence."

"And that is what you call mess jackets at midnight?"

For the next ten minutes or so, Captain Sellon described this arcane procedure—or midnight ritual, as I might call it. Let us say that the offender had been charged with conduct that might bring disgrace on the regiment if it went to a public hearing. One of the junior captains—Sellon, perhaps?—would be appointed president of the court. Four lieutenants would be its other members, rather than the nine more senior officers at an official hearing. Another captain would be prosecutor, and the defendant would be allowed to choose any other officer in the regiment to represent him.

When the rest of the officers and the servants had retired for the night, three tables would be arranged round three sides of the mess room and draped in green baize. They would be set out with papers, carafes, and glasses, and legal reference works, just as if this were a properly constituted court. The wicks of the oil-lamps would be trimmed and those present would wear formal mess-jackets and medals, as at an official tribunal. Witnesses would sit outside in the ante-room until they were called, sworn, examined, and cross-examined. All those involved were automatically assumed to be under an oath of secrecy, as a matter of honour. Some honour, I thought!

How could anyone not see the dangers of this drum-head ritual? I imagined myself being tried privately by such gadflies as Jock and Frank with Sellon as my judge! And, of course, there was no right of appeal to the world outside, let alone the Courts-Martial Appeals Court. But far from being a black mark against a regiment that settled its own problems in this sinister way, it seemed to be thought of more highly.

Yet even if a defendant was convicted, how could a collection of subalterns have any legal redress against him? They could not cashier him, unless he chose to send in his papers and resign. They could not imprison him, let alone shoot him or hang him. They would, apparently, have kept him under escort so that he could not "do a bunk," as Frank put it, until the trial was over. But what then?

I tried to imagine what had happened in the 109th Foot to bring about such a midnight charade. The regiment had been in India for seven or eight years and would have returned to England by now but for the emergency in Afghanistan. It had been stationed near Lahore, living among the local community. It occupied British army barracks such as might have been found at home in York or Colchester or Canterbury.

It seemed from my companions' conversation that there had been a scandal, six or nine months ago, involving the regiment I was no longer to join. It had ended in this macabre ritual. But whatever the offence and whoever the culprit, what could the outcome of the so-called trial have been? Captain Sellon would bite his tongue out rather than tell me. All the same, he seemed anxious that I should understand the uses of such a secret court.

"I don't think you quite grasp the point, sir," he said more patiently: "it is no substitute for the legal process and, for myself, I cannot condone it. But a man who misbehaves without committing a felony is often given the chance of putting things right privately. A chance of being dealt with quietly by his own kind. It may seem a privilege in its way. He avoids public disgrace with his reputation at issue."

"He welcomes this secret trial?"

"I will give you an example. Some years ago, a young lieutenant was mess treasurer in a regiment brigaded with my own. He was a decent enough fellow in most respects but not as well endowed with money as most of the others. To keep up appearances and pay his mess bills, he pilfered the funds of his comrades which were in his trust. In the circumstances and at his age, it was folly rather than villainy. It could not be ignored, but a formal public trial at brigade headquarters would have destroyed his reputation and career."

"It would," said Frank, nodding emphatically but still smiling.

"I speak of what I know, doctor," Sellon continued. "As a matter of honour, his name and misconduct were never revealed by those other subalterns who judged him. He was tried by his equals and convicted. Indeed, he admitted his guilt."

"And what was his sentence?"

"He was to go ten rounds against a junior captain who had been a school and regimental boxing champion. No one could compel him to do so, but it was the price of avoiding a public trial."

"He agreed?"

"He did. Of course, he was no pugilist and after that half hour he had been badly beaten. Yet he had tried to hold his own against a superior antagonist. In this he had shown a good deal of pluck. By doing so, he won back much of the reputation which he might have lost through an act of folly—as I choose to call it."

"What happened to him then?"

"He remained in the Army, though not in the same regiment. He transferred and began again. I think you do not understand, perhaps, that such rituals are also the way in which the Army protects its own."

I certainly understood how much I still had to learn about India and the codes of its British rulers.

"What happened in the 109th Foot?"

Captain Sellon leant forward again.

"Since you are no longer joining that regiment and have heard nothing so far, I think we may leave the matter there. We have talked enough of these things to give you an understanding. You will forgive me if I do not choose to make them a matter of gossip. If you ever discover the answer to your question, it will not be through me."

His two juniors were unwilling to contradict him, in his presence. As for me, I was about to face life and death somewhere beyond the Khyber Pass. Joshua Sellon was right. Regimental tittle-tattle was something best avoided. Or so I thought.

About half an hour before reaching Lahore, we stopped at a remote junction on a wide and fertile plain. There was a loop in the line where our train was held back, waiting for an on-coming set of southbound coaches to pass us on its return to Delhi or Bombay. As we sat there, our carriage door was opened by an officer in the uniform of a brigade major. He summoned Captain Sellon out to the platform. They spoke for a moment about something that was evidently confidential. Then, as the door was closed from outside, it became evident that Sellon had been commanded to join a conference further up the train.

While we waited for the southbound train to pass, I knew that Jock and Frank would never keep their mouths shut in their captain's absence. As for Joshua Sellon, I was never to see him alive again.

2

*J*ock gave Frank a nudge.

"You ass!" he said, gasping and grinning before he looked at me again. "It's all right, sir. Not your fault. You weren't to know about old Josh."

"What about him?"

"He's only Provost Marshal's Corps! That's all! Snooping into black-guards, as they say. He's done court-martials, but he won't tell tales."

"The long and the short of it was the Putney-Wilson case," said Frank, eagerly but quietly, as if Sellon might still be listening, "that's what happened in the 109th. You'll hear about it anyway in Lahore. But I daresay the tale reached the English press. Emmeline Putney-Wilson?"

"I don't believe so."

"Really? Not the suicide? It surely must have done."

"I think not. At any rate, I cannot recall it in the papers."

"Well, Emmeline was married to Major Putney-Wilson of the 109th. He was seconded to Delhi for several months. She was a pious sort of lady, it seemed, devoted to the two little children. First row of the garrison chapel on Sunday morning, hymn-book open. Voice of a prima donna and looks of a pretty horsebreaker. Also a voice for amateur drama but nothing too racy. He and she were a real pair of uprighters. You couldn't imagine her breathing the same air as so-called Colonel Moran."

"Why is it," Jock butted in, "when a hymn-singer and her tambourine fall from grace, it's for a bounder? Perhaps she thinks it's the only way to save him."

"In a nutshell," Frank resumed, "Rawdon Moran was a rotter. Some fellows seemed to think him likeable. In other words, he paid for their pale ale and they laughed at his talk. No one thought him straight. After all the women he'd had, he must have found Emmeline Putney-Wilson easy to pick off. But she, poor little girl, got herself into a tangle. Love and guilt, I suppose. Wanting him and then feeling foul when she'd got what she was after. If ever the balance of a mind was disturbed, it was hers."

Jock took his chance.

"Of course he left her, as anyone with any sense knew he would. From being pretty and prim, she began to look grim and sick. The garrison chapel saw the last of her because she couldn't face the talk. And, of course, Putney-Wilson wouldn't be on detachment in Delhi for ever. A month or so went by, and every day she seemed more wretched at what would happen when he came home. The affair with Moran was over, but the tittle-tattle wasn't. Even if someone didn't tell him outright, sooner or later Putney-Wilson was going to hear the whole story by accident."

"And Moran?"

"Oh, he forgot her after a few weeks. Except when he was laughing with one or two cronies over having a high-style, nose-in-the-air saint on her knees in front of him. To cut a long story short, the night before Putney-Wilson came back, she couldn't take any more. She hanged herself from the bannister of their bungalow. She'd given laudanum to the two children, I suppose to prevent them growing up to hear of their mother's shame. Mercifully for them, the dose was too small to do the job."

"He destroyed her," Frank chimed in; "everyone knew that. They kept his name out of the inquest and made it look like simple madness. People do go mad out here, you know. Men and women. More often than you think."

To me, this pathetic story seemed worthy of a Greek tragedy. I was fascinated to see how the mere telling of it had sobered these two young rips. It was truly appalling.

"So the subalterns of the 109th put him on trial at midnight?"

Jock nodded.

"They took him by surprise, or they'd never have caught him. Two junior captains put him under arrest and escort. They held him in his own room until that evening. He was not allowed to speak to anyone. His meals were taken to him. There wasn't much documentation, and the case was simple. He had never hidden what he did."

"What about the regimental commander?"

"Colonel Tommy? I daresay he'd be glad to get rid of Moran at any price. Officially, he knew nothing about the trial. Unofficially, he must have known. Still, he was a good sort, the last man to interfere. Most of them hoped they'd see Moran kicked out of the regiment. A piper playing the Rogue's March while they cut off his buttons and epaulettes. But without Emmeline Putney-Wilson to give evidence, there was no simple proof of a crime. What Moran had done seemed worse than most crimes, but he put it all on her as an hysterical little girl who couldn't handle a bit of fun. Even in front of the court, the wretched fellow took a high tone. He wouldn't answer any charge or enter a plea. He refused to recognise the court or to have any part of it. They gave him an officer for his defence. Captain Learmont, from the support company. Captain Canning, the adjutant, was elected president with four lieutenants to sit with him. It took them just one session, a couple of hours, starting at midnight."

"But there must have been a charge?"

"Conduct unbecoming an officer and a gentleman, I should think. It doesn't sound much on its own, but they can tie a lot more to it."

"Such as?"

"Is there such a thing as constructive murder in the common law?"

"I daresay."

"Look," said Frank, "why should it matter what they called it? Her death was his crime. Of course, it could have gone to a general court-martial. But what good would that do? He might have got off Scot-free. Whatever old Josh Sellon thinks, better deal with it quietly and not let the poor woman's name be dragged through a court. As though the inquest wasn't bad enough."

There was a horrible fascination in the tale, if it was true. I looked at Jock.

"What could they do to him? They couldn't sentence him to death or imprisonment."

I then listened to an extraordinary account. It was easy to picture the closed velvet curtains drawn against the deep silence of a sleeping world, oil lamps casting their glow on regimental portraits and silver. Elegant dining chairs were set at long tables draped in green baize. The five members of the court in dark blue mess jackets, with Captain Canning as president, sat along the top table, the prosecution and defence on either side. Volumes of military law. Decanters of water and glasses. The president's gavel and "Colonel" Moran's surrendered sword. All these made up the high table's setting. A junior second lieutenant sat by the door to the ante-room, beyond which the witnesses waited.

As my two informants described it, the outcome of the case was never in doubt. Captain Learmont had been left to construct a defence of bricks without straw. Moran refused to answer for his association with Mrs. Putney-Wilson, but he had boasted of it to his toadies. To them he preached a simple gospel of worldly experience—all men are scoundrels at heart and every woman will sell herself if the price is high enough.

I shall have so much to say of "Colonel" Rawdon Moran that I had better describe him at once as my two lieutenants depicted him to me.

He was plainly older than the misguided young men who looked to him for wisdom. Perhaps about forty, with dyed whiskers. He posed as a jolly, rollicking fellow who had knocked about the world. He took little care to hide his viciousness. In appearance, he was tall with a well-developed chest, broad shoulders, muscular arms, and heavy square hands, a vigorous growth of fiery red hair on the backs of his fingers. It was his prematurely wrinkled face that betrayed the coarseness under the easy manner and jovial laugh.

No one got the better of him, he promised them that. Good old Randy Moran could turn his hand to anything. He had been everywhere and knew everything—and everyone. Was there a successful West End play? He knew the leading actress. Was there a sensational divorce suit or a murder trial? He knew the leading counsel on both sides. In any conversation about game-hunting, foreign cities, money, the law, great families and their houses, he was there before you, always knowing more than you did.

Moran had several times lent money to younger officers, perhaps to keep them under his influence, but those who accepted his good-natured offer would never have dared to delay repayment. There was something within the good-humoured look that inspired fear—no less than that. The very way in which he cut a cigar or scraped his boot suggested the act of a man who would stick at nothing, once he felt himself cornered. As for meeting women, however playful his introduction, it was not long before his arm was round their waists.

Such was the defendant in the subalterns' court. The evidence against him was proven. He never bothered to deny that he had taken his pleasure with a foolish, lonely wife who was flattered by his notice. She was not an innocent child, after all. All her evangelical gentility counted for nothing against that. Unbalanced as she became, her fault was merely a failure to understand that all good things must come to an end, as Moran described it to his cronies. She gave way to some innate moral hysteria that was none of his making. Her mind distracted, she destroyed herself. He invited the world to show him where his fault lay, in law or common sense.

However noxious he might be, the procedure of the so-called subalterns' court was no match for his wickedness. According to the account now given to me, evidence was admitted in this midnight court which any English judge would have ruled out as mere hearsay. There was ample testimony which blackened Moran's character, but it proved nothing. He had ridiculed women as creatures who would dance at a court ball one night and abase themselves before a money-lender on the following morning. If a husband could not support them, they would readily sell themselves. If that was impossible, they would rip the clothes from their own mother's back and tear the jewels from her throat in order to shine as the stars of the next evening party.

But men were no better. Moran assured his young friends that a pillar of the community would sell his wife and children, his own soul, to get money for some favourite lechery. It might be the gambling saloon, the stock exchange, a particular woman who could offer a special gratification not to be found elsewhere. Such men would sell the coats off their backs to gratify themselves with the sort of women whom they knew would take their money while regarding them with contempt.

I was a young man when I heard all this. The portrait of Rawdon Moran seemed to me hardly less evil than that of Satan. And if such a repellent form of Satan were at the bar of subalterns' justice, perhaps I would not have cast my vote strictly according to the rules of evidence.

Of course, the midnight court found him guilty of conduct unbecoming an officer and a gentleman—absurdly underrating his crime! It also convicted him, in some form, for causing the poor young woman's death. But then what was to be done with him? In one view, death itself would hardly be excessive. In another, it was doubtful whether they had grounds to do anything at all. In their enthusiasm to avenge Emmeline Putney-Wilson, they had not considered the dilemma in which they would find themselves.

And so Captain Canning and the four other members of the lamplit court had withdrawn to consider the verdict and sentence. It was late by then. Indeed, it was almost two o'clock in the morning. When they came back, Moran stood up even before they could command him to do so. Then Captain Canning looked him directly in the eyes. The so-called colonel was now found guilty of causing the death of the young woman by a means far crueller than many forms of murder.

Had he anything to say? He had not, except to deny the authority of these "boys," as he chose to call them.

What of the sentence? He might deserve to die, but officers of a British regiment cannot murder such a man in his turn. As they faced each other, Captain Canning had the courage not to be daunted by the ferocity of Moran's savage glare. Indeed, the captain continued to look the criminal in the eye and denounce him for conduct unbecoming a British officer and for moral homicide, whatever that might be. There was no sentence this court could pass which would be adequate to that crime—but pass a sentence it must.

It was therefore the judgment of his comrades that Rawdon Moran, sometime colonel of the Rajah of Kalore's Militia and now captain in the 109th Albion Fusiliers, should be required to send his papers in forthwith and leave the regiment. Within that regiment, meanwhile, he was to be outlawed. Whatever retribution was inflicted upon him, no officer would contribute to the detection, detention, or punishment of the person who carried it out. So long as he remained within their reach, he should be a target for their vengeance.

It was an extraordinary sentence, vindictive but surely ineffectual. There was one thing more. Should Moran ever again make application to serve Her Majesty the Queen, in a military or civil capacity, any member present would be absolved from his oath of secrecy. The proceedings of the present tribunal would be communicated to the unit or body considering such application. From respect to the late Mrs. Putney-Wilson and Major Henry Putney-Wilson, those proceedings should not otherwise be made public. An oath of secrecy would presently be taken by the members of the court and the other officers in attendance. Unfortunately, with so many excitable young men present, these oaths were not worth the breath expended in uttering them.

This promised to be a comprehensive destruction of Rawdon Moran's career. If ever there were an outcast, it would be he. But standing there at that moment, he looked round at what he seemed to regard as a litter of yapping puppies. His words were smoothly contemptuous and he almost spat the syllables in their smooth young faces

"In time, gentlemen, I may take my leave of this regiment. Meanwhile, I have no intention whatever of sending in my papers. Now that this pantomime is over, I shall be obliged for the return of my sword. If not, I shall report, as a matter of honour, that it has been stolen by a common thief among you here."

Honour was soiled in the mouth of such a scoundrel as this! But the bluff of the subalterns' court-martial had been called. These young officers had applied justice intended for minor social misdemeanours to a form of murder—and it had failed them. Then, before any of them could speak, a tall, pale, dark-haired man stood up at the far end of the prosecutor's table. He had sat quietly and almost hesitantly throughout the proceedings without once offering to take part. This was Major Henry Putney-Wilson.

"Mr. President, sir, I am not a member of this court. However, if you will allow me, I will lay aside for a while my obligation to the manual of military law and even, as some will think, my regard for the Christian religion. Since he scorns common decency and common justice alike, I require Captain Moran to afford me that satisfaction which one gentleman owes to another."

The onlookers watched in silence. This formula had only one meaning. Major Putney-Wilson had challenged Moran to a duel. By this date, duelling was illegal and seldom heard of between British officers. Such exchanges as occurred were invariably fought with pistols. But Major Putney-Wilson was no kind of shot. Moran could cut the heart out of the ace of spades at thirty-seven paces. If ever a man deserved the cliché of signing his own death warrant, it was the major at that moment.

Captain Canning was about to intervene, but Moran was there first. The mess-room rang with a short burst of scornful laughter.

"Duelling, sir, is a game for schoolboys. A game of chance. At twenty, I could shoot the buttons from a man's epaulettes at thirty paces and never singe his tunic. But I was once challenged in my Oxford days at Magdalen College, and I fought a duel. We met in Christ Church Meadows at dawn. I shot at this idiot who had called me out. The distance was not thirty paces. Yet I missed. The other fellow was a milksop who had never truly handled a pistol in his life. Look at this!"

He pulled back his tunic cuff and undid the link of his shirt. There was a small track upon the skin over the bone where no yellow hair grew, rather as if it had been shaved. He buttoned his sleeve and looked round at them all.

"I knew no better at twenty, gentlemen. A close-run thing indeed! But now? Duelling? No, thank you very much! Let us rather roll a pair of dice or cut the cards!"

Though he was fierce enough in his humour, the worst of Rawdon Moran was a terrifying moral chasm in his character, a bottomless depth of hate and harm.

So they stood motionless for a moment, like actors taking a curtain call at the end of a play's final scene. He had the whip hand over them. Everyone was looking at Moran, scarcely noticing one another. While they hesitated, he took his sword and thrust it into its scabbard. He swung round and walked towards the door that led to the ante-room. No one tried to prevent him leaving. Despite his contempt for duelling, they knew he would kill at that moment if he had to. And the law might find in his favour. The second lieutenant who was standing by the door closed it behind Moran and then, in an unexpected movement, stood with his back to it and with his arms folded, as if to prevent anyone else from following.

Presently there was a shout from beyond the closed door and the members of the subalterns' court looked at one another. They heard a gasp and trapped-animal sounds of a struggle which lasted a full minute. The lieutenant standing at the door remained quite still with his back to it, to prevent anyone from following. Then their hearts jumped as there came a terrible cry and a roar of anger pierced by pain. A second roar followed that might have been agony in another man but was fury in this one. So long as Moran was in the mess room, almost all eyes had been upon him. Only now did most of them realise that Putney-Wilson was no longer there. He had not been part of the proceedings, and no one had thought his quiet departure important.

The door of the ante-room swung open awkwardly. Two powerfully built soldiers, not wearing regimental insignia and unfamiliar to the onlookers, were standing over a figure lying on the floor. A military farrier, also from some other regiment, stood upright with a branding iron in his hand. The bright heat was fading rapidly from the dull metal. Major Putney-Wilson, having seen justice done, had begun walking away into the night.

The figure on the floor struggled to his feet. Moran's tunic had been torn where the buttons and epaulettes were cut away. They had "played the rogues' march" with him after all. But the tunic had also been stripped from his right arm and the shirt torn from that shoulder, which was not part of the custom when a man was drummed out of his regiment.

On the yellow-white flesh of the upper arm and shoulder, there was a crimson swelling, two or three inches across. Moran's face was mottled red and white with anger and shock. He swung round as if he might knock down the lieutenant who had guarded the door. But that guardian had now drawn his Webley service revolver from its holster and was holding it in Moran's full view.

The junior lieutenant by the door could see what his comrades could not. The crimson swelling on the upper arm bore an imprint, a brand. The farrier's iron customarily carried three digits, one for the number of the regiment and two for the number of the horse. Major Putney-Wilson was a devout man, and the insignia which the glowing iron left behind was one that the world might recognise. It was "666," the Mark of the Beast from the Book of Revelations. If memory served, those who bore the mark of the Beast were condemned to the lake that burns with everlasting fire and brimstone. Meanwhile, until the day of his death, Moran's own body would burn before the world, proclaiming him for what he was.

And still no one in that mess room moved. Then Rawdon Moran swore, softly but clearly. The tone of his voice counted for even more than the words.

"By God, my turn shall come! I'll be revenged upon the whole pack of you—you and all your kind!"

He swung round and lurched towards the outer door, then stumbled into the night.

"And they never saw him again," said Jock, the young lieutenant facing me from his horsehair banquette. "No one knew whether he only swore harm to the men in that room or to all the world. Strictly speaking, he was absent without leave after he left his quarters, but who would mind about that? Colonel Tommy must have sung hosannas. And the less said about the subalterns' court, the better. Officially, it never happened, you see. Unofficially, even with an oath of secrecy, you can't stop a story like that from going the rounds!"

"Good riddance to bad rubbish," Frank butted in; "except that a cove I knew in the 109th swore it would be like trying to say good riddance to the devil himself! You can't do it. He may be anywhere at any time, watching, waiting his chance. And just for a while, before they got their common sense back, every man in that mess room—almost every man in the regiment—was afraid of what Rawdon Moran might do."

By the time we reached Lahore, I ended my journey a good deal more thoughtful than I had begun it. Even so, I could not see that this story would ever be my concern. If it was true, all this had happened a year before my arrival in India. It was history. The headlines now were full of Isandhlwana and the Zulu War. Moran was stale news. There had been no sign of him after that dramatic night. By now he might be in England, or still in India, or anywhere in between. He had vanished into the darkness, like the wounded beast of his own hunters' legends. His last words were a promise of revenge, but what revenge had there been? He seemed done for. Yet I daresay many people would still have offered a good deal of money to know exactly where he was now and just what he was doing.

Jock and Frank had held my attention by the moral of their story. We went our separate ways, and I was left alone with my thoughts. By the time I reached Peshawar, I decided I had probably been treated to a highly coloured dramatisation of events. Did the God-fearing Putney-Wilson really have his minions in attendance to mark Moran for life if the villain should refuse to answer on the field of honour? It was the sort of tale one tells a sprog, a newcomer to the regiment, for the fun of seeing him grow pale and appalled. I was soon preoccupied by my onward journey and my passage through the mountain passes to Kandahar. How trivial was the legend of "Colonel" Moran when compared with the scenes I was soon to witness in that fateful battle of Maiwand!

3

I need not dwell on that infamous encounter of two armies, except in so far as it affected my own future. Sufficient to say that after the death of the latest Amir of Afghanistan, his son Ayub Khan rose up against his brother, the lawful successor. His first target was the old capital, Kandahar, where our regiment had been cooling its heels. Ayub was still forty miles off, but with a growing army and a detachment of artillery. He far outnumbered us. Our own "loyal" Afghan troops were deserting to him by battalions at a time. Even so, in July we were part of a brigade ten thousand strong under Brigadier George Burrows, ordered forward to cut off our enemy's advance. And so I came to the Helmand, the desert and scrub that lie west of Kandahar.

Two mornings later, we woke to find that our remaining Afghans had deserted, down to the last man. Our flank on the Helmand River was open to attack. General Burrows must confront Ayub that morning, before matters grew worse. So our column turned towards Maiwand, eleven miles off, rough hills on one side and the Registan desert on the other.

There were no fortifications at this site. We should have to fight in the open wherever the two sides met. And so it was. The battle lasted from just after eleven o'clock in the morning, when the artillery on both sides opened fire, until about three o'clock in the afternoon. By then, Ayub's followers had increased to some 25,000 men, against our 10,000, and his reserves were easily able to outflank us.

General Burrows had got us into this fix, but the folly of the British Army in the east was to rely on mercenaries. Three quarters of our infantry that day were still Afghan or Indian troops. They had no taste for fighting their own people. Turning tail almost at once, they caused fearful disorder as they fell back through the ranks of the British infantry.

On every horizon, Ayub Khan's banners flew above dark masses of his riflemen. He had lured us into terrain where there was little cover from enemy fire except among the desert thorn-bushes. The 66th Foot took shelter as best it could along the river water-courses, which were bone-dry in the summer heat. The Grenadiers crouched or lay in the open.

In my own case, our regimental field hospital was under canvas and sheltered in a shallow ravine. Two medical orderlies were my only assistants. There were so many casualties in the first hour that the best I could do in most cases was to apply temporary dressings, leaving surgery to be carried out when the firing stopped.

My own wound came towards the end of the conflict. The last time I had looked at my watch, it was half-past two. I had been on my feet for more than three hours. By this time, the jezailchees had outflanked our position. No part of the camp was now beyond the range of their rifles. Half a dozen times, a bullet entered our tent with a *zippp!* as it punctured the canvas. I had been advised not to flinch from this sound. At such speed, the bullet that you hear is never the one that hits you.

I was stooping over poor Major Vandeleur of the 7th Fusiliers, whose chest wound extended into his lung. Before I could do more for him, I felt as if someone had punched me hard enough in the back of the right shoulder to knock me off balance. I was about to twist round and give the offender a piece of my mind when I saw splashes of blood on my overall and collecting on the ground. What I had felt was a bullet that pierced the green canvas of the tent, smashed my shoulder bone, and grazed the sub-clavial artery.

With my right arm done for, all hope of treating my patients was gone. There were three casualties in the dressing station at the time. Two were walking wounded, and the major was stretched before me. I made arrangements for one stretcher and two pairs of sticks. Then I allowed the orderly to dress my own wound as well as time allowed. To my great sorrow, Vandeleur died of his wounds soon afterwards.

My memory of what followed is intermittent, thanks to the administration of morphine to dull the grating of fractured bone. Without the use of it, the jolting progress of forty miles to Kandahar would have been too excruciating to bear. A bugle call sounded. I recognised it as a command for the baggage train to withdraw from the field of battle while the infantry remained to cover a general retreat. In my growing confusion, I felt two bearers pick up my stretcher and begin to run with it. They were shouting that the "ghazis" were upon us. Less fortunate invalids lay about on the ground, abandoned to the hands of our murderous enemy.

Armies in retreat are seldom disciplined or resolute. In the emergency of this evacuation, supplies and equipment were abandoned everywhere. The baggage animals were being unloaded and pressed into service to carry the injured. The ground was littered with their abandoned stores, unopened boxes of ammunition, mess supplies, cases of wine, kitchen utensils, and linen sheets. I saw wounded soldiers in rags and bandages sitting astride donkeys, mules, ponies, and in one case a camel. Ammunition wagons had become makeshift ambulances. A party of officers' servants was drunk from stolen liquor. Yet there was valour among all this. On the escarpments, the Grenadiers and the riflemen covered our retreat, sometimes forming squares and fighting to the end with their bayonets. They paid with their lives for a shilling a day.

In the camp, it seemed to be every man for himself. I should have been left to my fate had it not been for Murray, my orderly. A pack horse had just been unloaded for use as a mount. This dear brave fellow heaved me across it. Then, with my revolver in his hand to deter looters or marauders, he led me through the confusion and joined the long, miserable column of refugees to Kandahar.

I shall not soon forget the vicissitudes of that night. Stories of prisoners in the bloody hands of Ayub Khan sufficed to keep us moving. My friend Lieutenant Maclaine of the Royal Horse Artillery was less fortunate. His remains were found close to the site of Ayub's tent, where he had been butchered as the so-called Amir looked on.

We covered the remaining miles and arrived at Kandahar in safety during the evening of the next day. Fortunately, Ayub's men had been dazzled and delayed by the abandoned treasures of our camp. Had our enemies put their minds to it, all of us in the retreat would have been dead.

For more than a month, the white walls of Kandahar were surrounded by Ayub's men and it was impossible to evacuate the wounded to the Indian frontier. There was a curious lack of morale among our leaders, who acted as if our present position was lost. We might indeed have been overrun, but for Lord Roberts, winner of the Victoria Cross at Lucknow. Major-General Roberts, as he still was, formed up a column of ten thousand men, plus artillery. This column marched 313 miles in three weeks, over hostile terrain, to save us. Lord Roberts routed Ayub Khan in short order, secured the high passes, and opened the route to India.

So I took my place in an ambulance convoy which made its way south through the pass and at last to Peshawar. I really believed I was doing well at the base hospital, walking about the wards and reclining on the invalids' veranda. I should be back with my regiment before the year was out. Yet my weakness from a bullet wound put a stop to all that.

I fell prey to enteric fever, which accounts for more British lives than all the jezail bullets. It came closer to killing me than the Afghans had ever done. No one who has endured this illness and survived will need to be reminded of the ordeal. My temperature rose to 107 and I was delirious. At that point, most of the fever victims die. The lucky patient's temperature, on the other hand, drops a degree or so, and then a slow recovery begins. My temperature remained stubbornly where it was for several days, and I lived a half-life of sleeping and waking.

I have indistinct memories of being scalded in hot baths, my limbs being rubbed as the water cooled. I was taken out only to be lowered into another bath of heat that scorched the skin. Then the process was repeated. Peritonitis was spoken of, though not in my hearing, and death within twenty-four hours.

I came through the crisis without explanation but at a heavy cost. For a month, I was weak as a rabbit. I could scarcely stand, let alone walk. Every medical officer who examined me hinted that my days of soldiering were certainly done. In the end, my case was put to me bluntly. I should not recover as long as I remained in India. Indeed, there was a strong possibility of a recurrence in such a climate and, without doubt, it would carry me off.

A medical board of three officers came to examine me. One of them kindly suggested that if I went home, perhaps in time I might recover sufficiently to soldier in England. The looks of the other two said not if they knew it. It was agreed that I should be sent home and kept on the Army List for another nine months in England to see how I did. I was certain that they would then discharge me.

So I was invalided in uniform to Bombay, and my passage on the troopship *Orontes* was arranged. During the long sea-miles,

I reflected how different this was from my mood of expectancy on the voyage out. There was precious little to look forward to. If only I had heard of Sherlock Holmes and guessed the adventures that might lie ahead!

During those months of convalescence in the hospital at Peshawar, I had been given ample time to think of all that had happened since I left Portsmouth with the cheers of the crowd in my ears. I was at first too weak to do much more than lie in the warmth of the blankets, sometimes dozing and sometimes half-awake. I had grown up at a time when children and their teachers still lived in the long glory of Waterloo. The British Army had proved invincible, and the Empire which it garrisoned now stretched across the globe. Yet as I lay in that hospital bed, my own misfortune was small compared to the calamities of empire at that time. In restless days and long nights, I had ample time to go over and over the extraordinary sequence of reverses which had overtaken our troops in Africa and Asia in the months since I left England.

Between the hot compresses and sips of water that the orderlies administered, the spoonfuls of kaolin and opium mixture, I continued to dream and think.

Soon after the terrible news of Isandhlwana there was a further tragedy. I read in the press how the Prince Imperial, claimant to the throne of France, had been entrusted to Lord Chelmsford on a visit to South Africa, only to be cut to pieces on patrol in Zululand. That was not all. To be sure, I had escaped with my life at Maiwand. Yet the British envoy and all his staff had been assassinated at the Afghan capital of Kabul. Even at Kandahar, we had had every prospect of sharing their fate, cut off and surrounded by the brigands of Ayub Khan. But for the energy and audacity of General Roberts in his dash for the city, that is just what would have happened. Lying there immobilised in my hospital bed, my throat would have been slit along with the rest.

When I had first been ordered to Afghanistan, I imagined my comrades and myself riding confidently as benevolent imperial rulers over this ill-favoured territory. There would be respect for us and our empire. In the case of a doctor, there would be particular gratitude. I did not envisage my hurried and undignified exit from military glory, slung over a pack horse by my orderly, my shoulder smashed and bleeding, the knives of the pursuing jezailchees glinting not far behind us.

I was not the only one who thought of such setbacks with incredulity. I read a report from a Court correspondent on how the news of Isandhlwana had reached Queen Victoria at Osborne, during breakfast on 11 February 1879. "How this could happen we cannot imagine," the poor old lady wrote, describing this "great and unnatural disaster" in her journal. Among the list of the slain were several officers who had been her guests at court. More tragic still was the assassination of the Prince Imperial and the Queen's terrible task of consoling his distraught mother, the widowed Empress Eugenie of France.

And Afghanistan? Without Lord Roberts of Kandahar, we would easily have lost our only base there. Indeed, part of India itself, including the city where I now lay, would have followed. As the Queen said of these events, "The more one thinks about it, the worse it gets."

There was even more to come in southern Africa. The army that had won glory at Waterloo and Sebastopol met defeat in war against the Dutch settlers. At the treaty table, we surrendered to the Boers our Transvaal with all its mineral wealth of gold and diamonds. It seemed to be the last in a series of terrible coincidences. What of our African colonies now? Indeed, what of India itself?

If only I had met Sherlock Holmes at that moment! In such matters, he was not a believer in coincidences. Reason was everything to him, causes and effects. The fine steel point of his logic probed behind the excuses of coincidence and chance until it found such causes—and, behind the causes, the perpetrators.

4

*S*o much for my days of soldiering. And what of Holmes? Though I was not to meet him until my return from India, it is not strictly true to say that I had never heard of him before I left for home. Let me explain.

While I was convalescing at Peshawar our attendants used to wheel us out in our beds every morning on to the balconies of the wards. The clear air from the Khyber hills and the mild breezes from the fertile plains of the Punjab were supposed to invigorate our constitutions. There was little to do but lie propped on the pillows, talking or reading.

One morning my neighbour, a captain from the Somerset Light Infantry, was sitting on the edge of his bed in his dressing-gown and cap reading a copy of *London Life*. This was an illustrated periodical full of the gossip and humour of the day at home. Its features relied much on news or pictures of the West End stage and the London season. It was sent out monthly to the mess-rooms and clubs of the British Army in India, no doubt to boost our morale in what was now being called "The Second Afghan War." Captain Coombes handed his copy to me, his finger indicating a small paragraph at the foot of the page.

I read what followed.

W. S. Scott Holmes is an English Shakespearean actor now entertaining the best society in New York. He sends us a puzzle. His grandfather, William Sigismund Holmes, lived a hundred years ago. It was a world before steam engines or telegraphs. In 1786 the good Sigismund bet one of his creditors a hundred guineas that he could send a letter fifty miles in an hour. At this time, a carriage horse would only cover six miles in an hour, while at twenty miles an hour the fastest racehorse would be exhausted in a few minutes. A ship under full sail in a strong wind would not even equal that. How did Sigismund Holmes do it? See the answer on page fifty-four.

I leafed my way through the magazine and came to the solution.

Sigismund employed the twenty-two young men who had represented the varsity teams of Oxford and Cambridge at their first game of cricket. They appeared dressed in white flannels and shirts, with caps and padded gloves, on the Old Steine at Brighton. Here they formed a line, twenty yards apart from one another, a quarter of a mile in all. All this was done under the eyes of the Prince Regent himself— a sportsman if ever there was one! The letter was enclosed in a cricket ball. It flew with great speed and accuracy from one expert fielder to the next, along the line and back, over and over. At the end of the hour the letter had travelled fifty-one and a half miles. The ingenious Sigismund Holmes was a hundred guineas less in debt. Any doubters may find this feat confirmed by the celebrated sporting writer C. J. Apperley, popularly known as "Nimrod."

NB: For every curiosity of this kind printed, the proprietors of the London Life will be pleased to pay the correspondent two and a half guineas.

I was amused by Sigismund's trick but gave not a second thought to his grandson. As his admirers will know, in those early days W. S. Scott Holmes was the stage name of William Sherlock Scott Holmes. He returned to the chemical laboratory of St. Bartholomew's Hospital and resumed his career as a criminal investigator after a year on the boards in America with the Sassanoff Shakespeare Touring Company. Thereafter, as a consulting detective, he chose to be known more simply as "Sherlock Holmes."

Those who have read my narrative of the Brixton Road murder, given to the public under the somewhat sensational title of *A Study in Scarlet,* may recall something of the events which led to my first meeting with this future friend. When I had disembarked from the *Orontes* at Portsmouth, I was classified as a military invalid with little or no prospect of a further career in my chosen profession. Until their final decision was communicated, the Army medical board left me to lead a comfortless London existence at a private hotel in the Strand. The place was no better than a boarding-house for impoverished widows and widowers in their last years. My princely income was an allowance of four pounds and six pence a week.

During convalescence in hospital, I had managed to put aside most of my pay and my invalid supplement. There had been little opportunity to spend it. Even the comfort of a pipe and tobacco was forbidden me. Yet as the weeks of 1881 passed in London, this little stock of capital ran lower and lower. I had no family in England, except a few distant cousins down in Devonshire.

I had no expectations of a legacy and no one to whom I could turn for immediate assistance.

A city with as many attractions as London is not an easy place in which to do nothing. Week after week, I seemed to spend more money than I had meant to. My state of mind may easily be imagined, as I contemplated the loss of both health and independence. As for marriage and a settled existence, what woman of any sense would have a man with my prospects?

In this frame of mind I walked down Piccadilly one January morning, wondering what I should do. That famous avenue was busy with people who all seemed to look far richer than I should ever be. Swans-neck pilentum carriages passed me, drawn by glossy bay geldings. A coach with armorial bearings upon its door rumbled by. Even the hansom cabs were almost beyond my means to hire.

At that moment, the course of my future life was decided by a single stroke of coincidence. As I returned from the trees and carriages of Hyde Park Corner, the clocks struck twelve. I resolved that my first economy must be to leave the private hotel for cheaper accommodation. What could be cheaper? Goodness knows whether I should find anything short of a common lodging-house. All the same, I would celebrate my decision to live more cheaply by allowing myself a final luxury. I pushed open the door of the old Criterion Bar in Coventry Street, off Piccadilly Circus.

The stroke of coincidence was a tap on my shoulder and the friendly voice of young Stamford, who had been a surgical dresser under me at Barts Hospital before my days in the Army.

We exchanged all the formalities of friends long parted and then began to talk. I described my military experiences in Afghanistan and the situation in which I now found myself. I knew him well enough to mention that I must move from my present hotel to another abode—I knew not where. At once he told me of his acquaintance, a certain Sherlock Holmes. Holmes had informed him that very morning that he was in search of lodgings. More to the point, he had found a very nice set of rooms, in Baker Street, but must have someone to go halves with him in the cost. Stamford rather thought that Holmes was inviting him to share the rooms; but Stamford was already suited, as they say.

I recall, as if it were only a week ago, my excitement at this chance of solving my own problem so easily. If I could chum with someone, it would halve the cost straight away.

"By Jove!" I said with a laugh. "If your friend really wants someone to share the rooms and the expense, I may be the very man for him. In any case, I should prefer going halves to living alone!"

That afternoon, in the chemical laboratory of Barts, I came face to face with a studious-looking individual, a little over six feet in height. He was so lean that it made him look, if anything, taller still. The eyes were sharp and penetrating, the nose thin and hawk-like. His features made him appear at once alert and decisive. His jaw was firmly set, as if resolute and determined. In the matter of his physical strength, the moment of our first handshake convinced me of that!

I was not in the least surprised that he later proved to be an expert swordsman, boxer, and singlestick player. As for the power of his hands, I shall never forget our visit from a bullying strongman, Dr. Grimesby Roylott. This bully emphasised his threats to us by taking the poker from our fireplace and bending it into a curve with his huge brown hands, his arteries swelling and face purpled. After his stormy departure, Holmes ruefully picked up the distorted metal from the grate and with a careful effort bent it straight again.

From the start, I knew that Holmes was a man who never admitted failure or defeat. I have sometimes been asked to describe his appearance and manner by those who had not known him. I have suggested that they should imagine the stance and manner of Sir Edward Carson, QC, that most vigorous and astute of cross-examiners, combined with the combative and self-assured manner of Lord Birkenhead, the former Mr. F. E. Smith. There was also a dash of the late Lord Curzon with his taste for what he called effortless superiority. But even all that does not do him sufficient credit for his nobler character. Holmes would put away ambition in order to work tirelessly and without reward on behalf of the poorest and humblest client. Indeed, it was "poor persons' defences" which gave him the greatest satisfaction and which he undertook, without reward, for pure love of justice.

When Stamford introduced us that afternoon in the chemical laboratory, the great detective's fingers were blotched with acid and stained a little by what looked like ink. Among broad low tables, shelves of bottles, retorts, test-tubes, and Bunsen burners with their blue flickering flames and odours of gas, he was in his element. After our brief introduction, he quite ignored me in his excitement at explaining to Stamford the success of some experiment on which he had been engaged. He confided to us that he had identified a reagent which was precipitated by haemoglobin and by nothing else. In plain terms, it would now be possible for the first time to identify blood stains long after the blood had dried.

It is not my intention to say more of this first meeting, for I have done that elsewhere. Let me just add, for the benefit of those who have not met him before, that Sherlock Holmes dwelt in alternating spasms of fierce intellectual excitement and moods of brooding contemplation. The problem is that life cannot always be lived at a pitch of fierce excitement. In the most active career, there are days or weeks of tedium. Other men might have turned to drink or sexual vice in these doldrums. Sherlock Holmes preferred the less complicated palliatives of music or cocaine. I deplored his use of the narcotic, but I came to see that the drug was not his true addiction. It was merely his substitute for a more

DONALD THOMAS

powerful cerebral stimulation when he was engaged upon a case. Then he needed nothing stronger than his faithful pipe.

As to his mind, it was possessed of a profound knowledge of chemistry, an adequate acquaintance with anatomy, and a practical familiarity with the English criminal law. In morbid psychology or psychopathology, he had a firm grasp of mental alienation. He read Krafft-Ebing or Charcot in psychiatric medicine as other men read the morning newspaper. Nor did he ignore the analysis of human darkness in such literary imaginations as Edgar Allan Poe, Charles Baudelaire, or Robert Browning.

Perhaps his most formidable gift was an ability to master any form of knowledge in a matter of days or hours. He who had known nothing of astrology or joint stock companies or the effect of amberite cartridges on gunshot wounds would be a master of the subject within a week.

Holmes exercised his brain as other men would have used a chest-expander or a set of dumb-bells. For example, he would set himself the great unsolved problems of mathematics. If he did not find solutions to age-old mathematical paradoxes like Fermat's Last Theorem or the Goldbach Conjecture, I believe he understood the nature of those riddles better than any other man living.

The most astonishing thing about him, from the moment of our first meeting, was his clarity of insight combined with a power of logical deduction. I remember the first illustration of this vividly. Almost the first thing he said to me, when Stamford introduced us and we shook hands in the laboratory, was "Dear me, sir! I see you have just been in Afghanistan. You were lucky to come back from Maiwand alive, despite your injury."

We were total strangers! Two minutes earlier, before Stamford and I walked into that laboratory, Holmes had not even known of my existence. How the devil could he tell me of Afghanistan, let alone that I had been at Maiwand? Even Stamford knew nothing of my part in that battle. I said as much to Holmes. He laughed

92

but would not enlighten me just then. Stamford later remarked that Holmes was forever teasing his acquaintances with these curious displays of deductive power. It seemed he was seldom if ever wrong in his conclusions. I thought it was surely some trick that he had learnt. What else could it be? I was naturally determined to find out how that trick was done.

To return to our adventure, however. Holmes had found vacant rooms at 221b Baker Street, handy for the streets of central London and the Metropolitan Railway, as well as agreeably close to the open spaces of the Regent's Park. The arrangement of the rooms was convenient for two tenants but, as he had discovered, too expensive for one. We went together to Evans's Supper Rooms that evening and over our meal agreed to inspect the new premises next day.

He told me about himself as we ate. His first rooms—"consulting rooms," as he grandly called them—had been in Lambeth Palace Road, just south of Westminster Bridge on the far side of the river. He had still been an apprentice then, but these lodgings were convenient for the chemical laboratory of St. Thomas's Hospital. He was not a regular student but was allowed occasional access to this laboratory on the basis of grace-and-favour. This was by virtue of a legacy to the governors in a bequest made by one of his kinsmen. How or why he had transferred to Barts Hospital, he did not yet say.

For a couple of years, this young researcher would return every evening from St. Thomas's to the terraces and tree-lined vistas of Lambeth Palace Road, a favourite abode of our young physicians. It was here that he scored his first forensic triumph in the case of Dr. William Smethurst, an avaricious and philandering medical man. Dr. Smethurst's wealthy bride had died in suspicious circumstances. The autopsy revealed large quantities of arsenic, and Smethurst had been the only person to have access to her in her final days. He was tried, convicted, sentenced and waiting to be hanged in a few days' time. Sherlock Holmes, the young consulting detective, was employed as a last resort. In a sensational conclusion to this first case, he was able to prove that William Smethurst, though a thoroughly repellent individual, was as innocent of murder as the babe new-born. The arsenic had come not from the body but from items of the apparatus used to carry out the post-mortem tests.*

From then on, he never looked back. Perhaps he lost his footing when St. Thomas's Hospital grew anxious at the macabre nature of some of his experiments and drove him elsewhere. If so, this never impeded him. He confessed that shortly before our arrival at Barts on our first afternoon, he had been belabouring a cadaver with a truncheon to establish the extent to which bruising might be produced post-mortem!

So much for his past. Next morning, the two of us travelled to 221b Baker Street and viewed the first-floor rooms on offer. There were two comfortable bedrooms plus a large and airy sitting-room with use of an attic storeroom. We should be provided for by a quietly spoken but agreeable housekeeper of Scottish extraction, Mrs. Hudson.

Baker Street was less fashionable than the Strand, but I was pleased to find that I should be paying less than at my so-called "private hotel." I was so taken with this new arrangement that I agreed to the terms at once and arranged for my things to be moved to these premises the same day. Sherlock Holmes followed on the next morning.

I took an early opportunity of asking my new friend what made him think that I had lately been in Afghanistan and—indeed—at Maiwand. On one of our first mornings, I suggested at breakfast that someone must have told him. He shook his head: "No, my dear fellow. Why should anyone have told me? for they could not have known we were destined to meet. To begin with, I merely deduced that you came from Afghanistan.

---

* "The Ghost in the Machine" in Donald Thomas, *The Secret Cases of Sherlock Holmes.*

Why? My reasoning was very simple. Here was a gentleman of a medical type but perhaps in low water. His clothes are not new, even his waistcoat has seen a good deal of student wear. The nap is worn just where a stethoscope might hang. But there is also the air of a military man, one who holds himself upright as though having learnt to drill and march. Clearly, then, the probability is that we have an army doctor of some kind. Where has he been lately? He has probably just come from the topics, for his face is dark and that is not the natural colour of his skin, for his wrists are fair."

He made a vague gesture with his right hand as if the problem had been almost too easy for him. Then he resumed.

"Our medical man has also undergone hardship and sickness. Pardon me, but the sunken eyes and his haggard face say that clearly. His left arm has been injured. He holds it in a stiff and unnatural manner, but he can hardly have set out with it in that condition! Where in the tropics, in the present state of affairs, could an English army doctor have got his arm wounded? Most probably in Afghanistan. What battle has been fought there recently ending in a rout of our troops and injuries to many of them? You see? It could only be at Maiwand. The process is really very simple."

"Very plausible, at any rate," I said ironically. He demurred at once.

"Of course I could not be certain of all this, but where else would the path of reason lead me? If one follows it, one almost invariably reaches the correct conclusion. There is no trick to it, I assure you."

Soon afterwards, I was able to put this theory to the test. Until then, I still thought there was a certain boast and bluster in his claims. Little by little, Sherlock Holmes's associations with Scotland Yard and the extraordinary abilities of which he repeatedly gave evidence made me think again. On this second occasion, however, we were looking down from the sitting-room window one morning. A man in plain clothes, carrying a blue envelope, was evidently looking for a number on one of the house doors.

"I wonder who that fellow is after," I said, thinking aloud.

"You mean the retired sergeant of Marines?"

How absurd! He could not possibly know that the Royal Marines had been the man's career, unless he knew this visitor already. That seemed unlikely, for the man appeared to be having a little trouble in finding the right door. I saw my chance when this messenger crossed the road and there was a loud rap on our street door. Then came the sound of voices and footsteps on the stairs. A tap at our sitting-room door heralded the appearance of this wanderer. Determined not to be forestalled, I crossed the room and opened the door. There was our visitor with the blue envelope in one hand and his walking-cane in the other.

"For Mr. Sherlock Holmes, sir," he said, handing over the envelope.

I had my chance now.

"One moment, if you please! What is your trade?"

"Commissionaire and messenger, sir. Uniform away for repairs just now."

Good! I thought.

"Any previous occupation?" I inquired.

"Yes, sir! Sergeant, sir! Royal Marine Light Infantry, sir! No answer to the message? Right, sir! Much obliged, sir."

He brought his heels together, raised his right hand in salute, and went back down the stairs.

The face of Sherlock Holmes was all innocence.

"Very clever," I said. "But how could you know, unless you had met the fellow before?"

We were standing at the window again, watching the man as he walked slowly down the busy street towards the Metropolitan station.

"If you had observed more closely, Watson, you would have seen an anchor rather distinctly tattooed on the back of his left hand. Only a sailor, I think, would submit to wearing that. On the other hand he walks with a military step, does he not, rather than a seaman's roll? He also sports army side-whiskers of regulation cut. Who would combine all these traits? Surely a Royal Marine. Clearly he is no longer in the service, therefore he has retired. Indeed, he is a commissionaire and messenger. Now watch him as he goes. That poise of his head and the swing of his cane give him a certain authority and command. Does not that suggest something more than a common ranker? Not an officer to be sure, therefore a sergeant. It is a matter of simple deduction. Nothing more."

"And I daresay a matter of luck."

He smiled gently.

"My dear Watson! Lady Luck can play the deuce with us all!"

He gave his attention to the blue envelope, slitting it with a paper-knife and drawing out a single sheet of foolscap. It was a letter from Inspector Tobias Gregson, "the smartest of the Scotland Yarders," as Holmes described him. It solicited an opinion in the case of the Brixton Road murder. In the view of my new friend, Gregson and Lestrade were the pick of a bad lot at the Yard. Even so, he had been obliged to extricate Inspector Lestrade, when the inspector had got himself into a fog over the Bank of England forgery case some years before. After that, he was visited by this tenacious officer several times a week, bringing the latest news of London crime for his views upon it.

If I had doubted the purpose of his "consulting rooms," I did so no longer. They were the apartment of a private detective, who made himself available for hire as surely as a barrister or a hansom cab. Until a few days earlier, I would have told you that such people exist only in stories sold on station book-stalls. Now it seemed I breathed the excitement of crime and detection as surely as the air of Sherlock Holmes's shag tobacco in our sitting-room.

The new rooms in Baker Street received our first clients. My Army medical board discharged me with a pension which would not support me on its own. My only other qualification lay in medical practice. But a practice means a partnership, and such a partnership requires purchase money. I caught myself thinking that if I could somehow work with Holmes for the time being, a modest income from detection would combine with my little pension to keep me alive. After a while, I might save enough to establish myself as a physician again. Perhaps I could buy myself a place, if only as a junior in a country town. There were the cousins in Devonshire. I had not seen them in a good many years, but I daresay they might help me to establish myself as a small-town doctor.

Alas, how greatly I underestimated the fascination of detection! Holmes and I were in partnership from the very first days of the Brixton Road murder mystery. There were certain understandings between us, of course. We almost always turned away marital disputes and divorce actions, which are the lot of so many "inquiry agents." It also took me a considerable time to get used to Holmes's insufferable air of superiority in the act of discovery. There was still a little too much "brag and bounce" in his demeanour, as it seemed to me. But the longer we knew one another, the better we got on.

I resigned myself to his bohemian ways, his unexplained absences and his habits of working at all hours of the day and night. All day he gathered information, and much of the night he passed in restless calculation. How often did the night walker or the policeman on his beat in Baker Street glance up and see the familiar silhouette of Holmes in profile against the drawn blind of our first-floor room! It was the shadow of a man pacing rapidly to and fro, his hands clasped behind his back, his head bowed by a weight of thought.

Those who caught sight of this familiar outline invariably imagined the subtle detective brain forming a pattern of clues to foil a new challenge by the underworld. Yet Holmes was human and, in his way, fallible. Like many successful men, from time to time he liked to sigh and confess that his true ambitions lay elsewhere. If he had his time over again, it would be a life of bee-keeping in a fold of the quiet Sussex Downs. His cottage would be within sight of the glimmering sea and with the sound of its waves carried to him on a temperate breeze. For the time being, nothing pleased him more than to see his initials at the foot of a page in *Notes and Queries* or *The Classical Quarterly*, a few paragraphs on some obscure but learned topic, probably of interest to not more than fifty people in the entire world.

Yet while we were putting our detective partnership on a secure footing, in such cases as the decipherment of the Musgrave Ritual or the retrieval of the Admiralty plans for the Bruce-Partington submarine, stolen from Woolwich Arsenal, the world outside our rooms was moving on. It was becoming a more dangerous place.

In particular, to one who had seen something of imperial warfare, all was not well with Britain and her empire in South Africa. The shadow of defeat which had lain over Isandhlwana soon extended elsewhere. This was all the more important because it coincided with the discovery and development of the new diamond fields and gold mines by the Dutch Boers of the Transvaal. Their territory had been annexed by Britain, but I arrived home from India to hear of the uprising against British rule and an invasion of our own South African province of Natal by the Boers themselves.

After a British column was ambushed and almost wiped out by Boer Commandos, a momentous battle followed at Laings Nek. British casualties were numbered in hundreds and those of the Boers scarcely in dozens. So complete was the rout that Her Majesty's colours were never carried into battle again.

As I read of this in *The Times* or the *Morning Post*, I truly wondered whether there was not some purpose or pattern of events behind it all. Isandhlwana now appeared like a prelude to the loss of the whole of southern Africa. And what would follow in India and elsewhere? I said as much to Holmes several times, but he was not to be drawn into this discussion. He was less interested in British imperial policy than in the identification of bloodstains by haemoglobin.

In any event, before my question could be answered, there was a decisive encounter at Majuba Hill. British losses included the death of their commander General Sir George Colley. These losses once again ran into hundreds. Those of the Boer Commandos amounted to only half a dozen.

A returning medical colleague assured me that the enemy's fire had been so accurate and lethal at Majuba that burial parties after the battle found five or six bullets in each skull of some fallen Highlanders. Red-coated infantry were no match for camouflaged guerillas. There could only be one outcome. Two months later, the vast territory was lost and the enemy was in Natal. Within three months, our surrender was signed. So much for the boast of General Sir Garnet Wolseley that "so long as the sun shines, the Transvaal will remain British territory."

Even then, being settled into Baker Street, I assumed that I had heard the last of my own military career and everything to do with it. I had little enough to do with the dreadful events in Zululand or the Transvaal. Our detective practice continued to prosper. The case of the Brixton Road murder came and went, followed by a succession of lesser mysteries which wait to be written up. Before I could set my pen working on these, I received a letter which assured me that certain horrors of the past were anything but forgotten.

5

*T*he letter in question came from Mr. Samuel Dordona. It arrived following breakfast on a cold March morning, some time after my return to England. Sherlock Holmes had been studying several envelopes. He never overlooked the evidence of an unopened letter. The skeletons of two kippers lay on his neglected plate.

"I beg your pardon, Watson, this one is for you. See what you can make of the address."

He handed across the table an envelope of ivory bond paper, such as one buys in any good stationer's shop. It was directed to me with punctilious care, my precise medical qualifications following my name. Someone had clearly "looked up" my history. Before opening it, I studied the handwriting.

"It seems nothing out of the ordinary, Holmes. However, I believe my correspondent is not in his first youth. The script has an italic slope which the younger generation no longer acquire or, if they do, it is abandoned for something more casual once they are out of tutelage."

"Well done, Watson! Just so! The death of English copper-plate hand!"

"The address . . ." I studied it carefully. "The form of address is courteous, almost deferential. I am usually 'Mr. J. Watson' or perhaps 'Dr. John Watson' to my correspondents. This time we have the whole bag of tricks. John H. Watson, Esquire, M.B., B.Ch., St. Bartholmew's Hospital, but directed 'care of' our present Baker Street address. Our new friend has clearly found me in the *Medical Register.*"

"Who, then, I wonder?" Holmes inquired benignly.

"A man of some little education," I said condescendingly. "Also of extreme politeness. In my mind I think I see a clergyman. Not one of the Established Church, I feel. A Methodist? A Baptist, perhaps? Something of the kind. Will that do?"

He chuckled with such quiet pleasure that I grew uneasy. When Sherlock Holmes chuckled, it was usually an ill omen for someone. Taking a clean knife, I carefully slit the cover and drew out a single sheet of paper, written on both sides. I laughed as I saw the concluding signature.

"The Reverend Samuel Dordona of the Evangelical Overseas Medical Mission! You see? I was right!"

He slapped the table-cloth with his hand.

"Congratulations, old fellow! Were this the school's exami-nation-room, I should unhesitatingly award you 'Summa cum laude.' The instinct for divination runs in your blood at last. What can he want? Has someone rifled his Sunday collection plate or stolen his hymn-board?"

I remained suspicious of his enthusiasm. Glancing at the top of the letter, I saw that Mr. Dordona had pinned a newspaper cutting to the page. It was two inches of a single column.

"Our correspondent has sent us this as well."

"Yes, indeed," Holmes said airily; "I felt the enclosure as I passed the envelope to you. I believe you will find it is clipped from a page of one of the weekly papers. The newsprint of the weeklies is of so much better and fuller weave than the dailies. One feels the difference in quality quite easily, even through the covering of such an envelope."

This air of superiority irritated me a little, but at least I should make him dependent on me for hearing what it was the newspaper had said.

"'Captain Jahleel Brenton Carey, 98th Regiment, of unfortunate history in Zululand, has, we regret to hear, died under mysterious circumstances in India, a victim of much persecution.' That seems to be all."

I read it to myself again. Captain Jahleel Brenton Carey? It was a name I had heard. For the life of me, I could not place it just then. Certainly I did not connect it with my own time in India or Afghanistan. But even before Holmes could interrupt my thoughts, it came back to me.

While I was convalescing at Peshawar, I had read a magazine article. It was in that radical weekly, the *Pall Mall Gazette*, I believe. The editor attacked the military authorities at the Horse Guards over various cases of injustice in the Army. If I remembered correctly, one of them was to do with the death of the claimant to the French throne, the Prince Imperial, in Zululand. Zululand!—that fateful name again! Much chance the poor young fellow ever had of sitting on the throne of France. His father had lost it after the French defeat in the Franco-Prussian war of 1870. The royal family had been exiled and the Third Republic had replaced it a dozen years ago.

The young Prince Louis Napoleon was generally known as the Prince Imperial. He had been prepared for a military life from his infancy. It was everything to him. Though an exile, he had entered Woolwich Academy as a French cadet in the British Army—and in a British uniform. Of course, he still dreamed of the day when he might be Emperor of the French. Meantime, he longed for the chance of fighting someone. When war came to Zululand, he insisted that the Zulus would do as well as anyone else.

His widowed mother pleaded against this. Our own Queen protested. At last the Duke of Cambridge, Commander-in-Chief at the Horse Guards, agreed to let the young man go out "on his own hook." He was to be a battlefield tourist in the uniform of a British lieutenant. In other words, a pestering nuisance to those who would have to look after him. For the weekly picture papers, he dressed the part to perfection, complete with the sword which his great-uncle, Napoleon Bonaparte, had carried at Austerlitz in 1805.

All this had been in the newspapers that reached us in Kandahar. It was already three months after Isandhlwana. The Zulu tribes had been taught no end of a lesson by a British punitive expedition. As for the Prince, the radical press howled, "What if this feckless youth gets himself killed in Africa?" Impossible— but then defeat at Isandhlwana had seemed impossible!

So that was how I had read of Captain Jahleel Brenton Carey and the 98th Regiment of Foot. This young captain had been the commander of Lord Chelmsford's mounted detachment, whose sole duty was to accompany and protect the royal visitor. In plain English, Carey's head had been on the block should anything go wrong. But, once again, our troops had long since gained the upper hand. Whole areas had been cleared of every Zulu in sight. Their villages, or kraals, had been destroyed. Isandhlwana had almost been avenged.

Prince Louis Napoleon, carrying the hopes of Imperial France with him, embarked at Portsmouth. At the end of March 1879, he set foot in South Africa. By the beginning of June he was dead! Again the world asked: "How could it have happened?"

All this came back to me in far less time than it takes to describe. Holmes strode across to those bookshelves which ran along one wall of our sitting-room. Its scrapbooks and works of reference were his curiously assorted library. In a moment more, a folio lay open on his table, pages pasted with small newspaper cuttings, in every printer's type. He closed the volume with a look of satisfaction.

"As I suspected, Watson, this is a minor item cut from the foot of a column in the *Army and Navy Gazette*. Unlike the rest of the military press, the editor is a barrack-room lawyer who tries to salt the Horse Guards' tail once a week."

"I was in Afghanistan at the time," I said helpfully. "Did this make as much noise in England as the newspapers pretended?"

"Enough to put another nail in the coffin of Mr. Disraeli's administration. Dizzy was out of office soon after, and Mr. Gladstone was in."

He stood with his back to the fireplace and gave a faint sardonic smile.

"*The Times*, the *Morning Post*, and *tutti quanti* carried reports of the inquest and court-martial. For a few weeks, the Prince Imperial's assassination made enough noise to bring fire down from heaven! Then it was forgotten."

He paused to charge his pipe with strong black shag tobacco. Drawing upon the lighted match, he continued:

"They rode out—the prince and his guardians—to map an area of safe territory near the Blood River. The Zulu war was effectively over. King Cetewayo was in hiding. They caught him but never harmed him. Lord Chelmsford taught him to wear a silk top hat with morning dress and polished shoes. He was got ready for a voyage to England to be inspected by the Queen and given lunch at Windsor Castle."

"Preposterous!"

He shrugged.

"The area of desert scrub had been thoroughly searched for the prince's outing. There were no Zulus there nor anyone else. He was only going for the day, carefully escorted. The imperial party dismounted for lunch near an abandoned village by the Blood River. An hour or two later, having eaten their rations and drunk their picnic wine, they prepared to mount. At that moment the impossible happened, as it so often does in that strange country. A platoon of Zulus, with spears and captured British Army rifles, burst from the undergrowth. But still these fellows were on foot, thirty or forty yards away. The prince with his boot already in the stirrup should have got away without difficulty."

"No one was with him?"

"Captain Carey and all but two of the escort made off together in one direction, startled but uninjured. They believed the prince was galloping alongside them. How could he not be? Even in the confusion they were sure they had seen him vault into the saddle. Or rather, they had seen his boot in the stirrup and the harness strap in the hand of this first-rate rider. He had never fallen from a horse in his life. What they did not see was that, as he pulled against the harness to swing himself up, the strap had broken. He fell back instantly, sprawling on the ground. Once he was down and his horse had bolted, it was all over in half a minute. The poor young fellow died fighting on foot with a half-empty pistol. His body was found next day."

"I never heard the details in Kandahar."

He stood in silence for a moment, as if paying a private tribute. Then he quoted softly, "A hopeless encounter but a hero's end. 'For how can man die better than facing fearful odds, for the ashes of his fathers and the temples of his gods?'"

"Lord Macaulay, *Lays of Ancient Rome.*"

"Quite so. This poor young man was brave to the last in the face of certain death. When he was found, there were seventeen assegai wounds in the front of his body and none anywhere else. He never turned his back to the foe. He was wearing his great uncle's sword, Napoleon Bonaparte's. That sword has never been seen since. Poor devil! He died a death that Bonaparte would have saluted. But the young prince was worthy of better things."

I was so enthralled by the story that I fear the Reverend Samuel Dordona's letter was lost in my determination to hear the end of this account.

"The court-martial of Captain Brenton Carey," I said at last: "that was what I had read about in the *Pall Mall Gazette*."

Holmes sighed.

"In truth, a field court-martial—a drum-head tribunal. It found Carey guilty as charged. Misconduct in the Face of the Enemy. But all the evidence suggested that there was no misconduct. All those men had to ride for their lives when the tribesmen appeared, and each felt sure the prince was with them. Before they knew otherwise, he was dead. As always in such circumstances, a scapegoat was needed."

"And the press?"

"The press did what it does so well—and so often. It changed sides and had the best of both worlds. First it demanded that heads should fall, Captain Carey's to begin with. After the court-martial, there were doubts as to who was truly to blame. The press then raised a hullabaloo over Carey having been sacrificed to shield the incompetence of his senior officers. The verdict of the court-martial was quashed. From the start, there was something rum about the evidence. Had I been there to defend him, I should have asked further questions. Most importantly, how did so many Zulus come to be in a place where they could not possibly have been, unless someone put them there? The ground had been scoured by military scouts. The whole area was within view."

He waved aside a drift of pipe-smoke and resumed.

"Unfortunately, Watson, in the week when the poor young man was killed, I was elsewhere. Indeed, I was acting Hamlet's father's ghost on the boards of McVicker's Theater in Madison Street, Chicago."

"And Captain Carey himself? What happened to him after the verdict was quashed?"

He handed back the cutting.

"According to the inquest upon him it seems that he remained in the Army, in a more menial capacity in India. A lowly pioneer corps officer, commanding fatigue details and hard labour. Come, old fellow. In all this excitement we have forgotten our evangelical clergyman. Pray be good enough to read out his letter."

He turned and sat in his favourite chair by the fireplace. His long legs were extended and crossed at the ankles, his fingers were placed together as if in prayer, and his chin was lowered on his chest in that attitude which always reminded me of some patient bird of prey, sharp-eyed behind drooping lids. I began to read the studious italic script of our reverend gentleman.

"My dear Sir,

"Conscious of what a busy man you must be, I ask you to forgive this letter from a total stranger. My request concerns information, to which I have unwillingly become a party. It relates to the strange death of Captain Jahleel Brenton Carey, late of the 98th Foot.

"I heard of you by chance as a medical man in military service, who has now sent in his papers to become a partner in a consulting detective agency. I confess that I do not know quite what that means. If I am correct, you can help me in your present profession more than you ever could as a physician. If you cannot assist me, then I fear no one else will. My story is hardly one that I can take to the Metropolitan Police. I believe that only a man who has seen service in India would believe it.

"The manner of Captain Carey's death will require a fuller explanation than I can give here. However, I listened to his dying words. The poor gentleman lingered almost two days after sustaining the frightful injuries that killed him. I am now assured that the accident that caused his death was no accident at all—but who would believe this after the inquest, least of all the police?

"I am quite sure that the occasion of Captain Carey's disgrace, when the young Prince Imperial was under his care and yet was cut down in a Zulu ambush, cannot have been a chance encounter with Africans. Like Captain Carey's own subsequent death, it was no accident."

I paused and stared at Sherlock Homes. Could even he, with his intuitive genius, possibly have known that the letter would contain such a sentence? The room seemed cold and quiet as I read the conclusion of the message.

"I believe that the knowledge I now carry exposes me to danger and indeed the threat of death. My only defence is in sharing it so that my adversaries may be assured that the truth will be published if anything should happen to me. It has been my calling to serve God in India rather than in England, but I have been away too long. I now come back to London almost as a foreigner and am attending the medical 'First Aid' short course at the London Mission School. After an absence of eleven years, there seems no one else but you in whom I can safely confide.

"I beg, sir, that I may call upon you and your colleague Mr. Sherlock Holmes on Tuesday the 27th of March at 2 P.M. Should this not be convenient, I entreat that you will reply by return. In that case, I would ask you to nominate at once any other hour that might better suit you.

"I remain yours faithfully,

"Samuel Dordona, B. D., Evangelical Overseas Medical Mission

"49 Carlyle Mansions, London SW."

"The deuce!" said Holmes thoughtfully, as I finished reading. "Our clerical friend has a turn for melodrama worthy of the stage of the Hoxton Britannia, has he not? You have never heard of him before this, I take it?"

I shook my head. "Indeed I have not. Nor have I the faintest idea where he can have heard of me. But this letter is so curious. Why would an overseas medical mission be housed in a block of mansion apartments in Victoria?"

"I daresay it is our client's *pied-a-terre* during the month or two of his meagre furlough in England, before he returns to the Indian climate."

"He is to be our client, then?"

Holmes's mouth twisted a little with impatience. "To tell you the truth, Watson, we are not overburdened with clients just now."

"You do not think that the whole story of a mystery in Captain Carey's death might be schoolboy nonsense?"

"The *Army and Navy Gazette* seems not to think so. It talks of a mystery, but I daresay the libel laws prevent it from putting the details into print."

With that, he turned and stared past me at the curtained window for a moment. Then he said, "Captain Carey was not otherwise mentioned to you during your time in India?"

"My dear Holmes! We had more urgent business! When the Prince Imperial was killed, our brigade was marching to meet Ayub Khan at Maiwand! It was all over before I saw another newspaper from home."

"Of course," he said quietly, "you are quite right."

"I recall there was small talk among the fellows convalescing at Peshawar about how quickly the loss of Isandhlwana was followed by the death of the prince, one disaster coming so soon on top of another. Then, of course, those were followed by reverses in our battles against the Dutch Boers at Laings Nek and Majuba Hill, only a little distance away from the first two. By rights, we should have beaten the Boer farmers hands-down. I call that curious."

He stared into the fireplace.

"No, Watson. Not curious. Tragic, certainly. Dangerous to our military and imperial reputation indeed. But the word 'curious' might imply that these improbable disasters have no common connection. On the contrary, I should say that a common connection almost certainly unites them all."

"Where is your evidence? Where is the connection, at least?"

We had not talked of evidence as yet. He sat upright in his chair and the languid indifference dropped away.

"That, I cannot yet tell you at this moment. However, the Reverend Samuel Dordona interests me. He knows far more than he has told us—of that you may be sure. I believe it is of some importance that we should probe his story at our earliest convenience. I cannot speak for you, of course, but two o'clock tomorrow afternoon would suit me admirably."

He refilled his pipe, struck a match, and crossed to the net-curtained window of our sitting-room. There he stood, staring down into the street, watching the passers-by in the silence of his thoughts for a full half hour.

6

*N*ext afternoon, we played host to our clerical correspondent. Long before Mr. Dordona's arrival, Sherlock Holmes had made good use of *Palmer's Index to the Times* and annual volumes of the *Army List*. These held details of Captain Carey's career and death. The manner of that death might seem tragic, but nothing so far suggested that it was sinister.

Thanks to Holmes's archives, we compiled a fuller account of Brenton Carey's last days. Long after the battle at Maiwand, the Amir of Afghanistan continued to play us false. More British regiments were brought up to the North-West Frontier towns of the Punjab. According to the *Army and Navy Gazette*, the 98th Foot had been ordered to the forward reserves. Its troops began to move camp from Hyderabad to Quetta, the first stage of a journey to the Frontier and the Khyber Pass.

Brenton Carey and a junior captain had been left in Hyderabad to supervise two fatigue details in dismantling an encampment of bell tents. It was a laborious but commonplace duty. As I knew from my own experience, a bell tent usually provides sleeping quarters for one officer or for two or three other ranks. Officers' tents have a flooring which consists of two wooden semi-circles jointed together.

The London press had been full of the military inquest on Brenton Carey, held at Hyderabad Camp in the week following his death. According to the evidence, the jointed wooden flooring of one of the tents had collapsed as the fatigue party was hauling it aboard a waiting wagon. It had not been adequately secured beforehand. It was also said that one of the two men lifting it had stumbled on slippery ground. A pair of dray horses was standing between the shafts.

From that point, there was some confusion in the evidence. The two horses were startled by the crash and by the sudden vibration as the wooden semi-circles fell against the wagon. They backed and kicked out in brute panic. No one saw precisely what followed because Captain Carey was standing alone on the far side of the vehicle. Somehow, he was caught up in this sudden movement of the beasts and the jolting of the vehicle. He lost his footing and was trampled before he could roll clear. Having some acquaintance with Army transport in Afghanistan, I could see all too easily how such a tragedy might occur.

It is a terrible fate to go under horses' hooves. A cavalry mount is trained so that it will not trample a fallen rider, but these were beasts of burden. Worst of all, from the medical view, Carey was dreadfully injured by blows in the abdomen from their hooves. Unlike a broken arm or leg, abdominal or intestinal injuries are exceedingly difficult to treat. As a rule, one can only hope the intestine is not ruptured and will repair itself.

According to the inquest reports, Captain Carey lay senseless from the blows. He regained consciousness after a stretcher-party had carried him back to his bungalow in the camp lines. There was never any great hope for him. Following alternate periods of lucidity and semi-consciousness, he died late on the following day. His wife, Annie, and the regimental surgeon were by his side much of the time. For all his adventures and notoriety, the poor fellow was still only thirty-six years old.

It had been a cruel accident. Yet, through carelessness or bad luck, such things happen all too often in these fatigue duties. Indeed, any mishap in handling a team of wagon horses is an invitation to injury. But I still could not see why the *Army and Navy Gazette* should think this accident was mysterious. Its causes seemed all too obvious: inadequate packing and the ill-chance of a man slipping on wet ground. That was as far as we had got by two o'clock on the afternoon of the 27th of March. As I was standing with Holmes at our sitting-room window, he said casually: "Tell me, Watson, would you not say that Mr. Dordona looks the very pattern of an impoverished evangelical gentleman?"

He was not looking down at the street below us, where a cab would usually pull in, but northwards to the trees of the Regent's Park. A tall, plainly dressed man in a black coat and hat was walking briskly away from a hansom that had drawn up fifty or sixty yards distant. He looked upright but certainly impoverished. His black umbrella, which he used as a walking-stick, was not neatly rolled but untidily open. It flapped at every step. Yet he was taller and more confident than I had imagined. But I think I had expected the stage caricature of an unmarried, unkempt, unworldly clergyman, probably of a humble denomination whose superintendents could afford to pay him only a pittance.

The cabbie, who ought by now to have whipped up his horse and driven off to collect another fare, drew a clay pipe from his overcoat pocket and lodged it between his lips. He pulled a blanket over his knees in the cool March day, folded his arms, and allowed his chin to repose on the breast of his brown overcoat. He was preparing for a long and patient wait.

"If the gentleman in black is our client," said Holmes gently, "I believe he is here on a very anxious mission. He seems in fear of some kind. He can hardly be afraid of *us* or he would not have come. Who, then?"

I was still watching the progress of this down-at-heel cleric.

"He gives no sign of anxiety, let alone fear."

"You think not? His clothes mark him out as a worthy but impecunious saver of souls. Interesting, then, that he has indulged in the luxury of paying a trusted cabman to wait an hour or more until his business is done. You have known what it is to be on half-pay, Watson. Carlyle Mansions is the address our client gives us. One among many mansion blocks of apartments in the Victoria district. As you also know full well, a twopenny bus from Victoria to Camden Town passes down this street every twenty minutes or so. In our client's situation, would you not have taken the bus and saved your money?"

"He might have come from somewhere else that required a cab."

Holmes smiled, and I guessed that I had stepped into a trap.

"So he might, doctor. But he would surely pay off the cab and hire another when he leaves us. There is a rank five minutes away at the Regent's Park, another outside the Metropolitan Railway station. Much cheaper, for a man with little more than the clothes he stands up in."

"Then perhaps he does not intend a long visit."

"No, old fellow, that will not do. His letter makes plain that he has a tale to tell. But he needs the same cab and a driver to take him home. Why? Because he does not know who the driver of the next cab may be. In his present plight, whatever that is, he wonders who may be lying in wait for him. Our man has also taken care to be set down at a distance. It gives him a better chance to detect if he is being followed. Now, who does he suppose will follow a loyal but dull minister of religion—and why?"

The bell of the street door ended this speculation. During a customary pause, Mrs. Hudson's maid took the arrival's dilapidated hat and coat. It was the housekeeper herself who tapped at our door.

"The Reverend Mr. Dordona, sir, to see Dr. Watson."

This was the first visitor who had come to consult me rather than Holmes. I shook his bony hand, introduced him to my colleague, and motioned him to a chair. I needed no convincing that Samuel Dordona was all he claimed to be. The worthiness of the Evangelical Overseas Medical Mission was, as they say, written all over him.

Seen face to face, he was more than average height. A little more stooped than I had first thought, but he held himself well. His narrow, lean, perpendicular frame put me in mind of a grandfather clock case. In appearance, he bore the sallow tan of a fair skin that has passed ten years or more in the tropics. His dark, threadbare suit was brushed and neatly darned. The black hair was punctiliously plastered at the sides into two stiff, obstinate-looking curls, by the aid of a little macassar oil. Above his forehead, it formed what is called by hair-stylists a "feather" but is more apt to look like a ridge-tile. The pale face, shaved clean of whiskers, made the dark hair-line on his upper lip a distinguishing mark.

Natural caution gave his conversation a sharp and abrupt turn. Samuel Dordona did not waste his words. Once installed in an easy-chair, he did not lounge, as Sherlock Holmes was in the habit of doing. He sat forward, erect and solemn and as steady on the edge of his seat as if he had been nailed to it. There was a businesslike air. He was ready now, and impatient for conversation.

We exchanged a few preliminaries. He had been eleven years in India, for the most part near Hyderabad. He was not a medical man, but he repeated that he had enrolled at the London Mission School to study for their assistant's medical diploma in "First Aid" during his furlough in England. As for his evangelism, his work had been among common soldiers with an enthusiastic cast of faith, and very often among the less fortunate in the Provost Marshal's cells.

It did not surprise me that, in the relatively small English population of Hyderabad, Mr. Dordona should have encountered

Captain Carey. A few minutes that morning with *Crockford's Clerical Directory* informed us that the captain's late father had been a minister of the Church of England with a taste for evangelism. The parents were determined that only a strong Old Testament name would do for their son. Young Jahleel was destined for a childhood of moral discipline and the career of a Christian soldier.

During Mr. Dordona's account, Holmes sat with brows drawn down as if not a word must be missed. When there was a pause, he looked up.

"Very good, Mr. Dordona. But I still do not understand what you expect of my colleague Dr. Watson—or of me—that you could not get elsewhere. Why would Scotland Yard not believe a man of your openness and honesty? Do they think you have come to England to kill somebody?"

The movement of Holmes's mouth was both humorous and scornful. I could not tell whether Holmes intended a joke in poor taste or had aimed one of those terrifyingly accurate insights by which he penetrated to the inner mind and secret thoughts of his witness. As they stared at each other, neither he nor Mr. Dordona batted an eyelid. It was a joke, surely.

Our visitor wore an uncomfortably wide white collar, so starched and shiny that it looked like gloss-painted enamel. He eased his chin forward over this rather aggressively, like a man determined not to be put off.

"Mr. Holmes, I want nothing for myself. I bear a message from the late Captain Brenton Carey to anyone who will listen. Scotland Yard would not do so; the War Office will certainly not."

"Dr. Watson and I will, however?"

"You shall judge, sir. I was with Captain Carey when he died. On the previous Sunday, I had come from Lahore to address a prayer-meeting in the garrison chapel at Hyderabad. These were soldiers about to leave for Quetta and the battlefield. I had not yet returned to my duties in Lahore."

Samuel Dordona paused just long enough to let Holmes understand that he would not be pushed, as they say. When he told his story, it was as if he had rehearsed it in his mind many times on the voyage home, fearful of forgetting any detail.

"Captain Carey and I had known one another for some time. I had a high regard for him. On the Tuesday afternoon, I received a note from his wife asking me to come at once to the bungalow, which they occupied in the camp. You will know from the press that his fatigue party had been striking bell tents vacated by 'B' Company the day before."

"We have read the press reports of the inquest."

"It was said in evidence that as the floor of a bell-tent was being lifted, one man in the fatigue party lost his grip because his foot slipped on the muddy ground. Did they have that detail in the gazette?"

"Not that it was muddy, I think."

"I walked on the same ground the next evening. It was bone-dry, sir. We had had no rain for more than a month by then. There was no mud. Nothing that would cause a man to slip that evening or the previous day."

"Rain, Mr. Dordona, is not the earth's sole lubricant. But pray continue."

I intervened on my client's behalf.

"You know a good deal about soldiering in that area," I said to Mr. Dordona. "Had you ever known such an accident happen before?"

He looked at me and shook his head. "Never before, sir. However, when working with a heavy wagon-team, the first rule, of course, is that nothing must startle them."

"But you were not an eye-witness?" Holmes suggested. "That is to say, you were not at hand when Captain Carey fell into their path?"

"Mr. Holmes, I spoke to two men who had been witnesses. They could only tell me what you already know. By the time I arrived at the bungalow, the regimental surgeon had attended my friend. Even as a medical man, he could only give me his best conjecture. Everything depended on the damage to the intestines. He hoped and believed that there was no rupture."

"If it is not too much trouble," said Holmes casually, "would you please write down the surgeon's name? Indeed, would you write down all the witnesses? I think we had better have a list of the *dramatis personae.*"

I was alarmed at my friend's tone, which seemed part scepticism and part downright churlishness.

"Their names? I do not think . . ." Our visitor was plainly upset at this novel suggestion that he should be the one to take a copy of the evidence he was giving.

"If you please!" Holmes insisted, as if about to sigh with weariness.

"I will do it," I said, taking out pencil and notebook and wondering what the devil my colleague was up to. "Leave Mr. Dordona to tell his story."

Samuel Dordona followed my pencil.

"The surgeon was Major Callaghan. Mrs. Carey you already know."

"The surgeon remained with Captain Carey?" I asked.

"At first, Major Callaghan remained, but he had other duties. Annie Carey or I watched by her husband that night. The captain slipped in and out of consciousness; but when he was awake, his words were never rambling. It was only the inquest which suggested they were—and that was wrong. Once he had woken, he had complete and lucid command of his faculties. He knew what he was saying as clearly as you and I do at this moment."

There was a silence and then Holmes spoke, still rather coldly:

"You, sir, are the minister of an overseas medical mission. You do not yet claim, I take it, to be a medical man? Or do you?"

I flinched again at his tone. Mr. Dordona sat like stone on the edge of his chair, upright in threadbare clerical suit, hands clasped, dark eyes intently on Holmes, black hair absurdly sculpted in its ridge-tile peak.

"Sir, I have used my furlough to study for the First Aid Diploma. I hope to be of some extra use to my people when I return to India. That is all."

"You were not called by the court of inquiry into the accident?" I asked.

Mr. Dordona glanced at each of us in turn, as if wondering whom to trust.

"That court of inquiry was held quite some time after the inquest. I was on the high seas by then, returning to England. I should not have been called anyway. I had no conclusive evidence to offer. I was not, as you say, an eye-witness. What Captain Carey said to me during that last night could not be corroborated and was perhaps best not repeated in public just then. Unfortunately, the regimental surgeon had already assured the inquest that the injured man was never more than semi-conscious after the accident. In other words, rambling. That word again! I carried no credit against that, gentlemen, and so I have kept my evidence for you."

"Tell us about the prognosis after the accident," I asked him. "Do you think Captain Carey knew that he was going to die—or was likely to die? As a matter of law, that might make a real difference to the validity of his uncorroborated words as evidence."

"Not at first, I think. To begin with, Major Callaghan thought he would pull through and indeed said so. He said that as long as the intestine was not ruptured, there was hope. He instructed the orderly to use hot fomentations to relieve the abdominal pain. But nothing more."

"As I should have done," I said approvingly.

"His wife, Annie, however, was very distressed by his condition. Poor soul, she asked if a mild dose of laudanum could be given to ease the unhappy man's ordeal. The surgeon advised against laudanum. It would relieve the pain, he told her, but it would also mask any further symptoms."

"That was correct again," I said, "so long as there was still hope for him."

"The rest of that first day, it still seemed there was no rupture. The doctor's exact words were that it would be looking on the black side to think there was such serious damage. That night we were advised to keep applying hot fomentations and to administer sips of hot water. But poor Carey looked dreadful by this time, eyes sunk and cheeks drawn in. I believe there was what is known as the *facies Hippocratica*, so the inquest called it, a sure sign of the worst. I saw that for myself. Next morning, his condition had not improved. However, they administered turpentine internally."

I shook my head. "That would do no good. It would be too late. Did his temperature sink?"

Samuel Dordona nodded. "It continued to sink after that. Of course, the diagnosis now changed. His intestine had been ruptured after all. The surgeon acknowledged that it was peritonitis, for which nothing could be done. He explained to me in confidence that in an hour or two Captain Carey would lose consciousness and by that evening he would probably be dead. So it was."

There was a moment of silence before Holmes inquired more gently, "And in the meantime you had become his confessor?"

"I simply happened to be with him for the greater part of the night, Mr. Holmes. Poor Brenton Carey would have talked to anyone. His wife, Annie, was exhausted by then, and I persuaded her to go and get some sleep."

How often have I, as a physician, known such situations! However poor and shabby he might appear, Samuel Dordona had been a good friend to the dying man and his wife in these misfortunes.

"During that night," he went on, "Captain Carey talked to me. He was in pain. From time to time he dozed fitfully. But I swear that he spoke of what he knew. The only thing he could not tell me was how exactly he came to sustain the accident that killed him. It had come upon him like a thunderbolt from the blue and knocked the senses out of him. Those were his words. He came round to find himself in the bungalow. The shock of the incident—and the morphine he was at length given—fogged his memory."

"But he spoke of the Prince Imperial?" my friend prompted him.

"He did, Mr. Holmes. I wrote down the exact words he used, immediately afterwards. I committed them first to memory as best I could, and then to the flames. I have a good memory, you know. It comes as a matter of habit. It would never do for a minister to read out a sermon, let alone a prayer, that he could not otherwise remember. In those hours, Captain Carey told me a story that he swore he had told to no one before. Not even to his own wife, for fear that the knowledge might put her in danger. But knowing he was likely to die, he was determined that the truth of murder must not die with him."

Holmes brightened up. He opened his cigarette case and leant forward to offer it to our guest. "Murder, Mr. Dordona? Indeed? Pray continue your most interesting account."

"Captain Carey's patrol had ridden out on that day, when the prince met his death. So much had been done to protect this young man that the idea of his being killed went round the Blood River camp like a joke. A few days earlier, he and Captain Carey came into the camp just as General Sir Evelyn Wood was mounting. The general called out to him 'Well, sir, you've not been assegaied yet?' The prince laughed and called back, 'No, sir! Not yet!' You see what I mean?"

"Who rode with him on that last day?" I asked.

Mr. Dordona now intoned his account, rather like a child who has learnt his lesson and must repeat it.

"Captain Carey had a patrol of troopers from Bettington's Light Horse and another six Basuto riders. They rode out over grassland at first, the Prince Imperial and Major Grenfell at their head. Major Grenfell kept them company until the point where he turned off to another destination. They had also brought a native guide who could translate for them if it became necessary. They were following a ridge with an open landscape below them. They would have seen any tribesman a long way off."

"The tribes had no horses?"

Samuel Dordona shook his head. "No, doctor. The warriors go on foot. They could never have caught up with a mounted patrol. When Major Grenfell went off on his own business, he made another joke to the prince, something about not getting shot. The prince laughed again and said something like 'I know Brenton Carey will take very good care of me.'"

"Afterwards they stopped for lunch?"

"Before that, they took a wide sweep of the surrounding countryside through field-glasses. They were on the top of a hill, at the end of the ridge they had been following. The landscape was still deserted. Even a distant sound would have carried well in such a quiet place. They made sketches, mapping the land around them for an hour or so, until it was time for lunch. Just below them was a deserted village of five native huts. The escort searched the huts but found only three native dogs running wild. No one had been there recently. The troopers fetched water from the river and made a fire. Then they brewed coffee and ate their rations."

"How long were they there?"

"By all accounts, about three hours. Though Captain Carey was uneasy at remaining so long, the prince was in no hurry to go. Carey was the senior officer in command, but it was not easy for him to overrule the Prince Imperial. That was at the root of the tragedy. The prince treated this survey as a picnic rather than a patrol. Just then, the native guide reappeared and said that he thought he had seen a single tribesman coming over the far hill."

Mr. Dordona lowered his eyes, as if to prepare us for what lay in store.

"Even this was no cause for alarm at such a distance. All the same, Captain Carey insisted that they should gather their horses. They did so and began to mount. The prince himself called out 'Prepare to mount.' Just as if he had put himself in command. Each man had his foot in the stirrup and one hand gripping the saddle. At that moment there was a crash of rifle-fire, though the shots went wide. The tribesmen lack experience of firearms and are poor marksmen. However, several of the horses were startled and tried to bolt. Then thirty or forty Zulus burst towards the patrol from the tall grass just short of the village."

"Thirty or forty tribesmen who could not possibly have been there?" I asked.

"I cannot see how they could have got there—so many of them. Nor could poor Carey. The place had been searched for a possible ambush."

"Indeed," said Holmes quietly, in the tone of one who needs no more evidence. But Samuel Dordona was not to be denied a hearing.

"The first casualty was Rogers, one of the troopers. He lost hold of his horse when the animal bolted at the explosion of the rifles. All the rest managed to restrain their mounts in one way or another. Of course, Rogers was helpless on foot. It seems he must have run back into the cover of the huts and fired his carbine before one of tribesmen pierced him with a spear. A few of the Zulus were carrying Martini-Henrys captured at Isandhl-wana, but they fought mostly with their spears to which they were accustomed. One of them then hit Trooper Abel in the back with an assegai and brought him down from his horse. He was probably dead by the time he hit the ground."

"And the Prince Imperial?" Holmes inquired thoughtfully: "Where was he in all this confusion?"

"The prince caught his horse before it could bolt, Mr. Holmes, and he was a first-rate rider. He made as if to vault straight into the saddle. He had done it hundreds of times and it should have been child's-play to him. When Captain Carey saw this, he never doubted that the prince must have mounted. So Brenton Carey turned and led what he believed to be his entire patrol to safety at a gallop—excepting Rogers and Abel. He swore to me again on his last night alive that he had been sure the prince must be with them. Looking back presently, he saw Rogers and Abel lying dead but no one else."

"And the prince?" I asked.

Mr. Dordona came unwillingly to the truth.

"There was a native hut between the patrol and the tribesmen. It hid the details of what had happened. But then Captain Carey saw the prince's horse, Percy, cantering out of the kraal without a rider. He guessed that the prince must have fallen as he was mounting. The young man was helpless, but he fired the last shots from his revolver at the attackers. Thirty or forty of them. In a few seconds, he was overwhelmed and killed. A matter of seconds, gentlemen. Whatever a court might say, Captain Carey protested to me that there was nothing he could have done to save him, even if he had given his own life. Nothing. Carey was a brave man, and he spoke the truth."

"Nothing to be done except to have foreseen such an ambush," Holmes said as he turned his brooding deep-set eyes upon our visitor.

"Mr. Holmes! By all the laws of military logic, those tribesmen could not have been there. Do you not see that?"

"I find that an interesting assumption, Mr. Dordona. I see at least half a dozen ways in which an assassin might have put them there—supposing, of course, that there had been an assassin, of whatever tribe, or race, or nationality. However, I believe, as you say, that Captain Brenton Carey had done all one could expect of him in safeguarding the prince. Will that do for you?"

I watched Samuel Dordona closely. I will not say that he smiled with relief, but a great burden seemed to drop from him.

"At last, Mr. Holmes!" he said gratefully. "You are the first person since Captain Carey himself to suppose anything of the kind."

"Then so far," Holmes said carefully, "we have lost two troopers, Rogers and Abel, and the prince. Correct?"

Mr. Dordona nodded. "Correct, sir. There was nothing that could have been done to save any of them. And after this sudden attack, it seems that the Zulu tribesmen fled at once. No doubt they were in fear of being caught by armed horsemen. Captain Carey led his survivors back to the camp at the Upoko River. They met first of all Colonel Redvers Buller and General Evelyn Wood. To my own knowledge, both are brave men and winners of the Victoria Cross. Buller simply told Brenton Carey that he deserved to be shot. Others refused to believe the story. One of the subalterns from the 98th went into the mess-tent for dinner that evening and told the dreadful news. The rest thought he must be joking—because there had been so many jokes on the subject. The subalterns laughed at him and pelted him with pellets of bread."

"Forgive me," said Holmes coolly. "A good deal of this story was given to the court of inquiry and the court-martial, as I recall. Wherein lies the mystery now?"

But the tension had eased, and Samuel Dordona was not quite so upright on the edge of his chair. He sat back a little. His words became slower and quieter.

"No one at those courts spoke of the horseman, Mr. Holmes. A horseman on the hill above, seen by one of the patrol while all this was going on below. A horseman from whose appearance poor Carey seemed to seek relief by talking to me on that last night of his life."

He paused, as if marshalling every detail in his mind before giving us his account of the murder.

"Mr. Holmes, the hill above the abandoned kraal was the same one from which the patrol had mapped the surrounding countryside that morning, just before lunch. It is the only vantage point for miles around. A horseman sitting up there could not have failed to see the Zulu ambush gathering below—and he would surely have warned his comrades down there. No warning was received. Instead, gentlemen, was not this rider in a position to ensure that the Zulu attack took place—and to verify that it had done so? That was poor Carey's question in his last hours. Do you not see what I mean?"

"Perfectly," said Holmes quietly. "And who saw this horseman?"

"Trooper Pierre Le Brun, a Channel Islander. He was one of those who spoke French, and for that reason he was often detailed to attend the Prince Imperial. This rider on the hill, whoever he was, never dismounted. He wore something that might have been the uniform of the Natal Volunteers, though such items of headgear and clothing are common enough in that country. The horse was light-coloured, perhaps dappled. Trooper Le Brun was the last man in the flight from the kraal, and he would have had a view of that hilltop after the others had gone under it, riding closer to the foot of the slope."

"And where is Trooper Le Brun now?"

Mr. Dordona shook his head. "Captain Carey could not tell me that. No one knows, sir. It appears that he went absent before the court-martial; but his story remained one of many legends of the war. For some time before he disappeared, Le Brun had talked of throwing in his lot with the Boer pioneers of the Transvaal. So did many other soldiers. Gold and diamonds were thought to be lying in the streets there for the taking. Rumours thrive in the aftermath of any battle, Mr. Holmes, and the truth is not easily found. Visions are reported in the sky at moments of such intensity—angels, horsemen, burning swords."

"And this one?" I inquired.

"This one may simply be a copycat rumour for a story that went the rounds after Isandhlwana a few months earlier. In the last minutes of that fight, Lieutenant Melvill took the regimental colours of the 24th Foot from Colonel Pulleine to carry them to safety. As they stood together, the colonel thought he saw the first outrider of Lord Chelmsford's column mounted on the col above the camp. Melvill's servant, who escaped with his life when his master died at the Buffalo River, was standing by and heard this curiosity pointed out. A single rider sitting astride a dappled horse, as if watching the last act of the tragedy from above. Sitting at the salute. That was all."

"All this came from Captain Carey and nobody else?"

"It did."

"Captain Carey, who is now conveniently dead. I am bound to say that we are singularly unfortunate in our witnesses, Mr. Dordona. How they desert us! Lieutenant Melvill. Trooper Le Brun. Captain Carey. It is so often the way with ghost stories, is it not? Everyone knows someone who has seen the elusive spectre, but what man can vouch for it from the evidence of his own eyes?"

For a moment, Samuel Dordona looked as if we had deliberately encouraged him, only to dismiss his account.

"I tell you the story as it was told to me, Mr. Holmes. I am no more a believer in spectres than you are. Perhaps because he was dying, Carey's last words to me were about the phantom, if a phantom it was, above Isandhlwana. Goodness knows where the tale of this apparition came from. Officers never believed it, only the few survivors from those lower ranks who had died in their hundreds that morning. Those survivors had heard of this ghostly sighting on the col."

"I am relieved to hear it, sir. All the available evidence, then, points to a horseman being within sight on each occasion of a disaster. Is that so remarkable? There were enough horsemen around, in all conscience. Perhaps he was an outrider thanking his lucky stars that he was not part of the encounter, and keeping clear. Or perhaps he was a sensible fellow who felt that this was not a fight of his making. What good might he do, when everyone else was running away? Captain Carey would have been very foolish to rely upon such a man riding into a skirmish and offering himself to be butchered when he could so very easily save his skin."

"Do you tell me, Mr. Holmes, that you do not believe me?"

The tone of my friend's voice changed at once. "You misjudge me, Mr. Dordona. I do not believe readily. I confess that I was sceptical in the matter before your arrival—and until I heard your complete story. Who would not be? Almost all the doubts that I have now are on your side. I cannot vouch for Isandhlwana, of course. Such catastrophes may happen for the most ordinary reasons. The death of the Prince Imperial is another matter. Let us stick to that."

Mr. Dordona waited, still as a sphinx on the edge of his chair, to hear judgment passed. Sherlock Holmes spoke quietly.

"Let us have done with apparitions, sir, and stick to the art of war. A score or more of men with rifles and spears cannot remain concealed while advancing over such flat and open terrain unless they are assisted. A man on a hill, as you describe it, is no spectre. Hidden from Captain Carey's patrol by the ridge of that hill, he alone has the whole landscape in sight. How easily he may communicate directions to the assailants and those who command them."

Samuel Dordona continued to watch him closely as Holmes concluded.

"But how convenient afterwards to be dismissed as some phantom of the veldt or a figure of common soldiers' folklore! The litmus-paper test, sir, if I may borrow a chemical term, is simple. Surely if there was such a rider who was innocent in this matter of the prince's death, he would have reported what he had seen immediately on his return to whatever camp he had come from. At the very least, he would have told the story to some friend or other. Why should he not—if he was innocent? The court-martial, for all its faults, seems to have been scrupulous in tendering evidence. I think we may be certain that no such report was ever made. Whether he was a spectre or flesh and blood, your horseman was no friend to Captain Carey. Again, would he not have tendered information to defend an innocent man's honour at his trial?"

For the first time, Samuel Dordona smiled. "Thank you, Mr. Holmes. Thank you, sir."

My friend silenced him by a raised hand. "And let us not forget Trooper Le Brun. From all you have told us, I cannot see what the man had to gain by inventing such an apparition. Therefore, if our mysterious horseman is not a phantom, it seems to follow that he can only be a villain."

Mr. Dordona had been waiting for something. Now he took the plunge.

"Will you come to Carlyle Mansions, Mr. Holmes? Will you and Dr. Watson come and see for yourselves a proof which will surely persuade you of the truth? The truth of a horseman on the ridge and on the col? The figure whom survivors of Isandhlwana call Death on a Pale Horse! I cannot say more at this moment, but I believe I shall convince you that Captain Brenton Carey knew the truth of something monstrous."

"My dear sir! I will come this minute, if you are prepared to convince me!"

Our visitor held back.

"The evidence is not there yet, Mr. Holmes. Have no fear, it will be. It is in safe-keeping. Will you come tomorrow? Shall we say at three o'clock in the afternoon? I shall prove to you that murder was done on that patrol at the Blood River. And once the facts are in your possession as well as mine, the truth will be beyond the power of our enemies to destroy. But so long as those facts belong to me alone, I am in peril, and so is that truth."

I was about to accept this invitation, but the gaunt missionary in his threadbare black had not quite finished.

"Captain Carey persuaded me that the Zulus no more committed murder on the Prince Imperial than the gunsmith whose trigger is pulled becomes the assassin of an emperor on the streets of Moscow or Paris. And is there not something far stranger than even poor Carey hinted at? Does it not strike you?"

"Indeed," said Holmes in the soothing tone of a keeper humouring a lunatic.

"Mr. Holmes! Isandhlwana! The Prince Imperial! The disaster to come at Laings Nek! The worse catastrophe at Majuba Hill! The dismal surrender at Kimberley of such large tracts of our empire and the treasure they contain. All in so brief a space, like an orchestrated campaign."

It was an eerie echo to hear this quiet, unworldly man listing the omens that had troubled my own mind in the past twelve months.

Samuel Dordona stood up and looked at each of us in turn.

"I shall expect you tomorrow, gentlemen. I do not think you will be disappointed."

Sherlock Holmes remained seated.

"The police will not believe you, the Army will not believe you. But precisely what was it, Mr. Dordona, that persuaded you to honour us with your patronage? I do not recall that you have yet told us. Most unusual."

It was put in a tone more penetrating than any attempt to bar the visitor's way to the door, yet it did so. Samuel Dordona paused.

"I am here on the recommendation of the only other person in whom I have confided any part of the truth as I know it."

Holmes relaxed but did not quite smile his reassurance.

"Very good," he said. "And was that when this other person told you what became of that missing member of the fatigue party at Hyderabad Camp? I refer to the soldier whose foot slipped in the imaginary mud? The man who lost his grip of the wooden tent-flooring and precipitated the so-called fatal accident which mortally injured Captain Carey?"

I have said that Samuel Dordona's years of Indian service had bronzed his skin a little. That tan now changed to a faint blush. Holmes had trapped him. But the way out of the trap was the truth; and he was, I believed so far, a truthful man by nature.

"It was then that he told me. Why do you ask?"

"Because, Mr. Dordona, in your whole chain of evidence, the soldier who precipitated the accident is the one link you have omitted. What became of him, if I may ask? Why did neither the inquest nor the court of inquiry hear anything from such an important witness?"

"He was Private Arnold Levens, Mr. Holmes. The fellow disappeared that same afternoon of the accident with one other man. I believe they both feared facing a court to account for Captain Carey's death. And of course it is not hard to disappear in India. We are not talking about the Aldershot Garrison or the Horse Guards. The courts could not find either of the pair."

"How convenient!"

Samuel Dordona gave him what I should call a reproachful smile.

"Mr. Holmes, men who are detailed for fatigue parties have generally done something to deserve it. They are not saints. As I say, Private Levens and Private Moss were reported absent from duty without leave that very same day. It was at the evening roll-call, I believe."

"I am sorry to repeat myself, but what became of them?"

"Private Moss was never seen again. He may still be alive; he may be dead. A few months after the inquest on Captain Carey, the body of Private Arnold Levens was found in the new drainage canal just north of Calcutta. It was reported in the local press. The body had been there some time, and the cause of death could not be determined. He was identified by the contents of his pockets.

It is a common enough story when a poor fellow is on the run, at the end of his tether, befuddled with drink perhaps."

"He destroys himself?"

"Sometimes deliberately, Mr. Holmes, more often it happens accidentally. Something as simple as a fall into a canal while reeling drunk."

"And occasionally, no doubt, he is assisted. Thank you so much, Mr. Dordona," Holmes said with brisk courtesy. "Until tomorrow afternoon, then."

From the window, veiled by its net curtain, we watched Samuel Dordona walk slowly back to the waiting cab and begin his return to the mansion blocks of Victoria.

"He seems straight enough," I said, clearing papers from the table for Mrs. Hudson's maid-of-all-work to set down the tea things.

Sherlock Holmes still watched the street from the window. He spoke as though he had not heard me.

"I suggest Mr. Dordona no more wrote that letter than I did, Watson. It was written for him. Who can tell whether a colleague then posted it, leaving him no alternative but to keep an appointment with us?"

"How can you possibly say that, Holmes?"

"With every confidence, my dear fellow. Did you not notice his reluctance to commit his pen to paper in our presence?"

"That was nothing!"

"Was it? It is not just a matter of handwriting. Read his letter again. Then tell me whether the Mr. Dordona whom you have brought here could possibly have written it in his own person! Like his clothes, it is the letter of a clergyman from a stage comedy, not the resourceful client we have just met. There are two people in this. Who the other is I cannot yet say. But I have every intention of finding out before we go further."

"You think Samuel Dordona is a criminal? Surely not!"

"You misunderstand, Watson. I should call Mr. Dordona decent and honourable, a good friend to Captain Carey. A credit to his calling. Paradoxical that he should also be such a calcu-lating deceiver. An honourable but deliberate liar. A charming combination, is it not? Worthy of Robert Browning's honest thief or tender murderer."

I stared at him as he turned away from the curtains, but knew that he would say no more just then. I said simply, "We shall see for ourselves at Carlyle Mansions at three o'clock tomorrow."

He looked at me in astonishment. "I have no intention, Watson, of going to Carlyle Mansions at three o'clock tomorrow."

"I don't follow that, Holmes. You have already agreed to be there."

"You do not follow? Very well, I do not propose to be ambushed at Carlyle Mansions by Mr. Dordona or anyone else. Before three o'clock, I intend to know all there is to know about that estab-lishment. If there is any ambushing, Watson, rest assured that I shall be the one to do it."

A light tap at the door and the entry of Molly with the tea and muffins on a tray put a stop to this conversation for the time being.

As Holmes had previously remarked, we were not overbur-dened with clients just then. Much might depend on our success in the present investigation—possibly the entire future of our detective agency. During the rest of that afternoon, however, it seemed as if the assassination of the Prince Imperial and the death of Captain Carey had ceased to be worth further consid-eration. Holmes diverted himself for the next hour by taking his violin from its case and coaxing from it a newly discovered set of variations by the eighteenth-century Italian master Arcangelo Corelli.

Only when I knew my friend better did I understand an impor-tant truth of his character. If the "Scotland Yarders" whom he mocked were so far behind him, it was because they practised as a profession what Sherlock Holmes regarded as an art. It was precisely when his whole being seemed to drift into the sublime abstraction of the music of the spheres that there came to him those intellectual inspirations which led him into some of his greatest practical insights.

A little later, he announced that he might take a solitary stroll in the Regent's Park. From the tone of his voice, I knew better than to suggest that I should join him. When I looked down from the window, however, I could not help noticing that he was walking briskly towards the Baker Street station of the Metropolitan Railway.

7

*O*n the following morning, Holmes was up before his usual time. Shortly after ten o'clock, we walked to the Regent's Park and called a cab off the rank. Not a word had been spoken as to whom we might "ambush" by our early arrival in Victoria—or who might ambush us if we failed to be there first! I stared from the window of the hansom at the first pink flush of almond blossom brightening the balconies of Park Lane in the cool spring. Our cabbie took the parkside avenue at a brisk clip.

My companion made a gesture towards Green Park. "A survey of the field of action is never wasted, Watson. It would be a capital error to allow our rivals, if there are such, to establish themselves first. You will find a good many of these so-called mansion flats in Victoria. They tell me that mansions and underground railways are the peculiarities of that unfortunate district."

We were just then skirting the classic facades of Hyde Park Corner and passing the porticoes that line Grosvenor Place. Ahead of us rose the sooty residences of Carlyle Street and its neighbours, behind their Continental railway terminus at Victoria.

"For my part," I said, "I shall be rather relieved to find that the Reverend Mr. Dordona is alive and well. Whatever you may think, Holmes, I believe that he has put himself in peril for his friend, Captain Carey. And I do not see him as a liar."

Holmes gave one of his short grimaces. "An honourable liar," he said enigmatically. "I was careful to qualify the description."

Carlyle Mansions was a place of considerable gloom. Its five floors of darkened industrial brick and baked stucco lay on one side of a street in deep shadow. A similar building faced it, far too close. The narrow streets of the area were lined with modern pastiches of Venetian and romanesque in dark red brick and yellow ornament. Each set of windows looked out on to nothing more cheering than the front or back of the next building.

Yet the area had its uses. A man who wished to remain anonymous could choose no better locale. Mansion blocks were on the increase everywhere in London at this time. Their owners or landlords were as unidentifiable as their tenants. These buildings were not permanent homes, but lodgings or chambers, hired out for short periods to save the costs of hotels. Solitary officers or civil servants on furlough from India or the Cape would very often take a set of two or three rooms. Yet even these seemed a little expensive for Samuel Dordona.

There was also a constant supply of young men who came to town from the country to pass examinations for the Bar or the Foreign Office. They needed only a roof overhead and a peg to hang their hat upon. The tenants were bachelors frequently, spinsters rarely, married couples almost never. Here they lodged, attended by the porter at his desk in the lobby and the daily maid who dusted, laundered, and made the beds. A scattering of cheap cafés behind Victoria Street fed them from breakfast to supper for a few shillings a week. The tenants seldom spoke to one another or even knew who their neighbours were, nor did they know what went on in the world around them.

At this hour of the morning, the lobby doors of Carlyle Mansions were pegged open for ventilation. Standing alone just inside this entrance was a slightly built man of middle years with a sallow complexion and dark eyes. His mournful features seemed contracted by some deep frustration. His expression was worried and dog-like. He looked like a pug that has lost the scent of its master. This individual stood dressed in a brown jacket and cravat, exchanging intermittent conversation with the uniformed keeper of the porter's desk. There was something impulsive and ferret-like in the manner of the visitor's inquiries.

"I do believe," Holmes murmured, "that we have been ambushed after all. And who was more likely to do it?"

I had already recognised the figure by the porter's desk as our Scotland Yard acquaintance Inspector Lestrade. He and Tobias Gregson were the two whom Sherlock Holmes had described to me as the best of a bad lot in the Criminal Investigation Division. The inspector turned to see who had infiltrated the lobby behind his back. His eyebrows lifted as he recognised us.

"Mr. Holmes? Dr. Watson? You don't tell me you have some interest in this case, sir? The Carlyle Mansions Murder, as they're already calling it in the newspaper offices."

My heart almost stopped. I wondered with a shock which of our acquaintances might be dead. Surely not Samuel Dordona? Sherlock Holmes smiled.

"Are they calling it that?" he asked the inspector. "Are they really calling it that? Our interest will depend in the first place, Lestrade, upon the identity of the corpse. It has an identity, I presume?"

The detective dropped his voice, as if to keep the porter out of the conversation.

"Not yet, Mr. Holmes. To tell you the truth, we'd give something to know the answer to that, sir. Just at present, unfortunately, the dead man chooses to remain anonymous. From all the evidence upon him, he seems to have come here on his own with his pockets empty. Unless he was robbed down to his last halfpenny and bus ticket. Believe that if you like."

"But the case is still murder, is it not? An officer of your repute would not be here for less than that."

Lestrade became whimsical at our expense.

"It's murder right enough, sir. Unless you fancy he might have shot himself through the head and then hidden the gun to aggravate the Criminal Investigation Department. Unfortunately, our Sir Melville Macnaghten has not arrived yet. The Commissioner has a Home Office Committee this morning in connection with the Irish explosions. Apologies for absence are not acceptable. Most insistent Sir Melville Mac was that the investigation must not start without him. So, Mr. Holmes, nothing has been touched yet except by the police surgeon to examine the body. Who knows whether this unfortunate fellow might not be one of your friends?"

"A corpse without a name," said Holmes, deeply sympathetic.

"Most of 'em start that way, sir."

"And yet someone with a name must have hired the rooms that he now occupies."

I interrupted them.

"I have an interest in the Reverend Samuel Dordona," I said confidently, "as a client."

Lestrade's mouth twisted in a humorous grimace. "So you may have, doctor. But for all I know—or care—no such person as Mr. Dordona exists."

"Was he not the tenant of number 49? If not, who was?"

"Not your Mr. Dordona, doctor."

The inspector turned, still talking, and led the way to the stairs.

"According to the account books and the porter, the tenants are the Evangelical Overseas Medical Mission," he said cheerfully over his shoulder, "an organisation which according to our best information never came near the place and probably never existed."

I followed Holmes as he took the shallow granite stairs of the building easily, two at a time. The dusty light filtered through a glass dome above. We came to the landing of the fourth floor with its shabby patterned carpet, a parched fern in a terra-cotta pot and two upright wicker chairs. A uniformed sergeant, lounging on the post of a doorway painted chocolate brown, pulled himself up smartly as the inspector's head appeared above floor-level. The brass number on the door confirmed this as 49 Carlyle Mansions. Lestrade tapped smartly on its panel and the door was opened by a plain-clothes constable.

"Thank you, Constable Nichols, we'll manage for ourselves now. Keep your eye on the porter and his desk. See he talks to no one about the case. Make a note of anyone who comes or goes."

The inspector continued his commentary as he closed the door behind us.

"The dead man was found this morning, Mr. Holmes, between eight and nine. Before we could get here, that hell's-gate porter downstairs went out and sold the story straight to the stop press of the *Standard* for half a sovereign. It'll be all over the newsboys' placards before we can get a start. They'll have it up in print within the hour and on the streets in good time for the afternoon editions. No details, of course, but then it's the headlines that sell newspapers."

He drew back so that we might view the shabby interior of the room.

"Police surgeon's gone. We had Dr. Littlejohn as usual in this area. Bullet wound to the head. He won't know much more until after the autopsy. Everything stays put now until Sir Melville has been to see for himself."

He looked about him and sighed.

"Most of our murders get tidied up by lunchtime. Not this one. This isn't a straightforward case, gentlemen. No one could say that it was."

The sitting-room we had entered seemed all the larger and taller for its meagre furnishing and bare walls. A pair of sash-windows was overshadowed by Landor Mansions, the block on the far side of the street. What must be the bedroom and bathroom opened to one side, and what might be a kitchen on the other. Dusty dark-green paper, peeling a little by the picture rail, covered the walls. Its dado was a motif of faded summer flowers. The floor was covered by plain polished linoleum in bottle-green, with a rug before the stone fireplace and another beyond the desk. The furniture consisted of a round polished table with three dining chairs, placed between the windows. A day-bed in heavy mahogany and badly cracked black leather stood along the far wall. A sour smell of long-dead tobacco lingered in the curtains and fabrics.

"You might do better living in a dentist's waiting-room," said Lestrade helpfully.

Immediately before us, the knee-hole desk, with the fourth padded dining chair drawn up to it, stood clear of the walls. It was sideways to the nearer window. Petty crime abounds in such districts as this, and I had noticed that each sash window was equipped with an inset bolt. The frame could be lowered only two or three inches at the top unless this bolt was unfastened with something like a screwdriver. Two net curtains gave what privacy there was at present. They stirred a little in the draught as the door was closed behind us.

The murdered man still sat at his desk, or rather he lay forward upon it, as if he had decided to rest his head quietly upon his crooked arm and take a nap. He was looking away from us. I could see little more than the back of his head and the clothes that he wore. He was dressed in a russet-brown tweed Norfolk jacket with a belt at the waist and a pair of gaiters. It was the garb of a country gentleman who has arrived in London unprepared and has no clothes suitable for town. He patiently awaited the attention of the Scotland Yard Criminal Commissioner, Sir Melville Macnaghten.

Lestrade became helpful again.

"Shot first thing this morning by the look of it. Seven o'clock or so. Dr. Littlejohn knows a thing or two about guns. He did the case of the Fulham Laundry shooting last year. He reckons that this one hadn't long been dead when found. The wound to the head had hardly stopped bleeding. Have a look at him, doctor, if you'd care to."

The inspector stepped back, as if expecting me to confirm the police surgeon's diagnosis. I touched the dead man. The muscles of the jaw had begun to stiffen and the body to cool, confirming Littlejohn's finding of the time of death at about half-past seven that morning.

"That's right, doctor," said Lestrade encouragingly, "I tried the jaw. Just beginning to turn. We get to know these little tricks. You can't always tell, of course. Last year there was a woman down in Hoxton with instantaneous rigor mortis after an alcoholic seizure. She was found standing up, stone-cold dead, leaning against a door with her arms folded. In this case it's just his identity that's playing us up."

As I stooped over the dead man, shutting out the inspector's running commentary from my mind, Lestrade continued for Holmes's benefit.

"I can tell you how it was done, sir. We have the murderer's method taped. No shot was heard by anyone. Curious, seeing that the rooms on either side had been occupied from the evening before until after the body was found. No weapon lying around, of course. More to the point, no cartridge case. There was no smell of gunpowder. No sign of burning nor amberite on the skin. The spread of the wound suggests it was made at a range greater than the width of this room."

"Most, most interesting," said Sherlock Holmes quietly.

"And how was all that to be accounted for, Mr. Holmes? The logical conclusion, as it seems to me, must be that the gun was not fired in this room at all. How could it have been? No smell of powder, no skin burn, spread of wound too wide."

"How indeed?" Holmes asked admiringly. I guessed from his tone that he was preparing the unfortunate inspector for a *coup de grace*. For the life of me, I could not yet see what it was going to be.

Lestrade raised his forefinger like a man with a secret. "One has to box a little bit clever in a case like this, Mr. Holmes." He tapped the side of his nose confidentially. "Could our man here have been shot from across the street? That was the first thing I asked myself. Not shot by a bullet passing through the window glass, of course. No window was broken and no hole made in the glass. But as you can see, there is a gap where the nearer sash window-frame has been drawn down an inch or two at the top. That would be for ventilation, I daresay."

"Remarkable," said Sherlock Holmes coolly. "Next you will be telling us that a marksman in the opposite building had the victim in his sights, while the poor fellow sat at his desk just here. Your sniper was skilful enough to fire a bullet across the street, through the two-inch gap above the frame of this window sash, and into the victim's temple."

Lestrade appeared a little put out, for it plainly was his solution to the assassination. Now it seemed that Holmes had stolen it from under his nose. Yet the tone of my friend's words also suggested that the inspector's hypothesis was about to be reduced to ashes.

I ignored these two antagonists and gave my attention to the matted blood on the right-hand temple of the corpse. If Lestrade was right, to have hit the mark so exactly from the opposite building through such a narrow gap must indeed have been the work of a marksman.

"You have detained the occupant of the opposite room, I take it?" Holmes asked pleasantly.

Our Scotland Yard friend did not like this at all.

"Not yet, Mr. Holmes," he said huffily. "No sign of him. We have his details, of course, and we have a fellow on guard over there. We shall have the man we want the moment he appears."

"Of course you will," said my friend reassuringly—"if he appears, that is."

The inspector ignored this final comment. "A foreign gentleman, apparently. Mr. Ramon by name. Not present this morning, so far as we know. The commissionaire on duty in the opposite building is our source of information for all this. Naturally, he is also under our observation. After all, sir, who is to say that he might not have done it himself?"

Holmes sighed.

"Who indeed? Confronted by your accustomed cunning and audacity, Lestrade, the true criminal will not long evade you. And what have you concluded about the dead man?"

"Not known to us, sir, except for his presence in these rooms leased to this so-called overseas medical mission."

"Indeed. How did the murdered man get into this room, by the way?"

Lestrade was now visibly irritated. "He must have had a key."

"Ah, yes," said Holmes, "that would be it. Did you find a key?"

"The dead man's pockets were empty of everything, Mr. Holmes. Someone must have been through them."

"Of course, that must be it. His pockets were emptied by his assassin, no doubt, for who else could it have been? It would be a sharpshooter who came down from Landor Mansions opposite and up to the fourth floor of these premises especially to go through his pockets. How did he get in, I wonder? It seems he also had a key to this room. They must both have had keys. It could not be done otherwise. I do believe, Lestrade, that what you may have here is a most unusual case of one evangelical missionary assassinating another."

This was too much for the inspector. "Who knows how the dead man got here?" he said abruptly. "What does it matter? I daresay there must be another key hidden in these mansion rooms somewhere."

"Capital!" said Holmes encouragingly. "Of course there must be."

"At any rate, gentlemen, we shall make our full search and inventory on Sir Melville Macnaghten's arrival. Carpets up and curtains unstitched if necessary. Furniture dismantled. I can show you round in the meantime, if you choose."

Holmes shook his head. "Just tell me a little more about the fatal shot that was not heard in this building. Was it heard across the way in Landor Mansions?"

"Not that we know of, Mr. Holmes, but we have better evidence than just shots being heard."

"Have you, indeed? Excellent! Pray describe your better evidence."

"The measurements between here and the opposite building were taken by our men soon after the body was reported by the maid. Measurements across the street, between the two windows." Lestrade stood confidently again, staring up at the top of the sash. "There is a casement in Landor Mansions, the ones just opposite, slightly above this level and immediately across from us. From that window, our officers have taped a trajectory which crosses the street. It passes through the gap above the partly open sash-window on this side. It then almost infallibly enters the right-hand temple of the head of any person sitting at that desk."

"I see," said Holmes encouragingly. "And I daresay there was such a constant rattle and banging of cart-wheels in the nearby

Continental railway goods-yard that a murderer might choose a safe moment to fire without being heard. The clattering of iron wheels would drown the crack of his gun? That would be why the shot was not heard on either side of the street?"

"Yes," said Lestrade abruptly. "And what might be wrong with that?"

"Have you retrieved the bullet?"

"That must wait for the autopsy, which Dr. Littlejohn himself will carry out at the pathology department of St. Thomas's Hospital this evening, sir. At present the bullet presumably remains embedded in the dead man's brain. And seeing that it killed the man, where else is it likely to be?"

Holmes gave him a quick humourless smile. "Where else, indeed? I mention the bullet, Lestrade, because even I can see—and as Dr. Watson will tell you—there is more dried blood than one would expect on the surface of the dead man's wound. Will you take it from me that the injury was almost certainly inflicted by a soft-nosed lead projectile? Attend to it and you will see that the impact has left an expanded wound rather than a neat bullet hole."

"What of it?"

"A soft-nosed revolver bullet may have a lethal impact even when fired without gunpowder. Air weapons have been with us for two or three hundred years. They have often been preferred to gunpowder by a sniper who wishes to remain concealed. When he fires, there is no flash, there is no explosion, there is no sign of smoke, no smell of powder. Interestingly, these are some of the very things lacking from the scene of your present crime. I smell stale tobacco in the air. I do not smell the rather more pungent odour of gun smoke."

Lestrade had the look of a man who feels himself hooked and wriggling and does not care for it. Holmes pacified him.

"I wonder, inspector, whether you are familiar with the Von Herder air weapon. No? You are not? To be sure, at present it is something of a rarity in this country. Its use is mercifully confined at present to international criminals of considerable sophistication. Generally they prefer extortion or fraud to murder. Murder, when necessary, is a quiet business with them. The usual Von Herder weapon is a handgun powered by compressed carbon dioxide. It can fire these soft-nosed bullets at considerable velocity. Approaching the speed of sound but not exceeding it, for fear of setting off an atmospheric crack. Very effective."

"Not something I know of personally," said Lestrade, almost chortling at such a far-fetched theory. "Talk about a rarity, Mr. Sherlock Holmes! Oh, dear! Oh, dear!"

Of course Lestrade had never heard of Von Herder until this moment, but he resented a challenge to his solution of the case. He kept the unease from his voice but not from his face.

Holmes became reminiscent. "I was briefly acquainted with Von Herder in Berlin some years ago. He is a blind German mechanic of true genius but indifferent ethics. His handguns work upon compressed gas. This compression gives to a soft revolver bullet such velocity that it kills without a sound that could be heard beyond a closed door."

Lestrade was after him like a greyhound from a trap. "And I suppose you'll tell me, sir, that such a weapon could have been fired just as easily from either side of the street!"

Holmes looked troubled, as if he had been misunderstood.

"Dear me, no. I am as sure as I can be that the shot was fired in this room. The killer and his victim were face to face. The gunman was standing up, I imagine, and his victim would have been sitting down at the desk. The wound suggests to me that the range must have been very short and the barrel of the gun, not surprisingly, would have been pointing downwards. Of course I have not, as you correctly say, made an adequate survey of the premises. I cannot be more precise for the moment."

He dropped to one knee and smoothed his hand across the polished floor.

"And I cannot help thinking that this desk has very recently been moved. Quite innocently moved, perhaps, for the purpose of sweeping or polishing the linoleum. But it has surely not been moved back again."

Still poised on one knee, he took the edge of the rug beyond the desk and turned it back.

"It is as I supposed. Look just here. We have uncovered two small round blemishes on the linoleum forward of the desk. I believe we shall find that they are the matching patches, made by the pressure of the two forward casters of the desk over a period of months or years. They will prove a perfect fit when we move the desk forward; you may depend upon it."

"Meaning what, Mr. Holmes?"

Holmes stood up. "Suppose those casters now stood where they formerly did, on the two marks in the linoleum. The desk would have to come forward to accomplish that, would it not? A rough calculation in trigonometry, made from where I stand, tells me that as the victim then sat at the desk, his head would have been beyond the aim of a gunman on the far side of the street. The projecting corner of the window embrasure over here would have made such a shot as you describe quite impossible."

"Ifs and buts!" Lestrade exclaimed. "Who says that the desk was not moved for sweeping and then not put back?"

"Who says it was not moved after our poor friend was shot by a gunman confronting him in this room? Who says, my dear Lestrade, that you are not thinking at this instant precisely what the killer wishes you to think? One moment, please."

Sherlock Holmes crossed to the further sash window, which appeared to be tightly closed. Then, using the white cotton handkerchief from his breast pocket and extending his considerable height, he stretched upwards to the topmost glazing bar and carefully dusted it. The level was well beyond the unaided reach of a chambermaid. Next he raised his arms and gently pulled the window frame down as far as its two security bolts would permit. Returning to the nearer window, he repeated the process.

He walked back and offered two patches of debris on the handkerchief for the inspector's examination.

"I daresay it means nothing, my dear Lestrade, but you know better than anyone what a clever barrister might make of such a thing in court. Do borrow my magnifying lens, if you feel it will assist you. The further window, which is shut tight, now yields a deposit of street dust and soot, sufficient to require a constant passage of contaminated air to carry it into this room. It must certainly have been left open at the top for weeks, months, even years, but is now shut."

Lestrade stared morosely at the evidence on the white cotton as Holmes continued.

"Now consider the nearer sash. It yields only the amount of dust that might come from internal domestic sources. However, it also has several specks of dried white paint. These have surely been deposited since the surface was last dusted."

"In other words. . . ."

"In other words, my dear fellow, this nearer one is a window which was 'painted shut,' as slovenly tradesmen say, when the room was last decorated. It has been crudely and recently prised open. You may also see a little roughening of the white paint on the sash-frame itself. The fragments have parted from the rim of the wood. If you will step across to it, you will also notice that the further sash is painted but dusty. The nearer frame is cleaner but unpainted."

"And what is that supposed to tell us, Mr. Holmes?"

Holmes stood at the window and stared across the street.

"It has been clear to me since the moment I first entered this room that the shot must have been fired within these walls and not from across the street."

"Meaning what, again? They forced one window and shut the other?"

"Meaning that it suited the assassin for the police to believe that the shot came from the other building, though the porter has seen nothing out of the ordinary this morning. Let us leave that for a moment. From what I can see, there is also a curious punctiliousness about the arrangement of objects in this room. An exactness such as a busy housemaid in premises like these rarely attains. I believe that these rooms have been meticulously searched and the objects just as meticulously replaced, probably as soon as its occupant was dead."

I glanced up from my examination of the body and asked, "You think he had a secret to hide?"

Holmes frowned a little.

"The immediate cause of his murder was very probably that he refused to disclose to an intruder the whereabouts of something concealed in this apartment. Something worth killing for. He defied his adversary, believing—as you have believed—that no man would risk rousing the other residents of a fully occupied mansion block with the explosion of a revolver shot. He was wrong. One second."

He raised a forefinger to silence Lestrade, if only for that second. Then he strode across to the round table with its three dining chairs. He drew them out, one by one, and examined the upholstered seats. By way of placating the inspector, he tossed him another scrap of evidence.

"When you begin the search for your killer, Lestrade, look for a man not less than five feet and ten inches in height."

"Why?"

"I am rather more than six feet tall. When I did all that was necessary to examine the two windows just now, I found that I had a reach sufficient in length by more than two inches. A man several inches shorter would have needed a step-ladder. There is no step-ladder here. To move a heavy day-bed across would mark polished linoleum. I see nothing else to stand upon in this room but these three chairs. But then I see no signs upon the plush of the seats that they have been used for anything, perhaps even sitting on, since the maid's last visit. The tenant was presumably content with a day-bed and a chair at the desk. A man or woman standing on the other chairs would have left a tell-tale impress, such that there would scarcely have been time to brush the print out so immaculately."

During this conversation, I had continued my examination of the dead man. Holmes was right. The soft lead bullet had done considerable superficial damage to the victim's temple before burying itself within the softer tissue of his brain. The velocity of the bullet suggested a short range. Indeed, in this case the wound to the temple, supposedly inflicted from across the street, was so accurate that, other things being equal, one might assume the man had shot himself. But other things proved far from equal. As I turned my examination from "profile" to "portrait" of the face, forensic diagnosis was overtaken by a shock of recognition.

I had seen many dead men and women. Their mute faces, often open-eyed as this one was, seem to question the living. They seek to know, in the last moments of conscious life, why they have come to such an unquiet end as this and to understand what lies ahead. In their gaze, it seems, one last question pleads for an answer to the greatest mystery of all. So it was in this case. I had not wanted to interrupt Holmes's duel with Lestrade. Now I must.

"I know this man," I said quietly with a sense of shock as I spoke. The conversation behind me stopped. "I have solved one of your mysteries, Lestrade. I have seen him before. Only once, but for long enough to be utterly certain. Death has changed him a little, and I concede that our acquaintance was brief. But I swear that I am not mistaken."

They watched me as I straightened up from my examination of the body.

"His name is Joshua Sellon. In uniform, he was a captain in the Provost Marshal's Corps. In February 1879, we shared a saloon coach between Bombay and Lahore with two young Army lieutenants. According to them, Sellon was—or had been—a Provost Marshal captain. I had no idea he was in England at present, let alone why. When we met, he was knowledgeable about military law and crime. He talked to us about what they call a subalterns' court-martial. So did the two lieutenants. In this connection, the two young men described a man known to Sellon but about whom Sellon himself would not speak. His name was Colonel Rawdon Moran. He was as malevolently wicked as any man can be."

Sherlock Holmes gazed at the dead captain and sighed. "I believe we have found our second man of whom I was so sure."

I made no reply but concluded my explanation.

"By the same token, in his own military career, Joshua Sellon was as surely a criminal investigator as any of us in this room. I am certain from the evidence of my own ears that he knew of Rawdon Moran as a moral deviant and a corrupter of younger officers. I believe that his own path crossed with Moran's. Furthermore I suggest that it was in connection with Colonel Moran that Captain Sellon may have come back from India. Perhaps it is in connection with Moran that he has now been killed."

I could not prove the crime, but I spoke in the certainty of being right. The kaleidoscope of events in the past two days made only one pattern in my mind. For the moment, I would say no more.

Before Sir Melville's arrival, we pacified Lestrade by allowing him to show us the rest of the apartment. "For what use that may be," as Holmes softly and ungratefully remarked to me afterwards. What could we expect to find? The drawers of the desk were empty. Very likely they had never been used. Of course the dead man's pockets had been turned out. Had it not been for my chance encounter with Joshua Sellon on the Bombay, Baroda and Central India Railway, Scotland Yard would still be puzzling over whose corpse they had on their hands.

Carlyle Mansions, the office of the Evangelical Overseas Medical Mission, was just as I would imagine anonymous chambers hired by the day for the Provost Marshal's Special Investigation Branch. Nothing was left there, nothing was trusted. If they were Provost quarters, that was of course why Sir Melville himself insisted upon attending the anonymous corpse. There was nothing more personal here than the pots and pans, beds and chairs that go with such temporary accommodation.

"Well, there wouldn't be, would there?" Holmes muttered, as I gave my quiet opinion. "A Shoreditch burglar could search rooms like these and be on his way in five minutes. No one entrusts anything of use or value to such a place."

I nodded, but my thoughts were elsewhere. I recalled Lieutenant Jock's comment on Sellon during that railway journey to Lahore. I do not believe I had thought of it since. Immediately Sellon left our saloon coach, the young scamp whispered, as if I should have known already, "He's only Provost Marshal's Corps! That's all! Snooping into black-guards!" That phrase—"Snooping into black-guards." It was an odd one. It struck me at the time that Jock spoke as if it was well-known Army slang and we all secretly knew what it meant. As a novice, it had meant nothing to me. Nor did I hear it again in my short and invalid military career. Was it coincidence that the initial letters of the phrase were SIB? I guessed "The SIB" must be a common abbreviation of the Provost Marshal's Special Investigation Branch. Was that what Jock meant about Captain Sellon? Was that what had brought us all here? And finally, was that the profession for whose honour Joshua Sellon had chosen to die?

8

I stood between Holmes and Lestrade in the main room of the mansion apartment. The body of Joshua Sellon still lay like a Chamber of Horrors waxwork across the desk. Glancing at Lestrade, I wondered whether he believed a word I had said. Should I say more?

But before I could explain myself further, there was a patient beat of hooves from the street, growing slower and halting below the room in which we listened. The inspector drew out his watch, looked at it, and seemed to pull himself together.

"Twelve o'clock, gentlemen," he said solemnly. "It sounds as if Sir Melville Mac may have got back early from his explosives conference."

Until that moment, I had not consciously noticed a white hospital screen folded and propped against the wall by the door. Lestrade now took hold of it, like a man who has been neglecting his duty. He unfolded its panels to hide the desk and the corpse, as if for decency's sake. Satisfied that all was in place, he swung round and opened the door to the stairway.

"Sergeant Haskins!"

"Sir? Yes, sir. Hansom cab pulled up outside, sir. Gentleman at the desk. Not Sir Melville. Some other gentleman asking for number 49."

"Then make yourselves scarce. Up to the next floor landing. All of you. Eyes skinned and ears open. Let him alone unless he tries to leave the building again!"

He drew back, shutting the door quietly, drew a pass-key from his pocket, and locked it. Turning round to us, he put his finger to his lips and stood back against the wall level with the white screen. The inward opening of the door would hide him from the visitor's immediate field of view. For a moment he waited, pressed against the wall, and listened. I doubted that Lestrade would have asked permission to draw a firearm. Did he even know how to use one? He had had no reason at all to think he would need its protection this morning. But if this was the return of Joshua Sellon's killer, what a fool I had been to leave my Army issue "Webley Mark 1" revolver in a drawer of my Baker Street bedroom. A loaded six-shot with a hinged frame might prove extremely useful in a moment more.

It was a tense and distinctly unpleasant half-minute as a key rattled, the lock turned on the outside, the latch clicked back, and the hinges of the brown door creaked as it was pushed open. Then I exhaled and relaxed, for I had been holding my breath without intending to.

"Good morning," said Sherlock Holmes in his most courteous tone. "Good morning, Mr. Dordona. We are a little early for our rendezvous, I fear."

Samuel Dordona looked at the white screen round the desk and then his eyes jumped back to us. So far, he had not seen Lestrade, who was now concealed by the open door. The inspector was at the edge of the screen itself and had only to take a step behind it.

"Who let you in?" Mr. Dordona asked quietly.

Before Holmes could reply, I intervened. By drawing his gaze towards me, I hoped that he would not yet turn and see Lestrade.

"Mr. Dordona, there has been an accident. I fear that a man is dead. I have examined him. I believe his name and rank to be Captain Joshua Sellon and that he is a serving officer of the Provost Marshal's Special Investigation Branch."

All this hit him at once. As he stared at us, there came upon Samuel Dordona's face a look of stark fright. How can one describe such a spasm adequately? The apprehension in those tense and narrow features, the look in those dark volatile eyes, transformed him from a man who had seemed merely odd to one who now appeared grotesque. I shall never forget his quick neurotic speech and movements. The sallow tan of his skin grew paler, the double peaks of his dark pomaded hair seemed to stand on end, almost like an illustration of terror from *Varney the Vampire* or any other "Penny Dreadful" comic. There was even the suggestion of a winged predator in the abrupt hunch of his shoulders.

During our exchanges, Lestrade had moved silently out of view beyond the screen.

"And you, Mr. Dordona," Sherlock Holmes was inquiring courteously, "who let you in? Or should I say, who gave you the key to unlock this door?"

But Samuel Dordona glanced uneasily at the hospital screen and what must lie behind it. He ignored my friend as he muttered his own erratic questions.

"Is he still here? Is the body still here? How do you know it is he?"

"For the moment," Holmes said courteously, "I should like my own inquiry answered, if you would be so good. Who gave you the key?"

"The key!" I thought Samuel Dordona's voice might rise in a cry of anger, but it dropped away again. "Of course I have a key! These rooms are Overseas Mission premises! You know that already. What are you doing here?"

Holmes looked at him dispassionately.

"I know only, Mr. Dordona, that a man has been shot dead in these rooms this morning before our arrival. You or anyone else with a key to the apartment would have been able to come and go as you pleased. Does it not strike you that you will certainly be one of the first people to be suspected of the crime? It may even seem to the police that you have returned now to remove or to re-arrange some of the evidence of your guilt."

Now, of course, Samuel Dordona could not take his eyes off the white screen that concealed the desk and the image in his mind of what lay behind it.

"Is he still here?"

"Joshua Sellon? Indeed he is, and in a moment we must trouble you to look very carefully at him."

This promise turned his face a little paler still.

"What was he to you?" Holmes resumed. "Was he a colleague of yours? Another missioner of some kind as well as a military policeman?"

Mr. Dordona tried to speak. He began and halted. Then he said, with a perceptible tremor in his voice, "He was a good man, Mr. Holmes. A brave and trustworthy man. He was more than a colleague or a missioner. He was my friend."

Holmes spoke reassuringly. "I am sure he was, sir, but that is not quite the question that I asked."

"What would you have me say?"

"The truth, Mr. Dordona, if you would be so kind. I understand that you came to me yesterday with a view to becoming my client. Very well. My first advice to you was then, and must be now, to tell me the truth. Do you know the truth?"

"What truth?"

"In the first place, did you know that Joshua Sellon was a captain in the Special Investigation Branch of the Provost Marshal's Corps? Whether he supported your evangelical medical mission, I have no idea. Perhaps we never will know."

Samuel Dordona paused and then spoke slowly, as though renouncing everything he had said so far and starting again. I thought to myself that this was going to end badly for someone, perhaps for everyone concerned.

"Mr. Holmes, I am in England on my furlough. As you are already aware, I am using that time to qualify myself as a medical assistant. I do so in order that I may be of practical use in addition to my work as an evangelist."

But time was shorter than Samuel Dordona would ever know. Holmes had become impatient enough to break him.

"And how long, sir, have you been engaged in 'qualifying,' as you call it?"

"A month or so."

There was an intolerable weariness in my friend's voice.

"Very well, Mr. Dordona. I have played the game fairly with you so far. But if you will have it otherwise, it must be so. Answer me, if you please, at once! How many bones are there in the human body? The precise number, if you would be so good! Now!"

Something resembling a foolish half-smile appeared on the poor evangelist's face.

"How many bones? A great many, to be sure! It is not the sort of total one carries around in one's head!"

"Does one not? There are two hundred and six," Holmes snapped back at him, "as any *bona fide* student would tell you. Would you care to name twenty of them? That will do just as well. Before you make excuses, I may tell you that I visited the London Mission School in Holborn yesterday evening. You would have learnt the answer to my question in the very first week of the instruction in First Aid. More than that, you would have sat in class with the other beginners and chanted the entire list alphabetically until you knew it by heart, like your schoolboy twice-times table in arithmetic or your Greek verbs."

He was about to continue, but at that moment Samuel Dordona's nerve broke. The poor fellow turned and snatched the door open by its handle. He almost threw himself out of the room, closing and locking the door behind him in a single movement. Holmes made no attempt to prevent his escape. There were raised voices and hurried steps on the landing. Someone called out, "Stop that man!" There was the sound of a scuffle. The high cry that followed was not pain but Mr. Dordona's despair.

A key opened the lock of the door again. The fugitive reappeared, walking slowly with head bowed before the uniformed police sergeant. He was now crestfallen and apathetic, for all the world as though he might be on his way to the gallows. What a tableau the four of us made, the sergeant, the suspect, my friend, and I! Inspector Lestrade stepped out from behind the screen to join us.

"Very clever, Mr. Holmes," he said sardonically.

Sherlock Holmes waved Sergeant Haskins away. The door closed, and he addressed Mr. Dordona as if their previous conversation had never been interrupted.

"I made inquiries after you, sir, from the mission school authorities. They had no knowledge of any First Aid student by the name of Samuel Dordona. Only of one with that name who had attended Bible studies at the Mission School a dozen years ago. Where he may be now, no one knows. Did you take a dead man's name, perhaps, for your little charade?"

But Samuel Dordona, if it was he, had been well and truly frightened into silence. My colleague ended the pause.

"Very well. The school authorities had kept all their earlier records. These included an entry in that same year for the training of a nursing sister who went out to India. They knew her then as Emmeline Bancroft. You and I, and anyone else who cared to check the records of marriages at Somerset House, would perhaps know her better by her married name. She was the late Emmeline Putney-Wilson."

The stricken figure gave a gasp of shock, as if simply to empty his lungs and fill them with new breath. I could see that Holmes longed to be sympathetic but dared not.

"It grieves me, sir, that we should have to come to the truth by means that must be so painful to you. I still believe you to be an honourable man and a just man. Deceit does not become you, however necessary it may seem to you."

He paused and then addressed the frightened figure before him.

"For whatever distress I have caused you, Major Henry Putney-Wilson, I owe you an apology. You are in danger and you hoped a dead friend's identity might protect you. I think it will not. I beg you to leave this place and leave this city. Return to India or anywhere else away from England. You need not fear me, although you hoped to make use of me in destroying the man who killed your wife by the cruellest means. Leave that to the law, sir. It will come, I assure you. As for the secret of your identity, I need hardly say that it is safe with me. Until all danger to you is past, Henry Putney-Wilson does not exist for me. Except in the presence of my associate, Dr. Watson, and of Inspector Lestrade, I shall speak of you and think of you as the Reverend Samuel Dordona of Lahore. But I beg you will listen earnestly to what I have said. If I could trace the truth about you so easily, what might your enemies do?"

The poor man still stared at us. "You could not have known!"

Holmes shook his head sympathetically.

"I could not have *helped* knowing, sir! From the moment I met you—indeed from the moment I saw you walking down Baker Street—I did not believe that you were the man who had written that letter to Dr. Watson making your appointment. You do not have sufficient power to deceive, if I may say so. The letter is deferential, even obsequious. You are upright, forthright, firm, an air like Mars to summon and command. It is as much in your military stride as in your character. Did Captain Sellon write that letter for you? or, as I think more probable, did he compose it and did you persuade some other person to act as your scribe? I deduce that Joshua Sellon may have warned you not to let your own handwriting be publicly examined."

"But you could not know that!"

"I could and do, Mr. Dordona. Once again, if I do, how many others might do so?"

Our client's reply was little more than a mumble. "There are places in the commercial district of the city of London where men of means without the art of writing may pay to have letters written for them by clerks or scriveners. It is common enough. I made use of that to avoid discovery. Now, Mr. Holmes, I believe you know everything that I can tell you."

"I know something, Major Putney-Wilson. Not everything. I shall continue to wonder, as I did yesterday, whether you have left India to follow and kill a man. I was not joking when I asked you that. I am not joking now. Indeed, I might honour you for your intention. But there is a price attached, is there not?, and you may not be the one who pays it. So I must also wonder whether your crusade has already caused a brave man to give up his life in this room in order to save yours. Only you can tell me whether I am right."

While Holmes was speaking, I watched our client. Indeed he was our client. But yesterday he had been the absurdly disguised Samuel Dordona. Today he was the crusader who had employed two guards and a farrier to mark obscenely with a hot iron the man who seduced his wife and then drove her to hang herself. I was convinced he now sought that man's life. He had been terribly wronged, but we should not make the mistake of believing in him as a victim without the resolve to inflict justice.

But this knight was being turned back from his crusade by Sherlock Holmes. Resolve was giving way to despair. There was no response, only a deepening silence such as one hears when the pulses of an explosion subside. There were tears of disappointed honour on the bowed face of the suspect. He would not look at us just then. Lestrade saw this too. In the quietest and kindest voice I had ever heard our Scotland Yard friend use, he spoke to the man who had so recently been the Reverend Samuel Dordona. The inspector stopped just short of putting an arm round the bowed shoulders.

"Here, what's all this? " he said encouragingly as our prisoner wiped his eyes. "There's no need for that. No one's accused you of anything—yet."

9

*I*n deference to our client's safety, Holmes referred in future to what he called the "nom de plume" of the Reverend Samuel Dordona, rather than to Major Henry Putney-Wilson. In my own narrative, I prefer the truth, now that the drama is over and the secret is out.

Henry Putney-Wilson, with his key to the door of the mansion apartment, was inevitably the first suspect in the murder of Captain Sellon. It was very soon clear, however, that there could be no charge against him. Joshua Sellon was seen alive by a milkman on his rounds and the porter at the desk on his arrival at Carlyle Mansions. It was no later than half-past six in the morning. Major Putney-Wilson meanwhile was at the Ravenswood Hotel in Southampton Row, where he had been a single resident for more than a month. It was at least half an hour's cab-ride from Bloomsbury to Carlyle Mansions and back, plus whatever amount of time would have been needed for committing the murder. It would also require a cab to be waiting outside the mansions for his immediate return to Bloomsbury. No cab had been seen arriving, waiting, or departing.

At the Ravenswood Hotel, our client had still been in his nightshirt when the maid called him that morning just before seven. He had breakfasted in the public dining-room of the hotel from half past seven to almost half past eight. He then went out and scanned the day's press at Drummond's Reading Room in Russell Street between quarter to nine and quarter past.

Captain Sellon's body had been found by the daily maidservant a little before nine o'clock. Scotland Yard being close at hand to Victoria, Lestrade and his officers were alerted at once and had been on the scene well before ten. The police surgeon had come and gone shortly before Holmes and I arrived, at eleven. Joshua Sellon had therefore died between half-past six and quarter to nine.

It was one thing to clear Henry Putney-Wilson of murder, but quite another to persuade him to talk about Carlyle Mansions. What was the strange "overseas medical mission?" How had it attracted this devout widower of a woman cruelly driven to take her own life by the conduct of Colonel Rawdon Moran? How had it involved a serving officer of the Provost Marshal Corps Special Investigation Branch?

In his impersonation of Samuel Dordona on the previous day, our retired major of the 109th Regiment of Foot had promised to provide us with evidence of the murder of the late Prince Imperial of France. So long as Lestrade was present, it was clear that Sherlock Holmes would not discuss the matter, let alone invite him to produce the evidence.

Putney-Wilson was obsessed by the evil of Moran. He had sent in his papers, resigned from the Army, and entrusted his two motherless children to the care of his brother, a wine-shipper in Portugal. The terrible crime against Emmeline Putney-Wilson remained on the record. The major sought justice for what my two subalterns had called moral homicide.

Before he left Hyderabad to bring his children to Europe, the major had also heard of the terrible accident to his friend Captain

Brenton Carey. The two men had shared a belief and a cause. Our client had been present at the bedside of the dying man, not as Samuel Dordona but as Henry Putney-Wilson. Then he had gone to ground as Dordona, an absurd persona striving to shed the martial qualities of his creator. Perhaps it was not entirely absurd, if the evangelism of an overseas mission was close to Putney-Wilson's heart as an "uprighter." As for Joshua Sellon, was it old friendship? Had Putney-Wilson, on detachment to Army Headquarters in Delhi, been seconded to military intelligence?

He had tracked Moran from India to Africa during the Zulu War, then to the gold and diamonds of the Transvaal after the expulsion of the British. Some of his revelations I would rather not have heard. Moran was by then a professional criminal among canteen-keepers and wooden hotels that offered billiards and brandy to the rogues and the roués of the camps. He was well-matched by the "fathers" of crime, former convicts or the pickings of street corners all over Europe. They gambled on everything from animal fights and bare-knuckle boxing to cards, roulette, and coin-tossing. At intervals, the primitive and lawless townships were devastated by dysentry, typhus, and malaria, as surely as by devouring infections from houses of pleasure like The Scarlet Bar and The London Hotel.

Among other criminals, Moran and a younger business partner, Andreis Reuter, had little to fear. Law in the settlements was the justice of a lynch-mob, bought and paid for. The Volksraad or the Supreme Court of the new South African Republic might as well have been on the moon. The punishments of hanging and flogging became entertainments, performed for audiences of the brutal and the bestial. The weak and unknown lay at the mercy of the rich and influential. The hangman's profession was not restrained by rules of evidence or right of appeal.

Reuter had been a youthful speculator, known as a "walloper." He bought cheap from the diggers and sold at top prices to the jewellers of Cape Town, Amsterdam, or London. He became a prospector when there was hardly a law in the settlements, let alone a mercantile code. In swindler's *argot*, "watered stock" was one of his frauds. He advertised shares in the London press, took the investors' money, paid a promising dividend for the first year, and pocketed the rest as directors' remuneration. No gold ore extraction had taken place. No plant or machinery had been installed—and none ever would be. But not one in ten thousand of the investors could travel to Southern Africa to see for themselves.

With Moran's assistance, Reuter now "salted" a so-called gold mine. The cracks and crevices of two worthless diggings were plugged with gold and silver ore to make the "discovery" of deposits possible. Moran was the man for that. His work would have taken an exceptional metallurgist to detect. At first, the two partners could not risk selling the mine. Instead, they sold shares in an exploration company and options on land adjoining the digging. Andreis Reuter soon believed that with "Colonel" Moran as his partner, he had secured a prize among men.

Major Putney-Wilson saw his prey once and got no nearer Moran in the Transvaal. The colonel struck before suspicion touched him. He planned to rob his younger partner most efficiently. To do that, he must kill him. With Reuter dead, he might drain the funds and seize the shared assets.

The murder had an ironic resemblance to the fate of Emmeline Putney-Wilson. Young Reuter was as hard-faced as the older Moran; but he had a weakness, though not much affection, for certain women. Most envied among these was a maidservant, Seraphina. Her beauty as a favourite might be her downfall, but her moment of hope had not yet passed.

To Rawdon Moran, the trick was as easy as persuading a child to eat a poisoned apple. Age marked him almost as a father to the girl, and he played up to this. Through his dealings with Reuter, he became her confidant. Seraphina shared her secret ambition which was, in truth, no secret at all. She trusted him more readily when she discovered that she was pregnant by Reuter. She had no power over the man. Soon she might be lucky to have even a roof over her head. She could hope for no rescue but marriage.

Moran was wiser in the ways of the world than any man she had known. He promised to bring Reuter to the right state of mind. The younger man was susceptible, but there was no time to lose. He must be worked upon before she confided her secret pregnancy to him.

This simple and superstitious girl believed every word from one as confident in predicting as Moran. He understood the way these things are managed. He told her stories of "love-philtres" and their effects on the object of desire. A child in her ways, she would have believed him as readily if he had talked of wizards and dragons and magic spells.

He had such a philtre. It was a powder from the root of the African dandelion, Flower of the Forest, tasteless and harmless. He showed or read to the girl a passage in a pharmacopoeia. It confirmed all this. Hidden in Reuter's food or drink, it would begin to work at once. If it produced no effects after two or three days, she need only abandon it and her friend would think of something else. Even if this philtre failed, which it never did, she would be no worse off.

Seraphina must keep this to herself until she was sure the powder had worked. If her lover were to hear of it, he might be angry. All her hopes would end completely and for ever. Once she had succeeded, he would never be angry again. Even if he were to learn the truth then, he would be grateful to her for their happiness. They would laugh together over it.

In the face of advice from her kindly and persuasive mentor, Seraphina followed his instructions. Within a week, Andreis Reuter was dead. Under a brief and brutal interrogation by the township police, she was ready to tell the story of the philtre her friend had given her and which she administered to her lover. She could have done him no harm.

There was no pathologist in the township. Two doctors examined the white powder. It was derived from an ordinary weedkiller, in which four grains of sodium arsenite produced two and a half grains of arsenic. As for the appearance of the corpse, the dead man was shrunken, eyeballs sunk. He had swallowed three grains of arsenic on a single occasion.

Seraphina appealed to her friend. Rawdon Moran was nowhere to be found. Two days earlier, he had taken with him from their joint enterprise whatever of Andreis Reuter's mineral and financial wealth he could lay hands on. It was less than he had hoped, but he was beyond the jurisdiction of the Transvaal. He very simply denied knowledge of the so-called lovers' tragedy, except that he had long suspected Seraphina of robbing her master secretly. He had even warned Reuter, but the poor fool had been so besotted with his scullery princess that he had taken no action. A cursory examination by the constables showed that Andreis Reuter had certainly been robbed by someone of great things and small.

Had Colonel Rawdon Moran remained at the diggings, matters might not have gone well with him. But it appeared that he had left for British territory, less than a hundred miles away, with no intention of returning and in the knowledge that no British court could make him return. Then it was believed that he had reached Cape Town and boarded a Union Castle liner for England.

At this point, Major Putney-Wilson paused and looked round at us.

"You are mistaken, gentlemen, if you believe that my intention was to hunt the wretch and shoot him out of hand. I would far rather see him endure death by process of law. Joshua Sellon was my friend in Hyderabad and London. I was never far from him in the pursuit of justice. We worked separately but between us we traced Moran. He was never near British territory. He had headed north into Belgian jurisdiction. He reached the Congo, with such gold and cash as he had been able to loot from his partner. He did not sail to England but from Leopoldville to Antwerp. The Kingdom of Belgium sheltered him."

"And still does?" I asked.

Putney-Wilson shook his head. "He may be anywhere between Belgium and the Congo Free State—or the Transvaal—as his criminal business takes him. I may say, gentlemen, that I have not been idle. I can tell you that according to the shipping-lists, he was a passenger on the *Reine Hortense* bound from Leopold-ville to Madeira."

That was the end of our inquiry. Whatever his speed, even with the aid of the Trans-European express from Lisbon to outdistance a steamship, four days would still leave Moran on the wrong side of the English Channel when Joshua Sellon died.

What of the murder of Andreis Reuter? Putney-Wilson assured us that in the Suid Afrikaansche Republick, as the independent Transvaal was now known, Moran had retained well-placed friends and influence enough to laugh out of court the only story that Seraphina, as she became known in the law reports, could tell in her defence. Justice in the local "high court" was speedy and rough. Seraphina had never denied giving her lover the philtre. Indeed, she had admitted it at the first opportunity, sure that it could not be the cause of Andreis Reuter's death. On the evidence available, the tribunal was persuaded otherwise. Worse still, she had made a foolish attempt to incriminate a British officer of honourable rank and name who was not present to defend himself. As it happened, Moran was less concerned with honour and rank than with the discovery that Andreis Reuter was smarter than he had supposed: the account which held their working capital had been largely drawn upon by the young man who had felt the first doubts about his elder partner as a prize among men.

For Seraphina there could be no hope. Her local judges pre-sumed that she had acted in revenge against a man who had seduced her. An example must be made of such domestic "petit

treason," as the law called it. Crimes and executions were sufficiently commonplace in these primitive settlements not to cause
much comment. Seraphina was convicted and sentenced to be
hanged. Being pregnant, however, she was respited until the child
should be born, so that she need not be hanged until after its birth.

Major Putney-Wilson told his tale and looked at the horror on
all our faces. It was not the facts which convinced us, so much
as the manner in which he gave his account.

"Be assured, gentlemen, Colonel Moran does not hate the
young woman. He might not even desire her death in other circumstances. However, it became necessary to his scheme that she
should die—that scheme could not work otherwise. Therefore
it must be so. There is no anger in him on this occasion—just a
cold and bitter self-interest."

For the only time in my acquaintanceship with him, I saw
Holmes pause in asking a question because he feared the
answer.

"And has she died at their hands?"

"No, sir. Not yet."

"Then she must not and shall not! Brother Mycroft shall
answer for that."

10

*A*ll that remained was to elicit from Major Putney-Wilson the evidence of the Prince Imperial's murder. But Holmes looked at me with a hard and direct stare. In other words, as I had decided for myself, in the presence of Lestrade any such explanation must be postponed, nor did the major offer it. Better still, in the case of Joshua Sellon, the inspector seemed easily convinced of Putney-Wilson's innocence. It would require only proof of the witness's address and personal details before dismissing him from the case. All the same, Lestrade could not resist a brief reprimand.

"Let this be a lesson to you, sir, how you go about to deceive. Good-hearted and brave you may be. All the same, certain things are best left to those of us whose business is to deal with the world's wickedness."

Before Lestrade could develop this homily any further, Sir Melville Macnaghten, Commissioner of the Detective Division at Scotland Yard, arrived at Carlyle Mansions in a plain black carriage, a rolled umbrella in his hand. He entered the room upright as a guardsman. Indeed, he had far more the air of a brigadier than of a police commissioner. Neither Holmes nor I had ever met him before and, in any case, he was the last person to confide in a pair of private detectives.

Two uniformed constables and a sergeant had accompanied Sir Melville to attend to the evidence. First the body must be moved. In a moment more, Captain Joshua Sellon lay on his back, staring up open-eyed from the black leather day-bed with a stretcher underneath him. Having read the police surgeon's report, the Westminster coroner had now released the body to the nearby pathology department of St. Thomas's Hospital. Sir Melville's carriage had been accompanied by a hearse from the public mortuary.

While the commissioner and his officers made a survey of the rooms, Holmes addressed our Scotland Yard friend for Sir Melville's benefit.

"We are grateful to you, Mr. Lestrade, for your hospitality, but I doubt that anything further will be found here. We must look elsewhere."

As he addressed Lestrade, he still looked purposefully at Major Putney-Wilson. Direct conversation with our client was impossible just then, and that evening he was to be dismissed from the case. Before he left, in the company of Sergeant Haskins, he drew from his pocket a visiting card. It bore upon it the legend of the Ravenswood Hotel in Southampton Row.

"Should you wish to speak to me again, Mr. Holmes, you will find me here. I will give you the number of my room as well."

He drew a gold pencil from his pocket and scribbled on the back of the card. Holmes took it from him, glanced at the scribble, slipped it into his pocket and shook the major's hand. It was clear that Sir Melville wanted the premises to himself and his uniformed constables. He was in no mood to listen to the "theories" of Sherlock Holmes.

Even Lestrade was now instructed to make himself useful elsewhere by questioning the commissionaire of Landor Mansions across the street. Sir Melville had been quite taken with the notion of a sniper firing from the opposite window. Whatever the guardian of that mansion block had seen or heard was therefore of immediate importance to this theory, and he must be closely examined.

As we came out by the main door, Putney-Wilson was sitting in a cab with Sergeant Haskins, about to start for Scotland Yard. Holmes tapped the pocket into which our client had seen him slip the hotel card. Then he touched the brim of his hat in acknowledgement and the major, as it seemed, passed out of our lives. Holmes later boasted of extracting a promise from him of an early return to the safety of India.

Where Lestrade went, it was easy for Holmes and myself to follow. Presently we were sitting with the inspector in a cramped cubby-hole office behind the commissionaire's desk on the opposite side of Carlyle Street.

Holmes might be sceptical of chance encounters in criminal investigation, but the discovery of Joshua Sellon's body was not the only coincidence that day. I need not describe the commissionaire at Landor Mansions, for I have already done so. Albert Gibbons was none other than that retired sergeant of the Royal Marines whom Holmes had identified when the man brought us Tobias Gregson's message about the Brixton Road murder case, some months earlier. His commissionaire's uniform, which was being cleaned and repaired at that time, was now back in place, but there was no doubt of his identity.

Sergeant Gibbons had been pensioned by the Royal Navy, just as Holmes had guessed. He now supplemented this by such work as a dependable and honest man can come by. He was even privately employed on occasion by a Scotland Yard plain-clothes officer to carry routine messages. One of the kind had come to Holmes from Inspector Gregson. Yet it seemed that the sergeant was a stranger to Lestrade.

As for the anchor tattooed on the back of this messenger's right hand—there it was on Albert Gibbons. The splendid regulation side-whiskers of the non-commissioned officer were not easily forgotten. Like any master of the parade-ground, he stood back on his heels, not forward on his toes, and he walked like Major Putney-Wilson, as though to the beat of a drum-major's stick. This upright stature and air of self-possession portrayed a man willing to serve but never to be subservient. The security of his modest pension no doubt contributed to this air of stoical independence.

A man like our Royal Marine sergeant was unlikely to turn to crime—either from nature or necessity. With a sinking heart, I listened to Lestrade's hectoring interrogation for the next twenty minutes. It was increasingly evident that he had no idea of Gibbons as anything but the porter of a mansion block. Sherlock Holmes checked a yawn with the back of his hand and sighed. If Albert Gibbons could "give the devil himself the slip," as the inspector later complained, it was because he was plainly innocent.

"No, gentlemen," he said quietly, his sad eyes looking at us each in turn, "I heard no gunfire this morning. Nothing from here and nothing from across the road. And I've heard enough guns fired off in my time to know if one was discharged in this neighbourhood. It wasn't. Even with all the other street noises, there's something about a rifle or even a revolver shot that you can't mistake for a Christmas cracker nor a firework. Not if you've heard it coming at you from the Rhoosian infantry at the Alma or at Inkerman. Nor if you've had a taste of being in the Naval Brigade under the guns of the Redan."

I watched Holmes as he studied the strength of the porter's resolute, prognathous jaw, the high-bridged nose, and the cropped greying hair. His firm voice mingled the accents of the little streets in Lambeth or Clapham with an occasional archaic pronunciation, no doubt imitated from the officer class of his naval service.

"I understand your version of events, Mr. Gibbons," Holmes interposed quietly. "But please let us hear a little more about the rooms in this building. Have you seen inside the top-floor suite in the past few days?"

"And don't tell us you haven't when you have!" was Lestrade's ill-judged interjection.

Gibbons turned to Holmes, ignoring the inspector.

"I have not, sir. Nor has Mrs. Standish, the housekeeper. No key has been requested for those rooms. No services required."

"Is that not unusual?" I asked.

"No, sir. Not in this case, sir. The suite of rooms up the top was booked for a week by a foreign gentleman, Mr. Ramon. Spain was where he was coming from, I recall, so of course I never actually met him. Before he could get here and make himself known, there came another message from Spain saying that the rooms would not be wanted after all. Mr. Ramon was no longer coming over here. Gentleman taken poorly, I believe."

"Would the key never have been in his hands?" Lestrade asked sharply.

Albert Gibbons shook his large, impressive head.

"Hardly, sir. Not if he hadn't come here. Because we never let it out of our hands before that. But then a criminal wouldn't need the key himself, would he? His contact man—or contact woman—need only rent the apartment independently for a week or two beforehand. It might be the week before or the year before, come to that. With the key in their possession, they might take an impression of it in cobbler's wax while it's upstairs and then have a copy cut. From that moment on, never mind who had rented the premises, the criminals might come and go as they pleased. Being a police officer, sir, of course you'd know all that, wouldn't you?"

Lestrade gave him something uncomfortably close to a sneer.

"For a so-called innocent man, mister, you have a remarkable acquaintance with false keys and forced entrances. A bit too well informed, some might think!"

Albert Gibbons pulled a melancholy face at him and shook his head sadly. "And what sort of a Provost Sergeant should I have made, sir, in twenty years of service at Portsmouth Dockyard, supposing I had no knowledge of criminals and their ways? I can save you the trouble of checking my character, Mr. Lestrade, for you will surely look up my record when you get back to

Whitehall. Ask the Admiralty. They'll tell you. Twenty years, sir, helping to preserve law and order in Her Majesty's fleet. And when it comes to preserving the peace, I think you'll find we can hold our own, even with Scotland Yard."

Holmes sat back in his chair and chuckled.

"Well said, my good Gibbons! We shall make a consulting detective of you yet! What do you say now, Lestrade?"

The inspector said nothing, but the affability that Gibbons had shown subsided a little and he shook his head.

"No sir, not me, sir," he said quietly. "Consulting and detecting wouldn't do at all, not if I was expected to hold a candle to you, Mr. Holmes, and what I've heard of you. But as for this week, no one's come to that room, no one's gone from it, no one's there now. Your plain-clothes man saw that for himself."

It was soon evident even to Lestrade that he was wasting his time. By any standard of judgment, Albert Gibbons was honest and reliable. Better still, he was capable and efficient. He was disturbed at present only by the death that had occurred directly opposite in Carlyle Mansions. No one could appear more anxious to bring the criminal to justice. Yet he took this tragedy philosophically, like the news of a brave commander fallen in battle.

Lestrade's final response was to let him know that he was still under investigation. Our Scotland Yard man scowled as he got to his feet. That scowl, like his words, was directed at the former sergeant of Marines.

"You will say nothing of this to anyone, Gibbons. No chattering, no loose talk in taverns or saloon bars. You will not leave your present address nor your present employment without notifying us. That is an order, not a request. We have not finished with you by a long chalk, my man. I shall certainly want to speak to you again."

Gibbons turned upon him that same mournful look of watery blue eyes and fine mutton-chop whiskers.

"Thank you, Mr. Lestrade. As to loose talk in taverns and bars, it may assist you to know that I have no use for strong drink. I was born a Wesleyan Methodist and hope to die as one. You will find me in taverns and saloon bars only in the search for lost souls. If one day I find you there, sir, I shall hold out my hand to you."

We now went through a foolish charade in which the three of us got up and left the sergeant at his desk in the lobby of Landor Mansions. Inspector Lestrade turned towards Victoria Street and the Criminal Investigation Division of Scotland Yard. As soon as he was out of sight, Holmes swung round towards the apartment block we had just left.

"Quickly, Watson, before our only dependable witness disappears! Sergeant Gibbons is a man to be trusted, you may depend upon that. We must speak to him now without our friend Lestrade in attendance."

Presently we were back in the room behind the commissionaire's desk, occupying the same chairs from which we had risen a few minutes earlier.

"I promise you that you have nothing whatever to fear from us," Sherlock Holmes said reassuringly to Albert Gibbons. "The record of your military service speaks for itself."

Despite this assurance, the sergeant was far more nervous now than he had ever been under Lestrade's questioning.

"Sir?"

"Do you know in which room of Carlyle Mansions the body of Captain Sellon was found?"

"Yes, sir, the sitting-room of number 49. Slumped over the desk. Sergeant Haskins told me that much this morning. Very sorry I was to hear about it, sir."

There was a long pause before Holmes added,

"You are familiar with that room."

"Sir!"

"My words were a statement to you, Gibbons, not a question. At what time was it that you entered apartment 49 of the opposite block, perhaps using a copy of the key, possibly duplicated in the manner you described to Inspector Lestrade just now? Was it before the shooting this morning? or was the captain already lying dead by the time that you made your intrusion?"

"Sir? Who says I was ever in any room over there—or in that building at all?"

"I do," said Holmes firmly. "Captain Sellon was a serving officer of the Special Investigation Branch, Provost Marshal's Corps. As I am sure you know. You, unless I am much mistaken, were in his confidence. Mr. Dordona is in ours. Indeed, he is our client. We are, if you will excuse the cliché, all in this together. So we will now have the truth, if you please. You have my word again that whatever truth you tell me will not hurt you, but that a falsehood will destroy you."

Sergeant Gibbons looked from one to other of us, but Sherlock Holmes allowed him no respite.

"Please remember that Inspector Lestrade is looking for a neck to fit a noose. Very well. Did you enter that room before Captain Joshua Sellon was killed—before he arrived there, indeed? Or was he already lying dead when you let yourself in this morning with a key that had been copied for that purpose?"

"I was. . . ."

"One moment, if you please. You have told us, just now in the presence of Mr. Lestrade, that you are familiar with the methods used to copy such a key. But you did not copy a key to that room, did you, because you had already been given one? Almost certainly by Captain Sellon. Is that not so? Capital. Tell me whether you were in time to exchange any words with Captain Sellon before he was shot dead."

This questioning about Sellon and the key was one of those occasions when my heart missed a beat because I could not see how Holmes could know so much. From time to time in such exchanges he would take what seemed to be a gambler's chance with shots at random. But if luck was on his side, it was because during every phrase he uttered, he watched his victim's response like a hawk or a cobra. Then he would add one thrust to another as he saw his adversary's self-assurance falter.

Albert Gibbons said, "You are Mr. Sherlock Holmes, sir. I know that."

"Of course you do. Kindly answer the questions."

"And then you, sir, are Dr. John Watson?"

"Indeed. You and I met some months ago, when you brought my colleague a note from Inspector Gregson."

Instead of replying to any of the questions, Sergeant Gibbons got up and went to a small bureau in his commissionaire's office. He opened the lid and lowered it on to its supports. His hand slid into an empty cubby-hole that might have held papers or envelopes. There was a slight jerk as a spring gave way. Then he drew his hand back and moved out a section of hollow wood which had seemed to be part of the bureau's frame. It now appeared as a deep box-like drawer, a concealed compartment. From within it he drew a plain package.

When this brown-paper bundle was unwrapped, it revealed two items. The first was a strip of brown polished leather which gave off an aura of stables and wax polish. The second was a scarlet medal-ribbon. The scarlet of the ribbon was defaced at one end by a patch of rusted liquid. A medical man would know at a glance that the stain could only be blood. What was the connection between the two?

"This evidence was kept by Captain Sellon, never by anyone else," he said quietly. "Things hadn't gone well across the road. That was when the Reverend Mr. Dordona—if we may call him so—came and persuaded the captain to let you see these items. Mr. Sellon didn't agree at first, only in the end. He can't show it to you now, poor gentleman, so I shall do it for him."

Holmes leant forward a little, hands on knees. "Major Putney-Wilson is known to you. Let the name go no further."

Sergeant Gibbons drew a long breath.

"I supposed you'd probably twig that, Mr. Holmes. Is there anything you don't know?"

"Very little."

"What's to be done with these items now?, I ask myself. This is the evidence of murder, gentlemen. Assassination, if you prefer."

At a casual glance, the length of polished leather was a harness strap, a couple of inches wide. It was ordinary enough, except that at one end it seemed to have been torn or unstitched. I am no connoisseur of "horse furniture," but even to me it was plain that it resembled part of an officer's pistol holster, worn forward of the saddle. Yet this one was remarkable for two things.

First was the manner in which the end of the saddle-strap had been unstitched or torn away. A blade of some kind had been used and had marked the polished leather with a single deep cut. The stitching was not simply torn apart, but had been partially and skilfully cut through. The aim of these mutilations, if I may call them so, was that when the harness took the rider's weight, as he mounted his horse, the holster-strap would part company with the saddle girth, throwing him back on to the ground.

The second curiosity was less sinister but more striking. Embossed in gold upon the leather of the holster-strap were a Maltese cross and a crown. In other words, it bore the emblems of the exiled Emperor of France and his family.

In my mind, I heard again those conversations at the time of the death of the young Louis Napoleon, the Prince Imperial. As the tribesmen appeared from the bush, his horse Percy had bolted at the sound of rifle shots, as did most of the other mounts. He had run after the animal, clinging desperately to the harness and the stirrup leather. According to one account, he made repeated attempts to vault into the saddle as the horse galloped faster. Then the girth of the harness gave way and he was thrown down at the feet of his killers.

In another report, he had clung to the near-side holster and the stirrup until the weight of his swaying body caused the stitching between them to tear apart. Or did the leather simply tear in his hands? At that moment, he was hidden from Captain Carey and the others by intervening bushes and one of the native huts. No one saw exactly what had happened. In any case, whatever the explanation, the end was the same. What did the details matter?

Holmes spoke quietly to Sergeant Gibbons as these thoughts passed through my mind.

"The Maltese cross represents the royal house of France, Mr. Gibbons. As evidence, the condition of the holster strap can speak only of the crime of sabotage. The Prince mounted safely enough that morning when they left camp. When can the damage have been done except while Captain Carey's patrol rested after lunch, out of sight of their tethered horses? One man could have done it easily enough. Unfortunately, we have only this piece of the harness. Who will ever know what harm was done to the rest to make the tragedy certain?"

"And the red ribbon?" I asked.

"That, my dear Watson, is the medal ribbon of a crimson sash. Nowadays I believe the sash itself is worn over the right shoulder. Customs have varied. At all events, it is the cordon of the Grand Cross of the Légion d'Honneur. It is, perhaps, the most celebrated chivalric order in the modern world, instituted by the Prince Imperial's immortal great-uncle in 1802. The missing medal belonging to this ribbon has a silver star of five double points surrounding the head of the first Emperor Napoleon. In this case, its silver star now lies somewhere in the African dust."

There was a silence in the cubby-hole office. Then Sherlock Holmes resumed.

"It was no ordinary death. To all his supporters, perhaps to the majority of the French people by now, this young man was Emperor of France, Louis Napoleon, and therefore Grand Master of the Order. As a mere soldier, however, it seems that the poor fellow was as good as dead the moment he rode out on his last morning."

I shook my head. "Cutting the harness could not ensure that the prince would fall to his death. No murderer would trust to such a chance device as that. It might have held for a few seconds longer."

To my surprise, it was Albert Gibbons who replied. The handsomely whiskered face still regarded me sadly, as if I might have been a persistent member of the defaulters' squad on a barrack square.

"No one trusted to that, sir. You will observe that several of the tribesmen carried rifles captured at Isandhlwana. The aim mattered nothing. The shooting was necessary only to bring about the disorder which followed and to scatter the horses."

For me, this was far too simple an explanation. "If the prince mounted safely, as almost all the others did, what chance had these untrained tribesmen of bringing him down?"

The sad eyes now regarded me with a little more sympathy for my brave effort.

"You may be sure, sir, if shots proved necessary to kill him in the saddle, they would easily be fired by a concealed marksman who could bring a rider down with a single bullet at twice that range. A hunter. The credit for the killing would still go to the tribes. The identity of the actual assassin would be perfectly covered by the presence of these tribesmen firing in all directions. As it happened, not a single bullet from a marksman was needed. The strap broke."

My mind went back to our visitor on the previous afternoon. "A marksman? Concealed with his weapon on a hill-top overlooking the skirmish?"

So much for the stories of a lone horseman in his saddle, on the ridge above the kraal. Several further pieces of the puzzle fell into their proper places.

Albert Gibbons nodded. "If the prince was brought down from his saddle by a bullet, sir, it would surely be called a lucky shot by one of the tribesmen. For who else was there to shoot him but the tribes, according to the courtroom evidence? They had thought of everything."

I was about to ask who "they" might have been, but Holmes answered him first.

"Someone had thought of it, Mr. Gibbons. Someone who could shoot the heart out of the ace of spades with five successive shots at forty paces. But, as it happens, the very thing they planned for took place. The leather stitching broke and the hero fell among his assailants."

I looked at the broken strap and the dried blood on the scarlet ribbon of the Légion d'Honneur. "But surely the conspirators would destroy the evidence of their crime, rather than preserve it?"

Holmes shook his head.

"I think not, Watson. Not these conspirators. These are hunters of big game. Such items are hunters' trophies. Some time ago you were kind enough to entertain me with the story of a subaltern's court-martial. That tale had been told to you by a pair of jackanapes on a train from Bombay to Lahore. I recall your account of the trial of a certain captain—the self-styled Colonel Rawdon Moran. After he had been branded with the Mark of the Beast on the orders of a man whose wife he had destroyed, Moran's last words to his former comrades were, 'I'll be revenged upon the whole pack of you.' Correct me if I have got that wrong."

"You are entirely correct, Holmes, as the stories of revenge have been told. First at Isandhlwana; second at the death of the Prince Imperial; third in the Transvaal and the murder of Andreis Reuter."

My friend gave a humourless chuckle.

"Then let us take the scoundrel at his word. However, those who truly relish revenge cannot enjoy its delicacy unless the world knows that they have taken it. The most evil vengeance is often delayed for that reason. As the Italian proverb has it, revenge is a dish which persons of refinement prefer to taste cold. The most exquisite satisfaction of cruelty lies in knowing that those who suffer should know exactly why they are made to suffer—and by whom. They should also know that they are helpless to remedy their agonies of mind—and that those agonies will taunt them and plague them for the rest of their lives. Those who injure them must possess their minds for ever. You understand? Such triumphs are conclusive to the satisfaction of the psychopathic mind. Such are the murderers who taunt the police to 'catch me if you can.' You will find them in every nation and in each layer of civilisation."

"And that is the evidence we have before us?"

Again he gave a short laugh.

"What you in your wholesome way call evidence, Watson, is something else to them. These trophies of hatred belong in the world of mania. They are to be displayed, not concealed. They must be flourished in the face of defeated enemies, exhibited like the booty of war or its helpless prisoners before they are put to death at the conqueror's feast. The vanquished heroes in this case will be made to wish they had died a hundred deaths before they ever took up arms against Rawdon Moran and his kind. You understand now?"

We both turned to Albert Gibbons. The sergeant brushed a hand across his whiskers. His pale blue eyes still watered a little. He had listened patiently to every word of my friend's denouncement. He now spoke quietly but firmly.

"Whatever I know, gentlemen, you shall hear. That is all that I can now do for Captain Joshua Sellon. Until I was pensioned last year, I served in the Provost Marshal's corps at Portsmouth. To this day I remain at the disposal of those who choose to put their confidence in me. Sometimes I run little errands and sometimes I listen for information. Most of the time I am only the commissionaire of Landor Mansions. It is better that way. The Crown estates being the landlord here, I like to think that I still owe my employment to Her Majesty."

Then came the rest of the story.

"Captain Sellon was one of my gentlemen for the last few months. I entered apartment 49 in Carlyle Mansions last night before he had yet arrived from his post at Aldershot Garrison. I had kept my eyes open upon these buildings, seeing who came and who went. I felt, though I could not prove it, that our enemies were closing on us. Not much was ever kept in that room, but I had every reason to believe that the broken strap and the French medal ribbon were there."

"Why?" Holmes inquired.

"They were being kept for the major so that you might see them today. Acting as sentry, I took it upon myself to take them into custody during the small hours of this morning. No one else was in the apartment at the time. Captain Sellon arrived a little before seven. I was to report to him. I did not go across at once. The less we were seen together the better. My duty now is to turn these so-called trophies into evidence against the men who contrived so many deaths. I believe I did right."

"To be sure, you did," said Holmes reassuringly.

"So many deaths, sir. Mrs. Major Putney-Wilson's, Colonel Pulleine's, the Prince Imperial's, Captain Brenton Carey's among them. And now Captain Sellon's."

"How were you and Captain Sellon found out?" I asked.

Sergeant Gibbons shrugged.

"Given the time, it would not have been impossible for our enemies to discover who occupied those mansion rooms and for what purpose. A good many leases in quieter parts like this are known to be Army tenancies. Men like Captain Sellon do not rest. They move on, always a little ahead. This time he did not move quickly enough."

He glanced down at his hand and then looked up.

"I fear that the captain was killed this morning because he could not surrender these souvenirs to a man who stood over him with a gun—and he would not have surrendered them even if he could. I am to blame for that."

"But where did Captain Sellon get these gruesome souvenirs from?" I asked.

"From Mrs. Captain Brenton Carey. They waited for her in a postal packet on her return to England. There was no letter, just the assurance that neither the death of her husband nor that of the Prince Imperial was a stroke of misfortune. To make her live in the knowledge that she had been terribly wronged and there was nothing she could do about it, to the delight of her persecutor. To put her on his trail, to occupy her thoughts and dreams until he was nearer to her than the husband she had lost."

"And they had not counted on the poor lady taking these treasures to the Provost Marshal as evidence in a criminal conspiracy," I said hopefully.

But Provost Sergeant of Marines Albert Gibbons, as I still think of him, demurred at this.

"They had not counted upon the friendship and loyalty which had existed between the families of Carey and Putney-Wilson. They had not counted upon the good lady using a friend who had also suffered, using him as an ally to seek the assistance of yourself and Mr. Sherlock Holmes. That was a miscalculation I hope they will come to regret."

"The medal ribbon and the holster strap," I asked: "What is to become of them now that you have them?"

Albert Gibbons smiled gently at me.

"As to that, sir, I have instructions to follow. Mr. Lestrade knew nothing of them before he came over here with you this afternoon. With the greatest respect, sir, Mr. Lestrade is a civilian and the matter in hand is one for soldiers. By tonight, that strap and the ribbon will be put away carefully. Put away where it would take the Brigade of Guards to get them out again. It is sufficient to our plans that you have seen them."

And that, as Sherlock Holmes remarked when we stood outside the mansion block again, was exactly as it should be.

PART III

Death on a Pale Horse

1

I pride myself that my medical education and military training have made me more observant than most men in the face of a threat. I had scanned Baker Street when "Samuel Dordona" from the Evangelical Overseas Medical Mission arrived. I had watched him as he left. So indeed did Sherlock Holmes. Of course Major Putney-Wilson was absurd in his amateur theatrical disguise. It made him conspicuous rather than unobtrusive. Yet I saw no one who might have been his shadow or who paid him the least attention.

At Carlyle Mansions, Holmes would have been the first man to notice if we had been followed. Of course, it now proved that we and the entire street were under observation by Albert Gibbons, but this in itself should have been a protection against spies. Civilian and military police have what are technically known as "private clothes" personnel who wear no regimental uniform. I needed no persuasion that Gibbons in his commissionaire's livery was as much a sergeant of the Provost Marshal's Corps as he had ever been.

Sherlock Holmes certainly behaved as if there was no present danger from Moran or his associates. My misfortune was to assume that danger is something which all men and women instinctively avoid. But there are also those to whom danger is the breath of life and who deliberately tempt their foe to combat. They will fight a duel when they might as easily avoid it. Holmes fell precisely into this category.

No doubt Colonel Rawdon Moran had become our enemy. Yet he could not have murdered Captain Sellon if he had been on the passenger list of a homeward-bound liner which had docked at Funchal in Madeira less than five days before the captain's death. Holmes had easily confirmed from the shipping line clerk who knew the man: three days at sea and two more on the Transcontinental Express from Lisbon would still leave him on the wrong side of the English Channel at the time that Joshua Sellon died.

"Hence Ramon," said Holmes sardonically.

"I beg your pardon?"

We were sitting over our glasses of whisky and warm water two evenings later as the sitting-room fire burnt down to a final glow.

"Hence Ramon. The foreign gentleman who booked the apartment opposite Carlyle Mansions, from which Lestrade insists the bullet was fired. The man who booked it but never arrived to occupy it. You noticed, of course, that the name Ramon is a childishly obvious anagram for Moran?"

It had not occurred to me until that moment because my mind had been occupied by other things, but I thought it best to say, "Of course."

"It cannot have been Moran who murdered Joshua Sellon if he was not even in England. That is why he taunts us with his anagram. I doubt whether he any longer commits his own murders, except on special occasions. To use such a foolish pseudonym as Ramon is once again the old game of 'Catch me if you can.' We are not allowed to forget that he is the puppet-master of murder. He pulls the strings, and we are his marionettes who dance to his commands."

"What practical use is that to him?"

"The greatest use, old fellow. It is intended to rattle our nerves, to unbalance our judgment, and to tip us headlong into doing something foolish. Now, if you do not mind, I think I shall retire for the night with a volume of Mr. George Meredith. He is the only master of fiction who I can tolerate for very long. I have intended for some time to re-read *The Ordeal of Richard Feverel*, his first endeavour and in many respects still his best."

And so a remarkable few days in our lives came to an end, bringing in its wake what I think of as the night in question. A night of terror.

2

I had known fear on the battlefield, where I expected to find it. But then I had been in company with my comrades. Terror, I was to learn, is faced alone. There is no comrade to turn to, no rhyme nor reason to what is happening. The image of Captain Joshua Sellon's body lingered ghostlike in my mind, but that was far from the irrationality of terror.

I learned that terror is not the ghost before the eyes, like some student prank played with an owl's hoot and a white sheet. It is a heart-jump of fright at what has become inexplicable, as if one were waking in the silence and stillness of one's very own coffin. It is a brief irrational movement, alone in a familiar room, caught in the corner of the eye. The flicker is quick as a darting mouse, where there can be no mouse. Or a sudden shriek that teases the very edge of hearing, where no one else can hear it. Terror at its worst comes in solitude and silence. In terror, as in pain, each must feel his own.

Perhaps worst of all, terror is malignant because it pounces in familiar surroundings, like a loyal guardian turned traitor. It immobilises the brain and annihilates reason. On that night, in my own Baker Street room, I knew that what could not be happening to me was none the less happening. And yet I was a man who would laugh outright at a ghost beyond the window-glass or a spirit knocking on the wall.

It began when I woke drowsily and without apparent reason from an uninterrupted sleep. I felt as though I had risen suddenly and rapidly from a far greater depth of unconsciousness than usual. The speed of it had almost left me dizzy. I could not at first tell where I was or guess what the time might be, except that it was deep night. My surroundings were out of kilter. I could not recognise the dim landmarks of my familiar surroundings. Had the room changed its shape, or had I been taken somewhere else? Reason told me that I must be in the bed where I had fallen asleep.

I was aware at first only of light filtering into a dark room. If it was my own room, the bed and the light were in the wrong place and at the wrong angle. Nor was this the familiar reflection of yellow street lamps at my curtains' edge. The light was thick and tawny, as if I lay under foul water or something opaque had blemished my vision. Suddenly I could feel a cold draught where the curtains of the window above me might be. They were wide open, not pulled together as I had always left them when I went to bed.

My first thought was that there must surely have been an intruder. Where was he? I had the sense to lie quite still and give no indication of having stirred. I went back quietly in my thoughts through the first seconds of consciousness. I believed that perhaps I had heard a whispering at my ear and even a laugh. Yet now I heard nothing, nor could I see anyone. So after all I must be alone in my room, if it was my room. What of the objects around me?

As I looked cautiously, it seemed that someone or something had also changed the angle of a chest of drawers, if it was a chest of drawers. Perhaps that was what had made me think the bed had been moved. Though it was dark, I began to get my bearings again. Waking at night, I have always had some innate sense of time. I now felt that it must be three or four o'clock in the morning. But I could see no clock face and could hear no bell.

Someone, somehow, must be watching me. There was no sense to it otherwise. But why? I still made no movement to betray my consciousness. I listened meticulously. At this hour, no sound came from the street at the front of the house. A very faint mouse-like scratching was audible from the slates or brickwork outside the back wall. I could tell there was no moon but only starlight at the rear. It was framed by an open window with the curtain drawn aside, rising above me where there should be no window. I moved my eyes as far as I could. Had there been a burglar? I would surely not have slept through the coming and going of a housebreaker.

As my sight adjusted to the faint light of the stars, I made out something luminous. Or, rather, it was something seen in a faint and tawny glow. I saw now that the chest of drawers had indeed been moved to provide a flat surface. A murky half-light fell upon an object that seemed to be standing upon it. Yet the object had no explicable outline. I twisted my head a little. The thing was just above me, blocking my vision at this angle. The light was not falling upon it but coming through it. I saw that it was not even on the chest of drawers itself, but in the window embrasure.

Something had been left there or strung up there. Someone had come and gone. Now I was alone in the room. I pulled myself up and sat looking at the thing. It was not stationary, but moving or twisting at a slant as it came slowly into my view. What the devil was it? There was such an unclean light within it. I felt a shock of repugnance that it had been so very close all the time and I had not known it. It was like waking to find a snail moving on one's cheek or a rat licking one's neck.

The object was not even standing on the window-sill, within the casement or embrasure. When it moved as it did, I knew it must be suspended in the opening, not quite touching the surface. It was, after all, bottled in a jar of some sort, a curious amorphous shape, almost translucent, as if it had been fished from the depths of the sea.

I looked more closely at the only feature I could begin to distinguish from the rest. I doubted for no more than a second or two. It was surely a human ear that appeared to float before me in a tawny liquid. As I looked, it turned very slowly away. Wet hair, dark in colour, drifted about it, for all the world like weed in tidal shallows. Thick though the light might be, I knew my eyes were not playing tricks upon me. As it twisted away, I was looking at the upper section of a bare brown neck, severed from its shoulders. I had seen a score of cadavers in the course of my training, but never before one in which the entire head had been cut off so cleanly from the body to which it belonged.

I am not squeamish by nature. The thing had given me a fright only because it caught me with my guard down as I came to the surface of sleep. For a split second, I had thought I might be still asleep, in a mortuary nightmare of some kind. I had struggled to pull out of it. But what the devil was this object, suspended in the dim space of my own bedroom? A severed head? It turned a little more. I glimpsed in profile the curve of a dark-skinned cheekbone. The tip of a nose came next as the invisible cords that must be supporting its bulk unwound themselves a little more.

In reaction to this trick, as I thought of it, I now felt a growing anger with the object and the perpetrator. The grotesque image revealed itself a little further—or, rather, it was grotesque by what it did *not* reveal. It was not a head after all but, much worse, half a head severed vertically. The nose I was now looking at had only one nostril. The profile had only one cheek. The face had only one eye, which was open and blank as it stared at me with the pupil rolled upwards. The mouth had only half a cherry-bud lip at top and bottom. However horrible it might be, my defiance now drew me upright until I sat on the edge of the bed.

I was on my own ground now. This gargoyle of flesh and blood had got the better of me before I could rally my senses. My momentary instinct had been to call out for someone to come and wake me from a grotesque dumb-show. What a fool I should have looked, lying there petrified by some commonplace relic of the anatomy theatre—a joke at my own expense. The object continued to turn a little more, as if to give its expressionless eye a better view of me. The hair still drifted aimlessly as if in a yellow tide.

At last this "terror" was nothing but an anatomical specimen such as one passes in a bell-jar along a row of students in a lecture room. Still unwinding at the end of whatever cord suspended it, the jar gradually displayed the human brain that had been laid open for examination, a cerebrum the colour and texture of greyish-brown meat that has been first cooked and then served cold.

The tightness in my throat had passed as mundanely as a fit of indigestion. Now that I understood what was happening, it was nothing. As a medical student, I had a dozen times examined a brain laid open in just such a manner as this, preserved in a bell-jar of spirit. What floated before me was not borne aloft from the underworld of nightmares, but pickled in formaldehyde. The "thing," for I still caught myself thinking of the word, had no more power to harm me. The erratic beat of the heart that had woken me with a jolt was steady again. Reason no longer ran squealing into its corner, like the wainscot mouse on the far rim of human vision.

I put a lighted match to the gas-mantle. A pale glow strengthened. It fell across the window where the rear wall dropped to a little yard at the back of the house and the roof of a shed for coal and tools, a dozen feet below me. I neither heard nor saw a movement.

The severed head, or rather the wizened skin of its face, had a colour and texture which suggested that this had been an elder of some Indian tribe. I proved to be a little wrong in that diagnosis, but I was not to know it at the time. Now that I could see the bell jar more plainly, it sat in a shallow dish. The dish itself had been suspended by three chains from the lintel of the window, rather like a hanging lamp in the chancel of a church. That was how it had been kept aloft, apparently floating in the air.

Only a professional roof-top thief could have put this object and its container in place without rousing me from sleep. By now I knew a good deal from Holmes about the skills of London's so-called cat-burglars, quite enough to conclude that none could have climbed the outside wall without alerting either of us. Once again I confronted the sightless eye and its floating hair. How had this head been put there—and why—and by whom? No doubt the sole aim was to scare me out of my wits; but for what reason?

It was not a practical joke. For a second only, I imagined some ingenious pleasantry on the part of Sherlock Holmes. But his whimsies always had a purpose to them, and I was damned if I could see any purpose in this pathological monstrosity. Instead, if it had a dark humour it also had a whiff of mania about it. However eccentric his impulses might be, my friend and house-mate was no maniac.

I must wake him, of course, if only because the perpetrator might still be close at hand. I went to the open window and glanced out. There was no one in sight. I was about to draw away from my survey of the back yard when I saw by the faint reflection of gaslight and stars that there was a message of some kind written on the slates of the outhouse roof a dozen feet below. The night was cold and the roof slates had been humid enough to cause a chilly condensation. It was presumably a finger that had traced darker lines on the lighter moisture of the slates in large uneven capitals.

I COME IN SILENCE AND I KILL WITHOUT A SOUND
I VANISH LIKE THE SMOKE UPON THE WIND.
READ THIS, WHOEVER YOU MAY BE,
AND TAKE GOOD CARE YOU DO NOT CHALLENGE ME.

It seemed that the writer feared that he had still not made his purpose sufficiently plain. There was a further line, detached from the quatrain and drawn lower down across the roof. It

appeared to have been done as an after-thought, just before he
dropped softly from the outhouse guttering to the ground.

BEWARE ALL—I WARN BUT ONCE.

If I was to beware of anything, it was that the wretch might
still be down there waiting for me to appear at the window. I
found my key and unlocked the bureau bookcase, inherited
from my father. This piece of furniture had for years been my
companion as I slept.

My Army service revolver, a reliable and efficient Webley Mark
1, lay in the top drawer, carefully wrapped in lint, cleaned and
oiled only the week before. With this faithful friend loaded in my
hand, I felt more than equal to confronting any roof-top burglar
or any spectre of the dead alike. At such a range, I was confident
that my first bullet would settle all accounts between us.

I had no idea how Holmes would take to being roused from
sleep at this unsocial hour by such a wild story as mine. I had
still not consulted my watch; but as I crossed the landing, I heard
the distant winter chimes of St. Marylebone Church striking four
in the morning. I paused, then tapped gently at the door of his
room. I pushed it open without waiting for an invitation. I kept
my revolver drawn. For all I knew, he might be in mortal danger
from an intruder standing over him.

I realised, as he looked up at me expressionlessly from the pillow,
that he had been lying there wide awake during my silent ordeal.

"Holmes!" I said quietly. "We have had an intruder in the
house!"

"Indeed?" he said equably. "And has anything been taken?
Have Mrs. Hudson, Billy, and the maid been roused?"

"It is not what has been taken, but what has been brought!" As
I went on, my story sounded more and more fatuous. Holmes listened without expression or reply, patiently pulling his dressing-
gown about his shoulders.

"A bell-jar with half a human head, preserved in formaldehyde by the look of it, is hanging in my window. It was put there while I was fast asleep. I have heard nothing since I woke just now, and I have seen no one."

How ridiculous it sounded! What if the thing was no longer there when we went to investigate? He looked up sharply.

"Is that all?"

"All? Is it not enough? But no—it is by no means all. Someone has left a message written in the dew on the slate roof of the shed. Someone who claims to move and kill without a sound. He warns only once and this is our warning. It is mad; the whole business is insane."

He got to his feet and nodded.

"Good," he said thoughtfully as he shuffled into his carpet slippers. "Capital. I had been expecting something of the kind, Watson, visitors or messages. I prefer that they should not have kept us waiting."

"*Expecting* it? Preposterous! And who are 'They,' I should like to know!"

He was already leading the way across the landing.

"Not preposterous, Watson. I should call it inevitable in the circumstances."

"Why, in heaven's name? What circumstances?"

Before replying, he paused on the threshold of my room, looking across at the macabre souvenir in the window. He turned away and said, "I forsook George Meredith. I have lain awake until now, thinking. Night is the best time for it. Consider this. We may conclude that Captain Joshua Sellon of the Provost Marshal's Corps is dead because he believed, on the evidence of Major Putney-Wilson, that Jahleel Brenton Carey was killed in India in order to silence him. Captain Carey and perhaps his wife had come to believe that the killing of the Prince Imperial was not a chance encounter with Zulu tribesmen, but rather a carefully planned assassination. Major Putney-Wilson was the

Careys' natural ally, having suffered at much the same hands. Both men were stationed close to Hyderabad, and both shared a similar evangelical faith. I will bet a pound to a penny that they shared the same garrison chapel and, not surprisingly, a determination to rid the world of Colonel Rawdon Moran."

He stopped for a moment, as if to check that the room was truly empty, and then looked round at me.

"After Carey's death, Putney-Wilson adopted his absurd role of Samuel Dordona in order to hunt down the murderer of his wife. So far, he has done his best to get himself killed and accomplished nothing. No doubt he has resigned his commission, but the best place for him is safely back in India."

"And our nocturnal visitors?"

He shrugged and stared at the shrivelled head in its jar of formalin.

"Simple observation would have drawn them here. We entered Carlyle Mansions, the apartment of the murder, in public view. Who more likely to keep secret watch than the murderers? We have publicly associated ourselves with Sergeant Albert Gibbons, late of the Royal Marines, confidential courier—as and when required—to the Provost Marshal General. Who more likely to keep watch on us than those who knew his history? Did you really think we should not be noticed? For my own part I have counted upon it and should be disappointed if it were not so!"

"Even though the opposite apartment in Landor Mansions was not occupied?"

"Precisely *because* it was not. It had been taken by a certain 'Mr. Ramon,' that foolish anagram of 'Moran.' It seems he is not yet in the country, but how dearly he wants us to know the game has begun. This pickled head is his doing. Learn to know his mind. Moran is master of the revels, and mankind are his puppets. He reminds us tonight that we are his creatures, our very lives are at his beck and call. After Carlyle Mansions, did you truly believe we should hear no more of the matter?"

"I had hoped so. I did not quite see it as you do."

"Did you not? For myself, I was so sure of it that I have slept tonight—or rather I have not slept—with an efficient little Laroux pistolet under my pillow. It is a firearm better suited to a lady's corsage but handy enough in the circumstances. One cannot be too careful. Now let us see what we have."

He stood back a little from the window, regarding the severed and cloven head in its jar as though it might have been a work of art. After a moment or two, he passed judgment.

"Phrenologically, I feel quite sure that this fellow's origin is East African, though not, I believe, the Somali coast. That aquiline nose and the proud angle of the jaw would tempt me to suggest Ethiopia or even perhaps one of the many itinerant tribes of the southern Sudan. I would hazard that as a guess."

"Holmes! Who cares where the damned thing came from? What matters is that it is here!"

"I care greatly," he said in a murmur. Then he leant forward a little for a view of the yard with its outhouse. "And you say that you saw the message on the slates below us?"

"It is on the roof, just down there."

He shook his head.

"I only ask because I fear it is there no longer. It is a foolish but effective trick of writing on ice or dew or anything which will vanish in the warmer air. It makes the inscription useless as evidence and usually casts doubt on the credibility of the witness. As it will do upon you, if you repeat the story outside these walls."

"Fortunately, I can remember what was written, word for word!"

"Of course you can!" he cried soothingly, "and I should believe you without hesitation, in any case. But do you not see? It was essential to their purpose that you should read it while it was still there. I am quite sure that they watched you as you did so. They may be watching still, for all we know. That message—that challenge indeed—was the whole purpose behind tonight's charade. As for the rest. . . ."

"I come in silence and I kill without a sound," I repeated; "I vanish like smoke upon the wind. . . ."

"Just so. Certainly neither of us heard them come or go."

"Beware all, I warn but once!"

"Of course, they could not leave without a threat of that kind. These are men of some quality, Watson, however criminally deranged. We should do well to remember that."

"And we still have no evidence of the message they left!"

He looked a little put out by this. "I would not quite say that, my dear fellow. You have read the message and that is all. If proof of its existence became absolutely necessary, I do not think it would be beyond my powers of detection to provide it. I should be surprised if the finger which traced those wet words had not also disturbed the patterns of minute debris collected on the surface of the slates. A microscopic examination would, I think, reveal paths of lettering left in this process. For the moment, however, we have more immediate evidence to consider."

"The severed head?"

"The severed head indeed. Our visitor—or visitors—have departed, and I believe we shall hear from them again. But I do not think it will be tonight. They would prefer to see us tremble a little, first of all. Where is the fun otherwise? Therefore I propose to recoup a little of the sleep I have lost. Following that, I have no doubt what our next step must be."

I nodded towards the window. "That thing?"

"Indeed," he said. "Let that be our task."

"To do what?"

He looked at me with surprise.

"What else, Watson? To discover its origins. Why have we been favoured with that particular gift? If we can establish the reason, it may take us a good long way."

Breakfast on the following morning was a little later than usual. The exhibit in its bell-jar had been covered with a cloth and placed out of sight in an old leather hatbox in the lumber-room above our sleeping-quarters. On Sherlock Holmes's instructions, nothing was to be said to Mrs. Hudson or the rest of the household about the events of the preceding night.

"You believe that we shall experience some further intrusion of this kind?"

He shook his head. "Not of this kind. I think that most unlikely, Watson. Surprise is their weapon, and so these people seldom repeat themselves. We are merely forewarned and therefore forearmed."

I laid my knife and fork on the empty plate. "He came unseen and in silence," I said thoughtfully; "he vanished like smoke in the wind. How did he come?"

Holmes rattled the pages of his *Morning Post* a little impatiently and spoke from behind them.

"He was here already, I imagine."

"But how?"

He looked at me round the corner of the paper.

"Watson, you have already assured me that the ascent in silence to your window from the yard—or the descent from the roof-top—would be almost impossible while carrying a head in a bell-jar. Heads are heavier than people imagine. How then was it delivered?"

"How?"

"My dear fellow, were I to perform such a task, the *modus operandi* would be simple. I should enter when the house is open at various points, take cover, and then remain concealed. That is how I should go about it. I might choose the roof-space for my concealment. Until this morning, when did we last have occasion to open up the lumber-room? Even without that, how easy the access would be to those other dark corners under the tiles which Mrs. Hudson abandons to nature. Once in the house and their purpose accomplished, the departure requires only a doubled length of rope which may be used for the descent. This can then be cut through as one stands on the ground and the entire length drawn clear."

"These people have been in the house with us for all those hours, and we have not known it?"

"Quite certainly. Were we to search those abandoned spaces, we should no doubt find the evidence of it. Our time is too valuable at present to waste it upon foregone conclusions."

"How did they get in?"

"I was in conversation with Mrs. Hudson this morning. It seems the gas company sent two workmen yesterday afternoon to make a routine inspection of safety joints on the pipes. It is now an annual precaution, to ensure that we shall not all be asphyxiated in our beds. An hour later, these fellows took their departure. That is to say, they shouted a cheery farewell down the basement staircase and the outer door was heard to slam behind them as they—or one of them—left. No one recalls their appearances. They were just gasmen in gasmen's caps, like all other gasmen. How simple."

"And if they should return?"

"I do not believe they will take the trouble to disturb us again today," he said, sighing behind his newspaper. "You recall the message? Beware all, I warn but once. In that, if in nothing else, I believe them to be sincere. We have had our warning. Next time, I imagine it will be a question of whose throat is slit first."

"And what is to be done?"

He lowered the paper again and spoke thoughtfully,

"It is possible that Brother Mycroft may know more than I do about these matters. It is sometimes the case. We shall endeavour to find out presently. Today is the first Thursday of the month, when the committee of the Diogenes Club meets at 11 A.M. That is where Mycroft will be this morning. Let us therefore put Mrs. Hudson's Billy to the trouble of fetching the leather hatbox down from the attic— before he puts his best foot forward for the telegraph office."

3

The Diogenes Club is a secret society. Yet it stands at the heart of the British Empire. Its windows look out on to the fashionable pillared buildings, the gentlemen's clubs, and the carriages of Pall Mall. But you would more easily penetrate the secret rituals of the remotest tribes than the proceedings of its members. It is scarcely two minutes' walk from the dark-brick façade of St. James's Palace, the gilded clock, and the scarlet sentries. Yet the first rule of the Diogenes is that no member shall discuss its business with an outsider nor reveal its precise location. I shall say only that it stands somewhere between the intellectual elegance of the Athenaeum and the literary journalism of the Reform Club.

Mycroft Holmes was one of the six founder-members of this eccentric society. It had been whimsically named after that stoical philosopher of the ancient world who lived and died in a tub. Like him, the club professed an indifference to humankind and all its follies. When Alexander the Great came to ask Diogenes what favour he might bestow upon him, the ancient sage merely requested the Conqueror of the World to stand aside a little so that he no longer blocked the warmth of the sunlight. Holmes chuckled as he recalled this tale from Plutarch. He assured me that his elder brother would probably have made much the same reply.

As for Mycroft Holmes, I have no doubt that he will outlive us all, serving his Sovereign to the end of his days. As Her Majesty's Permanent Secretary for Inter-Departmental Affairs, he regulates the formalities of the Prime Minister's cabinet. He maintains the machinery of state in Whitehall and Westminster. From day to day, he advises the leaders of our government on every topic from Antarctica to the Zambesi. Indeed, as his younger brother Sherlock once remarked, he not only advises the British government, in many a crisis "he *is* the British government." In other words, governments may come and go, but Sir Mycroft goes on for ever.

Within his weighty intelligence, the policies of cabinets and the decisions of great leaders are filed and memorised. Cornered once by departmental inquisitors who required to inspect and approve the records and methods of his office, Mycroft replied innocently:

"Gentlemen, I will be frank with you: I do not find it necessary to keep records, for I have an exceptionally retentive memory. At this moment, your names, your faces, and your presumptuous intrusion upon my valuable time have been noted there. That note shall be at the disposal of the Prime Minister and Her Majesty's private advisers in deciding upon your future careers—in the event that you should still have future careers. To them alone I am answerable. Good morning to you, gentlemen."

Behind Mr. Gladstone, or the Earl of Beaconsfield, or Lord Salisbury stands this majestic *eminence grise*. Sir William Mycroft Holmes, Knight of the Order of the British Empire, is there as surely and securely as Cardinal Richelieu or Father Joseph were behind King Louis XIII of France two centuries earlier. Yet you would search the newspapers of the day or the volumes of *Who's Who?* in vain for a single mention of my friend's elder brother. When his time comes, an unobtrusive obituary in *The Times* will remember him only as a fugitive and wayward intellect. The eulogist will tell us merely that he enriched the study of ancient Greek particles by his note on "The resolution of Enclytic δε" in the *Classical Quarterly* and revolutionised Algebraic Philosophy by six pages on "The Methodology of Pascal's Wager" in the *Journal of Higher Mathematics*. Not a word will hint at the secrecy and power which he commanded at the heart of government.

Despite the value of his time, Mycroft knew that his younger brother would not have telegraphed him that morning without good reason. Within an hour, a reply came to Baker Street. Sherlock Holmes tore open the flimsy blue envelope, read the single line of the message, and looked up.

"Lunch at the Diogenes. One-fifteen precisely. In that case, Watson, it will be a private room. Under the second rule of the club, all conversation is forbidden in the public rooms. No one, not even a member, is permitted to address another except by invitation. You had better remember that."

It was a curious prospect. As our cab carried us and the leather hatbox towards Westminster, I wondered why men who preferred to avoid contact with the rest of the human race should ever have formed a club. Its inspiration had been the late Sir Cloudsley Clutterbuck, wealthy master of Cloudsley Hall, set in rolling fields between Oxford and Blenheim. He so arranged his life that he rarely saw, let alone spoke to, his footmen or the workers on his estate. Food was delivered to him from the kitchens by a revolving compartment in his dining-room wall. An ingenious system of bells indicated to the servants his precise wants, reducing the need for spoken commands.

The grounds of his park had been surrounded by a wall, six feet high. Village rumours spoke of secret orgies or the rituals of the black mass. But Sir Cloudesley merely wanted walls high enough to keep out huntsmen and riders, for fear that they might kill the wild animals on his estate. These were the only creatures to whom he talked freely and affectionately. In his will, he stipulated that he was to be buried in the grandeur of the family vault, not in a gold-handled coffin but in a plain "Diogenes tub."

Sir Cloudesley's Pall Mall club-house was a Grecian-style creation of the 1830s with half a dozen broad steps leading up to plain glass doors. In the high marble-tiled vestibule, Sherlock Holmes carried on a whispered exchange with the attendant porter, to whom he now entrusted the ancient brown leather hatbox, which had accompanied us on our cab ride from Baker Street.

We were led quietly up a further flight beneath a fine glass dome. To one side at the top I glimpsed the dining-room, its dark-red walls lined by oil portraits, no doubt commemorating famous men of silence. The seating consisted of individual tables each with a single chair whose back was to the wall. To avoid so much as an uninvited glance from other diners, every one of these chairs was sheltered within a hood, as though two porters might lift the occupant on poles and carry him off. Every table was also equipped with a reading-stand at its edge, so that throughout the meal the occupant might look across his plate and enjoy in peace the volume or newspaper of his choice. I noticed that the dining-room steward and his assistants glided soundlessly across the marble floor in ornamental felt slippers.

At the end of a first-floor corridor Mycroft Holmes sat alone in a traditional private room. Lunch was laid for three and sunlit windows opened on to the expanse of Horse Guards Parade. Mycroft's bulk was a challenge no tailor had come to terms with. The crumpled grey flannel of his suit encased him like a bag. Yet the massive head spoke of what Sherlock Holmes described as "Mathematics at Trinity, Cambridge; Classics at Balliol, Oxford; a laudatory first-class degree in both. Dining rights at All Souls. There's no knowledge but he knows it."

To all this was added the power of a supreme mandarin with a key to every government secret worth knowing. It was something of an anti-climax when he greeted us with his fork already in the air.

"I trust you will excuse me, dear Brother. Time presses for an afternoon conference with the Attorney-General on the Government of India Bill. I have chosen the stuffed vine-leaves and ordered them on your behalf. Dig in as soon as they come. In what way, gentlemen, did you suppose that I might be of some service to you?"

What an extraordinary pair the two of them were! Had I a brother—alas, I no longer had—surely I would have passed the time of day with him when meeting after several years apart? There was no family greeting whatever here. Mycroft paused just long enough to slide one hand under the table and press a discreet electric bell. In answer to his brother's inquiry, Sherlock Holmes leant forward and spoke confidentially.

"You might care to tell us something of Captain Joshua Sellon, dear Brother. That would be service enough."

Mycroft cut vigorously at the tight green roll of a rice-filled leaf.

"Ah, yes. I rather supposed he might be the subject of your visit. A bad business. Josh Sellon, eh? You have discovered, I am sure, that he was a Provost Marshal's man? He was first employed between our embassies as Queen's Messenger. As an official courier, he escorted the diplomatic bag between Whitehall and the four corners of the earth. More recently, he coordinated the Special Investigation Branch of the Provost's Corps in Delhi. What did you think he was?"

"Precisely that," said Sherlock Holmes sharply, "and please do not tell us that Albert Gibbons was nothing more than a Sergeant of Marines!"

Mycroft shook his head, cleared his mouth, and murmured: "Several years ago, the Provost began to recruit a military police. Non-commissioned officers who had served their time and had then enlisted in police forces. Some rejoined the colours. Most became uniformed military police officers in garrison towns or Admiralty dockyards. A few were chosen as special-investigation men in civilian clothes. Gibbons was one, not a high-flyer but a most reliable fellow in a tight corner. He was a City of Dublin policeman before his recall, which is presumably why your friend Lestrade never suspected him—or had ever seen him."

"So during his official retirement, he presides over Landor Mansions in Carlyle Street?"

"Over the whole of Carlyle Street, dear Brother. It will not surprise you that quite a number of our people are accommodated discreetly in these places when business brings them to London. Let us leave it at that."

The door behind me opened and two more plates of vine leaves were laid at our places. The menu at the Diogenes Club was *de rigeur*, as Holmes described it. In other words, it was Spartan and there were no choices. The man who had brought the *hors d'oeuvres* withdrew.

Mycroft Holmes pushed his plate back.

"To speak quite frankly, my dear Sherlock, I could wish that you had not blundered into this affair."

"Could you?" asked Sherlock Holmes indifferently. "Perhaps you would not mind pressing that most efficient bell again. There is something you had better see for yourself."

His elder brother obliged him, and the servant reappeared.

"Have the goodness," said Sherlock Holmes curtly, "to go down to the desk by the front door and retrieve a hatbox for me, which I lodged there just now. The duty porter is aware that I shall need it. Bring it to me here."

If Mycroft felt the least interest in this, he certainly did not show it. Instead, he mulled over the death of Captain Sellon. At last, he concluded, "You were, of course, correct, dear Brother. The bullet that killed our man Sellon was fired by a compressed-air weapon in the very room where his body was found. I concluded as much myself from the surrounding circumstances long before Dr. Littlejohn sent me his findings last night. The renting of a room in the opposite mansions was all part of somebody's disguise. Even so, Sellon's death was a shock. We pride ourselves that by offering a public service in renting out these apartment blocks to all and sundry, apparently as a *bona fide* agency, we can also conceal some of our own people there, among the rest. It seems that with Sellon, we fell into a trap of our own making."

"What was your man Sellon doing at Carlyle Mansions in the first place?" I asked. "And what, indeed, is the Evangelical Overseas Medical Mission?"

Mycroft Holmes spread a hand out sheepishly, as if he hoped the answer might materialise from thin air like a conjurer's hard-boiled egg.

"It is a useful form of words," he said at last. "Will that do?"

Sherlock Holmes's mouth tightened. "I think not, Brother. Men do not shoot one another so cleverly without good reason. What was Sellon's connection with the *soi-disant* Colonel Rawdon Moran? What had Moran himself to do with the disaster at Isandhlwana? Moreover, what had he to do with the death of the Prince Imperial? Not to mention those of Captain Jahleel Brenton Carey and a certain Trooper Levens who was in Carey's fatigue party? There are wild rumours and mighty few facts."

I quite thought Mycroft Holmes might be overwhelmed by this torrent of questions. But he seemed not the least put out.

"Whatever you think of Randy Moran, you may be sure he did not himself kill Josh Sellon. Yesterday he was still on the high seas, between Funchal and Antwerp. Do you know so little of the case, dear Brother?"

"I am confident that I know as much as you," said Sherlock Holmes, in the petulant tone of a nursery rival. "I suggest that you have it in your power to save me a good deal of time by confirming the details."

Mycroft was saved just then by the entry of two servants. The first carried a tray with three plates covered by *pommes de terre à la duchesse* and an unappetising form of boiled halibut. The second man bore our leather hatbox. When the two waiters had closed the door behind them, Mycroft sat back.

"Several officers of the Provost Marshal's Corps," he said, "have been working on a series of incidents with a common connection, such as you suggest. Captain Sellon had come too close to the truth for our adversaries to tolerate his presence any longer."

"And Owain Glyndwr?" Sherlock Holmes inquired.

"May one inquire, dear Brother, precisely what you know about Owain Glyndwr and how you know it?"

My friend got up and crossed to the side-table where the leather hatbox stood. Mycroft stared at it like an expectant child at a birthday treat. His brother unbuckled the top, lifted it back, and displayed the monstrosity to which I had woken on the previous night. By the light of day, this severed head appeared an inoffensive specimen. To my surprise, however, Mycroft helped himself to another forkful of halibut and mashed potato before greeting the floating relic with affectionate recognition.

"Oh, yes!" he murmured gently; "oh, yes, indeed! So this is the trophy of which your telegram spoke? He who came by dark? We know him, dear Brother! We know him, doctor! We know him very well indeed! He has been sadly missed by all his friends."

Mycroft Holmes was not much given to displays of humour, but he gave a plump chuckle at his own pleasantry.

I suppose I should not have been surprised to find that a severed head pickled in formaldehyde was not the least disagreeable to either brother on the table in the middle of lunch. But how Mycroft should recognise it was beyond me.

"He was in Abyssinia at the taking of Magdala in 1868," said Mycroft soothingly, as if he were consoling the cloven head for all its misfortunes. "The poor fellow fell to a swift sword-cut from one of our galloping hussars. I believe an officer of the 3rd Dragoons gathered him in when the burial parties were at work after the battle. The surgeon-major then performed his task of dissection and preservation. Our friend came to rest in the trophy case of the 24th Regiment of Foot. That seems to be his entire story until now."

"He was at Isandhlwana? At the battle?" I asked carefully.

In my own ears, I sounded as though I could not believe it. Mycroft turned to me, and whatever amusement I thought I had heard in his voice had vanished from his face.

"No, doctor. Not at the battle. That is the whole point, is it not? Despite the catastrophe, there were a handful of survivors. They are our witnesses. Several of them told the Provost Marshal's inquiry what was said and done in the camp on the day of the battle before the tribes attacked. Sergeant-Major Tindal was one of a small party of the 24th who escaped in a fighting retreat. He swore that he had reported an incident to Colonel Pulleine early that morning. During the previous night, an intruder had entered the mess tent of the 24th Foot. This delightful object in its glass jar had been removed from the trophy case. Owain Glyndwr had not been on general view, you understand. Indeed, he had always been treated with the respect due to a fallen warrior."

There was a moment of silence.

"And then?" Sherlock Holmes prompted him.

A look of deep self-satisfaction lay in Mycroft's grey eyes.

"I believe," he said, "I do believe they have made their first mistake."

"Who are they?"

"Owain Glyndwr," Mycroft ignored the question and gave the mediaeval name its full Welsh inflection: "in truth, an Abyssinian warrior. But the 24th Foot, being a Welsh regiment, gave him the name of their national hero. He belongs by right to the regimental depot at Brecon. They will be glad to see him back, when the time comes."

I was still out of my depth.

"But what has an Abyssinian to do with Isandhlwana? Who would want such a trophy? Not Cetewayo's tribes!"

Mycroft Holmes remained quiet and thoughtful. Then he nodded.

"Not the tribes, doctor. As you have discovered, we have a far more dangerous enemy, closer to home. We believe we know who some of them are, but we cannot tell precisely where they may be. It seems that they have thrown down this head as if it were a gauntlet. They are prepared for combat. These are resolute enemies, gentlemen, ready for victory or death. They are prepared to wager that, in a little while, either you or they will be dead. They propose that it shall be you."

"I still do not understand why," I said.

Mycroft scratched his large head, as if uncertain how to begin. "Do you not, doctor? After your meeting with Captain Sellon in India, he and several other intelligence officers were sent to the Cape to oversee the inquiry that followed our defeat at Isandhlwana. Evidence was collected by the Provost's Special Investigation Branch. Among witnesses, Lieutenant Teignmouth Melville's servant survived the escape in which his master perished. In the last minutes of the battle, he saw Lieutenant Melville take the regimental colours from Colonel Pulleine to carry them to safety. Poor young Melville was hacked to death even before he could cross the Buffalo River. The colours were found some weeks later in branches by the river bank."

"That much was in every newspaper," Sherlock Holmes said sardonically.

"Then you had better attend to what was not in the newspapers but in the survivor's evidence. As Melville stood with Pulleine, just before they parted, the colonel looked up for an instant and thought he saw the first outrider of Lord Chelmsford's column, mounted on the col above the beleaguered camp. You know that much, I believe? Melville's servant heard this figure spoken of as a last hope. Of course, there was nothing in it. The column was several hours away. Yet the tale persisted among survivors, the story of this solitary rider, sitting astride a dappled horse on the col. He seemed to be watching the last act of the tragedy from above but taking no part in it. That was all."

"Indeed," said Sherlock Holmes sceptically, "And you think Sellon was killed for hearing such a tale? That would not silence the others who heard it."

Mycroft shook his head. "Among the debris of the guard tent was a scrap of paper found by the first burial party and taken charge of by the Provost's men under Sellon's command. It was written at the last moment by Colonel Pulleine and hidden in the top of his boot. He knew that the tribesmen never bother to strip the boots from the dead because the tribes go barefoot. The hiding place was safe."

"And Sellon was killed for reading it?"

Mycroft shook his head again. "Not just for reading that."

Mycroft Holmes slid his hand into the inner pocket of his grey flannel jacket. He drew out a slim notecase of soft tawny Florentine leather. From this he took, with tweezers, a small folder of plain card. I saw a paper lying inside it. For our benefit, it was the original of the last message written by the commander of the doomed column in the final moments of defeat.

"In anticipation of your visit, I had this brought over from Whitehall by messenger," Mycroft said quietly.

CAMP ISANDHLWANA, 22 JANUARY 1879, 1.35 pm
WE ARE BETRAYED . . . FOR GOD'S SAKE LOOK AFTER
OUR PEOPLE . . . GOD SAVE THE QUEEN. . . .
Lt. Col. Henry Burmester Pulleine
Officer Commanding Her Majesty's 24th Regiment of Foot

"Do not touch it!" Mycroft added hastily. "Just read it. It is not to be touched!"

After we had stared at it for a full minute, he stood up and turned to the window with its view of Horse Guards Parade and an immaculate surface of sand-coloured grit.

"Look after our people?" I inquired.

"Our families, in other words," said Mycroft impatiently. "Not the entire British nation, which can well look after itself. There must have been a good few military dependents pauperised by so many deaths that day. It was a natural enough request by their commander."

"Then let us hope that King Cetewayo does better for his gallant people than we have done for ours," said Sherlock Holmes bleakly.

Mycroft glared at his fractious sibling.

"And you believe that Captain Sellon was killed for reading this final appeal?" I persisted.

"No, doctor, not even that. I have brought something more for your consideration."

In his hand was a short-bladed object in waxed paper. I recognised it as a turn-screw, of the sort that I had seen at Kandahar. It resembled nothing so much as a powerful corkscrew mounted in a metal frame. In truth, it was used by regimental quartermasters to open the crates of Boxer Mark III cartridge packets. Its condition suggested that it had lain exposed to sun, wind, and rain during the weeks between the battle and the burials at Isandhlwana. Such implements had been commonplace at Maiwand. As a medical officer I had never handled one, but I knew at once what it was. Its purpose was to open tightly screwed War Department crates of cartridge packets, used to re-supply the infantry pouches in battle.

"Surely," I said, "there must have been any number of these lying about the wagon-park."

"Indeed there were, doctor. A good number."

"Is there something remarkable about this one?"

"Just one thing. These screw-drivers and the broken remains of the very few ammunition boxes that had been forcibly opened were examined by three artificers at Woolwich Arsenal under Captain Sellon's supervision. The men who undertook the examination were sworn to secrecy. In any case, they were not told why they were doing it. The whole business was so sensitive that each man was required to sign a draft of the proposed official secrecy legislation, binding him to silence on pain of fourteen years' imprisonment."

"And the result?" Sherlock Holmes inquired laconically.

"When the blades of the discarded turn-screws were microscopically examined, they naturally bore signs of rust and encrustation from exposure for a few months. Yet most had never been used. They had been thrown down as useless at a time when the riflemen on the perimeter were crying out for ammunition. There was not the smallest abrasion on many of these blades consistent with having locked into the screws of the crates. Why were the quartermasters not pouring out a constant stream of cartridge packets to supply the ammunition runners? Why were a few of the crates laboriously forced open by bayonets and even smashed open by rocks? Others were left screwed down and abandoned. You see?"

"The wrong turn-screws?"

Mycroft nodded his large head mournfully.

"Can you wonder that the message in Colonel Pulleine's last note is one of treachery? Nor was that all. The two great faults with Boxer cartridges for these rifles was a tendency to absorb damp easily or for the bullet to fall out of its case before loading, in either event jamming the weapon. The Intelligence Branch of the Quartermaster-General's Department has inquired into this. So has Colonel Redvers Buller, VC. The handfuls of abandoned bullets that Joshua Sellon gathered in from the battlefield had been rendered useless. The answer to the riddle of defeat was in his possession. Someone decided he must pay for that information with his life. Will that do?"

This seemed too much to me.

"The ammunition train was tampered with?"

"That is your choice of language, doctor. I might have doubted, until Sellon was found with a bullet in his brain. His silence was ensured at so high a price."

We stared at one another while a detachment of the Life Guards crossed the Parade, helmets bright in the sun, to take up duty on Palace Guard.

"I'll be revenged on the whole pack of you," I said presently.

"I beg your pardon, doctor?"

"It is probably nothing, Sir Mycroft. Merely a form of vengeance that someone known to Joshua Sellon once promised to take upon the world."

But Mycroft Holmes had caught my every word, and it showed in his face. He gave a heavy sigh.

"Since you know so much, you had both of you better come with me," he said, pushing himself up from his chair. "Come and look at the evidence. This may get worse. Much worse. I suppose I must either trust you both entirely or not at all. I hope, dear Brother, I shall not regret it in your case. And bring that abomination in the hatbox with you. The Welshmen will want their hero back."

4

eremonial grit crunched under our feet as we kept step with Mycroft Holmes across the open ground of the Horse Guards Parade. Tall windows at the rear of White-hall faced the billowing trees of St. James's Park. Their candy-striped sun-blinds were drawn out in the fine spring weather to shade the servants of the Crown. It was for all the world as though we were approaching a grand hotel.

Brother Mycroft always walked as though his ungainly bulk was battling against a strong headwind. Scowling ahead of him, he kept his eyes fixed on some distant point between Birdcage Walk and the towers of Westminster Abbey. From time to time he glanced sideways at a passer-by who in his opinion had no business to be there. As Sherlock Holmes once remarked, his brother had a gift of conveying to the rest of the human race that he wished it were anywhere at that moment except in his presence.

Of course, Sherlock Holmes himself cared nothing for public life, let alone for ceremony or public men. The large and reas-suring buildings of government and administration left him cold. Early in our friendship, he had promised me that a nation was better led by a rogue than a reformer.

We turned into Downing Street and went up a broad flight of granite steps to another pair of glass doors. Mycroft paused at the top and jerked his thumb towards the prime-ministerial residence at No. 10.

"You may care to know, Brother, that a crossing-sweeper is still employed to clear a path across this street once every afternoon at 3 P.M. It is in order that Sir Robert Peel's boots shall be kept clean when the Prime Minister approaches his official residence. The fellow receives a lifetime pension to carry out his work—protecting the boots of a Prime Minister who has been in his grave these thirty years."

"You don't say?"

"Tradition dies hard, does it not? And a good thing too!"

A uniformed porter pulled open a glass door with his left hand and saluted Mycroft with his right. Within the domed lobby of the great building rose a double circular staircase, deeply carpeted in red to deaden our footsteps. I thought that their Lordships of the Treasury certainly did themselves pretty well.

A second porter was positioned on the landing, outside an entrance of white-painted panels, for fear that Mycroft Holmes should be tempted to over-exert himself by opening his own office doors.

As we stepped inside, I could see why my friend's brother was content to pass his life in these surroundings. His office was a long and elegant Georgian study with a white barrel-vaulted ceiling. Handsome bookshelves rose from floor to ceiling. Beyond its oriel window, there was a fine view of the park towards Buckingham Palace with the Royal Standard at its flagstaff rippling in a light breeze. The distance from the office door to his wide desk with its green-leather inlay seemed almost the length of a cricket pitch. And if this Permanent Under-Secretary should feel the need of a breath of fresh air, a private balustraded balcony in white Purbeck stone extended outside his window.

The porter carried away our overcoats and hats. Mycroft summoned his three secretaries. One was sent to fetch tea. The second was to inform the Attorney General that, most regrettably, the Prime Minister had found it necessary to postpone their discussion of the Government of India Bill until the next day. The third was to tell the Prime Minister that the Attorney General was unavoidably detained by a deputation of lawyers in the House of Commons on proposed amendments to the Supreme Court of Judicature Act. In two minutes the business of the nation was deftly set aside and Mycroft's official appointments had been abolished.

When tea had been poured, our host faced us and came at once to the point.

"We have recorded four relevant events in the murders of Captain Jahleel Brenton Carey and the Prince Imperial. If you do not mind, dear Brother, we will take them in reverse order. That is the sequence by which we were alerted to this conspiracy."

I noticed that this was the first time the elder brother had used the word "conspiracy." He did not yet say precisely what the aim of such a plot might be. Sherlock Holmes shrugged and Mycroft relaxed.

"First of all there was the discovery of the body of a so-called Private Arnold Levens in the Calcutta Drainage Canal, several hundred miles from where he had last been heard of in Hyderabad. Private Levens was one of the four men in a fatigue party commanded by Captain Brenton Carey at the striking of tents in the 98th Regiment's depot at Hyderabad."

"And what took Levens to Calcutta?" I inquired.

"Concealment, doctor. He was signed for as one of three privates and a corporal, unaccountably presenting themselves from a pioneer corps, when Captain Brenton Carey was mortally injured. The only men with a clear view of what happened on that side of the wagon were Levens and another private by the name of Moss. After the tragedy, Levens's name was taken as a witness. Thereupon, he and Moss absconded. It sometimes happens that private soldiers will desert rather than face a court of inquiry. They fear it may pin some blame on them."

"And a further curiosity?" Sherlock Holmes inquired.

"There was no Private Arnold Levens—no Levens of any kind—not on the regimental roll of the 98th Foot nor on that of the Hyderabad pioneer corps. But why would any other man choose to be there? You may be sure that money had changed hands. Men do not join a fatigue detail for the pleasure of the thing. Nothing further was known of Moss nor of this man Levens until the corpse was pulled from a drainage ditch in Bengal. Then his name was checked and discovered on the roll of Army deserters. His pay-book was found near the spot, though he had drawn no pay. Someone else had provided for him. By then he had been on the run for over a year; but that same person had protected him for their own purposes. Of course, whether this decomposing body was truly the Private Arnold Levens of Hyderabad we shall probably never know. We are told, however, that the man was probably dead before he went into the canal. A petty criminal gone to glory with the assistance of his friends."

The sun declining across the park glinted on Mycroft's gold-rimmed pince-nez.

"The trail then leads back to the death of Captain Carey, in consequence of the so-called accident at Hyderabad Camp."

He counted this second item on his index finger.

"The only two possible eye-witnesses had fled. Without them, it could never be established just how Carey's abdominal injury was inflicted by the lashing-out of a horse's hoof. Surgeon-Major Callaghan, the regimental physician, heard that the startled beasts had stampeded when the floor of a bell tent fell into the wagon. He attended Captain Carey and saw that death was unquestionably the result of blows to the abdomen which ruptured the intestine. Unfamiliar with animal behaviour, it did not seem to occur to Callaghan that this would require the wagon horse, most unusually, to kick forward rather than backward at the noise behind it. But the injuries had undoubtedly occurred. The blows from hooves were the only reason suggested. Therefore, as a medical man, he deduced that death must have been caused in that way. Captain Carey himself had no memory of being injured. Would that trouble you, doctor?"

I had not been expecting the question but the answer seemed plain.

"He may have been struck down by a blow he could not see coming. He may have been unconscious before the final damage was done. In any case, the shock of injuries severe enough to leave him unconscious might also wipe recollection of the incident from the brain when consciousness was regained."

"A horse's hoof or a blunt instrument would be all the same in its effect?"

"If the implement was chosen for that purpose, it probably would be."

Mycroft Holmes nodded and counted again on his forefinger.

"Number three. The trail then leads back to Carey's troubled murmurings on the last night of his life, his story of royal assassination at the Blood River in Zululand."

"The Prince Imperial," said Sherlock Holmes languidly. "We have read the newspapers, dear Brother. We know that Captain Carey himself was at first held responsible for allowing the tragedy to occur. We also know that while he was dying, he revealed to Mr. Dordona those secrets that might otherwise die with him."

Mycroft paused and managed a rare smile. He was pleased with himself and did not care who knew it. He shook his head. "I am aware that you have entertained to tea the Reverend Samuel Dordona."

"Are you indeed?"

"Come, Brother Sherlock! We may not be as clever as you, but we are not complete simpletons! Samuel Dordona, indeed! In other words, a well-meaning over-acting impersonator, Major Henry Putney-Wilson. Until the tragic death of his wife, Emmeline, the major was not too pious to take part in respectable theatricals at Lahore. It seems to have stood him in good stead. He once played the ruined hero, in Bulwer-Lytton's moral drama *Money*. It was performed at Simla as a compliment to the author's son, Lord Lytton, who had just come out from England as Viceroy. You did not know all this, dear Brother, did you?"

This was intended to irk his sibling, as they say. I glanced quickly at Sherlock Holmes. But not a nerve nor a muscle in his profile moved. Mycroft resumed.

"Of course, Brenton Carey can never have intended Putney-Wilson to keep the story of the Prince Imperial to himself. On the contrary, the major surely swore an oath to his dying friend that he would pass the story on to their mutual comrade in arms, Joshua Sellon of the Special Investigation Branch. That is perhaps the only item of the story which Putney-Wilson withheld when he told it to you in his absurd charade."

Mycroft sighed and pushed his tea cup away.

"I do not know how Rawdon Moran heard of any this. Yet I fear Brenton Carey unwittingly signed Joshua Sellon's death warrant by implicating him. We must now assume that Moran knows everything."

"Who else might know?" I asked.

Mycroft Holmes shook his head. "Perhaps Annie Brenton Carey. After the prince's death, Captain Carey retained his commission. As a servant of the Queen, he was forbidden from telling story-book tales of a man on a white horse. That was left to other ranks. There may or may not have been a figure on a pale horse above Isandhlwana, but it was a flesh-and-blood murderer who directed the tribesmen in their attack on Louis Napoleon."

He took a small key from his waistcoat pocket and stepped across to a cupboard set in the wall by his desk.

"What of the sabotaged holster-leather?" Sherlock Holmes asked coldly.

"You know of that, do you? I deduce it was substituted for the original while the horses were grazing and their riders were lunching. Substituted by someone who can handle a horse without disturbing it. It was certainly not the strap that had been tightened in place and inspected that morning."

The cupboard door was now wide open and Mycroft was struggling a little with what looked like an elongated cricket bat, wrapped in oilskin and tied with a cord. He continued his account.

"Even if the prince had escaped being thrown to the ground and speared, a marksman with a Martini-Henry on that ridge above the kraal could have brought him down from the saddle easily with a single bullet. The tribesmen with their captured rifles would most certainly have got the credit of killing him with a lucky shot from one of their guns."

A little breathlessly, he deposited his wrapped treasure on the desk-top.

"How many men thought they saw a figure on the ridge as they rode away?" I asked.

"One. Trooper Le Brun."

Sherlock Holmes intervened. "Le Brun was the last man to come alive out of the kraal. Therefore he was able to see the top of the ridge which those ahead of him were hidden from as they went under the hill. How unfortunate that, once again, there was no corroboration of his story."

Mycroft was picking at the cord that bound the oil-cloth. "Le Brun, if that was ever his name, was last heard of among ruffians and scallywags in the Transvaal gold fields. He is probably as dead now as Arnold Levens—and I daresay by the same hands."

He had loosened the knot and drawn the wrapping free. On his desk lay a rifle, its brown wooden stock polished as if it had been new. Its barrel was a breech-loader, shorter than the infantry weapons of ten years ago but common enough now. A neat steel plate on one side of the breech bore the imprint of the British crown and the letters "V. R." for Victoria Regina. Beneath that was the manufacturer's trade-mark, "Enfield 1870."

Mycroft patted the stock. "After the prince fell dead, Carey's party rode for their lives and never stopped until they reached the Blood River camp. A search party was not sent out until next day to look for the bodies of the prince and the two troopers. This weapon was also recovered on the ridge above the deserted kraal. Martini-Henry, .450 bore, British Army issue. According to Woolwich Arsenal, it had never been fired. It was no doubt loaded, but the round was ejected when the marksman saw that a bullet was not needed. The spears had done their work. A most efficient weapon, in its action. See here. The firing pin is cocked automatically as a round goes in over the breech. In the hands of a game-shot, the time between loading and detonation is very short. The gun is also extremely accurate. A short lock means that the marksman will almost invariably hit whatever he sees between the sights."

"Yet it was abandoned?"

"Abandoned, doctor? Yes. By someone who disappeared even more quickly than Captain Carey's patrol! Someone who was well aware that there might be other British Army riders in the area, who could be drawn to the scene by the sound of the tribes-men's gunfire. Our mysterious horseman would hardly care to explain to them how he, as a civilian, had come into possession of an Army rifle in pristine condition. Far better drop it on the ground and let the tribesmen take the credit for throwing it away as they ran."

Mycroft paused and then counted on his fingers for the fourth time.

"Last of all, Isandhlwana, the beginning of the tale. A similar figure to that reported on the ridge above the scene of the assassination had perhaps been seen or imagined above the battle. Mounted on a grey, he watched from the col. But the case is different. It needs no phantom on a hillside, gentlemen, to explain how Isandhlwana was lost. The mis-matched turn-screws and the sabotaged cartridges will do that."

He wrapped the rifle in its oilcloth again and tied the knots in the cord.

"Henry Pulleine acted with great gallantry. He knew he was condemned to die, but first he would write one brief note and conceal it where it might not be discovered by his killers before his body was found. He wrote of betrayal. And that was not all. A blade of metal no thicker than your middle finger was found on the ground by his body. There was no purpose for it in that tent except as a message. His fingers seem to have lost their grip of it in the moment of his death. Useless turn-screws of the same calibre lay among the grass of the wagon-park. Turn-screws that would never open those crates of cartridge packets to replenish the pouches of the infantry lines. Never in a month of Sundays."

There was silence in the sunlit room. The image of that last dreadful scene, men fighting the enemy back-to-back with their bayonets until the end, played like a lantern-slide in our imaginations.

"And Joshua Sellon?" I asked: "How did he come to Isandhlwana?"

Mycroft tested a last knot in the cord round the oilskin. He looked up and raised his eyebrows, as though surprised I had not guessed.

"Do you not recall, doctor, that you first met him in a saloon carriage of the Bombay, Baroda and Central India Railway?"

"Indeed I do."

"Captain Sellon was in the habit of noting the names of those he met and what they talked about. It was his profession as an intelligence officer—his second nature. Your name and conversation were entered in the notebook. You were proceeding from Bombay to Peshawar and the North-West Frontier, were you not? You talked of court-martials, he says, subalterns' court-martials."

"We did. Almost as far as Lahore."

He nodded.

"Do you recall that the train was delayed at a small junction, some distance short of Lahore?"

"It was. To this day I do not know why. Probably because a shorter train overtook us as we waited there, going in the direction of Bombay."

"Do you also recall that a staff officer, probably Brigade Major Anstruther, came to your coach? Captain Sellon was summoned to an immediate conference with his superiors."

"Correct."

"You do not know why Sellon was taken away?"

"I do not. When I next saw him—or even heard of him—he was lying dead in Carlyle Mansions with a bullet in his skull."

"Then it may interest you to know, doctor, that Joshua Sellon was not just a Provost Marshal's man: he was one of the best officers that the Special Investigation Branch had ever possessed. He was removed from your train because a wire from Calcutta—from the Viceroy's secretary—ordered his return to Bombay. The first suspicions about Isandhlwana had been raised in Cape Town. The few survivors had begun to talk. Captain Sellon was to be despatched from India to South-East Africa in charge of a Provost detail. He was to accompany the first patrol to the battlefield. A special train was despatched to your little junction from Lahore. A light cruiser lay at anchor in the harbour of Bombay. It waited for those whose skills were needed at the scene of the massacre. England was too far to send, but Josh Sellon could reach Durban, the nearest port in South-East Africa to Isandhlwana, long before you were with your regiment in Kandahar."

"I had no idea about him, at the time," I said slowly. "The young officers in my coach treated him as being rather a joke. A dull old fellow, was how they spoke of him."

Mycroft chuckled at my stupidity.

"A dull old fellow, eh? And what better disguise could such a man have? How fortunate for your two young buccaneers that they never came under his scrutiny. Joshua Sellon was asked for in South Africa by Sir Henry Bartle Frere, Her Majesty's Governor at the Cape. Sir Bartle had once had Sellon under him when he was Governor of Bombay. He knew his quality. When the rumours began after Isandhlwana, he cabled direct to the Viceroy in Calcutta and made his request. So Josh Sellon, Lieutenant Halliwell, and two of the Provost Quartermasters joined the first burial party that was sent into Zululand. They arrived there a few months after the disaster, the first troops to reach that remote scene. That was how it came about."

Mycroft Holmes laid the rifle on its shelf in the cupboard and turned round.

"Their investigation soon located several bogus turn-screws lying in the grass of the wagon-park. The difference in calibre between these and the .450 Martini-Henry ammunition might not be noticed at a glance. But these were put to the test as a matter of course."

This would not do, I thought. "But why had no one examined them or tested them in all the time that Lord Chelmsford's column was marching from the Cape to Zululand? Had they no occasion to fire their rifles in all that time, even in practice?"

He looked at me with a sad suggestion of pity for my obtuseness. It reminded me of Sergeant Gibbons.

"I think you do not quite understand, doctor. The fatal substitution of the mis-matched turn-screws was not made until after the final camp inspection had been carried out on the evening before the battle. That was the whole point. It must be done on the right day. The so-called hunter who performed it had first to assure himself that the Zulu impi was already in a position to advance on the following morning. He knew enough about the tribes and their tactics for that. It was what Moran waited for, night after night."

"For how long?"

Mycroft shrugged. "Who knows? He is a hunter, a tracker. No one sees him come or go. I know something of the fellow. That is my job. Randy Moran could cross a forest floor in pitch darkness without a single twig ever cracking under his foot. That same night, knowing that the attack was prepared for next day, he also entered the mess tent of the 24th Foot and removed the head in its specimen jar. He had no need to do it. It was the obsession of putting a signature to his work. We know him well enough to understand his ways. You had far better leave him to us."

Sherlock Holmes had been silent for an uncharacteristically long time. Now he shifted in his chair.

"Leave him to you? You seem remarkably sure of yourself, dear Brother, for one who has not yet proved a word of this story against Colonel Moran."

This time, Mycroft's chuckle had no humour in it.

"We know the scoundrel as well as we know poor Owain Glyndwr. True, his head is not yet pickled in a jar. That will be possible, I suppose, when the hangman has finished with him."

But his brother continued to scowl. "Then you have not found him?"

Mycroft bowed his head and pulled open a drawer of his desk. He took out a small pile of slim leather folders, chose one, and opened it. A large quarto-sized photograph showed the head and shoulders of a man in his middle forties. Even stilled by the camera's lens, a mesmeric coldness lay in those narrowed eyes. There was ferocity in the lines of the brow and nose, which seemed all the more powerful for the large size of the print. We confronted an image so lifelike that it seemed as if it might answer back at us, a virile yet sinister face. The model of a hunter and a killer.

The height of his brow was evidence of an intelligence to rival Mycroft Holmes. Yet the determined set of the mouth and jaw also bespoke a sensual leer that would corrupt intelligence or natural virtue. The shoulders conveyed the strength of a body which the portrait did not include.

"Colonel Rawdon Moran," said Mycroft quietly, "a bad enemy and a treacherous friend. A man of immense strength, his anger often masked but never appeased. Cunning beyond everything. A man who conquered the God-fearing Emmeline Putney-Wilson. The face that laughed into hers when she begged him not to desert her, not to betray her to the mercy of the world. These, gentlemen, are the eyes that taunted her into becoming her own executioner and almost the murderer of her own children. You see?"

Sherlock Holmes handed the portrait back. But Mycroft had not yet done. He pulled open another drawer and drew out a second folder. It contained bills of lading for consignments of goods to be shipped from Belgium, the port of Antwerp, to the capital of the Congo Free State at Leopoldville. As he turned the pages, I saw enough to understand that this was indeed the merchandise of death. Krupp 7.5-centimetre guns. Creuzot's 7.5-centimetre. A consignment of 3.7-centimetre automatic Maxims. Eight four-inch Howitzers. Add to that Maxim-Nordenfelt field guns and Krupp 3.7-centimetre mountain guns.

Sherlock Holmes looked hard at his brother. "And where did these papers come from? A reliable source?"

Mycroft sighed.

"A good man risked his life for them—and lost it in the end."

"Joshua Sellon?"

"Joshua Sellon. Since his return from the Transvaal, guns have been the trade of Rawdon Moran with that territory and with the moral leprosy of the Congo State. His old masters in Praetoria see themselves as the new Prussians of Southern Africa. The most brutal traders of Central Africa know that they are safe with

Leopold of Belgium. He may be the most depraved monarch in Europe, but that did not prevent the others from giving him the state of the Congo and its people as his personal plaything."

From one of the folders he drew out a page of a newspaper. I recognised the Berlin *National Zeitung*. He looked not at me but at my friend.

"The criminal confederation that you imagine, dear Brother, now proposes to extend itself into the dark continent, and Rawdon Moran is its agent. He prospered less than he hoped from all that was corrupt and tyrannical in the Transvaal. Yet the income of that republic from gold and diamond fields has increased a thousandfold in the last decade, from ten thousand pounds sterling to more than eleven *million*. Its power to make war upon the remaining British territories, or to blackmail them by threat of war, grows faster still. At first he directed armaments under the guise of importing agricultural machinery through the harbours of Portuguese East Africa. Now he prefers Belgium and her Congo Free State. The artillery has been armed; now it is the turn of the infantry. A shipment is pending via Antwerp of forty thousand Mauser rifles and twenty-five million rounds of ammunition."

Sherlock Holmes relaxed his scowl, though I could not believe that this tale of blood-money was new to him. "And where is Colonel Moran now, if I may repeat my request?"

Mycroft paused and then shrugged.

"Keep on going as you are going, dear Brother, and you may find the answer to that question sooner than you suppose and perhaps to your very great regret. I beg of you—leave him to us."

5

*I*n dealing with my patients, I find that there is sometimes an interval during which a man or woman can
worry no more about a particular threat to life or even
the well-being of a loved one. I suppose it is nature's temporary
protection during a long period of strain. I felt something of the
sort after our encounter with Mycroft Holmes. There were no
further alarms, and the drama seemed to blow away like a bad
dream. I felt like a hard-pressed rifleman in a long campaign—
willing to continue the fight, but longing to be taken out of the
front line for a few days' respite.

A little while later, Sherlock Holmes and I found ourselves
enjoying the pale sunshine of the pre-season race meeting on
Epsom Downs. Holmes had come by long-standing arrangement;
I was there to keep him company. I do not call myself a racing
man, nor indeed was my friend, but this was something of a
special occasion for him. A year or so previously, as my readers
may recall, Holmes had been of service to Colonel Sheffield
Ross. That gentleman's racing stables were on a barren stretch of
Dartmoor at King's Pyland, two miles west of the market town
of Tavistock.

Colonel Ross was still the owner of a four-year-old, Silver Blaze, so-called from the white "blaze" on his forehead. The previous spring, this horse had been tipped as favourite to win the Wessex Cup at the Winchester meeting. Indeed, the odds had shortened to 4–5 on. Just before the event, the animal was missed from its stable and the body of John Straker, a local man who lived close by, was found there. The blow that the man had suffered gave every reason for suspecting foul play. But thanks to the skills of Sherlock Holmes, this strangest of all murders was explained, almost innocently, as being no murder at all. The colonel's horse went on to win the Wessex Cup in the most unusual circumstances. Not since the impostor Judas Maccabeus triumphed in the Derby of 1843, disguised as Running Rein, had there been anything like this result in the racing calendar.*

The same Silver Blaze, fully recovered, had now been entered for the Surrey and Suburban stakes at the Epsom meeting. After his earlier success, the "ring" (as professional backers on the course are described) made him favourite to win at odds of 4–6 on. Nothing would do but that Sherlock Holmes must be there to see him run and to meet again his grateful client, Colonel Sheffield Ross.

If anyone had told me that this event could be connected with the murder of Captain Joshua Sellon, I should have laughed in his face.

On that Wednesday morning, we took the railway from Waterloo down through suburban Surrey to the Epsom course. We had also hired a drag, as they call them, to drive us from the railway station to the Downs. These antiquated conveyances are a rarity now. They resemble old-fashioned stage-coaches, and are little used except for show on such special occasions. As Holmes pointed out, one can park a drag by the side of the course and see the whole thing from the spacious comfort of its well-upholstered buttoned-leather interior. We had been

---

* "Silver Blaze," in Sir Arthur Conan Doyle, *The Memoirs of Sherlock Holmes*

provided by Fortnum's with a picnic hamper of game-bird, fruit, and Champagne.

The annual Surrey and Suburban meeting brings together a whole encampment of the disreputable class of the nation as well as the more raffish element of high society. Ascot is for royalty. Epsom is for the people. The Pearly King and Queen from the streets of London's East End appeared, selling whelks and jellied eels. Beside the roadway from the town, poles were still being driven into the ground and the last showmen's tents were going up. There were brightly painted gypsy caravans with flower-pots in their windows, and a litter of jars and copper pans on their steps. Thin horses and donkeys, turned loose or tethered, grazed on the ragged turf. Where the refreshment stalls ended and the entertainments began, the squalling sounds of the Punch and Judy show promised all the fun of the fair. The remainder of the booths stretched far across the sunlit downland that lay beyond the course.

We passed the flags that streamed out above the grandstand. Banners proclaimed the weighing-in enclosure, Tattersalls, and the bookmakers' booths. From the little canvas stalls, you could take your pick of Neapolitan ice, sold for a penny in silver paper, lemonade, or sherbet. A man in a chef's tall hat with a basket of lobsters was crying out "Champions a bob!" up and down the fairground. A whole town of canvas marquees advertised "Newsome's Equestrian Novelties" and side-shows from "The Hall of Mirrors" to "Beauties of the Harem" and the Fortune-Teller's booth. Puppet theatres performed such successes of the London stage as *The Corsican Brothers* and *The Daughter of the Regiment.*

There was enough to occupy us here even without the racing! However, the Surrey and Suburban was to be run at two o'clock, and we finished our bottle of Veuve Cliquot in good time. After so much of "Samuel Dordona" and "Randy" Moran, I felt new life had been breathed into me. A bell rang to clear the course and six runners trooped out from their enclosure. I glanced at the card and saw the entrants listed for the one mile and six furlongs of the race. There was Prince Napoleon-Jerome's Centurion, Mr. Augustus Newton's Rascal Jack, Colonel Armitage's Under-and-Over, the Earl of Craigavon's Dandy Dick, Mr. Seth Boyd's Shinscraper, and, to be sure, Colonel Ross's Silver Blaze, carrying his owner's familiar colours of black cap and wine-red jacket.

A thousand guineas was riding on the outcome. Small wonder that a roar of excitement went up from the stand as the starter's flag came down. Then the onlookers grew silent and I could feel the tension in the sparkling air. At the first bend, the rivals were bunched so tight that it seemed a wonder that they did not collide. The hooves pummelled the turf like padded thunder. Then, at the first straight, the line was strung out a little more. Gussie Newton's powerful bay, Rascal Jack, had taken the lead. But true to his title, he gave his backers the slip on the second bend and fell back gradually to last place.

Down past the grandstand, again it was Shinscraper who held the crowd's attention. All eyes followed him as the handsome grey led by a nose from Under-and-Over. Away they went, round the curve with the spaces between them lengthening now, inch by inch. We lost sight of them then until they came up over the brow and into the final straight that would take them past the famous old grandstand for the last time. The order of running had scarcely changed. Then, almost at the stand itself, Silver Blaze came on, as fresh as though he had only just left the starting gate. His jockey's knees were tight to the saddle, as he loped past Dandy Dick and then past Shinscraper. He came home by a length and a half, with Bobby Armitage's Under-and-Over just beating the French horse, Prince Napoleon-Jerome's Centurion, for second place.

The aftermath of such a close-fought contest is an anti-climax, but this had been a fine performance. For myself, I had been so absorbed in it that I realised afterwards, with something of a shock, how easily any of our adversaries could have put a bullet into me before I sensed the least danger. Sherlock Holmes must now leave me for an hour or two and seek out Colonel Sheffield Ross to congratulate our client on his splendid win. We should meet back at the hired drag.

"I have not the least doubt, Watson, that after such a run as that, we shall see Ross and his protégé back at Epsom for the June meeting. Next time, I promise you, it will be the Derby itself. A Derby winner in his stable will be the crown of his career!"

I had thought it best to leave my friend to the colonel, for my active part in the case of the missing favourite had been rather small. We arranged to meet at five o'clock, and I turned away to view the boisterous entertainments of the fair. A number of other silk-hatted swells were "slumming it" among the merrymakers. Every sportsman in this lower order of society seemed to have got out his fawn waistcoat and silver watch-chain for the occasion.

I had not walked two hundred yards when I came to the canvas walls of the "Royal Britannia Rifle Range." As a military man, marksmanship is a natural interest of mine, and this particular range was quite a grand affair. It stood high among the medieval jousts and gaming tents. The bull's-eye was quite fifty feet from the counter where the hopeful sportsmen queued up to take their turn. The wall at the far end was a proper "bullet-stopper" of packed earth, at least two feet thick. Upon this was the target scene, painted as a castle wall. There was a make-believe gateway at the bottom with a small red, white, and blue target roundel above it. A rack of prizes, from cheap dolls to china souvenir dishes, stood to one side of the aiming point. A barker in his moleskin jacket and cockney cap was the proprietor.

"The siege of Se-bast-op-ol, ladies and gentlemen! The famous Redan fortress correct in every detail. Who'll put a bullet through a bold bad Rhoosian? Who'll take a pot at the Tsar? Who'll shoulder a musket for Old England and the Queen? Every hit a winner!"

Curiosity got the better of me. I watched half-a-dozen working men detach their wives or women from their arms and pay their sixpence for a rifle with three shots. Five of them wasted their ammunition on various bricks of the castle wall. Each time this happened, the little entrance gate below the target opened and the face of a Beelzebub with his tongue sticking out appeared, followed by the derisive *cuckoo!* call of a novelty clock. The next man missed the bull's-eye with his first go—but hit it with his second. The little castle-door then opened and a Venus statue with a smile, holding a bouquet of flowers to cover the greater part of her nudity, appeared and bowed to him. There was a murmur of laughter as the man turned aside to claim his prize from a pale girl who no doubt kept company with the barker.

Then this cockney proprietor seemed to recognise someone passing by.

"Give us a shot, sir! Show 'em how it's done! Go on, then! Give us a shot, colonel! Colonel Moran, sir!"

If someone had touched me between the shoulder-blades with a chilled butcher's knife at that moment, I could not have felt a more poignant thrill of alarm. My first thought was that Rawdon Moran would not be in England. My second was the realisation that he could easily have returned from Lisbon on the Paris express by now. Walking away, quickly or slowly, I might only draw attention to myself. If I stood immobile with my back to him, I should do little better. But either he had seen me already or he had not. I moved slowly, as if idling my way unconcerned across to the far corner of the shooting gallery and taking shelter behind it. Once under cover, I turned and tried surreptitiously to identify him through the aperture between the canvas and the guy rope. After all, there was more than one Colonel Moran in the British Army, if only his brother Sebastian.

But there could be no mistake. This face, laughing scornfully among its companions, was the very image of the photograph that Mycroft Holmes had shown us the previous week. Perhaps he was a little older by now: closer to fifty than forty years, I would have said. Perhaps the impaling cruelty in those narrowed eyes was veiled just at the moment by the aimless smile he turned towards the barker. For an instant the ferocity in the lines of that brow and nose was softened to a look of amiable bravado. But behind all this was the virile and sinister face of that photograph. Why the devil had he ever allowed it to be taken? He must feel so sure of himself.

Did he really want the world to see him for what he was because he cared nothing for what it thought? Certainly he now had ten or twelve companions—male and female, young and old—about him. He was quite clearly the centre of a party that had come to the races and the noisy enjoyments of the fair.

As he tested the balance of a rifle in his hand, checking its "honesty," he remained the model of the hunter, pledged to kill or be killed. The tall brow with its air of intelligence would tip the balance in any fight for survival. The heavy lines of the mouth and jaw were unsmiling again. The strong shoulders were held back as he paid his sixpence and took his bullets from the barker. Yet there remained a seediness about him that belied his vigour.

Seen in life, rather than in a *carte-de-visite* photograph, the reddish whiskers owed more to the colour-bottle than to youthful charm. Only the tufts of hair sprouting on the backs of his fingers showed what the whiskers must once have been. The skin of those hands and of his throat betrayed a middle age which no cosmetic can disguise. The tone of his voice echoed a resolve and indifference to what the world might think. Jock and Frank had described to me the speech of a jolly, rollicking fellow who had knocked about the world and knew it for what it was. Now it rang hollow, coarse, and scornful. I guessed he was a man who laughed *at* people, never *with* them.

I stood back from the corner of the booth. He was certainly looking towards me, even if he could not see me. I felt a growing certainty that he knew just who I was and where I was hiding. In my foolish anxiety, I thought he seemed to point his rifle at me from his hip. But he was content to be the centre of attention among his acolytes. Two young women gazed at him admiringly, and their young men smiled ingratiatingly. There were also two older men and four women who now joined his admiring audience. They seemed expectant and submissive.

I tried to identify the rifle that he was holding. Was it a Purdy or a Scottish game gun, a Moore & Dickson perhaps? I could not tell, but I could swear he was still looking at me as he held it. At last he turned away. He treated his admirers like students in a lecture room. His voice was powerful in its self-assurance, yet not loud. He was telling them what to expect from his marksmanship.

"Now, d'you see, I once landed six shots out of eight in the crown of a hat held out for me. At 150 yards. In a regimental tournament with a gun very like this. The fellah that held the hat knew he was never in danger from me. D'you know that the Rifle Brigade are made to hold targets for one another to shoot at? You can be sure that a man who refused to stand target in his turn, as they say, would be dismissed the regiment as a lily-livered coward. At four hundred yards I have put four out of six bullets within eighteen inches of the same bulls-eye with no one holding it. I could find no one who would dare to at that range, not even in the Brigade. I myself have stood target twice at such a range because I knew my man with the gun. I did it for a bet. Which I am happy to say I won."

He paused, raised the long-barrelled weapon to his shoulder, lining up the front and rear sights. Even then, when most men would have given all their attention to their aim, he kept up his running commentary.

"This is nothing. I have often driven a nail into timber with a single shot at this range. There's no trick to it. Try it, some of you young fellows. Watch me. Raise the gun to the shoulder, hold it level. Do not grip it. View your target between the sights. You young men, imagine the V-shape rear sight as a pair of young lady's legs, open and waiting."

There was a snigger from one of the top-hatted men beside him as he continued.

"Now, keep the elbow level and as straight as you can. Just touch the trigger with the forefinger alone or else have nothing to do with such a weapon. A pop-gun and a cork would suit you better. Use only sufficient force to discharge the rifle. Do not grip it or grab it. Treat it as you would a woman. Let it be your coy mistress."

Before they could laugh obediently again, he had fired. I caught the metallic impact of the bullet hitting the bull's-eye above the painted castle gate. There was an excited outbreak of clapping from several of the watching men and women. It died away as he turned to them. I could see him well enough now, through a gap between the canvas and the timber of the booth's frame.

"Nimrod the mighty Hunter," called out a female admirer beside him, clapping excitedly.

He gestured at his chosen prize, a cheap brass ring, and the barker put it on the counter for him. He looked at the woman who had clapped.

"Hunting, my lady, is a serious matter about which I know a thing or two. Beware of it. You cannot always kill your beast with the first shot, however good your aim. Not if the creature is one of great strength. To hunt the elephant, let us say, is a supreme experience and a test of nerve."

Someone asked a question which I did not quite catch but Moran replied.

"Indeed I have, sir, times without number. Most memorably a fine bull elephant, in Africa with a Dickson rifle. These mammoths are slow to move but powerful and dangerous to anyone who does not know what he is doing. Use the dogs at first to rush past them and distract their attention. I fired from the saddle on one occasion and got a big bull elephant behind his shoulder. At first, he did not seem to realise what had happened."

There was an obsequious giggling from one or two of the others and Moran continued.

"Oddly enough, it seemed to lame him. He made no attempt to draw away but walked rather awkwardly into the trees. Then he turned to face me. Just looking at me. He had a fine big head. So I unsaddled and fired several times at his massive skull, while he just stood and looked at me, d'you see? The shots seemed to make no impact except that each time a bullet hit him in the head, he bowed it just like a 'salaam' and then tried to touch his wound with his trunk. Then he turned away, unsteady but not falling. I let him have six shots behind the shoulder and still he stood there. In the end it took a Dutch six-pounder to knock him over."

I listened with revulsion to this man's account of his cold-blooded murder of a noble creature. But he had not yet finished. He imitated a curious voice, a whining lamentation in mockery of the creature he had put to death.

"As he stood there, large tears formed in his eyes, which he opened and shut from time to time, and they trickled down his face."

Moran assumed a mournful expression and indicated the trickling tears with his fingers.

"Then his mountainous frame quivered convulsively, and he fell over on his side and expired."

Even from his gang of admirers there was silence. Were they as sickened by this narrative as I was? There was a murmured question at last and Moran replied.

"Fortunately, the ivory tusks weighed ninety pounds a-piece. I believe they fetched more than enough to set-off the cost of the day's expedition."

He took his smouldering cigar from the brass finger ring on the counter, where it had rested as he reminisced. He puffed it bright again and rested it again once more as he talked. I do not know how he chose his victim; but a little while later, as the group moved away, he called to one of the young women who had turned aside to watch a juggler on his stand. She was dressed like a servant by comparison with the rest.

"Be so good as to fetch me that new ring, m'dear."

She turned to pick up the metal circlet and dropped it again with a little gasp of pain, feeling the heated metal where the cigar had glowed against it. Moran gave a short laugh, and one or two of the others who had seen the trick coming chuckled obediently, for no great harm seemed to have been done.

"Dogs and women, Archie," he said to one of the older men: "no other way to teach 'em but hard experience. Eh?"

Such was Rawdon Moran. I was appalled and a little frightened by the extent of his callousness. Was this our self-proclaimed adversary? Of course he was a marksman, but I did not fear him for that. Even if he saw me, he could hardly shoot me dead on Epsom Downs. Of course he was a scoundrel, but Holmes and I had dealt with scoundrels. He was not a convicted criminal, but he was something worse than most convicts. At that moment, I would have bet my last sovereign that he had been responsible for the death of Joshua Sellon. Yet no court and no grand jury would have found an indictment against him on the present evidence. What spread from him, almost like a pestilence tainting the air around him, was a breath of self-confident evil.

Despite what he had done to destroy men and women, it was his tale of the bull elephant and his ridicule of its death which had moved me most. Sherlock Holmes, who had seen enough of crime and criminals in all conscience, was almost eccentric in his detestation of cruelty to the animal kingdom. He would more readily defend a murderer than a man who hunted a wild creature to its death as a matter of amusement. It was a small part of his make-up, but one that I now understood more surely than I had ever done before.

I drew out my watch and saw that there was almost an hour to go before my rendezvous with Holmes. What was I to do, except keep out of sight of our adversary? Moran had looked in my direction. He did not appear to see me, or recognise me if he did see me. I could not be sure. Was it merely a coincidence that he was on Epsom Downs? Or had someone been tracking me all the time on his behalf? Would he know who I was?

I felt sure he would have heard that Holmes and I had visited Brother Mycroft and, perhaps, Carlyle Mansions. He might not have been in England long enough to recognise me for himself, but I could not count on that. I must also assume that he knew of our visitors to Baker Street and of any correspondence we received. My best hope must be that he would not have expected to see me among the crowds at Epsom. If he did not expect it, then he might not have picked me out. I had kept my back to him at first. I had not turned round until I was behind the corner of the rifle range.

In truth, I could not be sure of anything. For safety's sake, the best solution was to keep under cover. From where I stood, the fairground stretched as far as the eye could see, giving me ample choice. It was not likely that Moran and his admirers would crowd into one of the family side-shows. It would be beneath their dignity. In any case, there was a good chance that I should see such a large group before they saw me.

I went the rounds of the tents. The Beauties of the Harem proved entirely harmless. *The Corsican Brothers* was a pleasant puppet-show of the Dumas comedy. I viewed the Stereoscopic Wonders of the World. I even entered the booth of Madame Palmeira, clairvoyante. My last plunge was into a simple maze, tricked out as a Hall of Mirrors. It was under canvas and ill-lit. I could swear that no one saw me enter except the gypsy woman who took my coin. Her custom had declined by this hour. I waited until I was reasonably sure no one else was inside before I entered.

The interior consisted of arched passageways hung with crimson rep pinned upon boarding, against which the mirrors were bolted. There was little subtlety in the display of convex and concave which grotesquely caricatured the reflection. At one moment I saw myself squashed to a midget and then elongated to a beanpole. A moment later, as I turned my head, the left-hand side of my face bulged out at me and the right-hand was no more than a wafer of colour. Presently I was upside down with my heels on the ceiling, and then I was ingeniously split in two so that each half walked with a single foot.

The design of this maze was simple enough, and whatever fun there might be was in the absurd contortions of the images. The one thing you could not do was to get from one passage to another adjoining it without going all the way round the system. That was the entire mystery of the entertainment.

Then I heard a family—or at least two children and two women together—laughing and calling somewhere to the right of me. I could hear their erratic footsteps on the thinly carpeted board which served as the floor of the display. Presently, the sound of their merriment faded as they made their way out and I was, as it seemed to me, alone in the place.

I must have been almost at the centre of the pattern when I heard one other person, walking quietly but steadily. Perhaps it was the woman at the door who had come to see if I was still there before she closed the tent. The footsteps came closer, in the adjoining passage. The design of the maze would lead me round the outer ring before I could come face-to-face with whoever was there but who was no more than two feet from me beyond the mirrored partition.

Then the movements stopped and a voice that I recognised began.

"It won't do, doctor. It won't do at all, you know. Believe me, you had far better give it up—whatever it is. You will only hurt yourself, you see. Leave such things well alone. Go back to your family mysteries. Go back to the lost inheritances and disappointed spinsters. Better still—go and heal the sick. That is what you have been trained to do, is it not?"

There was a pause. Did he really expect a reply? With a chill in my heart I stood absolutely still and said nothing. Once he could locate me by the sound of my voice or my own footsteps, it would probably mean a bullet in my ribs. I kept very still. A step in either direction and the creak of a board would give me away.

"Give it up," said the voice of Colonel Rawdon Moran again. "It won't wash. You may say so to your friend Mr. Sherlock Holmes, if you choose. Or you may keep it to yourself. That is entirely a matter for you. But your fate is no longer in your own hands. I beg you will believe me. Be warned, once and for all. Be assured, you will only hurt yourself."

Be warned once and for all! *Beware all—I warn but once.* Such were the words that had vanished with the dew before anyone else could read them. It seemed Moran could not have reached London by that night; but I knew he was the author of the message, as surely as he was the donor of the severed head.

I will not say that I was too frightened to reply to this sudden warning. I simply could not bring myself to do it. In any case, the invisible corridor beyond the partition was now silent again. It did not mean the coast was clear. The man was a hunter. What was it Mycroft Holmes had said? Randy Moran could cross the floor of a forest by night and never let a single twig crack under his foot. To be sure, he would not risk the explosion of a gun in a place like this—but Joshua Sellon had died without a sound. Moran would expect me to go onwards to the exit of the maze. In that case, my best chance was to go back, retracing my route to the entrance. Even with an air weapon, he would hardly dare use it while the gypsy woman was a witness. I tried to withdraw silently, the grotesque mirrored distortions of my appearance weaving back at me on either side. I stumbled once as I neared the pay-booth. Blinking in the sun, I saw only the head-scarved woman preparing to close her till.

"The gentleman who came out just now, a moment ago. Which way did he go?"

She looked up at me, strangely as I thought.

"No gentleman came out, sir. Not since you went in. Only two ladies and their little boys. There's no one in there now. I always make sure of that before we close up."

I glanced back. There was no sign of anyone behind me. Was he still in there?

"There's no one there, sir," she insisted. "You've missed your friend." She chuckled. "If he was in there, once it's locked, he'd be inside until tomorrow morning."

Had he found some other way through a gap in the canvas—found it or made it? But what a fool I had been. It now seemed plain that Rawdon Moran had had me watched every movement and every minute. The hunter always has the upper hand over the prey, and he had lived all his life as a hunter. Equally at home in the streets of London or the tracks of the African jungle. Holmes and I would do well to remember it.

As for Lestrade and Scotland Yard, what an idiot I should be to talk of a voice in a fairground maze without a shred of evidence to confirm that I was not inventing or imagining the whole thing!

I walked carefully back towards the waiting drag. Though it was probably too late to be cautious, I kept behind the shelter of canvas booths and fun-fair galleries on the shadowed grass. From time to time, I retraced my steps and took new angles. I dodged and ducked past the fairground structures of roundabouts and helter-skelter slides. At last there was nothing but one stretch of open ground between me and the ancient vehicle in which my friend must be waiting. The crowds were going home and Colonel Moran was nowhere to be seen. I crossed by the rails of the racecourse, looking back and seeing no one, concealing myself on the far side of the carriage before I entered it. Yet I was still haunted by the certainty that he watched me every step of my way.

6

I said nothing to Holmes as we rode away from Epsom Downs in our drag or on the train, partly because I felt rather shaken. To tell the truth, I was fast coming round to a view that these events were a matter for the resources of Scotland Yard or the Provost's Special Investigation Branch rather than for a pair of consulting detectives. Unfortunately, I hesitated too long. By the end of the evening, it seemed too late to describe my experience just then. And if I revealed the encounter with Moran belatedly, it might sound to my friend as though I were making a confession of having stupidly got into a scrape. That was true. I thought that I still did not know Holmes well enough to predict at what point he would think himself better off without such a foolish partner as I was proving to be.

In one corner of my mind, I even thought that Rawdon Moran might be right. I hope I am no coward; but, repulsive though the man was, had he not at least been correct when he said that by our present conduct we should only hurt ourselves? And what of danger to those who might be near and dear to us? There was a certain young lady in my life. Though fate was to play us false, I could not know it at the time. I could not tell what forces we were up against. Of course Holmes and I were partners and must act together. Yet the reader may bear in mind that our partnership was still relatively recent. I must be allowed a degree of discretion and independence in personal matters. I was sufficiently of two minds that I decided to sleep on the matter. Tomorrow should be the day of decision. I could just as well tell him my story then as now.

Next morning, uncharacteristically, it was Sherlock Holmes who was first at the breakfast table. I appeared at my usual time, having slept wretchedly, to find him already at the stage of toast and marmalade. His copy of the *Morning Post* had been read and laid aside. Against the polished silver of the milk jug stood an open copy of *The Ordeal of Richard Feverel*, chosen from the volumes of the Complete Novels of George Meredith which had long stood upon his shelves. He closed the book and looked up at me.

"I thought it best that you should sleep well, Watson. I trust you have done so, for you may not find it so easy tonight."

"Indeed?"

"I fear so. Colonel Rawdon Moran is back in England."

I could only play the part I had imposed upon myself: "Since when?"

"He has been here for a day or two at least. He did not, as expected, sail from Madeira to Antwerp. Masquerading as Sebastian Moran, I made urgent and brotherly inquiries for him by telegraph to the shipping agents in Leadenhall Street. Their passenger lists show that he disembarked at Lisbon last week and took the Iberian Express for Medina del Campo and Paris. He had only to travel a little further and board the steamer from Calais to Dover. He has stolen something of a march upon us."

"He has left France, then?" I asked awkwardly.

"Indeed. He was at the Epsom Spring Meeting yesterday afternoon."

If I looked astonished, it was for reasons which I hoped my friend would not find obvious. It was an unenviable experience to fence with him over truth and falsehood.

"You did not see him for yourself?"

"He was seen, my dear fellow. I hope it will not distress you to hear that he was closer to you than you imagined. You had not emerged from the Hall of Mirrors when he entered it."

"I did not see you there." That at least was true.

"I daresay not. You might, however, have noticed a young scamp of twelve or thirteen, wearing a braided jacket with a cap and muffler, loitering about the amusements."

"There were dozens of young rips like that!"

"Precisely. This one, however, was acting as a runner for an itinerant fairground photographer and was there at my request. 'Shadowing us' is, I believe, the vernacular expression. The boy is one of my young Baker Street friends who rejoices in the title of Skiver Jenkins of Lisson Grove. A promising lad. I should call him at least a sergeant-major in our Baker Street Irregulars."

"So that was it!"

"I fear so. Rawdon Moran is an habitué of the racecourse as surely as the card-table and would never miss the Epsom meeting if he were in England. I put him to the test. I can only apologise for turning you loose as a scapegoat with two of our young gentlemen keeping distant observation. I count upon the colonel's continuing interest in our movements. I can assure you that you were followed from the military rifle range by a pair of bullies until our friend Moran was able to detach himself from his party. He was on your track for at least twenty minutes. Skiver Jenkins was able to identify him from my description and a lamentably amateur copy that I had produced for the occasion from Mycroft's photograph."

"And what do you propose to do?"

"Nothing," he said with a shrug. "Our adversaries are impatient. Their intention is that we should now scuttle about like startled rabbits. By doing nothing, we draw them on a little further."

Though he had not so far mentioned his correspondence, there was one letter by his plate. It must have appeared of some

importance and he had apparently reserved it for his full attention. I contrived to read upon its envelope a return address. It was
the Ravenswood Hotel, Southampton Row. Major Putney-Wilson
had evidently thought it necessary to prevent his message being
tampered with surreptitiously: there was a red wax seal on the
back of the envelope.

Holmes finished his second cup of coffee.

"Our friend has written to us," I said helpfully.

"It would seem so."

He folded the *Morning Post* and with the envelope in his hand
went over to his crowded and disreputable "chemical table." There
he struck a match, lit a Bunsen burner at low heat, filled a glass
retort with water from a bottle and placed the vessel on the flame.
He watched until the water began to bubble gently. A cloud of steam
drifted from the nozzle of the retort. He held the unopened letter
so that the warm vapour played gently upon the hardened wax.
A moment later, the wax began to soften. Judging the exact point
at which to ease open the envelope, he took a fine steel blade and
prised the flap of paper from its pouch. He drew out a card with the
message upon it, read it, and then handed it across the table to me.

> You are quite right, of course. I have taken your advice
> and am returning to India. I shall pass what remains
> of my summer leave in the cool hills of Simla. My pas-
> sage is booked on the P & O liner *Himalaya* at the end
> of next week. Whatever is still to be done in England,
> I believe you are the only man to do it. I regret only
> that my foolish attempt to intervene may have served
> to make your task more difficult.
>
> I remain, sir,
Yours faithfully,
H P-W

"He has bitten the bullet, then!" I said as I passed the card back.

Without replying, he took up a magnifying lens and began to examine the wax as it cooled and hardened again. After murmuring something to himself, he slapped his knee and turned to me.

"Excellent! Admirable! Putney-Wilson has done as I told him; I do believe they have fallen for it!"

"Fallen for what?"

"My dear fellow, I had rather counted upon Colonel Moran or one of his satraps intercepting any letter which came via the postal service to this address from Major Putney-Wilson—let alone from Samuel Dordona!"

"But that envelope has not been intercepted, surely? The seal was unbroken. Had the envelope been slit open at its edges?"

"No. A Scotland Yard amateur would recognise that at once."

"What then? There are no broken fragments of wax, as there must be if a seal is removed. Do you mean that they have steamed it open as you have done?"

He shook his head.

"The wax seal has been replaced. Once it has been opened, it cannot be re-sealed with the original wax alone. It requires a new seal with a little extra wax on top of what was there before. To look convincing, the new seal must overlap the original wax imprint, however slightly. It is a serviceable method of deception—but for one thing: the old wax will have been heated twice and is therefore darker in colour; the new wax is melted only once and is therefore lighter. To those who know where to look— and how to look with an examining lens or a microscope—the slight discrepancy between the two layers betrays the secret interception. That discrepancy is here, as you may see if you care to borrow this glass. In other words, we are not the first people to read the contents of this note. Putney-Wilson has done as I told him. That is most, most gratifying, is it not?"

He handed me the magnifying glass and the envelope. As always, he was correct.

"How did you learn that trick?"

He smiled reminiscently.

"My investigation of the Maida Vale blackmail mystery, involving a fortune-teller and a private secretary to the Prince of Wales, pre-dates the happy occasion when you and I first made one another's acquaintance. In the course of that earlier investigation, I was introduced to the 'Black Chamber' of the General Post Office at St. Martin's-Le-Grand."

"The Black Chamber?"

He smiled.

"My dear Watson! Every government has such an office, of necessity. In our case it is a room where, for reasons of state, letters posted by suspected persons are opened by government officers on the authority of the Attorney-General and under the direction of an Official Examiner. They are scrutinised and then resealed and put into a special basket for the evening deliveries of the same day. The Examiner forwards a report to the Treasury Solicitor who normally requests the interception. Never make the mistake, Watson, of believing that a letter addressed to you has not been read by someone else first. Especially if it arrives by the evening post, rather than in the morning."

I handed back the lens and the envelope.

"Then our adversaries know that Major Putney-Wilson has withdrawn from the fray. Perhaps he may be safe, once he leaves England."

"We have time to save him. Unless they choose to settle accounts with him in Simla or on board the *Himalaya*. I think that is unlikely. They may do it at their leisure, though one must never underrate the sheer spite of such people. As for the story he might tell of Captain Brenton Carey's death, they must believe he has told it already, as is the case. So, my dear fellow, it is you and I alone who must now account for Colonel Moran."

Now I was quite prepared to tell him of my encounter with the colonel in the Hall of Mirrors at Epsom; but he seemed pressed for time just then, and the incident appeared less important. It could wait until after dinner.

It was a relief to be excused the duty of acting as nursemaid to Putney-Wilson. Holmes was to be otherwise engaged that day, and I felt unexpectedly liberated. The Army and Navy Club, to which I had belonged since the day of my first military commission, stands in St. James's Square just off Piccadilly. It is quite as selective in its way as the Diogenes. A serving officer who wishes to become a member must find a proposer and a seconder. He may be blackballed during the election by any member who knows of something to his discredit. No reason for this need be given, and the objector's identity is not revealed.

From time to time, when I am out and about in London, I take lunch with a friend at the Army and Navy by appointment. On other days I go alone and chance "pot luck" at a large round communal table at the centre of the dining-room. Those who are unaccompanied may dine together there for the sake of gossip.

Preoccupied by our present investigation, I had not been near the club for two or three weeks. It was time to show my face again. Even so, it was perhaps best not to travel alone in a cab. There is safety in numbers, and it is really just as convenient to take a first-class ticket on the underground railway, which people had begun to refer to as the "tube." To travel to St. James's Park from the Metropolitan station at the junction of Baker Street and the Euston Road was direct enough.

I walked along the busy pavement at my leisure and down the steps to the platform from the station booking-hall. I had only to wait for the next oncoming train to rumble out of the sooty brick arch of the tunnel into the brown glazed vaulting of the station. When one is travelling underground, Baker Street appears to be the centre of the civilised world. There is a line running east and a line running west, both of which end here. The stationary trains then stand side by side until the moment of their departure in reverse directions. This system is said to be the best for preventing collisions—and so it seems to be. Trains waiting at preceding stations do not leave their platforms until the electric telegraph signals that the space at Baker Street is "vacant."

There were trains waiting at either platform as I came down the steps and took my seat in a carriage of the westbound departure, which would be the second to leave. After a moment or two, I glanced up at the window of the adjacent eastbound train a few feet away from me. A blast on the guard's whistle would signal its departure in due course. My thoughts were far away from that adjacent carriage window, two or three feet distant. I was roused unaccountably by an open newspaper which a passenger sitting on that other train was reading. I could not see the face of the reader, or anything other than a man's hands holding the pages open as he read. The black headline was plain in its large bold type: VICTORIA MANSIONS MURDER.

What did it mean? It was a bizarre situation. I could see the headline well enough but I could not communicate with that other reader nor attract his attention. He and I were as isolated in adjacent trains as goldfish in two separate bowls. Had there been a second murder in the mansion blocks? Or was it merely a statement by Scotland Yard of some new development in the mysterious case of Joshua Sellon? It was neither. Though the columns of newsprint were too small to read at this distance, I saw that this could not be today's paper. At the top of that front page it was stamped in red "AFTERNOON EDITION." It was still only half-past ten in the morning. Afternoon editions do not come on the news-stands until after midday.

I managed at length to make out some of the smaller numerals and to see that the edition bore a date well past. It was the original report of Captain Sellon's murder. Why was someone now holding it open, as if for me to read? A sharp whistle-blast announced the departure of that other train, towards King's Cross and the banking districts. With a quickening of the heart, I convinced myself that should the newspaper be lowered, I would be staring into the malevolent features of Colonel Rawdon Moran. Those same eyes must surely have followed me from our rooms—perhaps in a slowly moving cab—with the quiet expressionless stare of the patient trapper.

That was absurd, of course. It was vastly more probable that someone else from London's millions had somewhere picked up a discarded out-of-date paper and was reading it. Yet I had begun to know the man since Epsom. I felt sure it must be he. He was not here by chance. I had ten—perhaps twenty—seconds before his carriage window glided out of view. But if I could see nothing else, I had a view of the back of his right hand as it held open that front page of the paper. In my mind, I tried to picture the hand that had held a gun at the Royal Britannia Rifle Range. I had kept in my memory the strong roughened fingers with a sprouting of red hairs on their backs.

There was time to focus on them. These were the same fingers, I could swear it. But they gripped the edge of the paper at just such a level that the upper corner of its page fell back upon them a little. Not enough to conceal them but, in this light and at a rapidly increasing distance, to suggest a reddish colour to those little tufts of hair that perhaps I was only imagining.

There was nothing more I could do—and he would have known it. That was what made me all the more certain. I could not see him but I would have bet my life that somehow, perhaps through a pinhole poked in the paper, he could see me register my astonishment before his train pulled into the darkness of the tunnel. Then I could only watch as that carriage slid completely out of sight.

Moran had surely kept me in his view, but any story I might tell to others would sound like the babbling of a delusional neurotic. He had contrived it all, if indeed it was he, so that I could not communicate with him or hold him to account. It was not twenty-four hours since I had heard that voice directed to me in the so-called Hall of Mirrors. Now I was being taught to understand that I should remain under scrutiny by his people in the London crowds, always at his beck and call. He had killed before—who knows how many times?—but always in such a way that he could not be touched by the law. From now on he would be constantly on the offensive, always driving me back. When my summons to execution came, I should be as powerless to evade him as I had been to confront him just now in our two "goldfish-bowls."

If I stop and read again the last paragraph that I have written, its words seem to me like the protests of an hysteric. Short of a growing obsession with our adversary, there was nothing to prove that it had been Moran. Had I imagined or misread the headline? No. I knew instinctively that this had been our second encounter and presumably my third warning. I was being informed that my time was up. Holmes was under sentence in any case.

As the half-lit stations slipped by, I tried to think as Holmes would think. In London, it is far easier than in any jungle for a determined man to stalk his prey. My friend had recently begun to make use of those juvenile ragamuffins and mudlarks whom he called his "Baker Street Irregulars." They could gather gossip, eavesdrop on conversations, and track a man who would never suspect a child among so many of them in the city streets. But then what Holmes could do, Moran could do. Which man, woman, or child in my vicinity might not be in the colonel's pay?

Someone in the busy crowd at Baker Street station might still have been watching me as the train pulled out—or might even be on the train. There was no question of what I must do—or rather what I must not do. They would expect me to scramble out of the carriage, run back up the street to our rooms and report everything to Holmes. I confess I was angered at the thought that they regarded me as the weakling of the two. Anger sharpened my wits. Holmes had deductive and forensic gifts far beyond mine. But a man who has been through the slaughter of

Maiwand and the siege of Kandahar does not take to his heels in the face of common criminals. It did me good to think of these masters of conspiracy as nothing but common felons.

I stepped down from the carriage only when I reached my destination at St. James's Park. I emerged from the steps into the sunlight with the park before me, Buckingham Palace to one side and Whitehall on the other. I did not think anyone had followed me up to the surface. Of course, there were dozens of people crossing the lawns, past the flower-beds, over the bridge and the lake to the Mall. A few were nursemaids with prams. Most were men whose suits and hats proclaimed them as going about the business of government. Almost anyone in that moving crowd might have been detailed to report on my movements, but I no longer cared. Past Marlborough House and the cabs of Pall Mall, I came to the club.

The rooms are quiet in late morning. Roebuck, the porter at the desk, took my hat, coat, and gloves. From force of habit, I glanced at the baize notice-board, where letters to members await collection, held in place by a wire mesh. There were seldom any for me. I did not correspond much within the club, and I give my Baker Street address to friends and acquaintances as a rule. I scanned the board and saw one envelope with my name on it. It would be the steward's bill for monthly expenses.

Then I noticed a postage stamp on the envelope and knew that this had nothing to do with club business. It also came as an unwelcome surprise to see that the address of the club had been written in the same copperplate hand as on the first letter which "Samuel Dordona" had persuaded someone to write on his behalf. It even had the same punctilious style. "John H. Watson Esq., M.B., B.Ch." The postmark confirmed that the envelope had been posted only two days earlier.

I did not think anyone could be watching me here. A stranger would be challenged if he tried to follow me into the club lobby. Moran himself would never have been so foolish as to put up for election to membership. His right to the title of "colonel" must have been questioned at once, even if his conduct had not been known. I slid the envelope from behind the wire and walked slowly up the wide carpeted marble stairs to the library on the first floor. I chose an armchair in a corner with a window view of lawn and trees at the centre of the square. That was where a spy might linger, but I saw no one. I slit open the envelope.

There was no letter—just a card of the kind used by doctors or dentists as a memorandum for appointments. Only the name and the date had been filled in, but I did not recognize the writing. Of course I had been prepared for threats or "warnings"; yet the five words on the card meant absolutely nothing. Had the envelope not been so precisely addressed, I should have thought that the message was intended for someone else.

In the space left for a name, someone had entered *Comtesse de Flandre*. Where there was a space for the date, there were instead just two words: *New Moon*. And that was that. I stared at the words, but I faced a stone wall at the end of a blind alley. What the devil was this? I could find no meaning to the name or date, and yet the circumstances of their delivery suggested they must be of importance. Whoever sent the card knew that I belonged to the club. Had it been sent by someone who also knew that an envelope delivered among all the others coming to the club would slip through without notice more easily than one addressed to 221b Baker Street? That suggested a friend. But was it from friend or foe? Was it simply a reminder that I was safe nowhere, not even in my own club?

I was determined that before I left the shelter of the Army and Navy I would know what this was all about. At least I could then write a message "to whom it might concern" and leave it in the trustworthy care of Roebuck at his desk, to be held in case I should suffer some unaccountable "accident."

I looked at those five words again. Why were they not explained? With sudden unease, I wondered whether they had been written in desperate haste by someone like Colonel Pulleine or Joshua Sellon, someone who had no time to explain them. Someone who knew that he—or she—would be dead in a minute more. A killer might search the place of his murder but would hardly bother with an appointment card on a mantelpiece.

I felt cold in that comfortable sunlit room with its leather arm-chairs and mahogany shelves of books. I thought of Moran again. Perhaps the card was from a killer rather than a corpse. A taunt or an invitation.

I was determined to have the truth of this. To begin with, I tried to remember who the Comtesse de Flandre might be. I had certainly heard—or read—that name. An old-fashioned club library was one of the best places to identify her. A few minutes with European aristocracy in the current volume of the *Almanach de Gotha* informed me that Marie Luise, Comtesse de Flandre, was a Prussian princess, forty-four years old. She was married to Prince Philippe, Comte de Flandre. He in turn was brother of the childless and dissolute King Leopold II of Belgium. The Comte and Comtesse de Flandre had five children, of whom the young Prince Baudouin was now heir to the Belgian throne.

But what could there be in all this? Anyone who read such sensational London newspapers as the *Pall Mall Gazette* knew of King Leopold II as a man of unsavoury reputation. His correspondence with Mrs. Mary Jefferies, the so-called White Slave Widow of recent infamy, had lately been read out at the Middlesex Sessions during her trial for keeping a house of ill repute. His character was even more widely known for the brutal treatment meted out to the tribes of his vast and newly acquired Congo Free State. It was the blameless Comtesse de Flandre herself who famously described this royal brother-in-law as the only man who could survive without such an organ as a heart in his body.

What on earth had she to do with our case? From what I could now make out, thanks to the *Almanach* and the bound volumes of *The Times*, the Comtesse de Flandre was a figure of domestic virtue and public philanthropy. King Leopold's sister-in-law would be as revolted as anyone by the stories of his Congolese tribesmen suffering amputation of a hand for returning without a full quota of harvested rubber. This unhappy land, dubbed "The Heart of Darkness," was also the centre of an arms trade to the Transvaal and elsewhere, the destination of Colonel Moran's Krupp field-guns and the heavy howitzers.

By now I was scanning the newspaper columns for any clue that might connect such a worthy lady with the hateful underworld of Rawdon Moran and his cronies. She was born a princess of Hohenzollern-Sigmaringen, sister of the present King of Rumania and of Prince Ferdinand of Bulgaria. Her father had been Prime Minister of Prussia.

The Comtesse's visits to England were reserved for such anniversaries as our own Queen's birthday or the military ceremonial of the Trooping of the Colour in St. James's Park. On their arrival at Victoria Station from the channel ferry and during their residence at Claridge's hotel, she and her husband were visited by foreign ambassadors and British statesmen from Benjamin Disraeli to Lord Salisbury, as well as by the most enlightened of our aristocracy. In her own country, she had been in the Royal Opera Box for the visit of the Shah of Persia and had been radiant at the opening of the Brussels Exhibition.

But what could this amiable lady have to do with the nightmare world of Moran? From what Henry Putney-Wilson had been able to tell us, a network of international criminals was deeply engaged in the trading of armaments via Belgium and its new Congo territory to the Transvaal and southern Africa. Had they encountered an obstacle which might be overcome by the removal of the Comtesse de Flandre? Was the note a warning from someone that harm was intended to this good lady at the next new moon—harm that did not exclude her assassination?

At least one or two of the pieces in the puzzle could now be put in place, thanks to our meeting with Mycroft Holmes. Moran had come away from the Transvaal with whatever he could loot from the estate of Andreis Reuter. The amount had been less than he had expected, because the young man had belatedly judged him for the rogue that he was. All the same, with the aid of his cronies, there had been enough to set up the "colonel" as an international trader in guns and ammunition. He became an agent of the cosmopolitan criminal brotherhood in which Sherlock Holmes had always believed—"the higher criminal world," as he was apt to call it. Moran's ambition was no doubt to seize the supreme governorship of that world, perhaps literally by force of arms.

Almost in the first week of our acquaintanceship, Holmes had ridden his favourite hobby-horse for my benefit. He believed firmly in this international aristocracy of crime. Such an intricate and worldwide association worked together for common purposes and was beyond the power of any police force to destroy. To my friend's own knowledge, it included Rawdon Moran's own brother Colonel Sebastian Moran; a further pair of brothers with a common Christian name, Professor James Moriarty and Colonel James Moriarty; blackmail and extortion was in the slippery and loathsome hands of Charles Augustus Milverton. Elsewhere the organisation embraced Giuseppe Gorgiano and the infamous Red Circle gang of Naples and Southern Italy; Hugo Oberstein, international dealer in such military papers as the Bruce Partington submarine plans; Captain James Calhoun, leader of a group of professional assassins from Savannah, Georgia; John Clay, an accomplished cracksman of Coburg Square in London's East End; and very many more listed in the personal archives of Sherlock Holmes.

Could such an organisation exist? A century ago, it would have been impossible. In our own age of international railways, telegraph wires, and ocean liners, it was impossible to prevent. A case soon came our way. A pair of the most determined felons gave each other alibis on opposite sides of the globe. Our friend

Sir Edward Marshall Hall gained the acquittal of one man charged with bigamy. Descriptions and photographs apparently proved that the defendant was in prison in the United States at the time. Two years later, I was in court with Marshall Hall for the trial of the Lambeth Poisoner, Dr. Neill Cream. My companion recognised him as almost a twin of he who had stood trial for bigamy and been acquitted; Cream had given him an alibi as an Illinois gaol-bird.

I stared long and hard at the oil paintings of Crimean generals on the library wall. Holmes and I were getting into this mystery deeper than we had ever intended. I could do no more good here. I slipped the card into my pocket, went down and called for my hat and coat, then set off for Baker Street. I would tell my story to Holmes and let him make what he could of it.

7

I explained everything to him. As usual, he ignored most of the evidence and seized on one item that was crucial to the entire narrative.

"The Comtesse de Flandre?"

"I fear she means nothing to me."

"Indeed? Does she not? There are others, my dear fellow, to whom she means a great deal. But few people are party to the secret."

He got up from his chair by the fireplace, where he had been listening in his usual attentive posture. His long legs had been stretched out, finger-tips touching in an attitude of payer, elbows resting on the arms of the chair, eyelids lightly closed. Now, turning up the ornamental gas-lamp below the picture rail, he crossed to the far wall of the room, whose long run of book-shelves made up his archive. The lowest shelf contained a run of large scrap-books, purchased at intervals from Appincourt, our Baker Street stationer. Other men might have filled the thick blank pages of these folio volumes with family mementoes or cuttings from favourite literature. In the case of Sherlock Holmes, hardly an evening passed without the appearance of a sturdy pair of tailor's scissors as he set about the daily newspapers.

From the pages of the morning's *Times* or the evening *Globe*, he would cut some item that had caught his eye. It might be the use of a refined form of strychnine by a French widow-robber, now making his last vain appeal to the Court de Cassation. Or perhaps there had been a sensation in the Place de Greve, after the desperate fellow had been strapped to the fatal plank and tilted forward under the hoisted blade of the guillotine. As his severed head fell into the basket, the felon's eyes were distinctly seen to turn and glare at Sanson the executioner. Most often, however, these brief paragraphs followed the progress of some petty villain who had risen from trivial burglaries in the slums of Whitechapel to the Olympian heights of homicide or extortion.

With a brush of his left arm, Holmes swept clear a space in the rubble of his chemical table. He lugged out from the shelves a tall volume in marbled boards. Spreading it open, his long agile fingers turned the crackling pages, stiffened by the newsprint with which they had been pasted. He stopped at a panorama of cuttings, annotated heavily in rusty ink. I caught the word "Reichsanzeiger" and knew only enough German to tell me that this was an official compilation of confidential memoranda. Thanks to his elder brother, Holmes acquired occasional documents and reports that were not yet for public inspection. He traced a line across a column and rested it under the words "Comtesse de Flandre, Marie Louise Alexandrine Karoline, Princess of Hohenzollern-Sigmaringen."

I looked over his shoulder and said, I fear rather foolishly, "Holmes, you have the advantage of me."

He chuckled and again flattened the surface of the broad page with his hand. "Happily for the good people of England, Watson, they sleep soundly in their beds. They are oblivious to those darkling plains of Europe where Mr. Mathew Arnold's ignorant armies clash by night. They do not yet know how close the powers of Europe came to a major war a matter of months ago.

We owed that crisis to Rawdon Moran and his masters, for there are even mightier villains than he. Such men have come close to accomplishing the greatest criminal conspiracies of modern times. The damage is still far from being undone. To this point, they appear to have been merely flexing their muscles for the grand assault that will one day come. These are the documents that prove the case."

"But why should they want a war?"

He looked at me with unfathomable sympathy.

"My dear Watson, why should a grocer want his customers to grow hungry—or a tailor to see his clients grow ragged? Who will profit from a modern war in Europe? Not the poor young heroes who will be slaughtered in their thousands by the devices of an industrial age. Not the householders who, with their wives and children, will be bombarded from the land, from the sea, and very probably in future from the air. But who else?"

"The merchants of murder!" I took up a phrase he had used earlier when talking of Moran or his kind and tossed it back at him. He nodded slowly.

"Very good, Watson. And whom do we know whose litany is a hymn of homage to the houses of Krupp and Maxim-Nordenfelt, Creuzot and Howitzer, Colt and Armstrong, Enfield and Webley? Why be content with the Congo and the Transvaal if all Europe is hungry for weapons?"

"But there has been no European war. What was their plot?"

He turned to another page.

"A few months ago, they decided to see what they could do, by forged despatches, to strike up the diplomats' dance of death. To bring two great power blocs of Europe to war, Austria and Germany on one side, France and Russia on the other, the old Turkish Empire and the straits of the Dardanelles with access to the Mediterranean to be the prize. The gateway to the East. If there were war, well and good. If not, the world would see how far a criminal clique could push the nations towards one.

The war was to be precipitated by a German prince claiming the throne of Bulgaria, Ferdinand of Coburg, kinsman of the Comtesse de Flandre. She is also sister to his closest ally, the King of Rumania."

"And her part in all this?"

"The Comtesse was the innocent recipient of forged letters purporting to be written by Prince Ferdinand. They were intercepted, as the authors intended, by secret agents of Tsar Alexander. Their contents were forwarded to St. Petersburg. Ferdinand appeared to promise his kinswoman that he had a secret treaty with Count Bismarck to defeat the Russian army in the provinces of the Black Sea. With perfect truth, the despatches pointed out that Russia could not sustain the cost of an all-out war longer than a few weeks. The so-called Prince Ferdinand therefore asked the Comtesse de Flandre to act as a loyal German princess and sister-in-law of King Leopold of Belgium. France would be quick to seek revenge for her defeat of 1870 by joining Russia against Austria and Germany. A Belgian army need only hamper a French advance in the Vosges for a few days. Only for as long as it took Germany and Austria to knock out Russia. A victorious Bismarck would impose terms. Belgium would never again have cause to fear her powerful French neighbour. That was the scheme outlined in the forged diplomatic papers by Moran and his associates. There was not a word of truth in this concoction, but it was so plausible that it nearly did the trick."

"It was close to the truth of what might happen in any case!"

"Precisely. The entire continent was set to go up in flames. There were also forged letters between Count Bismarck in Berlin and the German ambassador in Vienna, Prince Reuss, confirming the tale."

"And how was a war averted?"

Sherlock Holmes became modesty itself.

"At the eleventh hour, Brother Mycroft was kind enough to think that my own modest talents might be of some little use in saving the peace of Europe. What did I find? Our rulers are profoundly neurotic. Our adversaries must have been gratified at the mischief they were able to make with so little effort. Do not underestimate them, Watson! The forged letters from Prince Reuss to his master Count Bismarck were almost perfect. Those from Prince Ferdinand to the Comtesse de Flandre approached perfection."

"Yet they failed?"

"Only because of the suspicious ease with which they had fallen into the hands of the Tsar's agents. That should have alerted all the great powers. Conflict was avoided, but distrust between nations has immeasurably increased. The name of the innocent and admirable Comtesse de Flandre was cynically exploited. Next time—and there will be a next time—our enemies will have learnt by their mistakes."

"But there was no war this time."

He shook his head.

"It was close, Watson. The Russian High Command issued secret orders to its forward units to advance within sight of the Hungarian frontier. The Hungarian ministry replied with a confidential warning to St. Petersburg: 'If war should be forced upon us, Hungary will do her duty.' St. Petersburg at length offered promises of peace to the Austrian Emperor, but Vienna refused to suspend its military preparations in return for promises alone. It called up all reservists for ten days' training in the use of the new repeating rifle. Mycroft tells me that Lord Salisbury summoned the Turkish Ambassador privately to Downing Street. The Prime Minister promised that England would never consent to an alteration in the balance of power in the Mediterranean. The Royal Navy put to sea. It was nearly a bonfire of all the treaties and all the hopes."

He slid the weighty scrapbook back into its place on the bottom shelf. I stood there, trying to remember how it was that

I had not noticed his preoccupation with a great diplomatic crisis at the time. Of course! It had come and gone during that summer fortnight of my visit to the Devonshire cousins. I had lost myself in the pleasures of fishing for trout on Exmoor, among the steep rocky falls of Heddon's Mouth by the Bristol Channel, or facing the breeze on the links of Woolacombe golf club above the sandhills and the Atlantic surges. Now that seemed like another world. Over all my thoughts lay a sense of awe that this brotherhood of political gangsters had brought millions of their fellow human beings to the brink of destruction in the name of financial profit.

Holmes lay back luxuriously in his chair and sent up several blue-grey wreaths of smoke from his pipe.

"The Comtesse de Flandre," I said hopefully.

He stood up abruptly, his back to the fireplace, and frowned at the carpet. "Why not try the new moon?"

"I don't think I follow you, Holmes."

"Do you not? Consider the message that was waiting for you this morning. I believe that the last two words, concerning the moon, may be more important than the esteemed Comtesse de Flandre. They specify a time. In doing so they eliminate at least twenty-seven of twenty-eight possible dates in the month ahead."

"It would be dark at the new moon."

"Indeed it would. Perhaps we are to meet our foe during the hours of darkness, that is to say approximately between seven o'clock at night and seven o'clock in the morning."

He turned again to the bookshelves and took out a familiar cheaply bound volume. It was the current issue of *Old Moore's Almanac*, sold by the street vendors of Piccadilly. Flipping through it, he came to the tides and phases of the moon.

"For what it matters, Watson, the new moon is on 29 March, just a couple of weeks away. We may suppose that it is the next new moon which is indicated. If not, then this message would have very little value as information or as an ultimatum."

"And the Comtesse de Flandre? Why should the phases of the moon matter to her? At this time of year, she is probably on her way to the Swiss lakes or the Venice Lido."

He struck a match and furrowed his brow. Something was going on in his mind, but for the life of me I could not tell what. He shook out the match, drew on his pipe, and his brow was clear again.

"Riva," he said presently. "It is a picturesque little town at the Austrian end of Lake Garda. There was a brief notice not long ago in the Court Circular of *The Times*. If memory serves, the Comtesse and her children were to be guests of her Sigmaringen cousins at their lakeside villa there during the early spring."

"What can the new moon mean to her out there? Or anywhere, come to that?"

He walked across to the window and stood staring out across the reflected sunset of the foggy London sky. I knew better than to disturb him in such a mood.

"Fool!" he said softly, a moment later, and I knew he did not mean me.

He turned to the bookshelves again and drew out another flimsily bound handbook. It had the familiar livery of Bradshaw's railway timetable, but he did not turn to the usual pages. I could tell from their colour that he had found an appendix detailing international rail services to Paris, Brussels, or Berlin and the steamer times for the Continental ferries. He stood motionless and performed a little mental arithmetic.

"I believe, Watson, I owe you a very great apology for wasting your time over the identity of the Comtesse de Flandre."

"But not for revealing the activities of such political scoundrels as Rawdon Moran."

His face brightened a little and he looked up from the columns of figures.

"You are correct. I believe, however, that our Comtesse de Flandre is not the sister of the King of Rumania, nor the wife of

Philippe, Comte de Flandre, nor the mother of his five children. To be sure, she is a creature of the greatest elegance; but she has a heart of steel. She is also the property of a good many admirers."

He chuckled and I knew what was coming next.

"She also has two paddle-wheels, two funnels, and a two-compound diagonal engine capable of driving her at sixteen knots."

For the first time in the course of this case, he put back his head and laughed with all the power of his lungs. As for the ship, I had little difficulty in imagining her. In my Scottish childhood, the Clyde and the other rivers, as well as the islands and coastal waters, depended for their transport and supplies on these trim well-balanced paddle steamers. Named after nobility and heroes of legend, they plied from pier to pier among the little harbours of the western coast. They were about two hundred feet long and some thirty feet in the beam. At a speed between twelve and twenty knots, they could carry as many as four or five hundred passengers. Their build made them exceptionally manoeuvrable and, being flat-bottomed, they could work in as little as six or eight feet of water. Under the top deck, there were saloons and a bar, providing cover in wet weather.

He glanced at the timetable again.

"It appears that the ship is owned by the Belgian government and works the Ostend-to-Dover crossing with another paddler, the *Princesse Henriette*. Strange, is it not, that the ships are named after the chaste and worthy Comtesse de Flandre and her daughter? It is one more indication of the public distaste felt for the libidinous and cruel King Leopold of the Belgians."

"But suppose the message is an enemy's challenge rather than a friend's warning. After all, what can a passenger ferry matter to men whose ambition is to precipitate war between major European powers? Is it not far more likely that their target is again the Comtesse de Flandre herself, rather than a cross-channel ferry which happens to be named after her?"

He thought about this briefly and shook his head.

"Watson, your taste for writing up our modest investigations as a romance of crime is, as you know, a matter of indifference to me. But I remain a simple soul. Common sense tells me that a new moon is less likely to be of consequence to a royal lady than to a passenger ship, its captain, and its crew. The state of the sky, the position of the stars, and the phases of the moon are the rulers of their lives. I daresay you are right and I am wrong, but that is how I see it. Moreover, I prefer the promise of skulduggery on the high seas to an invitation from the Italian lakes."

"But have we not been given a time and place where we are challenged to go and settle accounts? Are we not invited to ride from a view to a death by a man who is master of the kill?"

"I believe you will find, Watson, that this is a message from a friend."

"And if you are wrong?"

He winced, as if at a spasm of pain.

"My dear fellow, I am not in the habit of being wrong."

He knew more than he was telling me, but his expression was as innocent as a sleeping child's. I tried again.

"Holmes, if what you say is true, the last thing we should do is to go anywhere near this ship or the new moon!"

His fingers beat a slow but impatient tattoo on the arm of his chair.

"You think not?"

"Suppose you are right and suppose this reference is to the ship. Our adversaries will watch us every moment from now on, as I am sure they have already done. If there are enough of them, the most amateur villains could accomplish that—and these are no amateurs. When the time comes, they need only lie in wait, as professional hunters do. For us, a ship is a natural trap if ever there was one. This may not even be the work of Rawdon Moran."

He raised his forefinger an inch from his chair-arm and spoke quietly.

"I think you are wrong there, Watson. This little matter has become personal between us."

"Well, then, he will have an alibi and half a dozen hired foot-pads whom we shall not know from Adam. On a ship of any kind, they have only to choose a convenient moment, shoot us through the head or hit us across it, and throw us overboard."

"They will most certainly have us in their sights," he said thoughtfully; "I assume that they will know our every movement. They will also choose a time and place to their own advantage. And in that lies the greatest danger to them."

8

*N*ot long ago, I should have regarded the glance of a passing stranger as accidental. I should have supposed that the attitude of some lounger against a pillar of the Lyceum Theatre was habitual sloth. Now, I looked twice to see how such people reacted as I passed them. Did they communicate by a furtive signal to a confederate behind me? My apprehensions could never prove anything of the sort, but that left me all the more uneasy.

I had gone to an exhibition in Kensington Gallery. I stood with my back to the door, studying a watercolour of a spirited young lady, "The Milkmaid of Cowes," braving a stiff breeze to catch the attention of a Royal Yachtsman. The disadvantage of a picture hung to face doors and windows is that it also mirrors the interior of the room and the admirer. I did not at first catch a reflection of the person behind me until he began to turn away. Seen in the glass, it was the build of Moran seen from the rear, down to the whiskers and the cut of the hair.

I swung round, hoping and believing I should confront a complete stranger. I was even prepared to find that it was Moran. Worst of all, this onlooker had vanished. In the time it took me to turn, it would have been easy for the image in the picture-glass to move deftly through half a dozen steps and disappear among the display-boards.

There were two or three other incidents of a similar kind. In none of them could I be sure of anything. I was walking home from Maida Vale by lamplight. I turned into Clifton Gardens, where the Regents Park Canal runs down the centre of this leafy avenue. The cream-painted Regency terraces rose on either side and a broad pavement extended before them. There was no immediate means of access to the other side of the water from where I was walking. Suddenly he was standing there. Was it "he," or not? The man wore a swell's costume of silk hat and crimson-lined black cape with a silver-knobbed stick in his hand. He was stationary, staring across the dark water in the lamplight—either at me or through me.

I hurried on to see if he would follow parallel. Half a minute later, I turned quickly and looked back. He had gone. I could see all the way to Warwick Avenue. But the broad walks on either side were suddenly empty. His only refuge would have been in one of the cream-terraced houses. But which one, if any? And was it he?

The following day, with no such thoughts in mind, I was passing a newly refurbished apartment block in a busy stretch of the Marylebone Road. If ever I saw the outline of Moran, it was the foreman on the flat roof, giving orders to a workman with a wheelbarrow. The odds were a thousand to one against it being so. Yet how easily a tile or a brick from the piles of material on that roof might slip off and brain a passer-by in the street below!

I came down to breakfast the next morning. Sherlock Holmes almost always rose late. Though he was apt to say that an exception disproves the rule, there were some occasions during a case when I would come down at my usual time and find him gone out on an errand of his own. So it was today. His plates were cleared away, but the *Morning Post* was smooth and unread.

All the same, I was not prepared to look across the room and find our Scotland Yard friend, Lestrade, sitting in my fireside armchair and reading my copy of *The Times*. He had the grace to get up as I came in.

"Good morning, doctor; I trust I find you well. Mr. Holmes and I met on the doorstep. I was arriving as he was leaving to keep an appointment with his brother, Sir Mycroft, at Lancaster Gate, or so he said. He was kind enough to suggest that I might sit here quietly and wait for him."

"Have you nothing else to do?"

The question sounded more discourteous than I had intended. I was not best pleased to find Lestrade in occupation of our sitting-room at such an hour. The inspector chuckled at my question and settled his jacket more comfortably upon his shoulders. I noticed that, unusually for him, he was wearing semi-official tweeds. I wondered where he might have been—or where he was going to. He sounded full of himself.

"We all have a good deal to do this morning, doctor, but my visit here is a great part of it. Now do not allow me to stand between you and your breakfast."

He made a gesture of invitation towards the table, for all the world as though he were the host and I a guest in his house. I had no intention of eating my breakfast as a performance where he was to be the audience.

"What brings you here so early?"

He sat down again without invitation, as if to establish an indefinite tenancy. I noticed that Mrs. Hudson's Molly had provided him with a cup of coffee.

"What brings me here, sir, is much the same thing as takes Mr. Holmes and Sir Mycroft to Lancaster Gate."

I had no idea why my colleague and Brother Mycroft had gone to the Bayswater Road. All the same, I was damned if I would beg an explanation. Something like an evil smile of triumph lightened the inspector's face. He almost wagged his finger at me.

"Ah," he said quietly, "I daresay Mr. Holmes has not told you about Lancaster Gate. Then I shall do so. I'm sure Mr. Holmes and I have no secrets from you."

The man was quite insufferable. Had I been fortified by a good breakfast, I should no doubt have dealt with him more robustly. As it was, I said grimly, "I shall be content to discuss the matter with Mr. Holmes on his return."

But there was no stopping him.

"Your channel crossing on Friday week, sir. The *Comtesse de Flandre.*"

It shook me a little that he should know of it already.

"What of it?"

He looked surprised.

"Well, naturally it has taken Mr. Holmes to Lancaster Gate. To discuss the arrangements with Prince Napoleon-Jerome's chief-of-staff. General Boulanger, I believe."

I was lost. Like anyone who had read the newspapers, I knew that since the assassination of the Prince Imperial, his stout and elderly cousin Prince Napoleon-Jerome, known to all the world as "Plon Plon," had become the claimant to the French throne. But I should have thought he was as far from being Emperor of the French as the poor young man had been, after two decades of the Republic. Of course the novelty of that Republic was more than a little tarnished. There had been a tumultuous movement in France in favour of the maverick General Georges Boulanger, winner of elections in that country. His great and popular promises even extended to restoring the Empire, in the person of Plon Plon as Napoleon IV, upon democratic principles.

Lestrade spoke quietly and confidentially.

"First thing this morning, Mr. Holmes took it upon himself to send one of his little ragamuffins to Leadenhall Street, to the shipping agents. Such firms open their doors almost as early as the railway stations. This little shaver was to engage accommodation for the two of you in the first-class saloon of the *Comtesse de*

Flandre on Friday week. Back comes the message that the entire saloon is already taken by a certain party. So you'll be travelling second class."

Having savoured the pleasure of our discomfiture, Lestrade continued.

"Mr. Holmes's budding spy kept his little ears open, asked a few questions of the messenger boys round those offices, and found out who that certain party is."

"Who?"

"Well, naturally, Prince Napoleon-Jerome and his suite, coming back to London from exile in Switzerland. As soon as Mr. Holmes hears this, a message goes to your colleague's noble brother. Sir Mycroft is to meet your friend at once. At the prince's town house in Lancaster Gate."

Lestrade beamed and chuckled, just as though this were the best thing he had heard in years.

"After all," he said at last, "you'll be crossing on the steamer anyway. Same crossing as Prince Napoleon. He's an exile and there's a law says he can't set foot on the soil of France. There's no way he can get between his estate in Switzerland and his mansion in London except by going through Belgium—and that means Ostend."

"Why should he need us?"

Lestrade looked very uncomfortable, as if he ought to say nothing.

"Put it this way, doctor. What's boiling up in France? General Bou-lon-geur hoping to be president next month and the monarchy brought back. That can't be done for nothing."

He illustrated the impossibility by a sucking sound and rubbing the tips of his thumb and forefinger together knowingly.

"Where's the spondoolicks to be found?" he went on; "where's the royal sparklers? They'll be needed down the pawn shop in England, because that's where the whole thing's got to be launched from. But suppose this restoration was all to go smooth as goose grease, then your friend's noble brother—and his friends— would be truly in the gravy for the help they'd given. I don't somehow think he'd mind being Lord Mycroft Holmes of Mayfair, with a Légion d'Honneur medal into the bargain, would he?"

He paused and put down his coffee cup.

"Still, I'm sure you know about this already, sir. Otherwise I should never have dreamt of raising the subject."

I left my breakfast aside but I sat down at the table. It had all come upon me too suddenly and too early in the day.

"Then Prince Napoleon-Jerome is our client." It was a bewildered statement, but it sounded like a question. Lestrade inclined his head and spoke consolingly.

"Only for a bit, doctor. Just from Ostend to Dover. Even if he was to come to the throne now, he wouldn't last long. For one thing, he's too old. And as for his health, it don't bear mentioning. What matters to him is getting his royal backside on the throne for a year or two, if you'll pardon the expression. After that they'd get some young princeling to follow after him. Someone that's every mother's dream and every girl's ambition. He could take his pick."

He chortled again.

"Not like the girl he's been keeping at Lancaster Gate—heard of her, have you? Cora Pearl? The Pearl from Plymouth, as she calls herself. The Pearl from Plymouth? She's named as Emma Crouch in our Special Branch dossier. Cautioned for a bit of naughtiness in the Haymarket with a gentleman of importance a few years ago. Pearl from Plymouth! I'd give the baggage 'Pearl from Plymouth,' if she belonged to me."

How I endured the next half-hour of these whimsies until Sherlock Holmes returned from Bayswater, I shall never know. Nor how I weathered a further half-hour before the inspector condescended to leave us and attend to his "busy" morning.

"Nothing is decided," said Sherlock Holmes reassuringly, as soon as we were alone together. "I raised the matter in a telegram to Brother Mycroft first thing this morning. Something had to be done."

"About the message at the Army and Navy club?"

"Just so. The *Comtesse de Flandre*. The period of new moon touches her steamer timetables on Friday week. I arranged for one of our little friends to slip away early this morning when no one was likely to notice him. I deduce that someone of importance is aimed at in this plot—but who? Our infant Mercury was to find out who had booked the first-class accommodation on the day in question. He informs me that the so-called royal saloon of the *Comtesse de Flandre*, which is in truth merely the first-class saloon on the after-deck, has been engaged for the Prince Napoleon-Jerome and his party."

"To what purpose?"

"Plon Plon, as they call him, is leaving his exile at Prangins in Switzerland by rail and steamer for his London house in Lancaster Gate. From there, he will underwrite the coming election campaign to put General Boulanger in the Elysée Palace and himself in the Tuileries, wearing the crown of France. He is shipping to England a significant election war-chest, which I believe is the term used for the finances of a *coup d'état*."

"What war-chest? Gold? Currency? Precious stones?"

"Not currency, I think. Other considerations apart, it would be too bulky. Also it would have to be in francs; and once this campaign to restore him begins in earnest, the franc will be destabilised. Gold bars to a sufficient value would be cumbersome. Whereas selected precious stones, packed in something no larger than a suitcase, might amount to a king's ransom. To judge from movements on the commodities exchange over the past few weeks, that is where the money has gone. We must remember that in its recent history, the imperial family of France has sometimes had to escape its enemies at a moment's notice. Even this prince once did so with the Queen of the Night in one pocket and a constellation of Mogul diamonds in his dressing case."

I had had enough of this.

"What about the meeting at Lancaster Gate with Mycroft and Boulanger? What are we supposed to do? Are we to guard this trumpery during the channel dash while Moran or some brother villain tries to steal it?"

He looked at me as if I should have known better.

"We shall be responsible for both, my dear fellow. I propose that the war-chest shall act as bait to our enemies. But the most valuable item on the ship will be the person of Plon Plon himself. His supporters, including some in the British government and a good many in Parliament, intend him to be the new Emperor of France before the season is over. One bullet put into him now would alter the course of history. Mycroft assures me that there will already be three armed guards in the mailroom to protect the treasure. That is normal. That mailroom is in the after part of the vessel, behind a locked steel grille. The Ostend steamers are operated by the Belgium government. They are designed and constructed to be secure."

"What about the French?"

"The prince will have with him Baron Brunet, his chief of staff, who carries a useful revolver. There is also His Highness's servant, Theodore Cabell. It will not surprise you to know that Cabell is a marksman and is also a captain in the royal bodyguard. His present name may be something of a *nom de guerre*. The principal danger would be from a sudden ambush carefully laid. Our task is to frustrate any such attempt. All in all, Napoleon-Jerome is thought to be safe enough at close quarters."

"As I recall, Holmes, the Prince Imperial was murdered in circumstances where he was thought to be safe enough."

He sat down, crossed his legs, and lounged.

"The very point I made to Mycroft. However, our government does not intend to lose its distinguished guest on a channel crossing. He is far less protected on a steamer than on an express train. His chief of staff and his bodyguard will sit with him in a locked and guarded first-class saloon until he is safely in Dover. One or two of our Scotland Yard friends will come aboard there. You and I will merely have a roving brief, keeping our wits and our noses alert for any whiff of danger during the voyage."

As international law then stood, Plon Plon would come under the protection of the British crown as soon as the *Comtesse de Flandre* entered British territorial waters. Thanks to Mycroft's discussions at Lancaster Gate that morning, such protection was to be represented solely by Sherlock Holmes, with my assistance, until we reached Dover. If the note waiting for me at my club was indeed a challenge, it was plain that his enemies as well as his friends knew well in advance of the prince's plans. In that case, I drew an uncomfortable conclusion. Either we should discharge our duty to the prince successfully, or we should probably all be dead before the *Comtesse de Flandre* docked at Dover.

9

*F*or the rest of the week, I found it difficult to share Holmes's enthusiasm for a fight to the finish. We might simply be victims of our antagonists' sense of fun. We should board the *Comtesse de Flandre* at Ostend and disembark at Dover eight hours later, just as though no villainy had been intended. We should watch in the darkness and fog without ever setting eyes upon Plon Plon and his little court in their "royal saloon." Perhaps whatever meaning we had read into the cryptic words *"Comtesse de Flandre"* and *"New Moon"* was entirely of our own invention. Only time would tell. Worst than that, we might land in England to hear that some monstrous robbery or homicide had taken place elsewhere; all our careful planning would have merely ensured that we were not there to prevent it.

I lay awake and tried to imagine why even the most inventive gang of criminals would announce to the world that it was about to board such a ship, hold a prince to ransom, overcome armed guards and a steel grille, and then escape in the middle of the sea. They would be fools to try it. Moran, whatever else he might be, had shown he was no fool. They certainly dared not remain on board when the steamer docked in England, for the harbour police would be waiting at Dover, supplemented by waterguard officers and reinforced if necessary by a party of riflemen from the duty regiment at Dover Castle.

It made very little difference to me when Holmes announced that he was going ahead of me as far as Brussels, a seventy-mile journey by rail. He would travel back by train to Ostend and we should meet at the pier an hour before the *Comtesse de Flandre* sailed. My friend's appointment, arranged by courtesy of Brother Mycroft, was with the British military attaché at our Brussels embassy. Though our mission involved a ship belonging to the Belgian government, it had been decided not to involve the authorities in Brussels or Ostend. Mycroft, always a prudent man, therefore insisted on having some diplomatic authority on our side in the event of what he vaguely called "complications."

On the day of our crossing to Ostend, I woke with an unexpected lightness of heart. All this would prove to be a fuss about nothing. If the final accounting came with Colonel Rawdon Moran, as it might well do, it would take some other form. At any rate, it seemed most unlikely to come yet.

As usual, I had packed my belongings and was ready while Holmes was still getting his things together. Despite my scepticism, I did not neglect to include my Webley revolver with its six chambers loaded.

"I suppose Belgian law is the same as ours," I said cheerfully: "one is permitted to carry a firearm for reasonable self-defence."

He shrugged this off: "I hardly think it will come to matters of Belgian law."

He then closed the drawer of his "chemical table," where he usually kept his Laroux pistolet. I had not seen it lying in its usual place and assumed he must already have it with him.

"It does no harm to be prepared," I said gently.

If we were credulous enough to believe what we had been told, we had a good chance in the next few days of encountering one of the most ruthless men we were ever to meet. He appeared to be as intent upon assassinating the pair of us as anyone I had ever heard of. Yet I sensed that Holmes was going into combat unarmed.

The next twelve hours were as uneventful as I hoped the rest of our escort duty would prove to be. The sea journey to Ostend takes the form of a direct fifty-mile crossing from Dover to the Ruytingen lightship, a point roughly parallel with the French coast at Dunkirk. There follows a stretch of some twenty miles eastwards, passing the frontier of France and Belgium. The tidal harbour of Ostend, between two steamer piers, lies just beyond it.

I cannot recommend a voyage to Ostend out of season. The air was bitter with an east wind blowing, for there is no high ground to speak of between here and Siberia. The sky had the colour of lead, and we were surrounded by a constant rising mist from a chilly sea. This vapour blotted out even coastal views of the flat land extending through Belgium and Holland.

It was the middle of the week and there were relatively few other passengers. However, this cross-channel service is maintained every day and night of the year, for these are the mail services of the Belgian and British governments. Our companions included a monsignore, in his uniform dress of cassock and biretta. He might be an assassin in disguise but I thought it more likely that he was a future cardinal. A party of schoolgirls travelled with two stout middle-aged chaperones. Hardly the stuff of which murderers are made.

The time during which I was on my own in Ostend, while Holmes went to make diplomatic arrangements in Brussels, did not show the resort at its most appealing. To be sure, it has become fashionable enough in the summer season with its raised promenade along the Digue, its Assembly Rooms, grand hotels, even a villa for the visits of King Leopold and the royal family.

Out of season, the bathing machines stood abandoned on the sands where a forlorn seashore is divided by wooden groins into separate beaches for men and women.

The docks consist of a tidal harbour with a steamer pier running out into deeper water at either side. A railway line extends along the eastern jetty and the Brussels train pulls in not more than twenty yards from the gangways of the channel steamers. Two ancient ironclad warships stood guard offshore, square gunports along their sides, a pair of squat funnels between their tall masts. A large-rigged sloop and an old bomb-ketch lay rotting on the mud of the shallows. Two other ferries had tied up already and were taking on stores.

I had nothing to do but await the return of Sherlock Holmes. I did this in my own room or else in the dining-room and lounge of the Hotel de la Plage. The service had been recommended to me as preferable to the Hotel de l'Océan, the only other first-class establishment on the shore.

Any reader of *The Times* will have noticed the number of letters complaining about the dismal unpunctuality of the ferry service between Ostend and Dover. To be fair, it is not the fault of the steamers but of the Belgian railway system. Frustrated correspondents complain of the consequences. Business mail is delayed, post is not delivered. Brokers in the City of London deal one or even two days late with transactions which in Paris or Frankfurt would have been punctually completed. Money is lost, and that is always a great thing.

It was something of a relief on the following day to see, through the mist, the shape of the *Comtesse de Flandre* moored at the eastern harbour pier, where the trains come in. She had probably sailed light from Antwerp, after coaling, and would remain alongside empty until sailing-time. Mycroft Holmes assured us that she would have been searched and inspected from stem to stern before even a single member of the crew was allowed back on board. To make assurance doubly sure, a pair of uniformed

Belgian policemen kept their watch by the ship's gangways, which was a customary precaution for international sailings.

As it happened, the two gangways were not yet in place, having been hoisted side by side on to the paddle-box amidships to prevent strangers coming and going while the ship was docked. Some of her crew had taken advantage of their afternoon shore leave, sauntering down the pier for the seaman's privilege of a few hours in the bars and cafés of the old town. No doubt the captain and the first mate would be the first allowed aboard to supervise the stokers, who must lay the fires and raise steam before she sailed.

As I surveyed her from the window of the hotel dining room, through the vaporous light, the steamer was smaller and lower in the water than the vessel which had brought us over the day before. She was, as I later had reason to know, about five hundred tons, a little over two hundred feet long, and at least thirty feet broad amidships. With the deck extending over the paddle-boxes on either side, the "waist" amidships on these ships is wider than those more recent ferries driven by propellers. There were two funnels, yellow with black "admiralty" tops to trap cinders. The first-class deck saloon stood aft of these and the captain's navigating-bridge forward. I thought that in the present calm sea, she would do well enough for the sixty or seventy miles of this channel crossing.

I still could not believe that this was the ship or the place for some great adventure. If I had any concern at all, it was for the state of some of the crew after their visit to the old streets of Ostend. No one had so far returned to the ship and, though I had seen my portmanteau with other cases being wheeled from the hotel to the jetty by a porter, the gangways remained drawn up. The brown-and-cream vans of the Messageries Impériales had already arrived, and the chests for the mail-ship's strong-room had been unloaded under the eyes of the three guards with guns in their belts who would accompany them.

Plon Plon's war-chest must be weighed before being loaded, and again at Dover Harbour, to ensure that the weights were identical. In this way, the ferry company was absolved from blame if things went wrong at some other point of the journey. Now was the time I would have chosen to stage a robbery. The baggage was in the open air, not locked behind a steel grille. The robbers had the whole of Belgium to escape into, rather than being trapped on a ship in the middle of the English Channel. But nothing happened. There were, after all, six or eight guardians of the law with pistols or revolvers to hand. Surely we had hoaxed ourselves into believing that some master-stroke of villainy was in prospect?

I was thinking I might as well sit it out until tea-time, when a liveried post-boy appeared at my table and saluted me.

"Doctor Vastson?"

I looked up and he handed me an envelope. Though it was of a different colour to the English kind, I had no doubt that this contained a telegram. Who but Holmes knew that I was here? I slit it open and drew out a flimsy paper with a longer message than I had expected.

JNQFSBUJWFUIBUJSFNBJOJOCSVTTFMTTUPQQQSFTFOU
TDFOFPGFWFOUJTIFSFTTUUPQPVSDMJFOUJOGPSNFE
ZPVXJMMCFUIFJSFTDPSTUUPPZPVSEVUJFTOPNJOB
MTUPQMFTUUSBEFPSHSFHFHTPOBUEPPWFSTUUPPQ
BDLOPXMFEHFNFNTOPUSFRVJSDFTUUPQIPMNFT

What on earth was this? A cipher from Holmes, of course, though nothing in it identified him. And where from? Brussels, presumably. But what about? Any telegram was obviously urgent. I stared at the jumble of letters in growing panic. There was not a single name hidden here, not a single word that meant anything. I had no idea where to begin!

Worse still, the use of a cipher presumably meant that our enemies were on to us after all. They had penetrated our defences so expertly that we could no longer communicate in plain English nor trust the officials of the Belgian telegraph service. This revelation brought me up short. Had Holmes sent me these few lines of mere gibberish as a warning of all this? But I must assume that the nonsense before me could be decoded. I glared at it, wondering what the cipher might be and where I should begin.

At the end of twenty minutes, I was shaking with mental exhaustion and apprehension. Despite the raw cold of the day outside, I was also perspiring a little from the concentrated anxiety. To start with, I had guessed that the last six letters would be his name, as they would be on any telegram. So IPMNFT probably equalled HOLMES. But these letters made no sense anywhere else in the message.

Very well. The sequence TUPQ appeared six times in five lines, at more or less regular intervals. I felt a flood of relief in the knowledge that a letter of the code would always have the same equivalent in the alphabet. Thank God! From now on it might be straightforward. If the encoding of every single letter had varied, I might try from now till Christmas without deciphering a word of this. The sequence TUPQ also appeared immediately before what I took to be the sender's name. In a telegram, this was invariably the punctuation STOP. At last I was getting somewhere and, surely, Holmes would not use a cipher that I had not a hope of breaking. Very well. I caught my breath and worked with a pencil on the back of a menu card until I began to get the better of this rampart of a hundred and ninety-two coded letters.

The letter F appeared twenty-five times. Other things being equal, that must be E, the most commonly used letter in English prose. Then J appeared twelve times, ahead of B at seven. I guessed that J was most likely to stand for I, made more frequent by its use as the personal pronoun. B was very probably A. With that last conclusion the system fell into place. I had soon divided the lines into words.

JNQFSBUJWF UIBU J SFNBJO JO CSVTTFMT TUPQ QSFTFOU
TDFOF PG FWFOUT JT IFSF TUPQ PVS DMJFOUT JOGPSNFE
ZPV XJMM CF UIFJS FTDPSU TUPQ ZPVS EVUJFT OPNJOBM
TUPQ MFTUSBEF PS HSFHTPO BU EPWFS TUPQ
BDLOPXMFEHFNFOU OPU SFRVJSDF TUPQ IPMNFT

He had simply replaced each letter with the one following
it in the alphabet. It was childishly simple now but not in
a moment of dismay when faced by an alphabetic rampart,
infinite possibilities, and very little time to spare! Of course
I had supposed from the start that he was not likely to send
me a message I could not unravel—but that start had been a
moment of panic. And if I could decode it, why was it that our
enemies could not?

I completed the transposition of the letters.

IMPERATIVE THAT I REMAIN IN BRUSSELS STOP PRESENT SCENE
OF EVENTS IS HERE STOP OUR CLIENTS INFORMED YOU WILL BE
THEIR ESCORT STOP YOUR DUTIES NOMINAL STOP LESTRADE OR
GREGSON AT DOVER STOP ACKNOWLEDGEMENT NOT REQUIRED
STOP HOLMES

And that was all. I had been right. Whatever might be going
on in Brussels, this was to be a channel crossing as uneventful
as any other in the ship's itinerary. All the same, I swore that I
was going to be the first passenger aboard the *Comtesse de Flandre*
and not a face that followed me should escape my scrutiny. Not
even if it were Holmes in disguise!

As a rule, passengers were permitted to board an hour before
sailing time. I reached the gangways as they were being lowered
into place, side by side, and made fast. I was dressed in my warm
Harris tweed coat and my hat and carrying my black malacca
cane, ready for the worst that the voyage could bring. My revolver
was in the pocket of the coat, but much use did it seem to be

now. Before I and a few others could get closer, the purser was at the gangway and his message was clear.

"Stokers' party and crew only just now. Thank you."

We waited until they were aboard—and still we waited. Then the reason for this became apparent. It was the arrival of a four-wheeler drawn by a pair of white horses. Several men got down, one of them a stout figure in a frock coat with a glimpse of astrakhan collar and silk cravat. He was holding a top hat as if to save the trouble of taking it off to acknowledge the crowd. This was my first sight of Prince Napoleon-Jerome, Plon Plon. The lamp-light caught a heavy face with mouth turned down and eyes mournful. His head was bald at the top and the dark hair grizzled. Yet the profile was strong and impressive. Here and there people clapped, but for the most part the onlookers were quiet. Most of them probably did not recognise the claimant to the French throne. Waiting passengers stood back for him to pass with three soberly dressed civilians and two officers in dark blue uniforms and gold insignia.

After an interval to allow the royal party to settle itself in the first-class deck saloon, the purser stood back and I was, indeed, the first of the other passengers aboard. I had decided that the best vantage point would be at the steamer's rail just forward of the paddle-box. From there I could see every face that came up the gangways, until each arrival stepped on to the deck a few feet away from me. I could even watch them as they waited on the harbour pier for their turn to come aboard. Perhaps because this was a Friday sailing, there were far more than had come across from Dover, but the second-class travellers would be confined to the forward part of the ship.

I truly had expected that Holmes might slip aboard in disguise; but none of these, whom I saw at very close range, resembled him in the least. I do not underrate my friend's capacity for concealing his identity. Yet there is one thing that cannot be disguised, short of bandages or dark glasses, and that is the eyes.

Not for nothing had I been a physician searching the gaze of my patients for hope, fear, or resignation. I looked at close range into the faces of those hundred or so who came aboard. I would swear on my life that none of them was Holmes nor, indeed, Colonel Rawdon Moran. His telegram seemed to have told the truth. The scene of events would be in Brussels.

As the light dwindled, the rising mist became a fog that closed upon us with the chill of a hoar frost. The ritual of departure began and with it came a fond memory of my childhood. It was low tide and the steamer had come in bows-first. To go astern in shallow water, against low tide and poor visibility, is unwise. Yet there was often no room for a ship to turn herself round in a small harbour where other vessels were moored. The answer is simple. A man in a rowing boat comes out, carries the loop of a heavy mooring rope from the winch in the stern of the ship to a bollard on the far quay. The winch is then used to wind the rope in and pull the stern round until the bows of the steamer face the tide. The loop from the bollard splashes into the sea, and the length of the mooring rope is wound in at the stern. How often had I seen the ferries perform this manoeuvre in the west coast harbours of my Scottish boyhood!

The oarsman in his little shell rowed out from the mole, collected the rope, rowed back, and looped it over the bollard. There was a clanking and a gust of steam from our stern as the heavy rope rose taut and dripping from the water. Our stern swung slowly round until the bows faced the sea. The loop was cast off by the oarsman standing at the end of the harbour jetty. The bridge telegraph above me rang "Half Ahead."

We faced the dark with several hours and sixty or seventy miles of fog-bound sea in a flat calm ahead of us. We should round the Ruytingen lightship off Dunkirk, then turn north for Dover. British travellers "going foreign," as the saying is, would have taken the shorter crossing to Dover from Calais. Unfortunately, our royal protégé, like all other claimants to the throne of France, had been permanently exiled by the laws of the Third Republic and was not to set foot on French soil.

The weather promised to be thick, but not so dense that the sailing had to be cancelled. As we eased past the end of Ostend's western pier, the bridge telegraph rang "Full Ahead" to the engine room and the two paddles picked up speed. Their wake frothed down either side of the ship as we slid into the seaway, past a tier of colliers and coasters. Presently we were steaming at about twelve knots, parallel with the flat winter sands. Behind a line of muddy surf, only a chain of lights from houses on the esplanade marked the shoreline that was fast receding into the gloom.

While I was leaning on the rail, watching our departure, the first mate had come to the foremast and hoisted a white oil-light almost twenty feet above the deck. He then turned, gave an order, and a second man standing behind him handed a box of lucifers to the ship's boy. The lad struck one of these and lit the green navigation light whose lantern was fixed to the forward edge of the starboard paddle-box. The seaman took the box back and went to attend to the red light on the port side.

On such Channel crossings in poor weather, I much prefer to "stick it out on deck," smoking a pipe, rather than go down to the miasma of the refreshment saloon. The vibration of the ship's reciprocating engines under my feet and the beat of the paddles on either side of the hull was comforting, even on such a journey as this. We passed very little shipping. From time to time I could just make out the drifting ghost of a fishing smack or a lugger, its ochre-coloured sails catching the faint breeze as it made its way out from Ostend or Dunkirk to the fishing grounds of the North Sea.

After twenty minutes of standing amidships, I had lost the lights of the shoreline. The sea-mist closed in until it condensed into a silent fog whose droplets hung on my hat-brim and lapels. They call it mist, rather than fog, but it was so thick that from the bows of the *Comtesse de Flandre* I could no longer see the red, yellow, and black of the Belgian flag at the stern. Indeed, I could hardly make out the two life-boats on board, hanging aft in their hoists, conveniently close for first-class passengers. The first-class saloon, at present the "royal saloon," was enclosed by a little metal gate across either side of the deck indicating to second-class passengers that they had reached the limit of their permitted territory.

I heard a voice behind me.

"Doctor Vastson, is it not?"

For a moment I expected to turn and see the liveried waiter from the Hotel de la Plage, but this was the younger of the two French military figures in their dark blue uniforms who had accompanied the Prince Napoleon-Jerome aboard.

"Lieutenant Theodore Cabell," he said reassuringly with a slight click of the heels and a respectful inclination of his head towards me.

It was an unexpected time and place for such formalities, but we shook hands. Lieutenant Cabell was a slightly built and flaxen-haired young man, more German than French in appearance. I thought he was the last person to be taken for an intelligence agent—or, indeed, a royal valet. He indicated the little gate to the first-class promenade, which now stood open.

"Come, please, sir. His Highness wishes it."

I should have been happier keeping watch according to my own rules, but I could hardly ignore a claimant to the throne of France.

Theodore Cabell repeated his invitation.

"You come this way, please. It is all right. His Highness merely wishes to receive you."

The very thing I had been hoping to avoid was to be held answerable for the measures we had taken to protect Plon Plon and his possessions. I hardly knew what the measures were, in the absence of Holmes himself.

Lieutenant Cabell slid back the outer door at one side of the first-class saloon and stood aside for me to enter. He followed and pronounced my name in his own way. At the far end of the casually furnished saloon, a bowed figure in formal frock coat and silk cravat looked up from his easy chair. I might easily have mistaken him for the manager of an important branch of one of our London banks. To one side stood a man in the uniform of the French general staff. Next to him was a middle-aged and formally dressed civilian, who I assumed to be General Georges Boulanger. These made up the "royal" party, so far as I could see.

"Doctor Vastson," the prince spoke as if in imitation of Cabell, holding out his hand but remaining seated, as befitted his rank.

I took the hand and inclined my head over it. It was a suitable compromise in acknowledging a man who did not yet wear the crown of France but might very well do so before the summer was out.

"Tell me," he went on in his casual and slightly accented English: "I am a small bit puzzled. There was to be Mr. Sharelock Holmes. He was recommended to me by his brother, Sir Mycroft. Now there is you but, I think, no Mr. Holmes?"

"My colleague has run to earth those who were suspected of trying to board this steamer. They are safely detained in Brussels and no danger to us. I have myself examined every passenger who embarked at Ostend. Now there is no port of call until Dover. Inspector Lestrade or Inspector Gregson of Scotland Yard will be waiting for us there with an escort. Mr. Holmes has arranged all that."

I hoped I was right.

"Run to earth?" Napoleon-Jerome, whom I continued to think of as Plon Plon, balanced the phrase delicately upon his tongue. "I much like that. Run to earth. I am pleased to hear it."

Theodore Cabell looked at me with a deferential smile.

"Very pleased," he said warmly.

Plon Plon looked up at him.

"Oh? Oh, quite so. Very pleased. I am very pleased. Since there is no Mr. Holmes, perhaps you would do a small thing for me, sir. I should like you to go downstairs for a bit. See that no one has opened the gate to the mailroom where my box is deposited."

I wondered why Lieutenant Cabell could not go down and take a look. Presumably his instructions were never to leave the prince unprotected.

"Of course, sir."

"You were brave in Afghanistan, monsieur. Sir Mycroft says so to me. A good deal brave."

"I hardly think that, sir. I was present when the battle took place at Maiwand. Not as a fighting man."

"But as a soldier!" He smiled as if at the comicality of my reply. "You must tell me everything about it soon. I should like that a great deal. I shall look forward to it."

He shifted himself in his chair, looking aside slightly at the man I took to be General Boulanger. Lieutenant Cabell touched my arm and bowed before his prince, rather as if at the altar of a church. Plon Plon did not look at me again as I lowered my head briefly and respectfully. Then I withdrew in company with my escort. I knew, of course, that the prince and I would never discuss Afghanistan nor anything else.

I went down the steps of the companionway to the lower deck. It seemed most unlikely that any of the guards would open the mailroom door to me in the middle of the voyage, let alone would they permit me to inspect the so-called war-chest. In that case, I should allow myself a glass of Highland malt in the ship's bar.

Below-decks, a ship of this kind, with its engine-room on view from the passageways down either side, is a wonderland of mechanical devices. Amid the smell of warm oil and the glow of copper piping, two massive steel pistons drove the heavy shaft that connects the weighty paddle-wheels at port and starboard.

Rising and falling, the two so-called diagonal cylinders with three hundred horsepower of steam behind them surged and retreated, rose and fell alternately, like captive beasts. No mere propeller could rival this display of mechanical might which had long ago conquered the ocean steamer routes to New York and Bombay.

Further aft, the port and starboard passageways came together at the glass doors of the dining-saloon. To one side was a steel grille or gate. Behind it were the "high-value" parcels and boxes, as well as the wicker baskets of registered post, bound for England from the Continent. The vertical steel bars of the gate were about six inches apart but connected by a redoubtable cross-piece and lock half-way down. This mailroom was a self-contained steel compartment in the stern of the ship. The three armed guardians of the Messageries Impériales were somewhere out of sight behind their partition.

Whether the prince's strong-box was secure, I could not yet see. A long curtain hung immediately inside the grille, cutting off most of the view. There was a small hatchway to one side, the barred guichet of the bureau de change. It seemed that its clerk had access only through the mailroom. But even that cubby hole was closed on this occasion and hung with a brusque notice—*Pas de service jusqu'au Douvres.*—closure until Dover.

There was no one in sight to answer inquiries. At one side, however, the curtain left a narrow gap. By taking a slant view, I could see most of the interior. Canvas bags of mail were ranged down one side. I made out a number of trunks, almost cabin-size, and a dozen or so wicker baskets which no doubt carried insured letters and small registered packets. Among the commercial consignments, there were a dozen or so wooden courier-boxes, reinforced by steel corner-pieces and lock-plates.

That was all, except for what at first I thought must be a coffin or casket carrying home the body of an unlucky Englishman abroad. The quality of the polished wood was infinitely superior to anything else in the room, probably made of oak. The other boxes had merely the agent's or banker's name painted in black on the lid. From this one, I swear I caught a glint of gold leaf. If that was not Plon Plon's "war-chest," I was mightily mistaken.

There was no means of calling attention. This was as far as I should get—or wished to get. I would go back, explain the situation, and suggest that Lieutenant Cabell should come down with me. He, at least, could try to make a formal request. I had nothing but my steamer ticket, no credentials whatever. No one would unlock that steel grille just to please me.

As I passed the dials of the engine-room again, the pistons had settled to a crossing speed of thirty-three revolutions per minute, still driving us "Full Ahead." The gleaming brass of the overhead telegraph dial, connecting the engine-room with the navigating-bridge, confirmed this. The engineers saw nothing of the outside world while on duty. A link that appeared like a bicycle chain connected the handle of the telegraph on the bridge with the hand on the repeater dial of the engine-room as the captain's orders jangled down here. The engineers themselves had now found their perches, one with a pipe, another with a newspaper, glancing up at the dials from time to time as if the ship would drive herself.

I put my hand on the steel wall to one side of this open view and snatched it off again. The heat would almost raise a blister. This was the partition of the passageway from the stokehold and the boilers. The crack of a metal door between the stokers and the engineers reflected an intermittent yellow flame-light.

Just then, the donkey-man was attending to the machinery with his oil-can and wad of cotton waste. The second engineer was reading his paper by the reversing gear, as they call it. The door of the stokehold opened. A man like a tall hobgoblin was standing in the alleyway that leads to the furnace. The engineer turned and shouted at him. I knew enough French to understand "Allez-vous en!" as the soot-faced scallywag was ordered back to his work. He was a tall rather bent fellow in vest and overalls, with a cap worn back to front. Truly he looked like something from the underworld. Soot covered his face until nothing was visible but the pink of his lips and the whites of his eyes. Very likely he had come aboard more than a little drunk. The engineer swore at him again and scouted him back to his duties, just at the moment all the stokers were needed to shovel up coal from the bunkers and toss it into the furnaces. I guessed that this malingering lout might be dismissed next day.

For a moment the man continued to defy the engineer, as if for the pure fun of the thing. It seemed he was demanding a "proper" drink, not the enamel jugs of water provided in the stokehold. He had presumably shovelled several hundredweights of coal into the furnaces since Ostend. But he was wasting his words. At length, having made his point, he shambled back down the narrow passage to the boilers, where reflected flames flickered on the white-painted iron. I thought after all that if I was con-demned to work in such conditions—and for such wages—I might well take to the bottle.

I was so far away in my thoughts that I almost jumped like a cat at a sudden voice behind me.

"Dr. Vastson?"

I turned and found myself staring into the spectacled face of the man who had rowed his boat from Ostend harbour pier to collect our heavy mooring rope. He had carried it back to the jetty, looped it over a bollard, and waved us farewell as the winch in the stern of the steamer turned our bows seawards and the rope was cast off again. He still wore his greasy cap, bulky donkey jacket, and moleskin trousers with worn-out knees. But I had watched him wave us off from the harbour pier, across a hundred yards of open sea, as we steamed away. He could never row after us at the speed of the ship's engines! How was he here? The face with its eyes vastly magnified by his lenses was one I did not know—or so it seemed, until a slight change in his glance and the removal of the spectacles betrayed him by his smile as Sherlock Holmes!

He turned his head away.

"Listen carefully, Watson, and do not appear to notice me."

Fortunately, we were leaning on the safety rail where the vibration of the engines made our words inaudible more than a few inches distant. I turned aside to survey the pistons.

"I watched every passenger up the gangway, Holmes. I swear you were not among them. The man who carried that rope back is still in Ostend."

"Indeed he is," Holmes said impatiently: "Sergeant Albert Gibbons of the Royal Marines is still in Ostend. It was I who rowed that cockleshell out to the ship to fetch the rope. I took it. While all eyes were on preparations for the ship's departure, I let my shell drift from the stern well-deck back to the platform of the paddle sponson at this level. A crewman climbed out to coil a sponson rope. A crewman climbed back. Not a glance came our way. It was Gibbons who rowed back with the mooring rope. Who notices the face of a dockyard scully? It was the easiest thing in the world, while the men at the winch gave that machine their full attention."

"And then what?"

He shrugged and smiled again.

"In weather as thick as this, a man could become invisible in a dozen places on deck."

"And the telegram? The code? What went wrong in Brussels?"

"I am happy to say, my dear fellow, that nothing went wrong. My coded message to you was betrayed in Brussels by a post office clerk for £100, just as we have been betrayed in London. That was essential. I would gladly have paid him myself to cheat us, though I fear the poor wretch may soon be lying somewhere with his throat cut after he has served his purpose. I have counted upon Moran or his underlings reading that telegram and deciphering it."

Then he sighed.

"I trusted your powers of perception, Watson. Why was my cipher made so simple? A schoolboy game! A babe in arms could transpose each letter with the next one in the alphabet and decode the meaning. Did you believe I could do no better than that, if I had wanted it to remain secret? You cannot have believed that what it said was true? Oh, Watson, Watson! I tell you again, you see but you do not perceive. Please listen to me."

I listened.

Holmes said, "I cannot find that Moran or anyone connected with him is on this ship. But there is an impostor."

"Who?"

"Why do you think I am standing here? You have just seen him!"

"The insubordinate stoker?"

"That man is no stoker!"

"He came from the stoke-hold."

"How long have we been at sea?"

"Almost an hour."

"Correct. That man's face was so covered in coal dust that only the eyes and the mouth were visible. After an hour of shovelling coal in intense heat, did you see a single trace of perspiration running down his cheeks? for I did not! A ship of this capacity requires two furnaces to raise sufficient steam for its two boilers—fore and aft. Each furnace requires at least quarter of a ton to travel the distance from here to Ostend. Does he look like a man who has worked in that heat, at that pace, for an hour?"

"No," I said reluctantly.

"Nor does he to me. He looks to me like a man who has applied soot to his face as an actor applies make-up, in this case to disguise himself beyond possible recognition. For the moment, however, his attempt to escape the stokehold has been frustrated. I shall watch him."

"But there are stokers already. He cannot stand idle in front of the furnaces."

"Of course not. Stoking is an art which he does not possess. I believe he is posing in front of them as what they call a trimmer, a menial who merely shifts coal from the store to the bunker and whose face does not get covered in coal dust like that. He has used it as stage make-up."

"Then who is he?"

"Let us be content that he is probably an impostor with the speech and manner of a dockland drunkard. Now if you will forgive me, I must leave you and attend to the safe-keeping of Plon Plon and his baubles."

"I should have thought he and they are safe enough from here to Dover."

"Would you? Then you have clearly overlooked the promises of 'Hunter' Moran. I assure you he has never yet failed to keep them. To lose that reputation might quite literally be the death of him."

10

I had my marching orders and went to resume watch on deck. Holmes would conceal himself below with a view of the mailroom grille and any reappearance of the drunken "stoker." In the absence of Moran, there was little else to do. My feelings were the dejection of one who knows he has been hoodwinked and wonders where the true robbery may be taking place. I went back up the companionway to the ship's rail just forward of the starboard paddle-box with its green riding-light. If Prince Napoleon-Jerome should need me, he would know where I was. Just above me, Captain Legrand of the *Comtesse de Flandre* faced all winds and weathers on his open navigating-bridge, which ran the width of the ship above the forward saloon deck. At intervals, I heard him ring down to the engine-room as he moved the brass handle of the telegraph to and fro.

Behind the bridge and below it, the helmsman stood on his platform, wrapped in the long jacket and hood of his sou'wester. Most of the ship's crew took this duty in their turn, for it was only a matter of turning the wheel according to whatever point of the compass was chosen by the skipper. With the ship's wheel between his hands, his head at the level of the captain's feet, a helmsman steers according to simple spoken orders. The commands may be given directly by the captain, or shouted down by a callboy on the bridge if the wind is high. For good measure, there is a repeater telegraph ahead of the wheel, on whose dial the helmsman can read the orders from the bridge telegraph to the engine-room. While it is true that he may see little of what is ahead of him, the duty of the man at the helm is only to do as he is told, according to compass bearings.

There may sometimes be a look-out in the bows who will "sing out" a warning of any minor obstruction in the water or small boat in the steamer's path. All crew members will give warnings when they think necessary, but they assume that the captain on his bridge can see larger vessels before they do.

For some reason not yet apparent, the bridge telegraph rang. We dropped to "Half Speed" ahead, and the steamer rolled a little as she lost way. The foremast hand walked past me, he who had given the boy a lucifer match to light the starboard navigation-lamp on the paddle-box. Like most of the hands, this fellow might be called on to relieve the helmsman or assist the ship to make fast at a pier head and attend the gangways. Just now, he was strolling towards the bows as if to take up watch, lighting his pipe as he went.

A few minutes later, we had our first encounter since leaving Ostend. A throbbing marked the approaching propeller of a screw-driven ship, not the beat of a paddle-steamer's wheels. The bridge telegraph rang "Slow Ahead." "Starboard helm!" was called back to the helmsman. At a snail's pace we passed our visitor about a hundred yards to port, her red riding-light just visible. I recalled the well-known verses of the Seaman's Litany, Thomas Gray's lesson in navigation. I had learnt it with every schoolboy in a Scottish fishing town:

> *Green to Green or Red to Red—*
> *In perfect safety—Go ahead!*

Only the dimmest outline of the other ship was visible, but the glimmer of her port riding-light continued to face ours through the murk. As we passed her, the captain of the *Comtesse de Flandre* reached up, pulled the whistle lanyard, and sent a comradely blast of sound and steam echoing across the lonely water.

There is nowhere so desolate as the sea on such a crossing. The stillness is eerie. A steamer's siren, a shout, even a gunshot, echoes back as if this place were the empty end of the world, far from home, far from help. The bridge telegraph rang again, and the *Comtesse* picked up speed with a rush of water from the blades of her paddle-wheels and the rising beat of steel on waves.

I wondered what Holmes was doing—or even what there was for him to do. I saw only a few more wraiths of fishing smacks and luggers on their way to cast their nets. Sometimes I thought I saw the same vessel on several occasions, but it was impossible to be certain. From time to time, our siren wailed across the quiet water and several calls were answered from different quarters of the opaque stillness. Often it was just a friendly shout from a lugger, fishing the shallows of the sands off Dunkirk. We kept strictly to our compass bearing. It is easy enough for a ship to go aground on these sandbanks and break her back.

I stood amidships, looking out across the paddle-box on which the passenger gangways had been stowed for use at Dover. My eye caught a glimmering of light on the sluggish grey tide through which our dusty red paddle blades were cleaving their way. Then there was a white gleam in the fog, higher than a ship's foremast. It grew to a distant blaze and fell away again. It must be the swivelled gleam of the Ruytingen lightship, nearer than I expected, searching forlornly for the horizon.

Though we were still on the Belgian side, the *Comtesse de Flandre* now pulled hard to port, as if to set a dead straight course for Dover. I was quite alone just then, except for the foremast hand, who had come back from his look-out and was trimming the wick of the red port riding-light behind me.

The man had scarcely disappeared down the forward hatchway of the crew's quarters when a commotion began. It is hard to imagine the tedium of such a crossing. Even the sight of the Ruytingen lightship had been an event worth celebrating. A dozen or so of the passengers had gone up to the prow, hoping for a view of it. I had just taken out my watch and read the time by one of the oil-lights on a tall standard when there was a shout from the watchers in the bows.

"Steamer ahead!"

I looked out across the paddle-box again. In the distance, a single green light appeared fleetingly on our starboard bow, vanished, then reappeared. It must be some distance away. I could certainly not make out the vessel or navigation buoy that might be carrying it. The channel through the sand-banks must have been buoyed. Perhaps the green light was merely assuring us that we were following the dredged channel. It was hard to tell in such a fog. Once again, however, the telegraph on the *Comtesse de Flandre*'s navigation-bridge rang its cautious command of "Slow Ahead," and we eased forward. There was no cause for alarm. If a ship was crossing our bow at that distance, it would be out of our path long before we reached its present position.

The mid-Channel vapour had closed in so completely by now that it would have been hard to know, except by one's watch, whether it was day or night. Our helm had been put hard a-starboard briefly to counteract the effects of the tide on our starboard bow as we rounded the Ruytingen lightship. Perhaps we were momentarily carried off course. Except for the captain at his compass, it might be impossible in these conditions for anyone to tell whether we were heading north, south, east, or west. It must be north, if we were crossing direct to Dover.

At that moment a sudden shout went up from the people in the bows. It was a cry, directed at the captain of some other vessel.

"Hoy! Hoy! Where are you coming to?"

I stepped aside for a view of what was going on. I could see less from where I was standing than those in the bows might. Yet the sea was so calm and the silence so deep that any captain on another ship in the vicinity must surely have heard that shout. But the green navigation light on that other vessel had gone and what I could see now, off our starboard bow, was red. I was reassured to see that it seemed to be going no faster than half speed, seven or eight knots. Perhaps it was only a warning light that we were passing on one of the sand-bank buoys. From its position, I supposed that any skipper crossing our bow did so in order to pass down our port side. That would be safe enough.

> Green to Green or Red to Red—
> In perfect safety—Go ahead!

But was he not going to cross our bow too close? I believe it was the shout of "Where are you coming to?" that had alerted our own captain. Immediately above me, I could hear him calling down to the helmsman on the platform just behind him.

"Hard a-port!"

The figure in the sou'wester held the wheel between his hands and obeyed. Then the captain reached for the lanyard. The steam whistle on our funnel blew a deep-throated blast. It was answered by three other ships, intermittently from various points of the compass, no doubt including the vessel ahead of us. This channel through the sand-banks now contained far more shipping than I had realised.

"Hold your helm!" The captain's order to the man below him was given with some uneasiness.

The helmsman's back and shoulders moved as he turned the wheel to its maximum but it was not enough.

"Hold on to your helm!"

I still assumed that it was a matter of the tide having carried us a little further off course than he had expected as we rounded the lightship.

"Hard over with it!"

The seaman remained on his starboard helm. Despite this, if the tide had carried us off course, we ought still to be showing our port light to the other vessel.

The bridge telegraph rang "Stand By." To stop the engines completely at this point would have left us helpless to manoeuvre against the tide. Again the whistle of the *Comtesse de Flandre* blew long and hard, a hoarse shriek this time and a blast of steam just above my head. As the note fell away across that quiet sea, the captain cupped his hands and yelled with all the power of his lungs at the oncoming skipper.

"Ease her! Stop her! Good God, man, where the devil are you coming to?"

A cloudy phantom materialised ahead of us, towering above the horizon, but at last turning away—or so it seemed. The warning shouted from our bridge must have carried across the silent stretch of water. But she could see no more of us than we could see of her. Then, by the oncoming beat of her paddles, I guessed she could not be more than a few hundred yards away, her outline still clouded. I held my breath as I suddenly saw all three of her navigation lights coming into view. Now it seemed as if she was travelling at the speed of an express train: white at the masthead, green to her starboard and red to port. Was she turning again because she had seen that there was no longer room to cross our bow? In a tight curve she was surely coming down our starboard side, very close and far too fast.

> When all three lights I see ahead,
> I Port my helm and show my Red.

But the next thing I heard from the bridge was the voice of the first mate.

"My God, captain! Look! That man is starboarding his helm! Port! Hard a-port! Stop her! Reverse the engines! Astern! Full speed!"

The captain had already reached these conclusions for himself. I saw him hurry to the starboard side of the bridge and grasp the telegraph handle. It jangled "Stop" followed by "Full Astern." I distinctly saw the position of the handle, and also "Full Astern" on the helmsman's repeater dial. I heard the verbal order. I heard the repeater ring below, the sound carried up through the engine-room ventilation hatch. I heard it ring twice more with orders to the engineers below.

I could hardly believe that the captain of the oncoming vessel was not mad or drunk or, perhaps, had handed the bridge over to some inexperienced junior officer. He was turning to starboard again, as if to cross our bow once more. The very thing that would bring catastrophe. At such an angle as this, his own bow would be coming at us amidships in a moment more. Even in the fog, he must see our three lights when we could so plainly see his. Why had he not held a simple course dead ahead to pass us safely? His red port riding-light was now on our green starboard quarter!

If to my Starboard Red appear,
It is my duty to keep clear. . . .

But that was too late. I saw what I could still hardly understand, as that ghostly giant rose through the mist, almost on top of our bows. Then I knew the worst and how it had happened. Coming down upon us was one of the newer and heavier railway steamers. From the low deck of our smaller ship, she seemed the height of a house. The red and green of her riding-lights, the white of her masthead light were glaring above. The starboard green wheeled away as she turned more directly towards us. I knew the answer! It was the height of her bows that hid us from her navigation bridge! A vessel that was so much lower might now be concealed from her captain's view. Her starboard light had disappeared; even the light on her foremast was hidden by those tall bows. Only her red port lantern glared ever closer.

The helmsman beside me had wrenched the wheel hard to port, in obedience to his orders. He must have known that it would never save us at so short a distance. At the best, it might make the angle of collision more oblique. The oncoming bow rode towards our starboard side. I never felt more helpless in my life. Holmes and I were playing a game of life and death with Rawdon Moran. Could this be some wild sport contrived by him? But what? Even he could scarcely bring two ships into collision as if they were no more than children's yachts on a pond in Kensington Gardens.

It was not a whistle but a howling siren call that hooted from the forward funnel of the oncoming ship, far too late. The whistle of the *Comtesse de Flandre* pierced the fog again. This time it rang on and on, in a crescendo of steam from its casing on the forward funnel, for all the world as if the lanyard cord were stuck. Our engines had stopped at the telegraph's command and we wallowed, helpless to move and avoid a collision. Then the paddles were just beginning their tantalisingly slow reversal without time to go full astern. The ship lay almost motionless, awaiting her fate.

Screams burst from the people gathered in the bows at what they saw coming upon them. There was turmoil on the deck. Passengers began to run for the stern, knocking open the low gate that enclosed the first-class promenade. They would not be safe anywhere on board, but they could not imagine what else to do in the last few dreadful seconds except to get away from the point of impact. I remember thinking that so long as the oncoming bow hit our paddle-box, our steel paddle blades might take the full force of it, and the wound to our ship would not be mortal.

Captain Legrand shouted down to the helmsman: "Let go of that wheel and look after yourself."

The helm was useless now in any case. Much good would the ship's wheel or rudder be in this predicament! But when I looked again, I saw that the helmsman had already taken flight without waiting to be warned.

And then the bows of the vessel above us drove into our paddle sponson. That is to say, it had missed the paddle wheel and carved through the wooden platform forward of it, where the ship's main deck is extended outwards over the paddle-box for twenty feet or so. On the bow of the other steamer above us was the name of a newly-built "luxury" ferry also constructed for the Belgian government, the *Princess Henriette*, no doubt bound from Dover to Ostend.

The starboard sponson of the *Comtesse de Flandre* crunched inward like matchwood under the sharp cleaving of the *Henriette's* steel bow. I snatched at one of the tall deck ventilators to steady myself. Oddly as it seemed to me, I felt no impact at first beyond a quivering of the deck planking underfoot. Perhaps we should be saved after all. I thought I had known much worse than this when a Scottish steamer bumped awkwardly against a harbour quay or an island pier. But then the heavy bow of the *Princess Henriette* was halted, as it came up with a violent shudder against the main iron frame of the *Comtesse de Flandre's* engine-room.

On the helmsman's platform, now deserted, the ship's wheel spun from port to starboard and back again. Lamps and bollards rolled about the deck. There was a smashing of glass and crockery in the saloons. Then I heard two distinct grinding sounds beneath my feet, short and sharp. I knew at once that this had been a mortal blow after all. Had it not been for the iron frame of the engine room, I fully believe the larger ship would have cut us clean in two at once and sent everyone on board to the bottom of the English Channel in the next minute. At a mere seven or eight knots, you might suppose that the damage from such a collision would be slighter, but there was a weight of almost a thousand tons of riveted iron and steel behind it.

How had it happened? I was to find out much sooner then I expected.

The captain of the *Princess Henriette* must have known our position from the blasts on our whistle to which he had responded.

He had appeared to slow down, for seven or eight knots was probably less than half the full speed of such a leviathan.

I drew away and by some instinct headed towards the port paddle-box on the other side of the deck. Napoleon-Jerome's party was well escorted, but there was something I must confirm before I searched for Holmes. I could not get Rawdon Moran out of my head. Could he be on board after all? I pushed my way through the groups of bewildered passengers as they jostled on to the deck from the saloon below. I walked round the port paddle-box to examine its forward edge, and saw that someone— or something—had extinguished the red port riding-light. I put my hand on the metal lantern, in case the impact had knocked the light out. But it was not even warm. I thought of the foremast hand trimming the wick and knew that the light had been put out a little while ago—deliberately.

This was no time for ancient history, but I recalled an instance in my boyhood of a collision at night caused by a ship's navigation light that guttered and failed—port or starboard, I do not recall. It was not a common cause of accidents at sea, but neither was it unknown.

And then—where was that foremast hand who had presented a lucifer to the ship's boy to light this starboard lamp and who had appeared to be trimming the wick just now? There was no sign of him. In the last minutes of our voyage, could he also have been the helmsman enveloped in the sou'wester? Could the captain tell, in such visibility and with eyes straining to see the outline of the oncoming ship, whether his orders were being precisely carried out? Could he be sure that some slight manoeuvrings of the helm would not carry us closer to disaster?

What had seemed to take a lifetime had been all over in a couple of minutes. As I turned, I heard a distant but ominous rushing sound below me. The sea was beginning to flood the bowels of the ship. Captain Legrand was stooping at the engine-room skylight on the deck, shouting directions to the chief engineer through cupped hands. Despite the wail of the ship's whistle, I caught his words.

"Evacuate the engine-room. Ease the safety valves if you can. Leave the furnace doors, open the tubes. The companionways are almost impassable. Evacuate yourselves and the stokers through the hatch in the forward stoke-hold."

I found myself struggling against passengers heading against me for the gangways, as though that would save them! Even before they could reach them, they were driven back by billows of steam from the wrecked starboard paddle-box.

I looked around in case Holmes was already on deck. Though the oil-lights still shone, it had become more difficult to see. There was a hissing curtain of steam rising between the joints of the deck planking as the water entered the fires of the after boiler. Then towards the bow there was an ominous roar as the remaining fires were drowned out by the incoming flood. The navigating-bridge was enveloped in smoke and steam from the cracked boilers. The structure itself had been knocked askew by the impact, and it seemed that the vessel now listed increasingly to leeward.

With a feeling of numbed anxiety I thought that if Holmes was still below and had been near the point of impact, he might already be dead. But if he had survived—and surely he had— he might choose to die rather than abandon his protégées. He would have tried to reach Napoleon-Jerome and his companions in the after-saloon. That was where he was most likely to be. I struggled to reach it, pushing my way through the confusion as fugitives from the lower saloons forced a passage up the steps of the companionway, adding to the bewildered crowd on the upper deck. Those in the so-called royal saloon on the after-deck might be safe if anyone was.

I found my way back to the saloon and slid open the door at its side. It is no cliché to say that my heart sank when I saw no sign of Holmes. Napoleon-Jerome sat more than ever like a banker or a gentleman farmer at one end of the sofa. General Boucher and Lieutenant Cabell stood on either side of him. Cups and glasses, some broken, were scattered on the carpet. Inside the saloon, it was more evident than out on the deck that the wreck of the *Comtesse de Flandre* had tilted several more degrees to starboard. Somewhat to my irritation, the prince folded his hands as if composing an address to an ambassador in precise and correct English.

"We shall not sink, I do not believe so, doctor," he said primly. "I know steam paddle vessels. They are flat-bottomed boats. They are like a wooden box. They float a very long time after an exchange of blows. I was in the Crimea, you know, in the war against the Tsar. Our monitor *Rochefort* was engaged and suffered an unlucky hit. Much of her side was blown away. She was disabled, but she did not sink. She floated until she became a nuisance to navigation and had to be sunk by our own gunfire."

To dispute with royalty, even if it has neither a throne nor a crown, is not easy. I tried to think how Sherlock Holmes would have put it to him. It was no good.

"Sir, I must go below and search for my colleague. The sea is coming in by the paddle sponson. It may not yet be flooding beneath the waterline, but it is very close. You can see from the steam outside that it has already filled the stoke-hold sufficiently to put out the fires. The boilers have cracked and steam is escaping from them as well. There is no pressure left to work the pumps, and the ship will fill with water below the Plimsoll line. That will sink her."

Lieutenant Cabell was blunter. "You must go now, Your Majesty. There is a boat just outside which we are attempting to lower."

The prince waved his hand side to side.

"They will come from the other ship and fetch us. I think they have boats enough. I will not have it said that I was rescued and that all the other people on this steamer were left to take their chance. We shall all go in the proper manner. I do not care a lot to be seen scrambling down the side of a ship to save myself. I fear every chance of an accident in such weather as this, and being myself in the water. I shall remain for a time."

I made one more effort and wished afterwards that I had not. "I too know something of ships, sir. This vessel is listing. The movement is gradual. But when the moment comes, she will go over without warning. You will not get as far as the door of this saloon. Whatever your decision, I am going down below at once."

"You will go down below to look for your colleague, Doctor Vastson?"

"At once, sir. I can do no more here. Please take the advice of Lieutenant Cabell."

Plon-Plon waved his hand side to side, rather like a fan.

"If you are going anyway, monsieur, there is a box belonging to me which I should like, if it is still there. It lies in the *coffres-forts* of the Messageries Impériales. It is consigned to myself at Lancaster Gate. There is an armed guard, but I expect they will have run away. It is marked with a crown."

General Boulanger intervened before I could reply. There was a chain at the belt of his morning dress, and from it he unhooked two keys on a ring.

"This, monsieur, is all the authority you require. I have an oil-lamp at my disposal. You will please take that for your safety."

Safety! There is a French phrase—*un mauvais quart d'heure*—which refers to an anticipation of disagreeable experiences. It describes precisely my feelings as I felt my way down the half-lit steps of the companionway. The fog had shown no sign of lifting, and no lifeboat had yet reached the stricken *Comtesse* from the vessel that had run her down. But the rush of passengers from the lower saloons to the upper deck had ceased and I had the lower deck pretty much to myself. Below-decks, the stricken steamer was silent now except for the wash of water that swilled to and fro across the planking. Only the echo of distant voices above indicated the turmoil and panic there. I found my way by a glimmer of mounted oil-lights overhead which the water had not yet reached and which showed me the way dimly.

The worst thing belowdecks was a fetid stench from the bilges of the sinking vessel, as the contaminated water ran erratically about the sloping deck. The engine-room passage stretching aft was more than ankle-deep in it. My lamp shone upon the heavy pistons of the ship's engines, now silent and motionless in mid-stride. There was a creaking of the hull as it seemed to heel over a little more. But that was no more than a tidal swell catching the flank of the vessel. Where was Sherlock Holmes? The deep well of the engine-room that lay beneath the heavy machinery was flooding steadily. Passing the paddle-box, I came to the open sponson. Here one could stand on the platform and step down twelve or eighteen inches into a lifeboat held alongside. But as yet there was no boat.

I came to the steel grille beside the *bureau de change,* guarding the mailroom and its high-value packages. I had no need of Lieutenant Cabell's key to open the gate. The three guardians had left the steel grille open as they fled when the bow of the *Princesse Henriette* crunched into the side of the steamer. What else should they do, as the sea began to flood this lower deck? They must have expected that the ship would capsize at any second, and they had run for their lives, leaving the mailroom of the *coffres-forts* unlocked. Who shall blame them for that?

The shouting on the deck above me had diminished. If I heard the sounds correctly, the two lifeboats of the *Comtesse de Flandre* were being lowered, and no doubt the first rescue boat from the *Princesse Henriette* had been launched. I shone my lamp on the cavernous cage with its high-value packages. Where was Holmes? My oil-lamp was giving out little more than a glow. Yet from what I could now see of the interior of this strong-room, everything was as it had been. Napoleon-Jerome's coffin-like war-chest lay in its place. Yet how was it to be rescued before the ship foundered? I should never be able to shift it on my own. I tried to lift one end, but only to ensure that it had not been tampered with. To judge from its weight, I was sure that it had not been.

"Watson!"

He was carrying no lamp of his own. I had neither seen nor heard him approach along the engine-room passageway.

"Leave that!" he called. "There is every chance that we shall break in two after such a blow."

I had expected that at the least we would lug the war-chest to the sponson, where a boat might be brought alongside.

"Leave Plon Plon's war-chest?"

I could see his aquiline profile against that failing glow of my oil-light.

"My dear fellow, there is nothing in that chest worth the loss of a human life. Not yours and certainly not mine."

"But there must be enough in there to start a revolution in Paris!"

He smiled, though at what I could not say.

"If it pleases you to think so—but not a revolution of the kind you suppose. To tell you the truth, I have been in possession of the keys to it ever since I left Brussels, thanks to Brother Mycroft. But you shall have your way, old fellow. And you shall carry away as payment however much of the contents you think worth carrying. Stand back."

He knelt down and I held the lamp closer. Apart from the polished brass lock-plate, there were subsidiary keyholes at either end of the glossy oak chest. The well-oiled levers of the locks moved smoothly and easily in obedience to the key, hardly touching the wards as they rose to ease back the bolts. Holmes took the edges of the lid and lifted it silently back. Napoleon-Jerome's treasure trove was covered by a sheet of heavy silver foil, for all the world like the lining of an ammunition box. He rolled this back, and I stared at the royal fortune that was intended to

317

restore the descendants of Napoleon Bonaparte to the throne of France.

The contents were wrapped in large parcels, set out in double rows and addressed to the Chaplain General's Office, North Camp, Aldershot. Each wrapper bore an identical printed label upon it: "Army Temperance Society Pamphlets. Series 9." And that was all.

Sherlock Holmes's eyes glinted in the yellow light as I stared at this display.

"My dear Watson! Did you really imagine that the Queen of the Night and the Mogul diamonds would be in here? I have gone to some lengths in Brussels to induce those who have betrayed us to our opponents to think so. That was the prime purpose of my visit. But that you should believe it is very singular—and indeed rather gratifying! Of course Colonel Moran cannot afford to ignore the possibility, having been assured of its value on the best possible information. He dare not turn back. But as for trusting Plon Plon's baubles to the Messageries Impériales, only consider. It needs just one guard to be corrupted. Or suppose the ship's captain—or any member of the crew—cannot resist the money offered by an international brotherhood of crime. No matter that his ultimate reward is likely to be a bullet in the head. What then? We already know there is a stoker on this ship who cannot be a stoker. A helmsman in his sou'wester could have been anyone. Above all, only a complete fool would trust a consignment of royal gems to a box that has been stamped and marked with a Napoleonic crown."

"Then who is beyond bribing?"

"The Prince's make-believe valet, if no one else. You have met the man already. Theodore Cabell, otherwise known as Captain Cabell, late of the Swiss military intelligence service, for the time being in the service of our client. A man whose bland manner belies tenacity and resolve. A sharp mind. It was he who first suspected the conspiracy of the forged despatches between Prince Ferdinand of Bulgaria and the Comtesse de Flandre eighteen months ago. My success in the matter owed more than a little to him."

He closed the lid again and locked it.

I believe it was the tension of what had gone before that now overcame me. I began to shake with laughter at the thought of the temperance pamphlets in the royal treasure chest—and the baubles no doubt on their way to the military security of Aldershot Garrison. I confess that it was not a healthy or wholesome laughter; even at that moment, it felt too close to hysteria. If I had stopped to think for a moment, I should have known, as Holmes did, that the worst dangers still lay ahead. When Rawdon Moran discovered how neatly he had been cheated, the matter would not rest there.

At that moment, the hoarse wail of the *Comtesse de Flandre*'s siren, which had diminished every minute as the steam pipe failed, faded altogether. It was a warning that the sea washing through the stoke-hold had put out the last fires. Apart from the scattered oil-lights along the lower-deck passageways and the upper-deck structures, the steamer was dead. Only the whistle of the *Princess Henriette* still carried its gusts of sound across the murky water. In the quietness around us, there was a sudden voice of command from the companionway to the upper deck.

"Holloa! Holloa! Is there anyone still down there? Make yourselves known! The ship is going over! Our last boat must cast off in five minutes! Are you there? Is anyone still there?"

Without waiting for a reply, the officer went back to the upper deck. Holmes had kept his forefinger to his lips to indicate silence. Now he lowered it.

"This is not over," he said softly. "Have you your revolver with you?"

"Of course. Have you?"

"No. I should like to borrow yours, if you would be so kind."

With a sense of exasperation, I gave it to him. We went slowly back towards the companionway steps, through the rush and swill of water on the tilted deck planking of the passageway. I guessed there would be no further warning before a sudden lurch and capsizing of the broken hull. We came up into the fog and the cold, between the funnels and the after-saloon. There was a haloed light here and there, but the vapour in the air seemed as thick as ever. No one remained in the first-class saloon. Plon Plon and his party were safe if anyone was. Two or three of the ship's officers and a handful of passengers seemed to be making their way towards the boat.

What followed next was beyond anything I could have imagined. We were standing behind the funnels just aft of the remains of the navigation-bridge. Lifeboats from the *Princesse Henriette* had come alongside the stern and taken off the passengers. The forward deck of our vessel was thankfully deserted. At the moment of the impact, the bow of the *Henriette* had not quite cut us in two. Now, beneath my feet I felt the timbers of the *Comtesse de Flandre* pulling apart; then I heard them screech and rend. Without further warning, the intolerable weight of tons of water in the depths of the ship on its port side twisted the broken hull beyond endurance. There came a deep rumble, though not a loud one.

Through the last drifts of smoke and steam that overhung the deck, unreal as if in a dream, I saw the bows of the steamer rise slowly and ghostlike before us. There was nothing louder than the dripping of water. The forepart sank gently back into the waves as it split away. Rolling aside, a thirty-foot length of the ship turned over slowly and capsized without a further sound. It was no longer part of the ship. Water streamed down the riveted steel of its flanks, as the bows disappeared from our view beneath the quiet waves. There was no turbulence and no echo in the depths. We watched like mourners at a burial.

Looking back on this disaster, everything I have described took far less time to happen that it takes to tell. And how can a few bald sentences convey the drama of it, except to those who have lived through such a quiet catastrophe? But fortunately, ships do not always "sink like a stone," especially if they are flat-bottomed steamers. Napoleon-Jerome was right about that. Also, thankfully, the sea was calm. Our heavy boilers had broken away and sunk with the bows. Lightened by this, the wreck of the *Comtesse de Flandre* floated, from the paddle-boxes and funnels back to the stern. The list to starboard was no longer quite so pronounced. In what time was left before the remainder of the wreck sank, the work of rescue might be concluded.

Not all of this rescue attempt had gone well. The second mate of the *Comtesse de Flandre,* an experienced sailor with a record of service in the Royal Navy, had knocked the starboard lifeboat off its chocks at the stern. It had then been swung out above the sea by its davits. By some miscalculation in handling it, the bow had abruptly dropped down with the stern drawn up high, and the mechanism had jammed. The boat had been left suspended from the side of the ship at an impossible angle. Fortunately the *Princesse Henriette* had by then lowered one of her after lifeboats into the waves on an even keel. Looking over the rail amidships, I could see that the sailors on both ships had also thrown into the sea anything that would float well enough to support passengers in the water until they could be picked up. There were several planks, a hen-coop, and even a small carpenter's bench still drifting within a few yards of us.

Through the fog, the dim shape of the other steamer appeared briefly and intermittently in the distant sweep of the Ruytingen light vessel. The two ships had drifted apart immediately after the collision, but the *Princesse Henriette* was only a short distance away and appeared to be intact. We had heard the rattle of her chain and a heavy splash as her anchor went down. When the indistinct gleam from Ruytingen swept the surface again, it illuminated briefly the outline of two or three small fishing smacks and luggers, which hove to in case they could assist us. It seemed that we had not been as isolated as I had supposed.

11

*I*n the fleeting phosphorescence from the light-ship, I made out a small boat that had come alongside our stern. The line of the *Comtesse de Flandre* dropped down at the after end to a small well-deck that accommodated the winch and its platform. The lower stern rail could also be opened at this point to give access for engineering maintenance. In the present state of the wreck, as the lower decks flooded, this had become the easiest point at which to disembark survivors into a small boat. Or, indeed, to embark *from* one.

We stood and listened behind the yellow funnels. The black "admiralty caps" round their tops were lost in the mist overhead. The scene around us was illuminated by the last glimmering oil-lights, two of them fitted just above the windows of the after-saloon. Their pale glow extended little more than a yard or two around us. Even here, the devastation was considerable. Not only was the navigation-bridge wrecked, but the wide ventilation skylight of the engine-room had been blown off by an explosion of steam from the boilers. Looking down at the flooded engine-room, I could just see that the rising water was now level with the blocks of the pistons that had driven the ship.

At that moment, my heart seemed to jump to my throat as the casing of an oil-light mounted above a square window of the saloon shattered without warning. There was no sound of a detonation as the frosted glass enclosing the wick burst apart, only the rattle of fragments scattering across the deck. A small pool of fire from the little oil reservoir of the lamp rippled, guttered, and expired on the planking no more than a foot or two away from us.

Then someone laughed in the darkness of the fog bank that lay on all sides.

Before I could ask Holmes what the devil was happening, another glass lamp-bowl disintegrated, high on a standard above the companionway opening. Specks of burning wick flew about like sparks from a forge. Then there was darkness except for a remaining glimmer above the starboard window of the saloon. But I knew who had laughed even before I heard the voice calling me.

"It won't do, doctor! It won't do at all! I have warned you more than once, have I not, that you had far better give it up?"

The launch alongside our stern had not come to rescue us. Without another sound, the square glass window of the saloon, by my right shoulder, cracked into three pieces and slithered inwards. Joshua Sellon had died without a sound, for I had examined the wound that killed him. I was now undergoing my first practical experience of Von Herder's carbon dioxide cylinder-pistol. No percussion wave. No powder flash. No acrid drift of cordite. And in the darkness of the fog, the marksman remained an invisible assailant, his soft-nosed lead bullets travelling almost at the speed of sound. Powerful enough to smash a window with a shot whose discharge was silent and invisible. Powerful enough, as I had seen for myself, to drill through a man's skull and blow the segments of his brain apart as though they had been no more than a cauliflower.

The voice came again, abruptly and from a different direction. I had not a hope of seeing him in such conditions. Stillness everywhere made it all the more difficult to guess the range.

"Doctor! I warned you that you would only hurt yourself! But you would have it so. You would not listen! And since you would have it so, it shall be so."

After the first smooth irony, the last four words were spoken with a snarl. Then there was complete silence again. Where the devil could he be? The voice certainly came from astern of us, but that told me very little. There was nothing of the ship's bows left. Forward of the funnels and the wrecked navigating bridge, the deck dropped to a vast and empty sea. In the dripping fog, a gunman could take fresh aim with every bullet and we should never see him. He had a store of cartridges and all the time in the world. Sooner or later, if only by luck, he would bring down one or other of us. Then we should be finished. Small wonder that the skill of Von Herder, the blind mechanic, was a legend in the European underworld.

I could make out Sherlock Holmes, motionless as a statue. His unmistakable gaunt silhouette was just visible in the veil of mist beside me. He had not bothered to draw my revolver from his pocket. A single shot, a flash from its muzzle, the crack of the explosion, would pinpoint our position for a man who was probably not more than twenty feet away. A man who could put five shots in succession through the heart of the ace of spades at thirty-seven paces. The fog remained our friend. As long as it persisted, Rawdon Moran must fire blind.

In a voice no louder than a breath, Holmes whispered.

"He will hit us sooner or later. We must lead him on constantly, bring him forward from the shadows. He will not resist the temptation to follow. The man is a hunter, and it is his instinct to stalk the prey. But we must move. Now."

As if to confirm this necessity, the glass pane in the other window of the saloon shattered. I had heard nothing of the bullet passing. But I remembered Holmes telling me that there would be no atmospheric crack until the velocity of the shot exceeded the speed of sound. All three targets had been within ten or twelve feet of where we stood. One question was uppermost in my mind. Why the devil had Holmes not got his useful little Laroux pistolet, as I had brought my Webley? Was it still in his table-drawer at Baker Street? Surely not. But if not, where was it?

He was moving away slowly ahead of me without a sound, gliding round the port side of the after-saloon, beckoning me on.

Then came that damned voice again! Was he such a fool as to believe he could torment our nerves until one of us shouted out or fired blind?

"Why could you not do as you were advised, doctor? Why could you not go back and heal the sick, as you were trained to do? Why could you not be content to marry your little sweetheart, Mary Morstan, or invest your little nest-egg in old Mr. Farquhar's Paddington practice? Even now it is not too late. I could wish you well and dance at your wedding, but you have given me no chance. . . . Oh, doctor, doctor!"

In those few seconds, I became badly frightened by this buffoonery. How it was, I knew not—but he had watched every moment and knew every secret. Miss Morstan and I were dear friends. Who knows what the future might hold? How did Moran know of her—and what could he know? Her name was now on the lips of a man who would send her to her death without scruple. Had he not sent Emmeline Putney-Wilson and almost the maid Seraphina—and others, perhaps, by his own hands? The brute need only watch patiently until that one minute in a thousand days when a woman was not under the immediate protection of a lover or her family. However constant the guard, such a moment always comes to one who watches patiently enough. Holmes was right. There was no safety except in the destruction of Rawdon Moran.

"Oh, doctor, doctor!"

Now there was laughter in that voice again, laughing at itself, laughter that was unhinged. Of course he judged me to be weaker than Holmes, and so aimed at me. He would break my nerve, frighten me to answer back, pleading for a chance to bargain, giving away our position. Then he would have us both. But I felt a sudden anger and determination. I accepted his challenge. Where was he? A brief luminance from Ruytingen across the waves lay upon the fog without piercing it. The wide surface of that cold sea was still and calm, except for the occasional wash of a wave against the listing wreck of the *Comtesse de Flandre*.

I heard him again as I followed Holmes round the side of the after-saloon. Now it was my friend's turn to be taunted.

"Have no fear, Mr. Holmes. As a man of honour, I do not take my opponent's life by an act of murder. I would not treat a beast of the jungle so. Stand your ground, both of you, and you shall both have your chance. Run like cowards and you must accept the consequences. Even you, my dear Mr. Sherlock Holmes! Would you prefer the readers of the obituaries and the penny papers to learn that, at the last, you had been a ninny, shot in the back running away?"

Despite the worst I had heard of him, I never expected this gibbering of the madhouse cell, for that was what it had become. The voice now seemed to echo from the starboard side and we were moving like ghosts towards the stern, under the port shelter of the after-saloon, keeping our backs to its wall. Then a fragment of deck planking snapped and splintered just beside my right foot. It was the impact of a shot at random from his silent pistol. He had moved round and was behind us suddenly. We continued to edge sideways towards the stern, presenting the smallest possible target. But in a moment we must leave the shelter of the saloon and come into the view of Moran's seamen by the winch. Holmes had instinctively drawn the Webley revolver, but it was useless to us now.

I had a mad idea that we could save ourselves by swimming for our lives. Without shoes and heavier outer clothing, we might dive from the rail and support ourselves if necessary on one of the floating planks. After a few strokes from the ship's side, the fog would close round us again. It could not be more than two hundred yards to the ropes that hung down the sides of the

Princesse Henriette for survivors to clutch at. Could we do it? I could swim further than that as a schoolboy or at Battersea baths as a medical student. But this dark sea held a bitter chill, and its unknown currents might carry us away from safety.

Holmes seemed intent upon his own plan. With long supple fingers that Paganini or Joachim might have envied, he was silently easing back the sliding door at this side of the saloon. There was no sound of our adversary, no derisive voice. Moran might be six feet away—or sixty. Had he come and gone? No. I felt sure he was still behind us. Keeping our heads down, we crossed the curtained saloon in darkness, its curtains still closed, and came out on the starboard side. Holmes was evidently making a circuit in order to follow our route again and then take him in the rear.

Coming out through that opposite door into the enveloping mist once more, we felt our way forward, our backs to the wall of the saloon again. We were coming to the point at which he had seemed to be standing when we first heard his voice. With luck, he was still following us towards the stern and we might track him unseen. Once in view, a single bullet would do the job. That, of course, was the moment when we might dive from the rails and save ourselves from the rest of his crew. But as I calculated our chances, my foot caught some object in the darkness and I almost overbalanced. It felt like a fallen log. I put my hand down and felt a human leg, then a jacket, and then the features of a face. The Ruytingen light touched the surface of the sea for an instant. In its brief reflection I saw the dead man's face. It was Lieutenant Cabell.

If I felt fear of any kind, it was not for a dead body. I had seen far too many for that. Rather, it came from the knowledge that something had gone wrong with all our plans. We were in the trap. Holmes had counted on our adversaries watching us every minute, reading our messages, decoding our cipher. He had counted on them believing that he would be on board the ship, no matter what he said. Had his judgment failed him now in the matter of the young lieutenant?

A whisper came at my ear, so quiet that it might have been Holmes. It was amiable, intimate, and soothing, coming from behind me:

"You would have it so, doctor, would you not? And, you see, it has come to this. You stand between Mr. Holmes and myself. He cannot shoot me unless he shoots you first, which I think he will not do. And he knows that if he does not lay his weapon down upon the deck this minute, then I—with more regret than I can ever describe—must shoot you here and now. And then, with more reluctance than I have felt in killing the noblest beast, I must shoot him."

I cried out at once, "Do as you must, Holmes!"

The moment the words were out of my mouth, I knew what a fool I had been. I meant him to understand that he must ignore me and take Moran to the land of shadows at all costs. Had I said, "Shoot him!" that would have done it. But it seemed as if "Do as you must" meant "Do as he tells you." To my dismay, Holmes laid my revolver on the deck and addressed our adversary.

"My congratulations, colonel. Your reputation as a hunter goes before you. It was remiss of me not to foresee that you might use Lieutenant Cabell's body as a bait to catch your prey. Sooner or later, even in this fog, we should stumble upon the poor fellow quite literally. The snare at which you waited would spring and you would have us."

Moran ignored the compliment. He came into view now, almost bear-like in his heavy military coat. He motioned us on with the pistol in his hand.

"A little further forward, if you please, gentlemen. Under the light."

In a situation so desperate and with the mind racing, there was nothing for it but to obey, moving an inch at a time and keeping one's nerve. With the heavy-looking weapon of Von Herder in his hand, Moran followed us, scooping up my revolver from the deck before I could prevent him.

Someone had now drawn back the curtains of the after-saloon, where the broken windows faced the ship's funnels, and a lamp had been lit. The space where we had first stood was hazily lit by the light from the interior. Holmes turned to face our enemy so that we stood with our backs to this illumination. Moran laughed, as if to assure us that such a position would not inconvenience him in the least.

Without looking down, he broke open the Webley and shook the six cartridges out. He dropped them into his pockets. Then, as if thinking better of this, he drew one back out and inserted it in the gun, spun the chambers, and closed the gun. It was as if he was performing some trick for our benefit.

With the revolver in his right hand, he raised his left and pulled the trigger of Von Herder's pistol. With less sound than a cork popping, the weapon discharged and I ducked my head as the remaining window behind us shattered. What was his game? For it was a game, a sport for an asylum of the criminally insane. Why not kill us then and there?

"You do not think well of me, Mr. Holmes?"

As coolly as if he was declining a second slice of cake at a tea party, Holmes replied. "I cannot say that I often think of you at all, Colonel Moran."

Moran chuckled. "You know that is not true, sir! I should be offended if it were. But however badly you may view me, I am a sportsman. I do not kill in cold blood—not even you. I might shoot you both now. But that is not my way with a man of your calibre, Mr. Sherlock Holmes, even though you have caused me some considerable difficulties. You deserve a better end."

Mad as a hatter!

"Indeed?" Again, Holmes made the word sound like an expression of polite boredom.

"We must have this thing over between us, Mr. Holmes. The world cannot any longer contain us both. That is all. But you shall have a sporting chance."

This time there was no reply, and Moran was left to continue his own demented monologue.

"There are two guns, you see? Mine and the doctor's. We shall duel at this distance. At so short a range, we may expect that the contest will soon be decisive. They tell me you are an opponent worth challenging to a match at firearms, Mr. Holmes. Very well. You are unfamiliar with the Von Herder pistol, I daresay, but no matter. You are very familiar with your friend's Webley revolver. Excellent. You shall have his revolver and this one bullet. And you shall fire first. You may check that the chamber brings the cartridge to the top in readiness. I have a certain knack of dodging bullets, but you will agree that if you miss me at this distance, you deserve neither your reputation nor your life. In that case, I shall have my turn after yours. Is that not fair?"

There must be a trick in this, though I could not yet see what it was. I knew that he intended to kill us both, but this game would also serve some peculiar vanity of his own.

"And in either event," Holmes inquired politely, "what is to become of my colleague?"

Moran gave another of his light-hearted chuckles.

"If you succeed, his difficulties are resolved. If not, then I fear we shall have to see what we shall see."

"And if I should refuse. . . ."

"You would be a far more stupid man than the world takes you for, Mr. Holmes! Now, do not disappoint me! You may miss me, of course. But even then, I may forego my right of reply. I am a hunter, sir, and more than half my pleasure is the thrill of the risk. I propose to be your executioner. But, as they used to say in the days of steel, the delight of an execution is not in the slovenly butchering of a man but in cutting the head from the shoulders with a single sword-stroke and leaving it standing in its place. Is that not so? Come, now."

Holding the Webley by its muzzle, he laid it on the deck and then with his foot sent it scudding across to the toecaps of Sherlock Holmes.

I measured the distance between us. I could never reach him before he fired at me. But the moment Moran raised his gun to take aim at Holmes, I would try to charge him down as I had charged many an opposing forward on the rugby ground at Blackheath in my student days. He might still shoot us both. But he must first turn and shoot at me before I could reach him. That would give Holmes just a moment's chance to spring and finish what I had started. It was a slim chance, but it was the only one.

The colonel's laughter seemed higher-pitched now, as he said "Come!"

Holmes was holding the Webley down, at arm's length, the safety catch released, the chamber carefully positioned. He began to raise it, his arm coming higher like a clock hand until it was horizontal. I watched for the forefinger to tighten on the trigger. But to my surprise, his arm kept rising. He would never hit Moran now! Higher and higher went the arm, until the gun was pointing at the sky. Then I could see that Moran was prepared to shoot first until Holmes called out, "Major Putney-Wilson, if you please!"

Moran would not have been human had he not paused to see what this meant. In a moment of surprise, he looked like a man who feels he has been harpooned. A second later there was a roar from the muzzle of the skyward-pointing Webley and a flash of fire. Holmes was not looking at Moran, but somewhere just beyond him. The colonel's eyes, which had been flicking here and there, now went still and round as marbles. With his pistol covering Holmes, Colonel Moran half-turned and saw a figure like a ghost in the vapour. The man took shape, tall and dishevelled, a cotton cap on his head, his body cased in a grimy boiler-suit, his face immaculately blackened by soot, the eyes and lips alone visible. In his hand was the silver Laroux pistolet of Sherlock Holmes.

In that same second, Holmes leapt at his enemy. The length of his reach was always extraordinary, but never more so than in this flying leap. His feet never touched the ground until the moment of impact. He was on Moran before the colonel could raise his gun. Moran was a ferocious hunter, but his skill was with his gun rather than with his fists—and with his fists rather than in his arms. Their collision enabled Holmes to knock aside the Von Herder pistol.

Each recoiled from the impact. Moran at once tried to snatch Holmes round the neck and double him over, imprisoning him in the traditional English wrestling grip of "chancery." But when he closed his arm round his opponent's neck, it had apparently dissolved into air. Holmes had dived and caught Moran round the waist, tossing him over his shoulder like a sack of coals. The colonel's teeth were brought together by the shock with a force that might have broken his jaw.

In a second more, Holmes threw him down on his back, knocking out his breath and catching him by the feet. What followed was more like a ballet than a prize-fight. The strength in Holmes's hands was daunting, as anyone would know who had watched him casually bend straight Dr. Roylott's distorted iron poker. From a spell of education in Germany, he was schooled in boxing and fencing as well as in the less common art of single-stick. In some forms of combat, Moran might have been his superior. But Holmes had waited for his chosen time and his chosen place. Despite his bulk, Moran seemed helpless as Holmes, with footwork quicker and more intricate than a dancer's, swung him by the feet in circle after circle at increasing speed. The art of it was to make the helpless victim gain velocity until he appeared to contribute to his own destruction.

At a precise moment, Sherlock Holmes released him and sent him hurtling into what I believe is called a "Tipperary swing." The colonel went head-first into the steel plating of the saloon. What damage was done to him I do not care to speculate, but it was surely the end of Rawdon Moran. So neatly had Holmes despatched him that the senseless body slid down and through the opening in the deck where the engine-room skylight had once been. The colonel fell like Satan into the darkness below, between the motionless pistons of the ship's engines. Knocked side to side, he crashed on to the barrel-shape of the steel condenser below them. I cannot tell at what point he was dead, but the white paintwork of the condenser showed him face down, head and hair washing to and fro in the rising flood. He was then as dead as any man had ever been.

The conclusion of that night's drama may be briefly described. As any reader of the press will know, the wreck of the *Comtesse de Flandre* was very nearly saved, perhaps in the belief that Plon Plon's baubles were on board. The breaking away of the bows, let alone the sound of gunshots from amidships, had been enough to frighten off Moran's two or three underlings who had brought the little boat alongside the stern. The captain of the *Princesse Henriette,* seeing that the remains of the other ship continued to float and hearing what sounded like a distress maroon, ordered two of his boats to carry across a pair of ropes so that he might take the wreck in tow. Holmes and I, with Major Putney-Wilson, took passage back to the anchored steamer in the first of these lifeboats.

It was still dark when the *Princess Henriette's* paddles began to churn. With her salvage prize in tow, she resumed her crossing to Ostend at half speed. The refugees from the *Comtesse de Flandre* were accommodated and fed, Napoleon-Jerome and his companions being consoled in the captain's quarters. Holmes and I were waited upon by the chief steward in a cabin of our own.

As for the strange adventure of Major Putney-Wilson, he had at first kept his promise to board the RMS *Himalaya* for Bombay. He then broke that promise at Lisbon and travelled to Oporto, where his children were cared for by his brother, the wine-shipper. Yet to see his children was surely forgivable. Someone, whom he would never name, then sent him two clues in a note such as I had received at my club. That benefactor also placed information for him relating to Colonel Rawdon Moran's activities in the Belgian arms trade. I looked hard at Sherlock Holmes and, I believe, detected a certain sheepishness in him as Putney-Wilson revealed all this.

My friend would only say that in the course of his own Belgian preparations, he had tried to account for every member of the *Comtesse de Flandre*'s crew at new moon. In taking on casual labour a week or two earlier, the Compagnie Belgique had engaged a hand for the stoke-hold. This humblest of the humble in the ship's company went by the name of Samuel Dordona.

Why had Holmes said nothing to me of Putney-Wilson, even as we studied the mysterious stoker who was not a stoker? Holmes looked at me as though I should have known better than to ask.

"My dear Watson! You had met Samuel Dordona, on two occasions. I confess I was a little concerned that Putney-Wilson might not pass muster last night. Therefore I said nothing to you but encouraged him to act his little part for your benefit. If he could deceive you, he could deceive all those who mattered. You never doubted him, not even when I pointed out that he was not the stoker he pretended to be. That was excellent! His part was all important, for he was to shadow those who shadowed us. I naturally entrusted him with the Laroux. If we could not account for Moran with your Webley, it was better that the pistolet should come upon him unawares rather than be taken from us in defeat. With such a man as Putney-Wilson behind us, I imagine we were never truly in danger."

"It felt very much like danger to me, Holmes! The only shot in our locker was the cartridge Moran returned to you in my Webley."

"A scoundrel like Moran gives his victims no chance. Logic therefore dictated that this must be a harmless Boxer blank, carefully separated in his pocket from the others. I still have the cartridge case. You may inspect it if you choose."

"You knew it was a blank?"

"What else? It came too easily from his pocket. Such a man would never allow me a chance to kill him! Far better to use that cartridge to summon our friends."

"But why play such a trick? He might have shot us out of hand and had done with it!"

"If you ever try, Watson, you will find that one man with a pistol cannot easily shoot two men at close range before one of them gets hold of him. On this occasion, in the fog, he might not hit his target at a longer range. Moran hoped that I would fire the blank at him, believing the round was live. While we waited for him to fall, he would shoot me and turn the gun on you, as you still waited to see him collapse."

"That was all?"

"By no means. Far more important was the act of firing into the air and calling out to Major Putney-Wilson—whom Moran had occasion to remember. You saw how the act and the name threw him off his balance for that vital second or two. Because I did not fire at him when I had the chance, he knew that whoever I called out to behind him must have a gun. He could not ignore the risk. He was, I like to think, a little bewildered. By instinct he half-turned, and by instinct he hesitated when he saw a figure coming through the mist behind him while two more remained in front of him. That gave me my chance. Not for nothing was Putney-Wilson a comrade of the Special Investigation Branch. He has lain very low in all this, but I am proud to have served— albeit irregularly—with such a man."

It was an extraordinary story, but I knew Holmes was right in one thing, for I had seen it myself. Whatever advantage Moran thought he might have over us was swept away by that inexplicable shot fired overhead. It was beyond his comprehension. In other circumstances he might perhaps have out-fought Sherlock Holmes. His downfall was that in no circumstances could he out-think him.

With that, my friend stretched himself out on the cabin settee, which his legs overlapped a little. He folded his hands and fell sound asleep. I sat and thought of all that had happened. A drama that extended to the scorching plains of Zululand and the banks of the Blood River, to Hyderabad and the Transvaal, to the dangerous underworlds of espionage, the murder of Captain Joshua Sellon, the dogged loyalty of Sergeant Albert Gibbons of the Royal Marines, and the devious policies of the Great Powers of Europe, was coming to its conclusion. As for that international criminal brotherhood which Holmes had identified—or imagined—its members had certainly lost a battle, if not a war.

Two miles off the harbour pier of Ostend, a tug came out to take the tow from us. Again I heard the rattle of a heavy chain and the splash of the *Princesse Henriette*'s anchor. It took an interminable time to complete the transfer of the wreck as a dim morning broke—if morning ever breaks in such weather and in such a place. We were still in our cabin, sitting over breakfast as though this might have been Baker Street, when there was a commotion on the upper deck. I went up and saw the rails of the ship lined with spectators.

Across the dull surface of the water, still a mile or two off-shore, the remainder of the *Comtesse de Flandre* was subsiding gradually into the depths. It did not capsize or turn turtle or any such exciting thing as we had been promised the night before. It sank slowly and evenly into deep water, taking with it, among other things, the mortal remains and secrets of Colonel Rawdon Moran. His grave was never to be disturbed, for the depth was too great and no one ever thought the contents of the wreck worth raising. Of Plon Plon's baubles, no more was said. A plain crate marked as containing surplus stock of the Army Temperance Society Tracts came safely to the Senior Chaplain at Aldershot Garrison.

12

*O*ur return to England was delayed by an inquiry at Ostend into the loss of the *Comtesse de Flandre,* held on the instructions of the Belgian government. Holmes and I found ourselves back at the Hotel de la Plage.

At the risk of seeming chauvinistic, such an inquiry would never have passed muster in London. It opened on Tuesday, four days after the collision, and following a single day of evidence it closed on Thursday. Its guiding principle seemed to be that the less said, the better. Sherlock Holmes always maintained that the authorities had a very good idea of the nature of the drama that had taken place, but were determined the world should never know it. This tribunal announced that the "valet" Theodore Cabell had died of exposure. The poor young man's funeral was over and done with even before the inquiry began. A final search of the ship was undertaken before the last lifeboat pulled away. It revealed the body of an unidentified man in the overcoat of an army officer, "horribly mutilated" but of whom no more was heard.

How had the collision happened? The captain of the *Princesse Henriette* swore that a trawler, moving at speed aslant the sea lane, had cut across his bow in darkness and fog without sounding its

horn or displaying a light. It had forced him into the path of the
Comtesse de Flandre. Another witness believed the guilty vessel
was a French customs launch heading for Dunkirk. As for the
moment of the collision, the two steamers had hit one another at
a combined speed of some ten knots. The distance at which they
saw each other was determined to be no more than sixty yards,
according to the ships' officers. The time between sighting and
impact was put at little more than ten or twelve seconds, giving
no hope of avoiding disaster. The mischief with the port riding-
light of the *Comtesse de Flandre* was known only to Holmes and
me. Because no port riding-light was showing, the larger ship
had been directed into the hull of the smaller one rather than
down its far side, which might have carried it clear.

Two pieces of evidence embarrassed the inquiry and were
quickly dealt with. An innocent witness had seen a fishing smack
pick up three men and their baggage from the stricken wreck. It
did not transfer them to the *Princesse Henriette* but sailed away.
The witness was not invited to enlarge upon this.

A further witness attributed his survival to a large parcel-post
basket, which was floating in the water by the *Comtesse de Flandre*'s
paddle-box. It bore him up until he could be pulled to safety in
one of the lifeboats. But a postal basket from the mailroom could
not be floating in the water unless the steel grille of that mailroom
had been unlocked by the fleeing guards and left open.

No one, it seemed, had noticed the stoker who was not a stoker.
However, Captain Legrand of the *Comtesse de Flandre* gave evidence
that the helmsman at the wheel before the collision was not
a regular member of the crew. The usual helmsman had asked a
friend to go in his place as it was the regular helmsman's night out.
Captain Legrand agreed to the substitution. The newcomer, said to
be an experienced seaman, took his turn at the wheel from time
to time during the crossing. He was thought to be one of those
crew members missing after the collision and it was proposed to
hold an inquest on him, albeit without a body.

The inquiry was concluded, though not without mumblings as to questions left unasked. Its commissioners replied that it had made a very exhaustive investigation of the circumstances under which the disaster took place. The commission promised that the results would be put into the form of a judicial report and forwarded to the state maritime authorities in Brussels.

At the first opportunity, Holmes and I took our leave of this charade and made our crossing to Dover. As we passed the Ruytingen light-ship, graced by a faint sun through morning mist, a small fleet of fishing smacks was still gathering items of baggage and wreckage that floated in the calm water. We heard that the second lifeboat from the *Comtesse de Flandre* had been sighted, but it was a floating wreck and had never been used.

Our arrival in London was something less than a Roman triumph. Sir Mycroft Holmes gave us a wide berth.

"Until we are of use to him again," said Sherlock Holmes laconically.

It was Inspector Lestrade who made us welcome, to the extent that he called upon us soon afterwards. He was persuaded by my friend that stolen property might be found in the apartments of Colonel Rawdon Moran, whose unaccountable disappearance from the London *demi-monde* had begun to be noticed.

"Conduit Street, I believe," said Lestrade, anxious not to be outdone.

Holmes drew the pipe from his lips. "Regent's Circus," he said coolly, "private rooms behind the Bagatelle Club. A gentleman of his stamp generally boasts more than one address."

Small wonder that he did! Late on the following evening, a four-wheeled growler set us down at the colonnades of Regent's Circus, in company with Lestrade and two other Scotland Yard officers, Sergeant Tregaron and Constable Blount, in regulation tweeds. These plain-clothes men pushed ahead through the crowd of loungers of both sexes who occupy the arcades after dark. A bright gasolier burnt in the fanlight above the door of the house ahead of us—the so-called Bagatelle Club. Our two officers stood back and waited for the clatter of the chain to allow an exit to several flashily dressed men, sporting a profusion of cheap "Birmingham" jewellery. Then the plain-clothes men pushed past the keeper of the door, allowing him no time to raise the alarm, and led us up the stairs to the brightness and babble of the floor above.

The houses in the four quadrants of Regent Circus are habitually home to the Seven Deadly Sins with all their friends and relations. This one boasted a gaming "hell" in which smartly dressed "bonnets" were employed by the management to entice the hopeful punters into play by their own apparent good fortune. The long room was brilliantly lit. To one side stood a buffet covered with wines and liquors. In the middle was the *rouge et noir* table. On each side sat a croupier, with a rake in his hand and a green shade over his eyes. Before him was an ornamental tin box containing the bank, with piles of counters or markers on either side.

As to Colonel Moran's apartment, the presiding genius of this casino could not have been more grateful—and helpful—on being told by Lestrade that the present interest of the police was not in the gaming parlour. A door which separated the apartments from the noise of the gamblers was sufficiently padded to impose a complete silence. The master of the premises almost fell over himself, as the saying is, to unlock Colonel Moran's rooms with his pass-key and put up the gas inside.

The large and rather vulgarly furnished drawing-room was just what I would have expected of Rawdon Moran. Windows and alcoves were draped with red velvet curtains, their lengths drawn back in heavy swags by gold-tasselled cord. Crystal pendants hung at every light. Each alcove contained a painting or statuette. One canvas typified them all. It was Giacomo Grosso's *Last Reunion*, which had created a small stir when exhibited at the Venice Biennale. An elderly man lay on his deathbed at the point of expiring, phantoms of his five mistresses from varying periods of his life standing naked round him. The focus of the collection, with the main window behind it, was a marble of Diana on a pedestal, a young female savage exhausted by the hunt, resting on a palm trunk whose upper branches shed mirrored light to illuminate her unclothed charms.

Holmes ignored these questionable treasures. A good deal of the room's ornamentation was oriental. A six-foot-tall four-square Chinese wedding chest drew his attention, its large bronze medallion surrounded by a bridal frieze of princes, princesses, temples, and bridges. It was not an item to which a man would entrust his fortune and was not difficult to unlock. No doubt, however, it had been well guarded by loyal subordinates in Moran's absence.

My friend rummaged busily, and then I heard an exclamation of satisfaction. At first I could not see what he had found. To judge from his posture, it was something large and long. There was a sound of metal. He turned and presented to me a white pith helmet marked by the gold insignia of a British field officer. Then Lestrade and his two men stood by in silence as Holmes lifted out something else and held it in both hands for me to see. He had drawn it from its immaculate scabbard, but I stared speechless at the gold guard of the sabre and the long polished blade.

"The sword of the Prince Imperial!"

He shook his head. "More than that, Watson. Also the sword which was worn by his great-uncle, the most renowned soldier of all time, Napoleon Bonaparte, at the glorious victory of Austerlitz on 2 December 1805!"

There was only one other thing to be done, and we were obliged to do it under the patronage of Mycroft Holmes. So far, Prince Napoleon-Jerome had shown no wish to see us again, either to congratulate or reproach us. Now the case had changed. We were summoned to the principal reception room at Lancaster Gate, its windows looking out across the Bayswater Road to the trees and shrubs of Kensington Gardens with their first greening of spring. When the interview was almost over, Plon Plon, in his own ceremonial uniform, inquired, "There is possibly some small token you would accept, Mr. Holmes, on your own behalf and that of your colleague?"

Sherlock Holmes's dislike of such flummery had no doubt been reported to him, and the prince had no intention of being rebuffed over a tiepin or a pair of cuff-links.

"Yes!" said Holmes firmly. Plon Plon looked as surprised as I felt.

"Something that is small?"

"I should like an assurance that the story of the sword and the helmet found by the Blood River shall remain a confidence between us. Is that small?"

Plon Plon almost smiled with pleasure, for he was no great admirer of his late rival, the Prince Imperial.

"But of course. That is the only small thing?"

"No. Five thousand pounds. It is a small amount for a prince to give."

"You wish me to give you five thousand pounds?"

"Certainly not! I wish it to be paid into a bank account in Johannesburg, to the credit of Miss Seraphina Heyden, lately released under a free pardon from Praetoria State Prison, having been declared innocent of the murder of Andreis Reuter. It is to go to her and to her child."

I had the impression that Plon Plon cared less about the money than the thought of paying it to a jailbird.

"And that is all?"

"No, sir."

Mycroft Holmes, who had arrayed himself for the occasion as Knight Commander of the British Empire, complete with sword and sash, tried to glare his sibling into silence.

"What then?"

"I should like a cheque for one thousand pounds to be paid to the Army Temperance Society for the service they have rendered you. Your property was conveyed safely to you by being packed in four boxes bearing their name and the address of the Military Chaplaincy at Aldershot Garrison."

Had the prince any idea that the contents of his war-chest had been conveyed to this society while his own royal coffer contained only evangelical tracts? I think perhaps not. Beyond doubt, however, he was relieved to have come to the end of Sherlock Holmes's demands.

Alas for Plon Plon's imperial ambitions, they are public knowledge. General Georges Boulanger's time as a political maverick and champion of the house of Bonaparte was passing. The fickle electorate of republican France drifted away from their allegiance. Boulanger might well have clung on until the tide of opinion changed once more. But his beloved mistress, Marguerite, Comtesse de Bonnemains, fell mortally ill with consumption. Politics and power meant nothing to him then. A few weeks after her death, the general drew up his final testament and shot himself beside her grave in Brussels. In the same year, the ageing Plon Plon also died, and with him the hopes of imperial France.

It was an awkward time in the partnership I had formed with Sherlock Holmes. I had undertaken to consider the purchase of old Mr. Farquhar's medical practice in Paddington. From time to time, I spent a week or two there as his locum. If I followed this up by purchasing a practice, my work as a physician would surely take up the greater part of my time. Of course I assured Sherlock Holmes that Paddington is hardly more than ten minutes' walk from Baker Street. I could not promise that I should always be available. As it was, I was merely committed to a further stint of a few weeks as Mr. Farquhar's locum tenens. Yet I was uneasy. Idle hands may do the devil's work. I thought of Sherlock Holmes without an investigation to absorb him after the adventure we had just been through—and that infernal cocaine syringe in its morocco case.

How often had I heard those words? "My mind rebels at stagnation. Give me problems! Give me work! Give me the most abstruse cryptogram or the most intricate analysis and I am in my own proper atmosphere." The alternative I knew only too well. The jacket removed and the shirt-sleeve unbuttoned. The sinewy forearm and wrist dotted with the puncture-marks of the needle.

Such were my thoughts as I made a pretence of reading *The Times* while drinking my coffee. I had noticed that there was a letter for him this morning, and now he was reading it. He looked up from reading it and chuckled.

"What a small world we live in, Watson!"

Without another word, he handed me a cutting from the *Journal for Psychical Research*, volume six, pages 116-117. It reprinted a letter forwarded to the editor:

British Institute, 26 Rue de Vienne, Brussels

In the morning of 29 March, after being wakened at the usual hour, I went to sleep again and dreamt the following.

I was staying with a friend by the seaside. The house overlooked the sea. It was a bright clear day. I was close to the wall watching two vessels on the sea. Neither vessel as they neared each other seemed to make room for the other. To my horror, one dashed into the other, cutting her in half. I saw the boiler of the injured vessel burst, throwing up fragments and thick black smoke. I saw passengers hurled into the water, making frantic attempts to save themselves. I noticed hats and other things floating on the water. Suddenly two bodies were washed up at my feet. I woke and it was exactly 8.30 a.m. I could not shake off the feeling of horror I experienced. The same afternoon, news came from Ostend of a terrible catastrophe in the Channel, the *Princess Henriette* and the *Comtesse de Flandre* had come into collision that same morning. One had cut the other in half just as I had seen it in my dream. I knew no one on board—but the lady with whom I was staying in my dream had three relatives on board. One was drowned and the other two saved.

Isabella Young.

There was a note enclosed with this.

I beg to confirm that Miss I. G. Young related her dream to me about the collision before we had heard anything of it. The news came that afternoon.

Meliora G. Jenkins, Superintendent,
British Institute, Brussels.

I looked at Sherlock Holmes, uncertain whether or not the whole thing was a joke to him. He beamed at me.

"We have a client! Such a client! Here is a matter far more to my taste than any criminal brotherhood or the baubles of Plon Plon. Here is a challenge to the ingenuity of the scientific mind! I shall write back after breakfast, offering this most intriguing mystery my immediate attention and soliciting the favour of an interview."

Truth is stranger than any fiction. So the spectre of the narcotic syringe faded. The earth turned on its axis once more. With any luck, there was more than enough intrigue in this case to occupy him until my return from a month as locum tenens in Paddington.

ACKNOWLEDGEMENTS

The National Army Museum, London; The Radcliffe Science Library, Oxford; Vita Paladino, Howard Gotlieb Archival Research Center, Boston University; Carol Thomas, editorial; Linda Shakespeare, photo credit.